KU-306-160

Dear Reader

Thank you so much for choosing The Apple of Her Eye. I hope you enjoy reading it and that you'll feel for the people in the post-war days of austerity. I can almost taste the vegetables that April pulled out of the ground for the pot and I hope I have managed to transfer this onto the page.

Although I'm not much of a gardener myself, I was hugely inspired by the gardeners I spoke to while writing this book. They're hardy souls who get out there digging and planting with no guarantee of success; there are so many pitfalls, including unseasonal weather and garden pests. But how lovely to have freshly cooked, home-grown produce on the table!

I discovered that some of today's vegetable growing procedures are different to those used in the era this story is set in and I have tried to stay true to the methods of the time. But, as regular readers will know, my stories are mostly about people; their lives, loves, disappointments and triumphs. I hope you like this new cast of characters. Maybe you'll even feel encouraged to have a go with the garden fork yourself after reading how it changed April's life. . .

I always enjoy hearing from my readers so, if you fancy getting in touch or would like to know more about my books, please visit my website: www.pamevansbooks.com

Warmest wishes
Pam

PAM EVANS was born and brought up in Ealing, London. She now lives in Surrey, near to her family and five beautiful grandchildren. The Apple of Her Eye is Pam Evans's thirty-first saga for Headline and all her previous novels are also available in ebook.

For more information about Pam and her novels visit
www.pamevansbooks.com

Pam EVANS

The Apple Of Her Eye

headline

Copyright © 2015 Pamela Evans

The right of Pamela Evans to be identified as the Author of
the Work has been asserted by her in accordance with the
Copyright, Designs and Patents Act 1988.

First published in 2015 by
HEADLINE PUBLISHING GROUP

First published in paperback in 2015 by
HEADLINE PUBLISHING GROUP

1

Apart from any use permitted under UK copyright law, this publication may
only be reproduced, stored, or transmitted, in any form, or by any means,
with prior permission in writing of the publishers or, in the case of reprographic production, in
accordance with the terms of licences issued by the Copyright Licensing Agency.

All characters in this publication are fictitious and any resemblance
to real persons, living or dead, is purely coincidental.

Every effort has been made to fulfil requirements with regards to reproducing copyright
material. The author and publisher will be glad to rectify any omissions at the earliest
opportunity.

Cataloguing in Publication Data is available from the British Library

ISBN 978 1 4722 1927 5

Typeset in Bembo by Palimpsest Book Production Limited,
Falkirk, Stirlingshire

Printed and bound in Great Britain by
Clays Ltd, St Ives plc

Headline's policy is to use papers that are natural, renewable and recyclable products and made
from wood grown in well-managed forests and other controlled sources. The logging and
manufacturing processes are expected to conform to the environmental regulations of the
country of origin.

HEADLINE PUBLISHING GROUP
An Hachette UK Company
Carmelite House
50 Victoria Embankment
London EC4Y 0DZ

www.headline.co.uk
www.hachette.co.uk

Acknowledgements

Many thanks to my lovely, enthusiastic editor Clare Foss who is such a joy to work with, and all the team at Headline who continue to publish my work so well. Thanks also to my agent Barbara Levy who has represented me from the beginning and has become a friend over the years.

Chapter One

Would the war never end, the British people wondered, as this, the sixth winter, dragged on the gloomiest of all with shortages of everything except cold weather. Fuel rationing often meant an empty hearth so the populace shivered in unheated homes in their outdoor clothes; families gathered around the wireless set of an evening in coats, mufflers and gloves.

But there was an underlying sense of optimism, despite the gloom, because everyone knew that peace was imminent albeit that occasional V-bombs still wreaked havoc in London. The beginning of a return to normality was now visible, most notably in blackout restrictions being lifted to half lighting.

There was certainly no lack of good spirits in the Blue Rabbit public house in Chiswick, West London, one evening in February 1945. The smoky public bar, which was almost exclusively a male domain, was packed, a darts game in progress, the whole place reverberating with raucous hilarity. Who cared if the beer was watered down: the war was nearly over, the men had finished their long working day, were off duty from civil defence and had escaped from the missus for an hour or

1

so to be with their mates, so they weren't complaining. Someone here always had a joke to tell.

Even the sound of the siren didn't unduly disturb these merrymakers which as it happened proved to be unwise. A terrible silence followed the explosion; most of the pub had been reduced to a smoking ruin.

Later that same evening April Green and her cousin Heather Miller were glowing pleasurably when they emerged with the crowds from a cinema in Hammersmith having just seen the film *Meet Me in St Louis*.

'What a lovely film,' said Heather dreamily.

'Yeah, I really enjoyed it too,' sighed April, a redhead with lustrous green eyes and a dusting of freckles. 'Judy Garland is one of my favourite film stars.'

'I always like American films. It seems to be so nice there; all those smart houses and gorgeous scenery and everything. We need their glamour to cheer us up,' said Heather, linking arms with her cousin and shivering against the bitter weather as they headed for the bus stop. 'There isn't much to smile about here.'

'It was only a film, Heather. I don't suppose it's so good in real life in the United States,' April suggested, though she also enjoyed the glimpses of America they saw on the cinema screen. 'Anyway, things aren't so bad here now. The war is on its last legs and we don't have to go down the shelter every night now that the bombs don't come very often.'

'There is that I suppose,' agreed Heather, a tall brunette with a shapely figure and deep brown eyes that were often spoiled by resentment as they mirrored her discontented nature.

'We are lucky; we've come through the war intact. Many people have lost their homes and relatives. There are a lot worse off than we are.'

'All right, you can spare me the lecture,' said Heather, taking offence as usual. 'I'm entitled to have a moan if I feel like it.'

'Of course you are. I was just saying that the outlook seems better than it has for ages, even though things are still a bit bleak at the moment.' They joined the queue for the bus to Chiswick. 'It's a fact of nature that the weather will warm up soon and, according to the news, the war is almost over so the boys will be coming home and we can all get back to normal.'

'I can't wait to see my Arthur again,' sighed Heather, referring to her childhood sweetheart to whom she was engaged.

'I'm longing for Ronnie to come back too,' added April. 'I haven't seen him for two years so it will be *some* reunion.'

'I shouldn't get too excited,' warned Heather.

'Why not . . . because the war isn't quite over yet, you mean?'

'No, not that.'

'What are you getting at then?'

'Well, you hardly knew him when you got engaged,' pronounced Heather. 'He wasn't around for longer than a couple of weeks before he went back to the war. It takes time to get to know someone well enough to get engaged to them. He wasn't much more than a stranger.'

'Trust you to try to put a damper on it for me.'

'I was only saying . . .'

'I know what you were only saying and I'm telling you that it was long enough for me to know that he's the one for me.' Speed was of the essence in such uncertain times and it certainly had been for April and Ronnie, who'd met at a dance when he was on leave from the army. Mutually lovestruck,

3

they'd gone ahead and got engaged before he went back. 'Anyway, we've been writing to each other and we are both committed. So if you are trying to spoil it for me you aren't succeeding.'

'I'm not trying to spoil anything,' denied Heather huffily. 'Why would I when I have a boyfriend of my own?'

Why indeed would her cousin so often try to take the shine off things for her, wondered April. Both twenty-one, they had grown up in close proximity because their mothers were sisters and lived in the same neighbourhood. Now that they were adults and could choose for themselves, they saw each other regularly but Heather often felt the need to give her cousin a verbal slapping. While April found it annoying, she was well able to defend herself and was fond of Heather as a relative so continued with the friendship.

The conversation was brought to a halt by the arrival of the bus and they moved with the queue to get on.

'Isn't it nice now that the buses have the lights on again?' observed April when they were settled in their seats and had paid their fare to the conductress. 'The lighting still isn't full strength yet but near enough to make a difference.'

'It is a bit more cheerful, I must say,' agreed Heather.

Looking out of the window at other lit buses, they seemed almost ethereal to April as they sailed through the night, the passengers now visible. After more than five years of total darkness any sort of light had a touch of magic about it.

They alighted from the bus a few stops earlier than they intended because the conductress informed them that the driver was forced to take a diversion due to an 'incident', which meant a bomb, and the main road through the town was closed. Sudden changes of plan were so frequent in wartime they took it in their stride and set off for home on foot, the air raw and pungent with the smell of smoke.

'I wonder where the bomb actually landed,' remarked Heather.

'On the main road somewhere I should think, as the bus couldn't get through,' said April. 'Not on our side of town so we'll still have a home and family to go to. Oh dear, that sounds so callous.'

'Just human nature. Anyway, I thought the bombing was supposed to be finished,' Heather complained. 'I hope this doesn't mean it's all going to start up again.'

'It'll just be a stray doodlebug, I expect. The government wouldn't have relaxed the blackout restrictions if they thought there were going to be any more manned bombers coming over.'

'That's true.'

They both lived in Chiswick in the serried ranks of Victorian terraced houses a few minutes' walk from the High Road. When they reached Heather's road, they parted company and April continued alone. Turning into the street where she lived, she gasped and broke into a run at the sight of a gathering outside her house, which meant trouble. It flashed through her mind that the buildings all seemed to be intact so it couldn't be anything to do with the bomb. What the hell had happened?

'We've been waiting for you, April dear,' said Mrs Willis, the Greens' next-door neighbour.

'Why?'

'It's your dad, love,' the woman explained, looking worried. 'The Blue Rabbit has been bombed and he was in there apparently. Your mum's gone to find out what's happening.'

'Oh my God, I'll go down there.' April felt sick and breathless. 'But where's Charlie?'

'Your brother is in our house with my boys so you don't need to worry about him. He can stay as long as it takes,'

'Thanks, Mrs Willis. Tell him I'll be back as soon as I can,' she said and turned and tore towards the town. There had been some frightening moments during the course of the war but this had to be the scariest. Her dad, her lovely, warm-hearted father, could be hurt − or worse.

It was a bleak sight at the far end of the High Road, a familiar landmark and one of the town's most popular pubs now just smoking bricks and rubble with only the saloon bar still standing. The bomb had obviously fallen earlier in the evening but there were still quite a few onlookers about, standing around behind the cordon. There was an ambulance on hand and April could hear men shouting to each other so she guessed that the rescue people were still trying to find survivors.

Frantic with worry, she hurried around in the dim light looking for her mother but there was no sign. An observer told her that some injured survivors had been taken to hospital so she thought maybe that was what had happened to Dad and Mum had gone with him. Determined to stay positive because the alternative was too awful to even consider, she decided that must be what had happened. She would go home now and wait for news with her younger brother Charlie.

When something catastrophic has happened to you, well-meaning folk think you need company and most people probably did. But Beryl Green's life had just fallen apart completely and all she wanted was to go home alone to her children April and Charlie. However, she was finding it difficult to extract herself from her sister Peg, who had gone with Beryl to the bombsite and now insisted that she go to Peg's house first to recover from the shock of the terrible news.

'You're not going anywhere until you're a bit less shaky,' stated Peg, a good-hearted woman of ample proportions with grey wispy hair and pink cheeks. 'Here, drink this hot sweet tea. It's supposed to be good for shock.'

'You shouldn't be using your tea and sugar ration on me,' said Beryl.

'Oh give over, these are special circumstances,' said Peg, who was bossy but well meaning.

They certainly are, thought Beryl, who was feeling battered from the blow. Could it really have happened? Had she just identified her dead husband in the light of a first-aid worker's torch after Jim had been brought out of the bombed building? Her glands tightened and she rushed over to the kitchen sink, heaving.

As soon as she'd recovered she said, 'If you don't mind, I really need to go home now, Peg. April will be back from the cinema soon and Charlie will be worried. I have to tell them about their dad.'

'I'll walk round with you,' offered Peg.

'There's no need. I'll be all right on my own.'

'You're shaking like a leaf . . . you need someone with you.'

'I'm fine, honestly. Thanks for offering and I expect I'll want company a bit later on but right now I want to be on my own with the kids,' she said.

'Fair enough. I need to tell Heather what's happened to her Uncle Jim anyway. As you say, the girls will be back from the cinema soon. You know where I am if you need me. Otherwise I'll come round in the morning.'

'Thanks Peg,' said Beryl and headed for the front door, a small, sad figure in a brown coat and woolly hat.

Slight of build, the shock had weakened Beryl to such an extent she didn't feel physically capable of putting one foot in front of the other but somehow she forced herself on. She had known Jim since she was sixteen and they'd never spent a night apart since the day they got married. A strong, sensible man with an amiable disposition, he'd always been her strength and she felt as though she was nothing without him. How was she going to manage for one day as his widow, let alone the rest of her life? In the seconds it had taken for the bomb to explode, her future had gone from being a bright and cheery prospect to something dark and daunting. But now she had to break her children's hearts by telling them they had lost their father.

As soon as April saw her mother's face she knew it was the worst news and for the moment she stood rooted to the spot, unable to move.

'What's happened, Mum?' asked Charlie, who was thirteen. 'Is Dad at the hospital?'

April watched her mother struggle to say the words, her dry lips trembling. 'Sorry both of you,' she began shakily, 'but your dad . . . well, he didn't make it.'

'He's dead, you mean?' muttered Charlie with a youthful lack of diplomacy.

'I'm afraid so,' said Beryl thickly.

Instinctively April and Charlie went to their mother and the three of them held each other close. From the age of fourteen April had considered herself to be an adult in that she had been earning her own living and paying her way in life. But this was the moment she knew that she had really grown up.

In the early hours of the next morning, in another part of the same town, greengrocer's wife Winnie Benson was contemplating the future with trepidation as she got into bed. Her husband Percy had been injured in the Blue Rabbit bombing and was in hospital. His injuries weren't life-threatening but they were serious in that he was almost certain to be disabled for a while at least and maybe permanently, due to a back wound close to his spine. They had removed the metal implanted by the bomb blast but said that the spine might have been damaged by it and there was nothing more they could do. He was told that the pain should ease off when the operation lesion healed but his mobility could well be impaired.

'You'll have to send for the boy,' Percy had said, referring to their twenty-three-year-old son George who was away at sea in the merchant navy. 'He'll have to come home and help you run the business.'

'He's on the other side of the world somewhere, Percy,' she'd reminded him gently. 'We can't get him home just because you're hurt, love, as much as we'd like to. I know what's happened to you is awful but I think they only give compassionate leave if someone dies.'

'Compassionate leave is no good,' Percy had said, missing the point completely. 'He needs to come home for good. It's his duty to be here looking after you and the business as I'm not in a fit state.'

'It's his duty to stay where he is, Percy, and you know that,' she'd pointed out. 'It is still wartime, remember.'

'I'm not likely to forget that, am I?'

'Of course not,' she'd agreed, looking at his sorry state, his face suffused with cuts from the debris and strained from the effects of pain in his lumbar region. 'But I think we both know that he won't be able to come home for good until after the war.'

'You're right, of course,' he admitted finally.

George Benson had gone away to sea in peacetime when he was fifteen. A few years later when war broke out, by which time he had been eligible for military service, he'd been unable to answer the call because the merchant navy had needed him; more than ever with so many men being lost in the heavy bombing of vital merchant ships.

'I'll manage, love,' she'd assured her husband. 'You just concentrate on getting better and I'll look after things at home.'

'What about the shop?'

A caring soul with a round cheerful face, blue eyes and a thick mop of greying blond hair, she'd put her hand over his gently. 'I'll look after that too so stop worrying. I've been helping you with it for long enough. I ought to be able to manage.'

'I've always run things and bought the stock.'

'So I'll do it until you're better,' she'd assured him.

'It's hard work, lifting and carrying,' he'd said worriedly. 'You're not built for that part of the job. You'll never be able to lift and carry the sacks of potatoes.'

This was true. Percy was a strong man. He carried the potato

10

sacks on his back almost effortlessly. No matter how bright and willing she was, she didn't have the physical strength to get the heavy stock from the store in their cellar up to the shop.

'Then there's the wholesale market,' he had fretted. 'You won't want to get up at five o'clock in the morning to do that.'

'I won't want to but I'll do it,' she'd said. 'You've done it for years. Now it's my turn.'

'You can't drive the van,' he reminded her.

She'd looked at him and squeezed his hand. 'Look, I can't promise to run the shop as well as you do, and yes there will be problems, but I promise you that when you come home Benson's Greengrocer's will still be going strong in Chiswick High Road. Now please try and relax and let nature and the medical staff here get you better.'

It was a daunting prospect, she admitted to herself now. Percy had always run the business while she looked after the home and just worked in the shop under his management. Now all the responsibility would be on her shoulders. It wasn't the hard work that worried her but the loss of Percy's strength. He had always been the tough one; he'd looked after her. Now their roles were reversed and she wasn't sure if she was up to it but knew she must do her best. She needed two things: some muscle for heavy lifting and at first someone to take her to Brentford Market to buy stock and teach her how to drive the van so that eventually she could do it herself.

What she wanted more than anything at this time was to have her beloved son by her side. George, her only child, who had inherited his father's strength but, thankfully, not his difficult nature. Percy was a dear and she loved him with all her heart but he wasn't always an easy man to live with and had never had a good relationship with his son. Maybe that was why she and George had always been close. Usually at a distance, it was true, but she always felt spiritually bound to him.

She reminded herself how lucky she was that her husband had survived the bombing. Others hadn't been so fortunate. She didn't know the numbers but there had been fatalities. Ironically, the Blue Rabbit wasn't even Percy's local. He'd gone there last night, apparently, because his usual watering hole had run out of beer, so she wasn't likely to know any of the other punters. Even so she felt for them and counted her blessings. Percy had been spared because he'd been in the saloon bar of the pub, some of which was still standing.

So now, in her late forties, she suddenly found herself with new responsibilities and was determined to honour her promise to Percy and keep the business going while he was out of action; permanently if necessary. 'Oh George, I wish you were here,' she murmured as she settled down to try and sleep.

Even as the first tears were still falling for the loss of Jim Green, the economics of the death of their main breadwinner had already occurred to his family. April had heard it said that good often comes from bad and she saw evidence of this the next morning when her brother came downstairs and made an announcement.

'I'll be fourteen soon and I'll be leaving school at Easter, Mum, so I'll be out working and bringing money home. You've no need to worry because I'll be the man of the house from now on.'

As kid brothers went Charlie was one of the best. Exuberant

and full of fun, he could be annoying at times but generally speaking he and April got along, give or take the odd sibling spat. One role she had never seen him in before was that of an adult. But now it was as though he had skipped the rest of his adolescence and grown up overnight. His pale brown eyes, so like their father's, shone with intent, his youthful face set in a grim expression.

'That's very kind of you, son, and I appreciate it,' said his mother, her voice breaking. 'But you're a bit young to be taking on that sort of responsibility. So don't you worry about me. I'll get a widow's pension and your dad has been putting a bit by since the day we got married in case anything happened to him. Always very aware of his responsibility as a husband was your dad. As a skilled metal worker in an engineering factory he earned well, especially these past few years with all the long wartime hours.'

'I'll try to give you a bit more each week if you need it, Mum,' offered April.

Beryl looked from one to the other, a sudden flush suffusing her face. 'I don't want to talk about this now, with your dad's death still so new; it isn't right,' she said, her voice ragged with emotion. Then she burst into tears and rushed from the room.

Charlie made as if to go after her.

'I think we'd better leave her for the moment,' suggested April. 'She needs to be on her own for a while.'

'Oh April,' said Charlie, struggling not to let himself down and shed tears, the worst disgrace ever for a boy of his age and class. 'Poor Mum. I didn't mean to upset her.'

'You didn't; it's just the way she's feeling at the moment and anything could have triggered it off. She'll be all right in a while,' she said, putting her arms around him and not meeting any resistance. 'We'll look after her, you and me. We'll get by together, the three of us.'

They stayed with arms entwined for a long time. April could feel her brother trembling and knew that he was sobbing but she made no comment. He was entitled to his pride even under these terrible circumstances.

Wanting to be strong for her family at this sad time, though the shock of the death had left her feeling physically sick and muddle-headed, Beryl managed to focus her mind on the organisation of the funeral and then the post-bereavement paperwork, finding it a calming distraction from the horrible reality of life without Jim.

'The allotment will have to go,' she announced to her children one evening in March over their meal. 'I'll go to the council and see about it tomorrow.'

'We can't get rid of Dad's allotment.' April was shocked. 'That was his pride and joy.'

'It was indeed,' agreed her mother, her countenance ashen against her black mourning clothes, the brightness of her greying red hair seeming to add to her pallor, 'but he isn't here to look after it now, is he?'

'But what will we do without all the vegetables he grew for us?' asked April. 'He kept us supplied for a lot of the year.'

'We'll have to take our chances at the greengrocer's like everyone else who doesn't have an allotment,' replied Beryl. 'We can't afford to pay for something we don't use.'

'We can't afford not to keep it, Mum,' April pointed out. 'It's cheaper to grow your own so that would more than take care of the allotment rent.'

14

'But who is going to actually grow the vegetables?' Beryl wanted to know. 'An allotment needs a lot of attention.'

'I suppose I could do it.' April spoke without much enthusiasm.

'You wouldn't want to take that on, though, would you dear? Not a young girl like you,' said Beryl. 'It's more the sort of thing for older men though I know that some women have been looking after allotments during the war.'

'I'm not too keen, I must admit, but I'd do it rather than give it up. I used to help Dad sometimes so I know a little bit about it. And he kept a chart in the shed listing everything that needs doing all through the year. There are books on the subject too, and all the tools are there.'

'Helping out for an hour or so at a weekend is different to being responsible for the whole thing. You're at work all day.'

'So was Dad and he did long hours of hard physical work whereas I'm sitting on an office chair all day so the exercise will do me good,' April reminded her mother. 'It isn't as though the allotment is a full-time job; it's only a hobby. Anyway I'm sure Charlie will help out . . . when he isn't playing football, and you might enjoy giving a hand sometimes, Mum.'

'Of course I will.' She paused for a moment. 'But as soon as I feel up to it I think I might look for a job.'

April's eyes widened. 'But you already have one.'

'Only home work and that is coming to an end now that the war is nearly over.' Because she hadn't wanted Charlie to be a latchkey kid, Beryl had worked at home assembling parts for a factory throughout the war, more to feel as though she was doing her bit than out of necessity as Jim was well able to support her. 'I'll earn more if I go out to work and there's no reason why not now that Charlie doesn't need me to be here when he gets home from school. I don't have any skills but I might be able to find some sort of work, in a shop maybe.'

'Are we that hard up then, Mum?' asked April.

'No, I've told you, your dad left me well provided for. With Charlie paying his way soon we should be able to manage very nicely but I feel as though I should make an effort. It's what women seem to do these days.'

'Only because of the war but if that's what you want to do, Mum, then you go ahead,' approved April. 'The company will do you good now that you don't have Dad.'

'That's what I thought,' said Beryl, who was actually terrified at the prospect of going out to work. When she'd got married it wasn't done for a wife to work but all that had changed with the war. So she felt obliged to put herself out and bring in some money. Besides, it might be nice to have an outside interest now that the children were grown up and she had lost her dear Jim. At forty-eight she was probably a bit ancient for the workplace but much older women than her were out working these days. As soon as she'd recovered from the death and felt stronger, she would look into it.

'How about I give the allotment a try, Mum,' April was saying. 'If I hate it or am hopeless at it then we'll give it up. But I think I should at least give it a go.'

'All right, dear, if that's what you want, we'll keep it for the time being,' she said, wishing she didn't feel so ill and exhausted. She needed to be fit to cope with her loss.

Dressed in wellington boots and a navy-blue raincoat with a hood, April stood in the rain, the cold wind blasting her face, and surveyed her father's allotment which was among many others on land next to the railway lines, everywhere deserted on this cold and wet afternoon, the sky leaden with low cloud. Dad's patch hadn't been touched since before he died; it had been forgotten until now, and was looking neglected though she could see the part that he had dug over before his demise and she noticed that some cabbages and cauliflowers were looking healthy.

Going into the shed that was so full of her father, she was overwhelmed by sorrow for the loss of him. There were his tools, his gardening books and a half-empty packet of Woodbines on the table with a box of matches, next to trays of seedlings. Added to her sadness was a feeling of panic because she had offered to take the allotment on and she had little more than a vestige of knowledge about how to do it. Having committed herself, she would go ahead and do her best but the whole thing was very daunting, not to mention dismal as there were other things she would rather be doing in her spare time.

Looking at her father's annual chart for March she saw that cabbages and cauliflowers could be harvested at this time. She opened the shed door to see the horizontal rain sweeping across the landscape. It wasn't essential that she do anything in this weather so the sensible thing would be to come back another day when it was dry. But she found herself picking up her father's spade and heading out across the muddy ground.

'You've been working at the allotment on a Saturday afternoon in the rain,' said Heather, who was at the Greens' house, sitting at the kitchen table waiting for her, when April got home soaked to the skin but with a glow to her cheeks and a basket of winter vegetables. 'Are you out of your mind?'

'Someone has to do it now that Dad isn't around,' said April. 'Anyway, I wasn't really working. I was only reaping the rewards of Dad's hard work last year. It might not be so much fun next time I go.'

'Next time! You mean you are going again?' Heather sounded horrified.

'I certainly am,' stated April. 'The allotment is my responsibility now.'

'Good grief; you'll be joining the land army next.'

'A bit late for that. The war will soon be over. What's wrong with looking after an allotment anyway?'

'Nothing if you're an old man, but it's a bit weird if you're a young woman.'

'Not these days,' said April. 'Women are doing all sorts of so-called men's jobs.'

'Men's jobs, yeah, but not their hobbies; how many girls did you see down the allotment today?'

April laughed. 'There was nobody else there at all because it's raining. I only went to see what sort of a state it was in but got interested and had a look at Dad's chart and his gardening books in the shed and did a bit of tidying up outside.'

'And she picked some lovely cabbages, cauliflowers and parsnips for our Sunday dinner and enough to last the week,' said Beryl, who was filling the kettle to make tea. 'Thanks dear.'

'That's all right, Mum,' said April noticing again how off-colour her mother looked: pale, heavy-eyed and so very sad. She'd always been such a bouncy, energetic woman. Now she was lacklustre and seemed almost ill. Still, grief was a kind of

18

sickness, she supposed. Charlie and herself were suffering too but not to the same extent as their mother. How April longed to see that sparkle back in her eyes. 'We'll all enjoy them so it was worthwhile.'

The back door opened and Charlie came in, wet and muddy but smiling.

'Another drowned rat,' said Beryl, tutting. 'Get those wet clothes off right away, and don't walk mud all over the kitchen.'

'Good game?' asked his sister.

He nodded, beaming. 'I scored,' he said.

'Well done,' said April.

'Good,' said his mother, somewhat absently. She was picking up his clothes as he peeled them off, stripping down to his underwear and looking embarrassed because Heather was there.

'Should I cover my eyes?' she said, laughing.

Turning scarlet he tore across the room and out of the door.

'He'd blush if next door's cat saw him get undressed these days,' said April fondly. 'He's at that age.'

'He still loves his football then,' observed Heather.

'Not half,' said Beryl. 'Still, it keeps him out of mischief. He's such an energetic boy, he needs something to channel his energy into. He's lucky to get into a game outside of school. There aren't the men around to run amateur football since the war.'

'I suppose not,' said Heather, who was an only child so envied anyone with a sibling. Her father had died when she was seven so it had been just her and Mum for a very long time. Unlike April, who until recently had had the full family set. 'Anyway, I just came round to find out if you fancy going to the flicks tonight, April.'

April hesitated because she still wasn't happy about going out and leaving her mother of an evening.

'Don't worry about me dear,' said Beryl, guessing the reason for her daughter's hesitation. 'I'll be fine. You've got your own life to lead.'

April caught her cousin's eye and, ignoring the warning look, said, 'Why don't you come with us, Mum?'

Beryl had lost her zest for life, not her sensitivity. She'd seen the look too. The last thing Heather wanted was her aunt tagging along. It was only natural and a generational thing so no offence was taken. 'Thanks, dear, but I'd rather stay home. I am still in mourning, remember.'

'People don't worry about that so much these days with so many losses,' April pointed out.

'Even so, I'd rather not go out if you don't mind,' she said, looking from one to the other and holding Heather's gaze momentarily. She knew her niece wasn't the kindest of souls; probably the result of being an only child and not having a father. 'But you two go and enjoy yourselves.'

'You're welcome to come along if you change your mind,' said Heather but Beryl knew it was only a token gesture.

'Yes, Mum, you really are,' added April and hers was a sincere invitation.

'Thanks, dear, it's kind of you but I won't change my mind.'

As frail as she felt, Beryl was determined not to become clingy towards her children. They had their own lives and she was going to make sure they lived them without worrying about her. But oh, how she wished she didn't feel so out of sorts.

When news came through that Allied troops had crossed the Rhine and soon after that the Americans and Russians had cut Germany in two, everyone knew that the war really was coming to an end and people were buying Union Jacks and bunting on the street and searching in cupboards for old ones.

Spirits were high everywhere. But not for Beryl Green, who had other things on her mind because she had just realised that her feeling of ill health wasn't entirely a reaction to her husband's death.

'I was so taken up with Jim's death I didn't notice that my period was late for a while and when I did I thought it was something to do with the change. I'm forty-eight so the age for it and that sends things haywire apparently,' she confided to her sister Peg. 'Pregnancy was the last thing on my mind until I realised my clothes were getting tight. I had the shock of my life.'

'It couldn't have been totally unexpected. I mean you must have . . . er done the deed,' suggested the plain-speaking Peg.

'Well of course,' said Beryl in embarrassment. 'It would have been at Christmas so I'll be about four months gone.'

'You don't seem very pleased.'

'Of course I'm not pleased! I'm absolutely livid,' she burst out. 'I'm too old for all that.'

'You've left it a bit late to get it seen to,' said Peg.

'I know and I probably wouldn't have gone down that route anyway. But I must admit I've jumped down the stairs a good few times to try and shift it. Oh Peg, what am I going to do?'

'There's nothing much you can do except get on with it, love,' said her sister. 'I'll help you with it once it's born.'

'But I don't have the energy for all those sleepless nights and nappies and stuff; that's a young woman's game.'

'Nature obviously doesn't agree or it wouldn't have happened.

Anyway, it'll be nice to have something to remind you of Jim. His last gift, you might say.'

'His last burden, more like,' said Beryl. 'I don't need a baby to remind me of him. He's always on my mind.'

'It might give you a new lease of life.'

'It might kill me off at my age. Everyone will be talking about me once I start to show, saying I'm too old, and what about April and Charlie?'

'I should tell them sooner rather than later before you start showing too much,' Peg advised her. 'They'll probably be thrilled. It's a new life, Beryl. It'll be nice to have a baby around the house. It might cheer you up.'

'Then there's the expense of it,' Beryl went on, unable to see a positive side. 'Another mouth to feed.'

'Worry about that further down the line. The first thing you need to do is tell the kids.'

'Yeah, I know. I'm dreading it. It will be so embarrassing.'

'You're not the first woman to get pregnant in her forties and you won't be the last.'

'I'm not up to it Peg; babies are hard work.'

'Beryl, listen to me,' she urged. 'You are the most maternal woman I know, a natural. Your kids have always been everything to you. Once the new one gets born, everything will fall into place and you'll love every minute like you did with the others.'

'I wish I had your confidence.'

'You will, once the baby is here.'

'I daren't think that far ahead.'

'You might feel better when you've told April and Charlie.' She paused. 'Don't tell them that you aren't pleased about it though, for Gawd's sake. It might come back and haunt you later on if you do that.'

'As if I would.'

'You'll have to paint a smile on your face then; you've looked as miserable as sin lately.'

'I am in mourning,' Beryl reminded her.

'Course you are but try and seem cheerful about the baby in front of the kids.'

'Will do.'

'You'll probably have to put the baby under lock and key in case I steal it,' joked Peg. 'You know how much I love babies.'

Now Beryl felt guilty for complaining about a pregnancy she didn't want when her sister would have loved more children after Heather, but her husband had died and she'd never met anyone else. She took her hand 'You'll see plenty of it, don't worry. You'll soon get sick of me coming round with it.'

'Then I'll chuck you out,' Peg said but they both knew she never would.

'I've got something to tell you both,' said Beryl when they sat down to eat that night.

April and her brother looked at their mother, who was scarlet with embarrassment.

'What is it, Mum?' asked April, slicing into a wartime sausage which they were having with potato mashed with swede to make it go further.

She cleared her throat and blurted out, 'You are going to be having a brother or sister.'

'Oh, are we adopting a war orphan?' asked April. 'That's a nice thing to do, Mum.'

'No. A baby brother or sister,' explained Beryl. 'Sometime in the autumn.'

There was a silence that was at first puzzled then shocked.

'Oh! What, you mean . . .?' began April eventually.

'Yes, I am having a baby,' Beryl confirmed shakily.

Four eyes rested on her.

'It happened before your dad died, obviously,' she explained. 'I've only just realised.'

'Uh, that's disgusting,' said Charlie, turning scarlet. 'I'll be a laughing stock among my mates.'

'Charlie,' said April. 'Don't you dare speak to Mum like that. Apologise this minute.'

'Women of her age don't have babies; that sort of thing is for young people,' he stated on the verge of tears. 'Everyone will whisper and laugh at me.'

'Don't be so selfish,' admonished his sister.

'They'll say things about Mum.'

'It's all above board, Charlie,' Beryl pointed out. 'It's just a pity your dad didn't live to know his third child.'

'But he isn't here, is he?' he said, his voice trembling. 'First we lose Dad then we have to put up with some screeching baby in the house. Why does everything have to change?'

'It's the way life is,' said his mother sadly.

'I'm going out.' He rushed from the table, leaving his meal half eaten.

'Little sod,' said April, making to go after him.

'Leave him be.' Bery, put a restraining hand on her daughter's arm. 'He's at a difficult age. He's having a lot of changes of his own to put up with as well as everything else. He's embarrassed about what your dad and I did to get the baby I expect. He'll come round in his own time. How do you feel about it, April?'

'A bit shocked to be honest, Mum, but I think I'll be pleased when I get used to it. How about you?'

Both her children seemed achingly young to Beryl, who felt older since Jim died, her age seeming enhanced by her present condition. She felt tired and ill and burdened while they were youthful and full of life and health. But she lied and said, 'I'm thrilled to bits. It will bring new life into the house. I do hope it looks like your dad. He'd be tickled pink. We always wanted another.'

'If you're pleased then so am I.' April got up and went to her mother and put her arms around her. 'Congratulations, Mum. It will be lovely having another sibling.'

Beryl didn't dare say a word for fear she would collapse in tears. She felt like an absolute fraud and wished she could somehow want this baby. But she didn't; she absolutely hated the idea and there didn't seem to be anything she could do about it. She was so ashamed of the way she felt.

Chapter Two

'How's your husband getting along now Mrs Benson?' inquired a customer at the shop as Winnie emptied potatoes directly from the brass weighing scales into her shopping bag, a sprinkling of mud dust falling to the floor.

'Not so bad thanks,' replied Winnie in the cheerful manner she adopted for customers whatever her mood. 'He's still in pain though and can't get about much but at least he's home from hospital so that's cheered us both up.'

'Can he get around indoors at all?'

'With difficulty, but yes, he can just about manage so he isn't completely reliant on me,' she said. 'We've borrowed a wheelchair for going out but he hates going in it. Says it puts years on him.'

'I suppose it might have that effect,' the woman said sympathetically. 'But it's only temporary isn't it?'

'I bloomin' well hope so,' Winnie replied. 'But they told us at the hospital it will take a while so he'll have to be patient. We both will.'

'He's always been such an active man too,' the customer remarked.

'That's why he gets so frustrated,' said Winnie, weighing some carrots that were on the customer's list she was working from. 'He wants to be down here in the shop doing this. Not sitting in his armchair upstairs in the flat.'

'What sort of a patient is he?'

Winnie's blue eyes sparkled with humour. 'Well . . . he's a man,' she replied.

'Enough said,' the customer laughed.

'Still, we're at the end of this awful war now thank goodness, so we've all got something to smile about,' said Winnie brightly. 'They say we can expect an official announcement any day now to say that the war is over.'

'Yes, I heard about that,' said the customer. 'I've got my best frock out ready for the celebrations.'

'That's one party that's really worth making the effort for,' said Winnie.

She finished serving her and cleared the queue then went outside to check the display to see what needed filling up. Before the war this would have been resplendent with colour from fruit from abroad. Now, as it was too early for home-grown fruit, it was just seasonal vegetables with a bunch of imitation bananas hanging up near the shop door as a reminder of better times. When they did manage to get a limited number of oranges they were reserved for customers with children and not even put out on display.

She paused for a while in the spring sunshine, enjoying the warmth on her face and noticing that the High Road had somehow managed to retain a certain elegance, despite the bomb damage and general shabbiness due to wartime lack of maintenance. When the news they were all waiting for was finally announced on the wireless the whole area would be awash with red white and blue. She had flags and bunting ready to put up.

Percy had been out of action for more than two months and she'd surprised herself by holding things together rather well. In fact she was enjoying being more involved in the business. The muscle she required came in the form of a pal of Percy's called Cyril who was the landlord of a local pub. He was nearly sixty but strong and knew how to drive.

Fortunately they were allowed a small ration of petrol just for business so every weekday morning she and Cyril set out at five for the wholesale market in the van with her in the driving seat under his guidance. He also lifted heavy goods when she needed it and she insisted on paying him for his help as it was so regular and useful. Soon she would be ready to drive on her own and she anticipated it with a mixture of nervousness and excitement. This independence lark was rather nice when you got used to it.

Of course she couldn't manage in such a busy shop alone all day so had a female assistant who worked for her part-time. So she had kept her promise to Percy and Benson's was still a presence in the High Road.

Fortunately he was able to keep the accounts in order and she handed the money over to him after she'd cashed up at night. She could easily do it herself but deemed it wise to give him something to take his mind off things and help him to feel that he was making a contribution. But now she needed to sweep the shop floor, which was almost permanently suffused with dust and mud from the vegetables.

At long last the war was over and the excitement was indescribable. April thought the feeling between people went beyond neighbourly goodwill as they crowded on to the street hugging each other and smiling at the sheer joy of it. There was almost a sort of community love. A mutual burden had been lifted so the day was something wondrous they could share even with those who had lost someone. There would be no more bombs; that in itself was cause for celebration.

The Greens joined their neighbours on a nearby bombsite and a pre-planned party for the big day was arranged. Money had been contributed by each family and people gave their sweet coupons and any tinned fruit or other provisions they had stored. A local grocer donated biscuits, tea and other provisions and residents brought out chairs, records and a gramophone and anything else they thought might add to the festivities.

The afternoon belonged to the children but in the evening the adults let their hair down in the light of a victory bonfire while candles in jam jars were spread around adding a celebratory glow. There was dancing, singing, drinking and a great deal of laughter.

Beryl, who was inside making sandwiches with the cheese donated by the grocer, was enjoying the day but naturally her husband was on her mind and she was sad that he wasn't here with them. She still loathed her pregnancy but had managed to accept it, albeit with reluctance. She was noticeably plump but no longer tried to hide it and wore maternity smocks with a kind of determined pride. She was carrying her husband's child so had nothing to be ashamed of, even though she did feel awkward about her age.

At first a few wisecracks about her advanced years had been made but everyone was used to it now including Charlie, who had come out of his sulks and apologised for his rude behaviour on first hearing the news. He was a good lad and now worked as an errand boy at a local brewery.

'Come on, Beryl, we need some more sandwiches out here,' said the Greens' neighbour Mrs Willis, poking her head into Beryl's kitchen, every door in the street open. 'You'd think the men hadn't eaten for a week, the way they are scoffing.'

'Coming up,' said Beryl, entering into the spirit of things and wishing she didn't feel so burdened by her pregnancy which made her feel isolated from and different to other people.

'We should have gone to the West End, April,' said Heather, who had defected from her own street party in favour of her cousin's. 'That's where the real celebrations are. We could have gone to Buckingham Palace to see the royals on the balcony. It's a shame you didn't want to go.'

'I told you, Heather, it wasn't that I didn't want to go but that I knew Mum wouldn't fancy the crowds in her condition and I didn't want to leave her on a day like today when I know she'll be missing Dad. We all are. Anyway it's nice being with people we know on such a special occasion.'

'Yeah, I suppose so.' They were sitting on the Greens' front garden wall taking a break from the celebrations and drinking weak sherry that had been watered down to make it go further. 'At least your party is quite a bit livelier than ours; we don't even have a bonfire.'

'It does add something extra to the atmosphere.' Watching the fire crackle and glow and seeing everyone enjoying themselves made April feel sentimental. 'I don't think I'll ever forget today. It feels so very special. Peacetime eh. The end of the old and the start of a new era.'

'Yeah, it will certainly go down in history and we'll be able to say we were part of it when we are old and grey,' agreed Heather. 'So now that the war is over, when do you think the boys will be home?'

'Well it won't be next week or next month, obviously,' replied April. 'It will take a long time to get them all back.'

'Not too long surely,' said Heather. 'They've been away far too long already.'

'It will take a huge amount of organisation, getting all those thousands of men back to England. Just think of the amount of transport they'll need, all the ships and so on.'

'Surely the military will have put plans into place; they've known it was going to happen.'

'I expect they have but it will still take a long time to get everyone back,' said April. 'There are so many of them and they are scattered far and wide.'

'But we've lost such a lot of time already,' said Heather in a tone of complaint. 'I want my life with Arthur to move on. I want to get married.'

April felt uneasy about her cousin's sense of urgency. 'Won't you need some time to get used to each other again?' she suggested.

'Of course not,' said Heather dismissively. 'Arthur and I know each other inside out.'

'I shouldn't start trying to get him up the aisle the minute he steps inside the door though.'

'As if I would.' She grinned. 'I'll give him at least a couple of days.'

April laughed, glad that her cousin wasn't completely devoid of a sense of humour. Heather was often too intense about things, which could be irritating for some people, especially a soldier who had been away fighting for his country. 'I suppose it will be strange for all of us. Exciting though.'

'I'll say,' agreed Heather. 'I can't wait for things to get back to normal.'

'No more air raid shelters for us,' said April happily.

Charlie swaggered on to the scene looking flushed, happy and a little bleary-eyed.

'Good party innit, girls?' he said, giggling. 'Are you enjoying yourselves?'

April nodded. 'So are you by the look of you. Have you been drinking?'

'Just a glass of beer.'

'You're fourteen, Charlie, and much too young to have alcohol.'

'The men running the bar said I could have it as it's such a special occasion,' he replied, swaying slightly. 'Anyway, I'm a working man now.'

Currently at a transitional stage in his development, Charlie tended to be a bit lanky but he still had the sweetest face, despite frequent cuts and grazes when his efforts with a razor hadn't gone well. His eyes were the colour of light ale like his dad's and he had the same wavy brown hair. He was a bit lippy at times, as were many lads of that age, but generally speaking he was a joy to have around, and was very good to his mother.

'You're working, certainly,' she said, smiling. 'But you've still got some growing up to do before you'll be a man.'

A group of boys came over before he could respond. 'Come on, Charlie,' said one of them, his face wreathed in boozy smiles. 'We're gonna see if we can find some girls.'

'Go on,' said his sister. 'Go and enjoy yourself but take it easy on the beer.'

'Hark who's talking. That isn't water you're drinking,' he reminded her and went off with his friends laughing and talking.

'He's growing up,' said Heather.

April nodded. 'He's a smashing kid. Very sweet to Mum now that he's got used to the idea of the baby.' She paused. 'Which reminds me, I must go and check on Mum. I don't want her hiding away inside.'

At that moment her mother appeared with a plate of sandwiches at the same time as someone started singing 'Knees Up Mother Brown'.

'Put those sandwiches down, Mum, and let's go and join in,' said April. 'It won't harm the baby as long as you don't go mad, so no excuses.'

As they jogged around singing at the top of their voices April felt her father's absence as a physical pain. He should have been here and there was a missing element because he wasn't. She knew instinctively that her mother was having similar thoughts. But life went on and they were at the beginning of a new age, so they owed it to themselves to embrace it.

Peacetime proved to be the same as wartime without the bombs but with even more shortages. There was no sign of rebuilding the bombed houses or sprucing things up with a lick of paint. But there was a lightness in the air because people now felt safe and had hopes of better things.

The man revered as the people's wartime saviour, Winston

Churchill, was rejected by them in the General Election in July when there was a landslide victory for the Labour Party which was promising good things in the peacetime era.

'Seems a shame after Churchill's leadership brought us through the war,' said April to her mother when the news was announced on the wireless. 'He must be very hurt.'

'Politicians are used to it, I should think,' said Beryl. 'It's a tough old game to be in. Churchill may well be a hero but he is also a toff and that could put people off now that the war is over. The country needs rebuilding and Labour is promising all sorts of changes for the better for the new world. That's what we need to hear.'

'I suppose so,' said April. 'I'm not very "up" on politics but I know that something drastic needs to be done about our poor, battered country. You can see it everywhere you look.'

'You still don't know when to expect Ronnie home then.'

'No. I haven't heard a word from him so I'll expect him when I see him. Heather is in a real state because she doesn't know when Arthur will be back. Every minute she's at home she waits for a knock at the door.'

'Always a drama with Heather,' said Beryl. 'She's a highly strung girl.'

'She certainly is. I'm dying to see Ronnie but in a warm and excited sort of way, whereas Heather is impatient and miserable about waiting for Arthur. All we can do for the moment is keep the Welcome Home banners up and look forward to seeing them.'

'That's the best way to be but I suppose Heather can't help her personality.'

'I suppose not,' agreed April. 'I'm lucky because the allotment keeps me occupied in my spare time. I know it's an odd thing for a girl to do but it's very relaxing, even though I'm constantly at war with the weeds and pests who'd eat everything that dares to rise above the surface if they could. Working in an office all day it's a complete change and I enjoy the fresh air and exercise. There's something so lovely about working with the soil. I can't really explain it. It's a different feeling to anything else that I do.'

'You're doing very well with it anyway,' said Beryl. 'We're having lovely vegetables every day.'

'That's mostly due to Dad for the way he looked after the soil before he died. But I've been lucky with some of the stuff I've put in. I really do enjoying growing things. I'm learning all the time but there's still an awful lot I don't know. I find out by reading Dad's gardening books and talking to the other allotment holders.'

'You must have inherited your liking for it from your dad,' suggested Beryl, who intended to help her daughter after the baby was born.

'Actually, Mum, at the moment we've got more vegetables than we need for ourselves and Auntie Peg so I was thinking about trying to sell the surplus. It will go off if we don't use it. We could do with the extra money to pay for seeds and other gardening materials. What do you think?'

'An excellent idea.'

'I think I'll pay a visit to the greengrocer's in the High Road.'

'You should set up a stall,' cut in Charlie, who came in from seeing his pals and got the gist of the conversation. 'I'd help you and it would be a laugh.'

'There wouldn't be enough produce for that and it won't be regular,' said April. 'No, a greengrocer is my best bet. Things are still short, so they might be interested. I'll get a lower price than selling direct to the public but it will be more straightforward.'

So it was that she found herself walking along the High Road on Saturday afternoon carrying a basket of 'samples', a few of each of her seasonal vegetables. She'd left it until late in the day in the hope that the shop wouldn't be too busy and fortunately there was no one in there except a woman with a weather-beaten sort of a face, curly fair hair and smiling blue eyes who April knew from hearsay to be the owner's wife.

'Your dad's allotment is it?' said Winnie, having listened to what April had to say and inspected her produce.

'It was Dad's but he was killed in the Blue Rabbit bombing so I look after it now.'

Winnie frowned. 'Oh love, I'm so sorry. You must have been devastated.'

April nodded. 'We were and we miss him something awful.'

'Actually my husband was in the Blue Rabbit that night,' Winnie said.

'Oh no.' April, looked alarmed.

'He survived,' Winnie assured her quickly. 'He was injured but he was one of the lucky ones.' She paused. 'Come on through to the back so that we can talk. I'll hear the shop bell if anyone comes in.'

April was led into a cosily furnished room just behind the shop with a sink and kettle on a small hob. 'This is our staff room; where we come for a breather and a cuppa when we are on duty. To save us going up and down the stairs to the flat every time we need a sit-down.'

'Don't worry about tea,' said April, conscious of the meagre rations as the other woman went to fill the kettle.

'Nonsense, you must have a cuppa with me while we talk about price. I won't rob you but neither will I pay as much you'd get for a direct sale.'

'I understand that,' said April, beaming. She was doing business and it felt good.

'I guessed you would. You seem like a sensible girl.'

'As I said, the supply will be intermittent . . .' April reminded her hesitantly. 'I'm only an amateur.'

'Every little helps in these hard times,' responded Winnie. 'The war is over but the peace is still a bit of a shambles. Once goods start coming in from abroad again things will be easier all round as regards food supplies but people always enjoy home-grown vegetables, even when things are plentiful, so whenever you can supply I'll buy.' She paused with a twinkle in her eye. 'As long as the standard stays high.'

'That goes without saying and and I'll do my best,' promised April.

She stayed quite a long time chatting, though they were interrupted a few times by the shop bell. After they'd agreed a price they exchanged some family details. Winnie told her about her adored son away at sea and how she'd been running the family business since her husband's injury; recently she had even taken a driving test and acquired a driver's licence. By the time April left, having arranged to come back later with the produce, she felt as though she had made a new friend and was looking forward to spending more time with her.

Winnie was impressed with April. Not many young women would spend their spare time growing vegetables to feed a family and keep up a tradition. Her mother had a diamond in her. Mrs Green must have had a hard time losing her husband then finding she was pregnant at her time of life. But Winnie guessed that April would be a comfort to her and was already looking forward to seeing her again.

When they did meet again, just as Winnie was closing the shop that same day, she burst out laughing because it was the strangest delivery of stock she had ever had. April had wheeled the vegetables here in an old pram lined with newspaper.

'Needs must when the devil drives. The stuff is too heavy for me to carry so I borrowed the pram from a neighbour,' she explained.

'I hope it isn't the one your mum is going to use for the nipper when it arrives.'

'Not likely! We might not be well off but we aren't that hard up,' said April. 'It's much too old and decrepit to put a baby in but it's just the job for vegetables. I might offer to buy it from the neighbour if the arrangement between you and me becomes permanent.'

'As I've said, if you grow it, I'll buy it off you,' said Winnie as April wheeled the pram inside to unload.

It was a glorious autumn day and Beryl was keeping April company at the allotment.

'I shall have you down here on your knees with me when you've had the baby and can bend down again, Mum,' warned April, who was weeding. 'So make the most of sitting there like the lady of the manor.'

Beryl laughed; she was seated on an old deckchair outside

the shed, enjoying the fresh air. The sun was low and golden and the colours of nature as rich as paint as the season turned. 'I shall do so of my own accord, don't worry. Anyway the winter will be coming in by then so you won't need me.'

'There'll still be work to be done here, according to Dad's chart,' said April. 'Not as much as in spring and summer of course, but more than enough.' She chuckled. 'Don't worry – I'm only teasing. I think you'll have quite enough to do with a young baby to look after.'

Beryl's smile faded but fortunately her daughter had her eyes on the job and didn't notice. 'Maybe at first until I get into a routine but we'll see how it goes,' she said.

'I can't wait to see my new sister or brother. You must be really looking forward to it now that it's getting so close, Mum,' said April with enthusiasm.

Total dread would be nearer the mark; the closer the birth got the more burdensome the idea of a baby became to Beryl but she said, 'Oh yeah, of course, but there's still a good way to go yet.'

'The time will soon pass, Mum,' said April in an encouraging manner, 'though people say that time seems to slow down towards the end of a pregnancy.'

Naturally there had been a lot of talk about the baby at home; would it be a girl or boy, and long discussions about choosing a name. April was very excited about it and even Charlie was taking a casual interest. It was only Beryl who viewed the future with gloom. This felt entirely different to her other two pregnancies. Then she'd been eager for her child to be born, longing be a mother. But that was a long time ago. She was well past that stage in her life, even though nature had decided otherwise.

'Yes, I expect it will drag a bit later on,' she said.

They moved on to other things. The allotments were well attended on this fine Saturday afternoon; all the other gardeners were men of advanced years. Most were friendly though and several came over for a chat. Beryl was glad of their company because it distracted April's attention from her mother and got the subject away from her forthcoming ordeal.

They had another visitor too. 'I thought I'd find you here when there was no one in at home,' said Heather, looking to be in good humour. 'Guess what! I've got the most amazing news. I've had a letter from Arthur. He'll be home sometime within the next few weeks.'

'Thank God for that,' said April in the way of friendly banter. 'Perhaps you'll calm down now and stop going on about it so much.'

'Calm down, me, don't talk daft. I'm so excited I don't know what to do with myself.'

'You can get down on your knees and give your cousin a hand weeding if you like,' suggested Beryl jokingly. 'That'll soon sort you out. April reckons it's very relaxing.'

'No thanks, Auntie,' said Heather with distaste. 'I'd sooner shake hands with a bacon slicer than mess about with dirt.'

'Mess about!' said April with mock offence. 'This is hard work, I'll have you know.'

'Don't do it then,' was Heather's answer to that. 'It isn't as though you have to.'

'I said it was hard work, I didn't say I didn't want to do it,' said April, knowing that her cousin would never understand her passion for gardening. 'But if you're too rude to me I might decide to cut off your supplies.'

'That wouldn't worry me,' said Heather. 'I'm far too excited to think about food.'

'You've really got it bad.' Beryl smiled.

'Be a dear, Heather, and get me a trowel from the shed to save me getting up,' requested April.

Heather made a face. 'I don't like sheds. They're smelly and dusty and there might be creatures in there. Spiders and cobwebs at least.'

'Oh for goodness' sake,' said April with mild impatience. 'You ought to be used to that sort of thing after all those nights in the shelter.'

'I'll go,' offered Beryl.

Heather put a restraining hand on her arm. 'No, I'll go, Auntie, don't you get up,' she said, not wishing to seem too unhelpful in the light of her aunt's condition. Gingerly she approached the offending structure, went in and came out quickly holding the trowel and throwing it over to April then brushing her hands together as though to remove some vile substance. 'Ugh, it's horrible in there.'

'It's a good job my dad isn't here to hear you say that,' said April with a grin. 'He loved that shed.'

'There's no accounting for taste, I suppose,' said Heather, then noticing that her aunt didn't look pleased, added, 'Sorry Auntie. I was only joking. No disrespect to Uncle meant.'

'Mum,' said April when her mother didn't reply and looked serious suddenly. 'She didn't mean anything . . . you know what Heather's like for putting her foot in it . . . Mum, what's the matter. Are you all right?'

There was a brief hiatus then Beryl said, 'Yeah, I'm fine dear, thanks.'

'So is Heather forgiven then?'

'Yes of course she is,' said Beryl absently, though the conversation hadn't registered properly because she had been preoccupied with a sudden pain in her lower stomach.

'Are you sure you're all right, Mum?' asked April in concern, because her mother had turned very pale.

'I'm quite sure,' she said as the pain passed and she relaxed, glad that it been nothing more than a twinge and not worth mentioning.

'Thank goodness for that.' April relaxed as her mother got her colour back. 'So Heather, what else did Arthur say in his letter, or is that too private to mention?'

'No, not really.' She paused with a gleam in her eye. 'Not all of it anyway. But he seems fine and is looking forward to coming home.'

'At least one of them is on his way,' said April. 'Perhaps Ronnie won't be long after.'

'He can't be very much longer, can he?' said Beryl. 'The war is over, after all.'

'Exactly,' said April, rising. 'In the meantime, we'll look forward to Arthur's return with you, Heather, won't we, Mum?'

'Not half,' said Beryl, smiling.

In the early hours of the next morning Beryl awoke suddenly with that horrible low pain again. Half asleep, she tried to ignore it and turned on her side to try and settle. It couldn't be the baby because she still had two months to go. When the pain persisted she went to the bathroom and, realising that she was bleeding, hurried to April's bedroom.

'Sorry to wake you, love, but I need you to go to the

phone box to call an ambulance,' she said, trying to hide her fear. 'It's the baby, something is wrong.'

April scrambled out of bed. 'Shouldn't I go for the midwife if it's the baby?'

'No. It's the hospital I need.'

Flustered and concerned for her mother, April pulled some clothes on and ran from the house to the nearest phone box.

All through the next agonising hours, as she went through labour knowing that her baby almost certainly wouldn't survive, Beryl castigated herself. This was her punishment for not wanting her child. Now the poor scrap wouldn't see the light of day. She had wished this on it. If it didn't survive she would have murdered it with her evil thoughts.

The hospital staff were noncommittal about the baby's chances but it was two months premature so Beryl's common sense told her that they weren't brilliant. A woman in labour was expected to get on with the job and not make a fuss or ask questions. When at last she did enquire about her baby she was told: 'Will you stop fretting, Mrs Green, and let us get on with our work.'

After months of loathing the idea of another baby, now she had never wanted anything more.

'It's out,' said the midwife after that last big push. 'It's a girl, Mrs Green; you have a daughter.'

Beryl heard her baby cry and was filled with relief and waited for the child to be given to her as was the usual procedure. There was muttering between the nurses and the cord was cut then one of them hurried away carrying the baby.

'What's going on?' asked Beryl.

'She's very small, Mrs Green, so she's being taken to the special care baby unit.'

'Oh I see,' she said fearfully. 'What's actually the matter with her?'

'She's two months early so she needs plenty of warmth and oxygen,' the nurse explained briskly. 'So now we'll get you cleaned up and then you can have a cup of tea and a nice long rest.'

'How can I rest when I don't know if my baby is going to live or die?' she said, sobbing now.

'That will be quite enough of the dramatics if you please. You'll disturb the other patients,' admonished the nurse. 'Someone will take you down in a wheelchair to see her later on if you behave yourself and do as you're told. You are not a young woman to be dealing with childbirth so you need to do as we say.'

'I'm not in my dotage yet,' she said bravely.

'You are as far as childbirth is concerned,' stated the nurse. 'So you need to take care of yourself.'

Beryl didn't need reminding of her age because the maternity ward was full of healthy young women and she felt about a hundred years old.

'Yes, nurse,' she said, feeling as though she had lost her identity completely the minute she had entered this hospital.

Much to her surprise Beryl did manage to sleep and felt a lot better for it initially, until she remembered her baby's circumstances. Then the anxiety returned. After some persuasion one of the nurses wheeled her down to the special care unit, a very warm room containing cots with transparent lids, and she saw her tiny daughter for the first time, a pink scrap of humanity who looked so delicate it didn't seem possible that she could come through this.

Beryl wept with love for her and knew that if she did live, her mother would be devoted to her. All her fears about not being able to cope had been replaced by a longing for her to survive and complete confidence that she could make a good job of bringing her up.

'What do you think about Lily as a name for your little sister?' Beryl asked April that evening when she came to visit, having been given special permission as Beryl didn't have a husband to come to see her. Visiting was normally restricted to the father of the baby.

'That's lovely,' April said. 'I think we should stick with that if Charlie approves.'

'I shall need you to get some things for me at the shops, love,' said Beryl. 'Nappies and the nightdresses that babies wear at first. With her coming so early I hadn't done the baby shopping for her yet.'

April was doubtful. She had just been to see her new sister and had been shocked at the littleness of her. 'Shouldn't we wait a while, Mum?' she suggested.

A shadow passed across Beryl's face. She was struggling to stay positive but she was also painfully aware of her baby's frailty. 'The staff here seem to think she's got a good fighting chance but yes, I suppose you're right. Perhaps we should leave it for a while longer.'

April leaned over and hugged her mother. 'Best not to tempt fate but I'm sure she'll be fine and I can't wait for you both to come home. Charlie is looking forward to seeing her too.'

Beryl smiled. She wanted to go home to her family so much with their new addition but she had never missed Jim more than she did now.

'I've been thinking about Dad,' said April, oddly in tune with her mother's thoughts. 'I wonder how he would have felt about another baby.'

'He would have loved the idea, I'm certain of that,' said Beryl, tears welling up. 'It's such a shame he's missing it.'

'But we'll think of him when we look at Lily. She's our little daddy's girl.'

Beryl struggled against tears then managed a watery smile. She took April's hand. 'I am so pleased to have her,' she said thickly.

'Me too, Mum,' April said. 'Me too.'

Of course April couldn't possibly imagine the magnitude of her mother's feelings, having never known how much she hadn't wanted another baby. That was something that no one except her sister Peg would ever know. Such was Beryl's love for her baby now, it seemed incredible that she'd ever had such negative thoughts.

Chapter Three

It was November 1945 when an extremely handsome young man with short blond curly hair and a tanned complexion strode along Chiswick High Road in the Saturday afternoon crowds with a sparkle in his piercing blue eyes. Dressed in civvies and carrying a travel bag he went into the greengrocer's.

'Hello, Mum,' he said, beaming.

Winnie, who was about to put a cabbage into a customer's shopping bag, let it slip from her grasp in joyful surprise and it dropped to the floor.

'George,' she whooped, flinging her arms around him, her face wreathed in smiles, her customer temporarily forgotten. 'How did you get here?'

'The usual way, Ma, through the door,' he said drily.

'Oh you,' she said, laughing and crying simultaneously. 'You know what I mean. You didn't let us know you were coming.'

'I've been away enough times for you to know that I like to surprise you when I come home.' He looked towards the customer, who had retrieved the cabbage from the floor and put it into her bag. 'You finish seeing to your customer, Mum, and I'll go on upstairs. Is Dad up there?'

'No, don't do that son,' she said quickly, suddenly concerned because there was something she needed to tell George before he saw his father. 'I won't be long doing this then I'll put the Closed sign up for a while. You go into the back room and I'll join you in a minute.'

'Welcome home, George,' said the customer, a housewife who had known him since he was a boy.

'Ta very much,' he said with a grin. 'It's good to be back.'

'You look well,' said the woman. 'You don't get a tan like that round here.'

'You certainly don't,' he agreed, having noticed how pale everyone seemed and how grey the streets looked.

'It's nice to have you home anyway.'

George was used to homecomings, having been away at sea so much, but this one was special because he had been away for so long and there had been many times when he hadn't thought he would make it back at all due to the heavy bombing of merchant ships. It had often been relentless and they had lost a lot of men. He'd had a good few near misses himself.

'See you in a minute then, Mum,' he said and headed for the back room.

'Why didn't you let me know, Mum?' asked George when Winnie had told him about his father injuries.

'I didn't want you to worry,' she replied. 'There was nothing you could have done, and it wasn't as though your dad was at death's door. I would have got in touch with the shipping company if he had been.'

'I should have been told though,' he said. 'But your letters didn't mention a word about it.'

'Because I didn't think it was fair to bother you with it as you wouldn't have been able to get back.'

'So how have you managed running this place on your own?'

'Quite well as it happens. Cyril from the pub helps with the heavy lifting,' she explained. 'He taught me to drive the van too so I go to the market to buy the stock. So what would have been the point of having you fret when everything was running smoothly here? Besides, I knew the war would be over soon and you'd be back.'

He smiled affectionately. 'You're quite a woman, do you know that?'

'Thanks, son. I surprised myself, to tell you the truth but I rather enjoy being in charge.'

'Ooh, Dad won't like that,' he said with a wry grin. 'He likes to be the boss.'

'Things will revert to normal when your dad comes back to work, of course.'

George's brow furrowed. 'He will be able to come back to work then, eventually,' he said in a questioning manner.

'We're hoping so,' she said. 'It's a matter of waiting for everything to heal. They told us it might be a long job.'

'Miserable for him, being laid up,' said George. 'He likes to be on the go.'

'He isn't happy about it so don't expect him to be all sweetness and light when he sees you.'

'He's never that, not towards me anyway. I'd better go up and see him though. I'll come down and give you a hand in the shop when I've shown my face up there.'

'I shall close early today in your honour,' she said.

'I was going to take you both down the pub tonight to celebrate but I suppose with Dad being out of action—'

'We'll take him in the wheelchair,' she cut in. 'He hates going in it but it's a special occasion so he might be prepared to put up with it. A celebration will do him good.'

The sound of someone knocking on the shop door interrupted their conversation. Winnie got up and looked through to the glass shop door.

'It's April with the vegetables,' she said, hurrying towards the door. 'I must see to her because she'll need paying. So you can go on upstairs to see your dad if you like.'

Picking up his bag he glanced through to the shop on his way to the stairs and stopped in his tracks when he saw a gorgeous redhead wheeling a pram into the shop. He followed his mother, who introduced them.

'April brings me home-grown on a regular basis,' Winnie explained. 'We do business, don't we love?'

April smiled and her face lit up. 'We certainly do.' She looked towards George. 'It was my father's allotment. He was killed so I've taken it on.'

'Good for you.' He wasn't a lecherous man but he did have an eye for beauty and he certainly saw it in her. She wasn't smart or made up but she had a lovely face and gorgeous hair. 'It must be quite a big job.'

'There is a lot to do but I enjoy it,' she said. 'It's just a hobby but I'm very keen.'

'So when everyone else is at home relaxing you're out in all weathers with your garden fork.'

'I'm not sure about all weathers but I'm not easily put off.' She looked at him. 'It must feel good to be back. I'm still waiting for my fiancé to come home.'

So she was engaged and that was a blow but never mind;

he wasn't looking for a girlfriend. 'I'm sure you won't have to wait much longer.'

'My cousin's boyfriend got back last week,' she said chattily. 'So the troops are beginning to come home.'

He looked towards the pram full of plump vegetables, turnips sprouts, spinach and cauliflowers, and smiled. 'An unusual method of delivery,' he remarked.

'I don't know how else to get them here,' she laughed. 'People must think I'm a tramp, walking through the streets wheeling this lot about. Still, it does the job.'

'Perhaps we could collect them in the van if you supply us regular,' he suggested.

'I'm only a small supplier and it is intermittent,' she explained. 'Even so . . .'

'I was thinking of offering to do that myself now that I can drive the van,' Winnie added. 'It wouldn't use much petrol as the allotments are so close.'

'I wouldn't hear of it,' said April. 'You have quite enough to do with the shop and your husband to look after. '

'I'll be around, for a while anyway, so I'll be helping out,' George offered.

She shook her head. 'It's quite all right really. I don't mind delivering.'

'We'll see,' said Winnie, then changing the subject added, 'How's your mother?'

'She's very well, thanks.'

'The baby?'

'She's coming on a treat now,' replied April, looking happy. 'She's putting on weight. The hospital says we can have her home soon.'

Winnie's face lit up with a genuine smile. 'Oh that is such good news.'

'Yes, we are all very pleased.' April looked from one to the other. 'Shall I wheel this lot through to the back and unload?'

'I'll do it for you,' offered George.

Winnie laughed. 'It's going to be useful having you around, George. I won't need Cyril to lift and carry now that you are home.'

A fleeting shadow passed across George's face but he smiled and said, 'You certainly won't, Mum.'

'You can help me put it out later on if you like,' said Winnie. 'It won't stay in the shop long. April's home-grown stuff just flies out.'

April waited until they had unloaded the pram then made her way home, pleased for Winnie that she had her son back to give her some support. It couldn't be easy, running the shop and looking after Mr Benson. April had only seen him once or twice and he'd not seemed to have the same cheerful disposition as his wife. Still, that was understandable considering his circumstances.

George seemed to take after his mother so that would be a comfort to her now that he was back. As a regular seaman she supposed he would be going away again, which was a pity for Winnie. Still she must be used to it, and she would have him around for a while.

'Oh, so you're home then, are you?' said Percy Benson, who was sitting in the armchair when his son walked in. 'About time too.'

'Nice to see you too, Dad,' said George, going to him and offering his hand in greeting.

'You mother and I have had a hell of a time,' Percy said after the brief, unenthusiastic handshake.

'Yeah, so she's been telling me. I knew nothing about it.'

'I told her she should have let you know but you know how soft she is when it comes to you. Always has been.'

George nodded. There was not a glimmer of warmth in his father's greeting, as was normal when George came home. He had travelled the world and met people from a variety of backgrounds. In the service he'd had great mates but he'd also encountered bullies of the worst kind. But no one could make him feel as worthless as his father did. He was the reason George had gone away to sea. He'd had to get away or lose every last shred of self-confidence.

'So, how are you feeling in yourself?' he asked, as usual ignoring his father's cold attitude. He had turned the other cheek many times over the years for fear it would come to blows between them, which would be wrong and upset his mother terribly.

'It's not much fun being stuck indoors,' Percy replied miserably.

'I can imagine,' said George sympathetically. 'I thought we could all go down the pub for a celebration drink tonight.' He paused. 'I'll wheel you down there.'

'Humph, I don't know about that.'

'See how you feel later on,' said George patiently. 'There's plenty of time. It might cheer you up though.'

'So, did you get much bombing out at sea?' Percy asked.

George nodded. 'A fair bit. More than one ship I was on went down but I managed to survive. The luck of the devil I suppose. The service lost a lot of men.'

'Mm, I heard something about that.'

'Still the war is over now and it's time to put all the bad stuff behind us and look to the future.'

There was no 'how are you, son', or 'nice to have you back'. There never was. His father was a very strange man. Often charming towards other people but always hostile towards his son. George knew he should be used to it by now but doubted if he ever would be.

Winnie swept into the room, beaming. 'I've closed the shop so let's get the kettle on, shall we? Are you hungry, George?'

'I wouldn't say no to a piece of your sponge cake if there's any going spare,' he said.

'Still a wartime one I'm afraid because ingredients are still short but I've got one in the tin,' she told him.

'I can't think of anything I'd enjoy more,' he said. 'Anything you make tastes good.'

'Ooh, you old flatterer,' she said, loving it. 'You always did know how to get on my good side.'

'Stop spoiling him, Winnie,' said Percy.

'I'll spoil him all I like.' Winnie was a loving wife but she was also a devoted mother and definitely no pushover. 'And I'll thank you not to make comment.'

Welcome home, George, he thought. Nothing much has changed around here. She's still a joy and he's the miserable sod he always has been, towards his son anyway.

'I met Winnie Benson's son today,' April told Heather, who was at the house when she got home. 'Cor, what a smasher! He looks like a film star.'

'April,' began Heather in a tone of admonition. 'What on

earth are you doing fancying other men when you are engaged to Ronnie?'

'I don't fancy him . . . well not with any intent anyway,' said April with a wry grin. 'But I'm only human and I couldn't help noticing how easy on the eye he is. Tall, blue eyes and blond hair. Very suntanned too.'

'It's a wonder you didn't find out what size pants he wears,' said her cousin sarcastically.

April grinned. 'I didn't quite get around to that. Maybe if I see him again . . .' she teased.

'You shouldn't be looking at other men,' insisted her cousin, missing the joke completely. 'Not when you're engaged to be married.'

April burst out laughing.

'It isn't funny.'

'It is very funny,' said April. 'You sound like some Victorian matron. Of course I notice other men. I didn't go blind when I got engaged. Any normal woman would notice George Benson. He's absolutely gorgeous.'

'Next time I have to buy vegetables I'll get them there so I can have a look,' said her mother, smiling and entering into the spirit of the banter. 'I'll let you know what I think, April.'

Charlie came in and put the wireless on so the cousins went into the kitchen to talk.

'So how are things going with Arthur?' asked April lightly. 'Is it all lovey dovey?'

'We have our moments,' said Heather primly. 'We're going to start saving up to get married.'

'That's quick.'

'Quick? We've been engaged since before he went away,' Heather reminded her.

'I meant it's a bit soon after him getting back,' explained April. 'I thought you might want to go out and have some fun together before you settle down, him having been away for so long.'

'No. We're starting to save as soon as he gets a job.'

April had had her little joke but as her cousin was in such an intensely serious mood she went along with her to avoid upsetting her. But she did think Heather was sometimes a little staid for such a young woman.

'So does that mean courting at home instead of nights out?' asked April.

'We'll go out sometimes I suppose but mostly we'll be staying in or going for walks. We haven't started it yet though so we're going to the pictures tonight.'

'Lucky you.' April guessed that her cousin was enjoying the fact that she had her man back and April didn't. It was just the way Heather was. Not malicious exactly, just insecure.

'What are you having, Mum?' asked George that evening when the three of them went to the local.

'I'll have a sherry please dear, if they've got any,' said Winnie.

'A pint of the usual for you, Dad?'

'Yes please.'

George went over to the bar, greeted on his way by locals welcoming him back. It was a nice feeling; kind of warming. He was waiting to be served when someone slapped him on the back and said, 'George my old mate. Well, you're a sight for sore eyes.'

'Johnny,' greeted George, swinging around and pumping the hand of a young man with mid-brown hair and a warm smile.

'I was going to go round to your place tomorrow to find out if you were back.'

'Got demobbed a few days ago.'

'Good to see you,' said George, meaning every word. He and Johnny had been best mates since primary school and there was no one he would rather have seen at that moment.

'You too.'

'I've brought Mum and Dad down for a few drinks,' he said. 'They've been having a rough time.'

'Yeah, I heard your old man had a spot of health trouble. I was going to go round to your place to see them and find out if they knew when you'd be back.'

'And now I'm here.'

'No big thing for you is it, coming home after a long spell away, you old rascal.'

'Not really, no, but it feels like more of an event this time. Probably because I've been away for longer and all the bombing at sea and danger from submarines.'

'Did you get much of that?'

'Enough. Did you see much action?'

'Plenty but it's all in the past now and I'm just glad to be back,' Johnny said.

'We'll go out for a few beers together sometime soon,' suggested George.

'The sooner the better for me mate,' approved Johnny. 'We've got a lot of catching up to do. We were never on leave at the same time during the war.'

The pub was packed and everyone was pushing forward to get served. George's turn finally came. 'What you having, Johnny?' he asked.

'A pint of bitter please.'

'Coming up.' George ordered the drinks for them all with a smile on his face. It was so good to be home.

George had been in bars in many parts of the world; the squalid, the smart and the exotic, in sun-soaked places and bitterly cold ones. But there was nothing quite like an English pub, he thought, when he took the drinks to the table. The place was dark, crowded, noisy and badly in need of redecoration but it was full of heart and welcome.

'Hello, Johnny,' said Winnie warmly when he came to the table to join them. 'Welcome home, love. It's been a long time.'

'Welcome home, boy,' added Percy with enthusiasm.

'Draw up a chair,' invited Winnie.

It was odd, thought George, that his father could offer a warm welcome home to his son's pal but not to his own son. Oh well, there was no accounting for people but his dad wasn't just anyone and it still hurt, even after all these years.

Although George was feeling pleasantly relaxed from the effect of the beer that night when he got into bed, he wasn't so far gone as to be able to blot out a nagging worry. He'd originally gone to sea to get away from his father and in search of adventure. But he'd been a seaman for a long time and it was in his blood now. When his leaves ended he was always more than ready to go back. It was a very hard life with no home comforts but it was right for him. He loved the atmosphere of the sea; the smell and feel of it made him feel energetic and invigorated. He enjoyed the camaraderie, visiting other lands and discovering new things.

But the way things were here at home, he wouldn't be able to go back, not for a good while anyway, because his mother needed him here. Even though she would never admit it, it was too much for her running the shop on her own and looking after Dad. He felt a stab of empathy that she had gone through the worry of her husband's injury and all that went with it and not a word to her son. She was a gem of a mother and deserved the back-up support he was going to make sure she had from him. It wouldn't be forever, just until the old man got back on his feet which they seemed to think he would at some point.

Oh well, only time will tell, he thought, drifting off to sleep.

It was a big day in the Greens' house. Today, a Saturday, little Lily Green had come home to her family and there had been a stream of friends and neighbours who had called in during the day to see her and wish her well.

'She's famous, aren't you, darling,' said Peg in an infantile voice, peering into her crib. 'All these people wanting to see you. Everyone wants to have a look at the best-looking baby in town, yes they do. Isn't she the loveliest thing you've ever seen, Heather?'

'She is sweet,' said Heather.

'You must be so pleased with her, Beryl, after such a worrying start,' said Peg.

More than you could ever know, thought Beryl. This little mite had changed her as a person. When Jim died, it felt as though her life was over and the pregnancy filled her with horror. Now Lily gave her joy and made her feel whole again. But she said, 'Oh yeah, I feel truly blessed.'

'Small babies don't really do anything, though, do they?' said Heather with her usual lack of tact.

'Nothing entertaining,' said Beryl. 'But she soon will be doing something new every day.'

'I think she's lovely,' said Charlie as though defending his new sister.

'Oh, so do I,' protested Heather. 'I meant that she'll probably be more fun later on.'

'You'll be next to have a little one, Heather,' said her mother. 'If you and Arthur are going to get married soon.'

'Yeah, maybe,' said Heather, but she hadn't actually thought past the actual wedding yet: the long white dress, the flowers and the fuss with her being the undisputed star of the occasion. There was also the exciting prospect of being able to sleep with Arthur, actually share a bed with him, all legal and above board. She didn't even want to consider the unromantic and messy business of motherhood yet.

The baby started to cry and April picked her up.

'You're spoiling her already,' said her mother.

'No harm in a cuddle,' said April as her baby sister fell silent. 'It's what she seems to want.'

'Babies always want that,' said Beryl. 'But she won't always be able to have it, especially when you are all at work and I have other things to do.'

'I can't wait to take her out in her pram,' said April. 'I'll take her down the High Road next Saturday to show her off.'

'I'll probably be glad of a break from her by then,' said Beryl. 'New babies can be exhausting.'

'You know where I am if you need some time off,' offered Peg. 'I'll be glad to take her off your hands for an hour or so as often as you like.'

'I'll bear that in mind,' said Beryl as Lily became fretful. 'Meanwhile I think she wants feeding.'

'I must go,' said Heather. 'I have to go home to get ready to see Arthur.'

'That takes all day too,' added Peg.

'M-u-m,' Heather objected.

'Whoops, now I'm in trouble,' said Peg. 'My daughter doesn't enjoy a joke.'

'Not when I'm the subject of it,' said Heather. 'Anyway, I'm off. Are you coming, Mum?'

'No, I'll stay for a while longer,' she said.' I'll be back in time to get the tea ready.'

After Heather left, Beryl said, 'She seems very keen on Arthur, doesn't she.'

'She's keen on getting married, I know that much,' said Peg then added quickly, 'But yes, she is very fond of him.'

'A wedding will be a good excuse for us all to get something new to wear,' said Beryl.

'I'm going down the allotment for an hour or so,' said April. 'Will you be all right with the baby on your own, Mum?'

Beryl gave her a look. 'I have looked after a baby before, dear.'

'But not for a long time,' said April. 'You had the nurses for back-up when you were at the hospital with her.'

'I'll be fine so you go and do whatever it is you have to do at the allotment on a damp December day, though what that could be I can't possibly imagine.'

'I'll find something, don't worry.' She left the house, glad to be out in the fresh air. There wasn't a frost so she would dig over some vacant ground ready for next season and fork the top soil over to aerate it and brings pests to the surface to be preyed on by birds. She also had some Brussels sprouts and leeks to harvest which she would enjoy. Wearing a thick coat and woolly hat she quickened her step, eager to get cracking.

'Surprising how April has taken to the allotment isn't it,' said Peg, back at the house. 'Not many girls of her age would want to be out digging on a cold day like this.'

'I'm surprised too,' said Beryl. 'But pleasantly so. She keeps us supplied with vegetables on a regular basis. And of course she makes a few bob selling it to Benson's. I'm very proud of her.'

'As well you might be,' approved Peg. 'You wouldn't catch my Heather getting stuck in like that.'

'I don't know if April will be quite so keen when Ronnie comes home though,' Beryl mentioned. 'She won't have so much spare time then.'

'If she's anything like Heather she'll live and breathe for him,' said Peg. 'Getting married to Arthur is all Heather thinks about. She's almost obsessed.'

'Mm,' said Beryl thoughtfully. 'Though somehow I have a feeling that April will still find time for the allotment whatever else is going on in her life. She's really taken to it since Jim died. It's almost as though she needs it.'

'There are worse ways to spend her time,' said Peg.

'Indeed,' said Beryl, thinking how lucky she was to have three such lovely children.

George and Johnny were having a few drinks together that night before going to the Hammersmith Palais to look for some women.

'So what happened to that girl you were going out with the last time we were in touch?' asked George. 'I thought that was serious.'

'So did I. But she met someone else and gave me the push. She ended it by letter while I was away at the war which was a blow but we live through these things, don't we.' Johnny sipped his beer. 'What about you? Any action in that department?'

'No, mate,' he replied. 'I can't really have a steady girl because I'm away most of the time and you can't expect a woman to put up with that.'

'But seamen do have girlfriends and get married, don't they?'

'Course they do but I don't see how they can make a good job of it if they are never around. I mean, think about it, if you're not together how can you share your lives?'

'Mm, there is that I suppose.' Johnny paused thoughtfully. 'But you're staying at home to help your mum run the shop so you could get someone steady now.'

'I'm not staying at home permanently,' George explained. 'Once Dad's back on his feet I shall get a ship. Not much point in getting serious about anyone, is there? But I'm hoping for some female company, of course.'

'Don't you ever fancy an ordinary, comfortable life on dry land?' asked Johnny.

'Sometimes I think it might be nice and I'll be all right at home for a while then I'll start to get the wanderlust again. It's strange. I've tried it before and I always want to go back.'

'I'm just the opposite,' said Johnny. 'I feel as though I never want to go away again after my time in the army. I'm making the most of my home comforts.'

'I suppose you want to find some nice girl and settle down?' said George.

'Eventually yeah, but I intend to have some fun before that. The army took a large chunk of my life so I want to live a little now that I'm free.'

'In that case we'd better get to the dance hall and hope we get lucky.'

'A man after my own heart.' Johnny was grinning but he became serious suddenly. 'I'm so glad you're back, mate. It was always us two in the old days.'

'It certainly was.'

'I'll make the most of you before you bugger off again.'

'Finish your drink then and we'll head off to the dance,' said George, his voice gruff with emotion.

They finished their beer and headed for the bus stop, laughing and joking like they did when they were boys.

April had a special mission the following Saturday morning. Wearing her best blue coat and the high heels she wore for work, she set off for a walk along the High Road with Lily in the pram, pausing every few minutes to allow locals to admire her baby sister who was very smart in her white knitted bonnet and mittens.

She stopped outside Benson's, put the brake on the pram and went inside.

'Is your mum around?' she asked George, who was busy serving.

'She's upstairs taking a break. Can I help?' he asked in a friendly manner.

'It's nothing important,' she explained. 'I'm out for a walk with my baby sister in the pram and I just called in to show her to Winnie. I promised I would when I was passing. But another time will be all right.'

'I'm sure she wouldn't want to miss that,' he said. 'Why not bring the baby in and take her upstairs. I'll give Mum a shout to let her know you are on the way.'

'If you're sure that will be all right, I'll go and get her,' she said, eager to show Lily off.

'Quite sure,' he confirmed.

Charlie Green walked along the High Road on his way home from playing in a football match with his mates when he saw Lily's pram outside the greengrocer's. There were lots of black high prams like that around but he knew it was hers because the pink rabbit he'd bought for her was in it. What caught his eye was the fact that the pram was empty.

He went into the shop looking for his sister while his pals walked on.

'Wotcha, son,' said George, guessing from the mud on his face what he'd been doing. 'Been playing football?'

'Yeah.'

'Just a kickabout or a match?'

'A match,' said Charlie. 'A local junior side. We play most Saturdays during the season if we can get anyone to organise it.'

'A man after my own heart,' said George. 'I used to play a lot of footie when I was your age.'

'Football is my passion,' said Charlie. 'I used to go to watch my team Chelsea play sometimes with my dad before the war put a stop to League football.'

'I'm a Chelsea supporter too,' George said.

'Sensible man,' said Charlie, sounding about forty. 'Dad got killed by a bomb so I don't suppose I'll be going to see them play when it starts again.'

'You can come with me and my mate if you like, if I haven't gone back to sea by then,' said George.

'Really?' Charlie beamed.

'Yeah, why not.'

'Cor, thanks.'

The shop was filling up with housewives with their shopping bags and baskets. 'So what can I get you?' George asked Charlie.

'I'm looking for my sister April. Our baby sister's pram is outside so I know she's here,' he explained. 'She said she was going to take her out.'

'Be with you in a minute, ladies,' George said to the queue, then hurried through to the back and yelled up the stairs for April to come down.

'What are you doing here?' asked April of her brother. 'You're filthy. You shouldn't be in a shop in that state.'

'It's only a bit of mud and there's plenty of that in here anyway,' he said, referring to the dust on the floor and the earth on some of the potatoes.

'Don't be so rude. Dirt can't be helped in a greengrocer's shop but you don't have to add to it,' she said, flexing her big sister muscles. 'So what do you want?'

'Can you lend me a ha'penny please, sis?' he asked. 'I want to get a sticky bun from the baker's and I haven't got any dosh on me.'

'Go and wait outside while I get my bag from upstairs,' she told him. 'I'm having a cup of tea with Mrs Benson.'

'He's all right in here,' George assured her while weighing up some parsnips. 'He's perfectly respectable.'

'I'll just be a minute then,' she said and hurried away while someone in the queue recognised Charlie and asked after his family and the new baby. Others joined in and it turned into quite a jolly conversation.

As a teenager before he went away, George had often found the chattering that went on in his parents' shop irritating because the place always seemed to be full of people when he went in and out and it curtailed his privacy. Now he found himself enjoying the sense of community.

April stayed longer than she intended with Winnie so she was in a hurry when she finally came down the stairs with the baby.

'I could talk to your mum for hours,' she said to George.

'Me too; she's very good company.'

'I'm in a big rush now though,' she said. 'The baby will need feeding and I've got a few bits of shopping to do for Mum. I've got things to do at the allotment this afternoon too.'

'Calm down or you'll upset the nipper.' He smiled, glancing towards the baby in April's arms.

'You're right.' She looked at him. 'It's nice to see your mum having some time off. It's been hard for her on her own. I bet she loves having you around.'

He nodded. 'At least she doesn't have to get up early every day to go to the market now that I'm doing it. I used to go with my dad when I was a boy so I'm familiar with the procedure. In fact there isn't much I don't know about the greengrocery trade, having grown up with it.'

'Are you back for good?'

'I'm not planning on staying indefinitely but I'll be around for a while.'

'Good,' she said giving him a warm smile which made his heart melt. 'I mean it will be nice for your parents.'

'It's good for Mum certainly,' he said, thinking how cold his father still was towards him.

'I expect your father enjoys having you around too.'

'Yeah, of course he does.' His manner suggested he didn't want to continue with the subject.

'I'll be off then,' she said.

'When is that boyfriend of yours due back?' he asked.

'Any time now. I hope he doesn't catch me in my gardening clothes. I didn't used to do anything like that before he went away.'

'I'm sure he'll think you look lovely whatever you are wearing,' he said, meaning it.

'Oh. Thank you,' she said graciously. 'I'm certainly having to wait a long time.'

There was a short silence then he heard himself say the unthinkable. 'Would you like to go out and have some fun tonight to take the boredom out of waiting? We could go dancing if you fancy it.'

Up went her eyes.

'Not a date, of course,' he explained quickly. 'I know you're spoken for and I wouldn't muscle in on the girlfriend of someone serving in the armed forces. I just thought a night out might ease the strain of waiting. No funny business, I promise. Strictly mates. You have my word.'

'Well I . . .' she began.

'No, of course you can't,' he said. 'It was a silly idea, spur of the moment. Forget I said it.'

April was quiet, mulling it over. She hadn't been dancing since she last saw Ronnie and she could certainly do with a night out.

'I can't see that it would do any harm,' she said, surprising him. 'So long as it isn't a date.'

'Absolutely not,' he assured her.

'Let's do it then.'

'So I'll call for you around seven thirty if you tell me where you live.'

She was tempted to suggest she meet him somewhere because of what Mum and Charlie would have to say about it but she decided she would be doing nothing wrong; just breaking the monotony of waiting for Ronnie.

'If you have a piece of paper, I'll write it down for you,' she said excitedly.

'Oh April,' said her mother later when she told her about her plans for the evening. 'You've waited all this time for Ronnie and now you're going to let him down.'

'I'm not letting anyone down, especially not Ronnie,' insisted April. 'I haven't had a night out for three years except to the pictures with Heather. I fancy letting my hair down for a change. It's just a night out with a friend who just happens to be a man. Nothing more than that.'

'It's all work at the office and the allotment for her,' added her brother supportively. 'I think she should have a night out. He's a nice bloke, that George Benson. He'll look after her. He won't step out of line.'

'Since when did you become the expert in such things?' asked his mother.

'I didn't,' he replied. 'I just want my sister to have some fun and I can't take her out dancing because I'm too young to get in.'

'Exactly,' said his mother. 'You know nothing about such things. She's engaged to be married so shouldn't be going out with any other men.'

But when that 'other man' turned up to call for April and assured them all that it was all above board and strictly platonic Beryl did a complete volte-face. And when he reminded Charlie that he would take him to see Chelsea play as soon as League football started again she melted completely.

'Seems a nice enough fella,' she said when the door had closed behind the couple. 'She'll come to no harm with him.'

'You've changed your tune,' Charlie commented.

'Yeah well, I hadn't met him when I said those things, had I?' she reminded him.

'I told you he was nice, didn't I?' he said. 'And I'll get to see Chelsea play again. Yippee!'

The Palais was a riot of colour and excitement, the dance floor crowded with couples, the men in civvies now outnumbering those still in uniform. Demobilisation was taking a long time to complete, so many servicemen were home from abroad but yet to be officially demobbed and given their demob clothes. Most of the women looked nice despite clothes still being on ration. Many had become adept at making the best of themselves and were very inventive with a blouse and skirt or an old dress. The coloured lights from the ceiling added a touch of magic.

For all his good looks and charm George wasn't a brilliant dancer but he managed to get around the floor quite neatly and liked to jive.

'It was a bit cheeky of me asking you out to a dance when I have two left feet,' he said. 'Maybe I should have suggested the pictures.'

'I'm glad you didn't; this is much more fun,' said April, who was wearing a white fancy blouse that enhanced the colour of her hair and a black skirt. 'Anyway you're not that bad and you're quite good at jiving.'

'I didn't go to dances abroad,' he said. 'Most of us blokes usually think that as long as we can get around the floor we'll manage.'

'As the purpose of going dancing is to meet girls rather than perfect your quickstep,' she suggested lightly.

'Exactly.' He grinned. 'But not tonight, of course.'

'No, tonight you've taken pity on a girl starved of fun.'

'Not entirely,' he assured her, glad that there was no visible evidence of the way he really felt about her. 'I wanted to go out and have fun as well.'

'What did you do for relaxation when you were in port and had a night off?'

'The lads and I would go to the bars mostly,' he said.

'A girl in every port eh?'

He laughed. 'Of course not, that's just a myth.'

'Girlfriends though?'

'I've had a few of those,' he admitted.

'I bet you have,' she said, giving him a knowing look.

The nearest thing April had ever had to a tan was freckles on her nose and sore red patches on her arms and legs from sitting on the kitchen chair in the back garden on one of the few sunny days they had in summer. She didn't know anyone with a tan either because of the nature of the British climate.

But his skin was evenly browned and it really set off the white shirt he was wearing with a shiny tie with bright patterns that looked to have been painted on. His suit was a lighter grey than those worn by British men.

'I bet you didn't get those clothes around here,' she said when they went to the pub in the interval.

'No, I got them in America. I suppose they are a bit loud for London but I like to dress like this.'

'They suit you.' She paused. 'Until the war I didn't know anyone who had been abroad, and you're the only person I know who's been to America.'

'That's the good thing about being in the service,' he said. 'You do get to see the world.'

'Is that why you joined?'

'Partly.' His manner didn't invite further enquiry.

'Perhaps we should be getting back to the dance,' she suggested, emptying her glass of gin and orange.

'Yeah, if you like.' He finished his drink and they left, both smiling.

To George's credit he behaved impeccably throughout the evening. He didn't even hold her close in the last waltz. When they walked to her place from the bus stop she said, 'Thanks ever so much for tonight, George. It's been lovely.'

'I've enjoyed it too.'

There was a sudden tension. They both knew that if things had been different he would, at the very least, have asked to see her again. But he just said, 'I suppose I'll see you when you bring the vegetables to the shop.'

'Yes.' She paused thoughtfully. 'By the way, thanks for offering

72

to take my brother to football when it starts again. He's absolutely thrilled. He misses his dad a lot even though he doesn't say much. They were both great football fans.'

'Yes, that's sad for you all. Mum told me what happened to your father.'

'The same bomb that injured Mr Benson.'

He nodded. 'Dad was luckier. Anyway I'm looking forward to having Charlie come along when the footie starts again. As I'll be home for longer than usual, I shall get back to doing traditional things.'

When they turned the corner into her road and neared her house, she said, 'Thanks again, George.'

'Pleasure.'

On a sudden impulse she leaned up and kissed his cheek in a friendly manner.

That was when she heard someone call her name; she turned and in the light from the lamppost she saw a soldier standing at her gate. It was Ronnie!

Chapter Four

Events moved with such speed April was powerless to stop the affray. Ronnie was like a man possessed and blows were being aimed at George who fielded them, offering no retaliation, just defending himself.

'Ronnie, what are you doing?' she shouted, trying to pull him away from George. 'It isn't what you think. George has done nothing wrong.'

'Stay back, April,' urged George as the punches kept coming. 'You'll get hurt.'

'You'll get killed if he doesn't stop,' she said, her voice shaking with fear. 'Please stop, Ronnie, I beg you. You've got the wrong end of the stick.'

Suddenly Ronnie drew back, stood for a few moments to catch his breath then walked away without a word, leaving April and George staring after him speechless. April started to go after him but George said, 'I should let him cool down before you try to explain. He probably won't listen at the moment. Leave it until tomorrow when he'll have calmed down and might be able to see things as they really were.'

'Why didn't you hit him back?' she asked.

'Because I was the one at fault,' he replied. 'I was with his girlfriend.'

'Not in that way.'

'He doesn't realise that, does he?' he reminded her. 'He only knows what he saw.'

'And came to the wrong conclusion.'

'Exactly, but he will have been through a lot,' said George, feeling entirely to blame. 'Look at it from his point of view: he will probably have been in some hell hole somewhere longing to come home, aching to see you. Then when he finally does set eyes on you again you're with another man. It's no wonder he blew his top.'

'I shall have to go after him,' she said. 'Right or wrong, I can't leave it until tomorrow; it's too important. I might be able to catch him before he gets the bus home to Hammersmith.'

'Shall I come with you?'

'Not likely,' she said in a definite tone. 'We've had enough rough stuff for one night.'

'What about you though?'

'He won't hurt me. I really am sure about that. He isn't normally a violent man.' She looked at George. 'Thanks again for tonight. Sorry you got hurt.'

'I've had worse.'

'G'night then,' she said, taking off her high heels then running down the street towards the main road, carrying her shoes.

Maybe it had happened for the best, thought George, as he walked home. At least Ronnie's intervention had stopped yours truly following his instincts and asking to see her again.

The last thing he wanted was to encroach upon another man's territory, especially a member of the armed forces who had been away doing his bit for his country. April was lovely though and he had already fallen for her. But those sorts of feelings had to be curbed because she wasn't free. Easier said than done, he thought, looking back over their evening together, which he'd found rather wonderful. Oh well, George, she's not for you so get used to it, mate. He was an even-tempered man, not usually given to moods, but he felt quite depressed when he reached the High Road. He was concerned about April too because that boyfriend of hers was very handy with his fists.

'Hello, April, what are you doing here?' asked Ronnie when she found him in the bus queue.

'What do you think?' she said, astonished by his mild attitude. It was almost as though nothing had happened. 'I've come to try and put things right.'

'My bus will be here in a minute and it's the last one of the night,' he said.

She stared at him in disbelief. 'You have just half killed a friend of mine and you're worried about your bus?'

'It's quite a step on foot. Anyway, I didn't hit him that hard . . . did I?'

'Hard enough. And it was completely uncalled for. You got it all wrong. There's nothing going on between us.'

'It didn't look like nothing to me.'

'Will you please come out of the bus queue,' she said, taking his arm and drawing him away. 'And I'll explain what the situation between George and me really is.'

Away from the eavesdroppers in the bus queue, she told him of the circumstances that led to her being with George earlier.

'So I really did get it wrong then.'

'Completely!'

'Sorry.'

'It wasn't me you punched.'

'Sorry for doubting you, I mean.'

'I forgive you,' she said putting her arms around him. 'So let's start again, shall we? Welcome home, Ronnie.'

She felt his body trembling and when she looked up at his face he was weeping. 'Oh how embarrassing,' he said thickly. 'I'm sorry. Trust me to ruin everything.'

'You haven't ruined anything at all,' she said. 'I'm just so pleased to have you back.'

'I'm glad to be back,' he said, blowing his nose. 'But if you don't mind I think I'd like to call it a night now. I won't bother with the bus though. The walk will do me good. I'll see you safely to your door first but we'll have a proper reunion tomorrow. I'll come and call for you in the evening.'

'All right, Ronnie,' she said gently. 'I'll look forward to it.'

Standing at the gate watching him stride away, a tall, slim figure with a terrible sadness about him, she was worried. His unexpected behaviour made her realise how little she really knew him. A draughtsman in civilian life and a mild-mannered man, he had never struck her as someone capable of violence. Two weeks from their first meeting to their parting was all the time they had had together and she could see now that they had been too absorbed in the magic of falling in love to really get to know each other. Now they seemed like strangers. She wondered if the fight might not have been entirely a result of her and George being together and may have been provoked by some sort of angst within Ronnie, who had seemed so strange.

So after all the waiting, hoping and yearning, their reunion had been a huge disappointment. But perhaps tomorrow would be better and if it wasn't maybe the next time. They would make things improve, together. She was determined.

Her mother was up feeding the baby when April got in.

'Have you seen Ronnie?' asked Beryl, looking concerned. 'He arrived just after you'd gone out. It was a bit awkward and I told him you'd gone out with a friend, omitting to mention that it was a man. He seemed very edgy and I could tell he was disappointed that you weren't in. He went off to the pub and said he'd come back later but he didn't.'

'He did. He was waiting across the road when I got back . . . with George, who insisted on seeing me home.'

'Blimey, that could have been dodgy.'

April told her what had happened.

'I've never thought of Ronnie as a violent man because he seemed such a gent,' said Beryl. 'He shouldn't have thumped George, of course, but you can understand why. I suppose he just saw the two of you together and lost his temper.'

'He seems different to how I remember him, Mum,' April confided. 'Sort of weird somehow.'

'Fighting in a war affects some men for a long time after, can even be for life. I remember people talking about it after the First World War,' her mother said. 'We can only guess what awful things have happened to him. I mean, imagine having to go against every bit of morality you've ever been taught and kill people, not to mention the horror of being on the battlefield and knowing you could cop it at any moment. He'll probably be his old self after a few weeks but if he does seem a bit different sometimes you'll have to be patient with him. Our boys have done their best for us; it's up to us to support them now.'

'I shall do my best for him, Mum.'

'What about George?' asked Beryl. 'Is he all right after his hammering?.'

'He seemed to be. I should think he's pretty tough. Poor man; he didn't know what he was getting into when he invited me out.'

'He did know that you were engaged, though, so maybe he shouldn't have.'

April felt an overwhelming need to defend George but she thought it wise to stay silent on the subject so she went into the kitchen to make some cocoa for them both. She would keep her mother company while she finished feeding Lily.

The following evening Ronnie called for April as though nothing had happened. They went to a pub so that they could talk and chose one on the riverside. It was a cold night but the pub was warm and cosy with a fire and people filling the bar. Because they got there early they managed to get a table in the corner away from the crowd. Through the window they could see the lights on the other side of the river, the reflection of the moon on the water a mass of pearly splinters.

'So here we both are,' she said when he had got the drinks.

'I thought the day would never come when we would be sitting here together. The waiting seemed to go on forever.'

'Yeah, it has been a long time,' he said.

'So when will you get demobbed?' she asked, because he was still in uniform.

'A couple of months, I think,' he replied. 'We all have to wait our turn. There are so many of us.'

'So now that you can look to the future, have you got any plans?'

'I shall go to the firm I used to work for to find out what the chances are of getting my old job back. When I went away they said it would be waiting for me after the war but that was a few years ago. Things change.'

'I'm sure they'll do what they can.'

'I hope so, though I've heard a lot of the chaps have come home to find they are out of work. It'll be a long time before the country gets back on its feet.'

She knew it would take time for him to think about the plans they'd made to get married; that had been during those heady days before he'd gone away. Now his work prospects were more important. Without a job he wouldn't feel able to move forward. A few romantic words from him would be nice though.

'You're looking lovely, April,' he said, pleasing her. 'Just as beautiful as I remember.'

'Thank you.' He was thinner than before he went away, she noticed, and the boyishness she remembered had gone leaving him looking rather gaunt, especially as his brown hair was army-style short. He still had a warm smile though and a deep voice with better diction than most people of her acquaintance. 'You don't look so bad yourself.'

'So what have you been doing with yourself while I've

been away?' He gave a wry grin. 'Apart from going out dancing with a platonic male friend.'

She chuckled. 'That was the one and only time, I promise you.'

'I believe you,' he said with a stiff, rather forced smile.

Steering the conversation on to safer ground she said, 'I took over Dad's allotment after he died so that's been keeping me out of mischief.' She gave him a wry grin. 'And please don't tell me it's an odd thing for a girl to do because I already know that and I don't care because I enjoy it.'

'If it makes you happy why not?'

'It keeps us well supplied with vegetables and earns a few pennies for the family pot.'

'So I've come back to a rich woman.'

'Hardly. Most of it goes into plants and gardening materials but there is a little left over.' She had already put him up to date with the situation at home. 'Vegetable growing at my level isn't about money. It's creative and an absolute joy, most of the time anyway.'

'That must be why my father spends so much time gardening,' he said. 'I always assumed it was to get out of the house and away from my mother for a break.'

'I think some men do probably enjoy that part of it; they like a good old chinwag with their cronies,' she said. 'I've seen them at my allotments.'

'I bet they like having you around.' He gave her a knowing look.

'No, not especially,' she said. 'They are all getting on a bit but they are very helpful to me as I'm a beginner. There is quite a lot of competition goes on between them though. They are very proud of their veg. They like theirs to be the best.'

'Marrows at dawn, that sort of thing,' he laughed.

'Not quite.' She grinned, entering into the joke. 'More like "my beetroots are better than yours". Though I don't go in for any of that. I'm far too much of a novice.'

'I think you're probably wise not to be too competitive,' he said. 'It could become a strain.'

'So can I rely on you to give me a hand from time to time then?' she asked jokingly.

'Depends on the weather.'

'A fair-weather gardener, eh.'

'I'm not any sort of gardener,' he admitted. 'I don't think I've ever even pulled a weed in the whole of my life. Dad's always looked after everything in that department.'

'Oh well, I might try and tempt you to come along in the spring when everything is fresh and things get busy.' Again, she was only joking. His lack of interest in her beloved hobby had left her feeling oddly flat.

'Don't bank on it,' he said predictably.

As she sipped her drink she saw George come in with a man of about his age. 'Meanwhile here's your chance to apologise to my platonic friend for beating him up.' She nodded in George's direction. 'He's over there.'

He followed her glance and frowned so deeply she thought he was going to fly into a rage. But he said, 'That's not such a bad idea,' and got up and walked across to George, who was standing at the bar.

'What was all that about?' asked Johnny when Ronnie had left after speaking to George. 'Have you been up to no good with someone else's girl?'

'No, not at all. You heard what the man said: he was sorry

for jumping to the wrong conclusions and thumping me, wrong being the operative word.'

'He also told you, in no uncertain terms, to keep away from her in future. Not a man to cross if he's so handy with his fists.'

'He's just guarding his territory and I don't blame him,' said George, who had been warned off in a very firm manner.

Johnny looked across towards Ronnie as he sat down with April. 'Is it that redhead?'

'Yes, that's her.'

'No wonder you were after her.'

'I wasn't after her. I took her out to cheer her up as a friend,' said George. 'We didn't know he was going to arrive home that night.'

'All right, I believe you,' said Johnny. 'Don't jump down my throat. She's lovely though.'

'She's nice with it too and I have no intention of trying to spoil things for her and her man.'

'Oh dear, you have got it bad.'

'Johnny, will you pack it in, I've told you she's just a mate,' objected George.

'Just pulling your leg,' said Johnny, who didn't have a malicious bone in his body.

'Even if she was free she's the sort of girl who would want, and deserve, commitment and I couldn't give her that,' said George wistfully.

'Just as well she isn't available then, isn't it?'

'Exactly.'

They drank their beer then Johnny said, 'It's a bit miserable not having a girlfriend to be with at Christmas, isn't it? It's only a week away.'

'There will be plenty of good cheer of the liquid sort to

help us on our way,' said George. 'But why don't we go and find some football to watch on Boxing Day? There's no League games, of course, but there might be some amateur matches on somewhere in London.'

'Yeah, I'm all for that.'

'Do you mind if a young lad I know comes along with us?' asked George. 'He used to go to football with his dad but he was killed in the bombing.'

'That's fine with me,' said Johnny. 'Who is the boy anyway?'

'April's kid brother.'

'Aah,' he said knowingly. 'So you're in with the family then. A wise move.'

'I'm not "in with them" but I do like them. April is a friend of Mum's. She's a vegetable grower and supplies us at the shop from time to time, that's how I got to know her.'

Johnny enjoyed banter and he and George had known each other for too long to ever take offence. But he realised now that he shouldn't tease his pal any more about April because he obviously did have some sort of feelings for her. Romantic or just friendly, he had no idea, but he would respect them whatever they were.

'So football it is on Boxing Day if we can find out where anyone will be kicking a ball about.'

George nodded. 'Shall we move on when we've had these,' he suggested because his eyes were constantly drawn to April and Ronnie might notice and fly into another rage.

'Yeah, whatever you like, mate,' Johnny said amiably.

Beryl could hardly bear the pain of Christmas without Jim on this the first Christmas Day since he died. The saving grace was Lily, who was an absolute joy. Being premature, she was a little behind in her development, though she was expected to catch up in time, but she could smile and respond to people now.

Peg and Heather spent the day with them as usual and Ronnie came round in the evening, having done his filial duty and had his Christmas dinner with his parents. Heather went to Arthur's for the evening but the rest of them played cards, had a few drinks, ate their pooled sweet rations, listened to the wireless and sang a few songs. It was jolly enough but Beryl found it hard going. Jim had been such a presence in all their lives it was hardly bearable without him. She found Ronnie difficult to get on with too.

She didn't know what to make of him. His courtship with April had been so short before he'd gone away she hadn't had a chance to get to know him then and she found him rather distant now. It wasn't exactly coldness; more as though he was somewhere else in his head and wasn't happy there. He went through the motions but he was tense and she'd noticed that he didn't light up when April was near as sweethearts usually did. A man of few words, he didn't have much to say to anyone and lacked the warmth they were used to in this family. It was probably the after-effects of his experiences in the war and she knew she must be patient. Anyway, April was the one who was going to marry him and she was old enough to know her own mind.

Not that there was any talk of a wedding but she supposed he hadn't been back long enough for that yet. His pre-war job was waiting for him after demob so she supposed they might be making plans after he settled into that. Oh well, Christmas Day was almost over, thank goodness. Boxing Day should be better. Charlie was going to watch some football with George and his mate so he was looking forward to that, bless him. George, now there was a man after her own heart; why couldn't April fall for someone straightforward like him?

She admonished herself for thinking ill of Ronnie and mentally trying to run her daughter's life for her and went upstairs to check on Lily.

April was also finding Christmas Day extremely tedious. She tried not to admit it to herself but Ronnie wasn't easy to be with, mostly because he kept withdrawing into himself. She sensed that it wasn't because he was bored with her personally and that it was something deeper and apart from their relationship. He smiled in all the right places but she could tell that he was deeply miserable. She would have to speak to him about it if it continued but not today which mercifully was almost over.

Ronnie didn't know exactly when he'd first started to feel depressed but it was at some point during his time in action. His nerves were always jangling during combat but the knotted stomach and overpowering sense of fear used to disappear between battles. There was no reason for him to feel like this now that there was no more conflict but his mind didn't seem to be able to accept that. The dry-mouthed symptoms of terror were uncontrollable and there was nothing he could do until the panic burned out, usually returning quite soon.

He tried to behave normally but sensed that April might suspect that something was wrong and didn't want to spoil things for her. When the symptoms were at their height he lost concentration and it was difficult to make conversation because he felt so isolated within himself. He loathed feeling like this; he wanted to feel normal again like he had before the war. But no matter how hard he fought against it the feelings just kept coming. Christmas Day with April and her family had been a huge ordeal and he was glad it was nearly over so that he could go home to his bedroom and cry. That was the only thing that gave him any relief and that was short-lived. Somehow he had to pull himself together but he just didn't know how.

Charlie was glowing when he got back from the football match the next day. April hadn't seen him this cheerful since their dad was around.

'I've invited the lads for a mince pie,' he announced and in trooped George and Johnny, the latter being introduced.

Suddenly the house was filled with life and laughter. To April it was like a breath of fresh air after such a dismal Christmas Day. She found herself feeling relieved that Ronnie wasn't coming round until later on, after the misunderstanding with George. Another one of those would upset everyone.

'Lovely mince pies, Mrs Green,' said Johnny. 'Just what we need after an afternoon in the cold.'

'Not half,' added George. 'It was freezing.'

'You must be mad standing there in the cold just to see a ball being kicked around,' said April with the deliberate intention of provoking them.

'It isn't just a ball being kicked around,' said Charlie.

'It's an art,' added George.

'Beautiful,' said Johnny.

'Oh listen to them,' laughed Beryl, entering into the spirit of the banter. 'Anyone would think they were talking about a statue or something.'

'Better than a statue, Mum, because it moves,' said Charlie. 'Anyway, you and April have watched me play enough times and you shouted loudest on the touchline.'

'That's different,' said April. 'You are our own special work of art.'

'Ugh, that is so embarrassing.'

'As embarrassing as when we shout for you at your matches?' asked his sister.

'Nothing is as bad as that.' He turned to his new pals. 'April only went and shouted at the referee. Can you imagine that?'

'Ooh, April,' said George in mock admonition. 'That really is beyond the pale.'

Everyone was smiling, even Lily who was awake in her crib.

'She's a little smasher,' said George.

'You can pick her up if you like,' said Beryl jokingly, thinking the idea would fill him with horror.

'Yeah, all right,' he said and went over and gently lifted Lily, carefully supporting her head.

This raised a cheer and the baby gurgled.

'You're a natural,' said Johnny as George cradled her, smiling and talking to her. 'You know who to come to for a babysitter, Mrs Green.'

'I certainly do.'

'You can come round when she's screaming her head off in the middle of the night,' suggested Charlie. 'She's got one hell of a pair of lungs.'

'I think I might miss out on that one,' said George. 'Not sure how I'd be with a crying baby. I like them all smiley and sweet.'

'Don't we all,' said Beryl, laughing.

They all had more tea and mince pies. April thought her mother looked happier than she had in ages. It had been a most enjoyable interlude.

'Thanks for letting Charlie tag along to the match,' she said to the men when she was seeing them out at the front door. 'He so loved going to football with his dad.'

'He didn't just tag along because he was good company,' said Johnny. 'He's a great kid and a true football supporter. He knows more about the game than we do.'

'That's right,' added George. 'I shall have to ask my mother for some Saturday afternoons off when the League games start again if I haven't gone back to sea by then. Then he can get to see his beloved Chelsea again.'

They went on their way, leaving the family feeling happy and refreshed.

The living accommodation above the shop at Benson's was on two floors. It was an old building with high ceilings and three bedrooms, a living room, dining room and kitchen and bathroom. The ground floor had an office as well as the sitting room they used for their breaks and a built-on lavatory at the back. The door to the cellar was in the hallway behind the shop.

The cellar was the most hated place in the house for George, who had bad childhood memories of it and had never forgotten the claustrophobic terror. It was, however, very satisfactory for storing fruit and vegetables, having stone walls and floor so remaining cold all year round. The only sign of modern life in here was a single electric light bulb that hung from the ceiling over the grey tomblike interior. One of its worst hazards was the sheer stone steps that led to it from the house. Many a person had acquired bruises from losing their footing and tumbling down.

George was in there early one morning in the New Year checking stock and getting sacks of potatoes and crates of vegetables ready to take up to the shop. He was deep in thought about the business as he worked. As his father showed no sign of being able to return to work at any time soon, it had become obvious to George that if the shop was to support the three of them for any length of time they needed to increase their turnover. Up until now he'd only taken a token wage because he'd earned well at sea and spent little so he had managed to put something by. But he would eventually need to earn properly in order to pay his way. He didn't have a lavish lifestyle but he did enjoy a drink with his mates, the cinema and enough cash to take a girl out if the situation arose.

Even apart from his own needs he could see that this business had the potential to be a little gold mine with the right management, especially when things got plentiful again. He needed to put more effort into buying, to search for stock. Now that the seas were safe for the ships to bring in goods from abroad, he needed to get hold of oranges and bananas which were still in very short supply. Everything was taking longer to get back to normal after the war than had been expected.

So he would go to Covent Garden market sometimes instead

of the local one. The basic petrol ration had been restored after the meagre wartime allowance so he would have enough fuel to do it a couple of times a week. He would shop around for goods. As well as being good business practice, the public needed greengrocery for a healthy diet. So starting tomorrow he would go in search of something a bit more colourful than seasonal British vegetables and fruit.

The real way forward was for Benson's to open another shop in one of the nearby towns. But that would be too much for his parents if he wasn't around and as he wasn't planning on being here indefinitely it wasn't really an option, even though now was the time to do something like that before the boom came and shops became scarcer and more expensive.

It struck him as odd that he was thinking along these lines because he'd never had so much as a hint of an entrepreneurial streak before. He supposed it must have happened because he'd been forced into working here and it had grown on him like other traditions of home he hadn't realised he'd missed so much: his parents, football matches, English pubs and the good old British sense of humour.

Oh well, he would do his best to make this shop more profitable and that would give his parents a boost when the time came for him to go back to sea. For now he had to get these goods upstairs and into the shop. He carried some crates over to the stairs and made his way up.

One cold February evening, Heather came to the Greens' house sobbing her heart out.

'He's chucked me,' she wailed. 'The rotten bugger. He doesn't want to marry me.'

April guided her towards the stairs so that they could speak in private in her bedroom.

'Blimey, she's in a state,' Charlie remarked to his mother after they'd gone. 'Why is she so upset over a bloomin' boyfriend? He wasn't much cop, that Arthur, anyway.'

'That sort of thing really hurts, Charlie,' said his mother. 'She'll be feeling bad about it for a while. You'll know more about it when you're older.'

'I'm better off sticking with football and my mates I reckon,' he said.

'For the moment yes,' she said, enjoying his naivety while it lasted.

'So it isn't so much that he doesn't want to marry you but that he doesn't want to marry anyone at the moment,' said April after her cousin had poured her heart out.

'That's right,' confirmed Heather, her voice distorted by crying. 'He wants to be free after being so confined during the war.'

'He isn't actually rejecting you then.'

'Of course he is. If he loved me he'd want to marry me,' she said. 'He was on about us being together for so long and neither of us having had a life as single people.'

April didn't know what to say to make her cousin feel better because the pain of rejection she must be experiencing wouldn't be soothed by a few soft words.

'It's the bloody war,' Heather went on. 'We'd have been married long ago if he hadn't had to go away.'

That was true, April conceded. It was a very fortunate person indeed who had not been negatively affected by the war in some way. But might Arthur have felt restless after they were married if it hadn't happened this way? Neither he nor Heather had ever tested the waters beyond each other and Heather could be very possessive.

'The shame of it,' Heather went on before April had a chance to speak. 'I'm just a cast-off. I won't have anyone in my life. I'll be the odd one out everywhere. People will be talking about me behind my back.'

'Don't worry about other people,' advised April.

'Easy for you to say,' Heather came back at her. 'You're all nice and cosy with Ronnie.'

Nothing could be further from the truth as Ronnie grew ever more distant and difficult. But she would never betray him by telling anyone about the anguish he caused her with his unpredictable behaviour.

'I know it's painful now but maybe it's for the best; you're a young woman and you might meet someone else you're better suited to than Arthur,' April suggested. 'It might be fun meeting some new men, getting to know different people.'

'Some new men,' she exploded. 'What do you think I am, a tart or something? I don't want go out with a string of men. I want to get married.'

'Is that why you stayed with Arthur, because you thought he was a safe bet as a husband?'

'I stayed with him because I loved him but of course I wanted the marriage part. It's what people do. I don't want to be left on the shelf.'

'You're too young to be on the shelf.'

'I will be if I don't hurry up and get a ring on my finger,' Heather stated categorically.

April was worried by this attitude that was guaranteed to

put most men off. Heather was an intelligent woman but she was very self-centred and seemed almost obsessed with the idea of fitting in with convention.

'You managed well enough when Arthur was away and you'll be fine without him now. I'll make sure you're not lonely. We'll go out to the flicks together and you must feel free to come round and cry on my shoulder whenever you want. We'll have some girlie nights in to chat.'

'You just don't get it, do you?' Heather blurted out. 'I'll be on my own, a single woman.'

'I realise that. I don't understand why you're so upset about that part of it though,' said April. 'Surely it's the missing Arthur that's the worst bit.'

'The two are one and the same. Love and status, both gone just like that on a whim of Arthur's. Don't pretend you don't care about convention because everybody does. Whenever you meet anyone new or someone you haven't seen for a while the first thing they ask is if you're married or engaged. We're at the age for it to be expected.'

'I suppose you're right,' April finally conceded but she hoped she herself never became so obsessed with appearances as her cousin.

'Anyway, I'll be here for you whenever you need me,' she assured her.

'Except when you're with Ronnie.'

'I'll find time for you both, I promise,' she said, genuinely concerned for her cousin's well-being.

Chapter Five

Dressed in a black skirt and cardigan with a white blouse and high-heeled court shoes, April was at the filing cabinets by the office window looking out at the sun-washed forecourt and wishing she was outside in the fresh air tending to her vegetables instead of working in the records department of a local engineering factory. She had been employed here since she left school and had always found her working day monotonous. But it was a job and you weren't expected to enjoy it. Going to work and paying your way when you hit fourteen was standard procedure for someone like her. It was only recently she had been so acutely aware of the boredom of the work, which was mostly filing, occasional typing and answering queries from other departments by searching the files.

It was almost the first anniversary of her father's death and nearly a year since she had taken over the allotment. There would always be an ache in her heart for her father but the raw pain had eased with the passing of time. Looking back on her first year's gardening she could see that it hadn't all been plain sailing but she hadn't done badly for a beginner. Now it was time to get busy again for the new season and she was longing to put her seed potatoes into the trays in the shed and dig over the soil with fertiliser ready for planting some early peas and broad beans, having burned all the woody refuse around the plot and dealt with the other winter maintenance. How she yearned to get cracking on it; but it was dark in the evenings when she got home from work so she would have to wait until the weekend. Most people of her age couldn't understand her passion for it, especially Ronnie who said she must be completely deranged to want to spend so much time in such a cold and dirty occupation.

'Miss Green, have you become incapacitated at the filing cabinets or are you intending to do any more work today?' the female department head was asking.

'I've nearly finished here,' said April.

'I should think so too,' retorted her superior. 'There's only so much time anyone can take filing a few bits of paper and you seem intent upon setting a new record. I have some typing for you to do, right away please.'

'Yes, miss,' said April respectfully, putting the last piece of correspondence into place in the file and closing the draw of the cabinet.

'I'm sorry, Heather, but no I won't go out dancing with you,' April stated firmly one day in the spring when the cousins were talking in the Greens' small back garden where April was pulling up some weeds in a tiny flower bed. 'The cinema certainly, for a look around the shops in the West End definitely, for a cup of tea and a bun in Lyons yes but a dance hall so that you can find a man is out of the question. It would upset Ronnie and he's moody enough without adding to it.'

'Oh I see, you're all right so blow everybody else,' huffed Heather.

'You know that isn't true,' April challenged. 'I spend as much time as I can with you and I am genuinely sorry about what happened between you and Arthur but I'm afraid you'll have to find someone else to go dancing with.'

'Who exactly?'

'You've other friends besides me surely.'

'They all have boyfriends or husbands.'

'What about the women at work?'

'Ditto.'

April was finding Heather something of a strain since she split up with Arthur. Desperate to find a replacement for him and lonely, she relied heavily on April for company, consistently pestering her to help her meet a man.

'Why not forget about trying to find a man for the moment and take up a hobby,' suggested April.

'What good will that do?'

'It might stop you feeling so desperate and a man will come along in due course, probably when you least expect it.'

'What sort of hobby do you have in mind?'

'An evening class perhaps.'

'Oh April, do me a favour,' Heather said scathingly.

'At least it would get you out of the house and you would meet new people.'

'Absolutely not!'

'What about a spare-time job as an usherette in a cinema then? You might even find a boyfriend that way. Single men do go to the pictures.'

'No thanks.'

'You can always give me a hand at the allotment if you are

really desperate to get out,' said April. 'There is plenty to do there at this time of the year.'

'You know I hate anything like that,' she wailed. 'I want to be a wife, not a carrot-grower.'

'I intend to be both simultaneously,' said April, then in an attempt to cheer her cousin added, 'Go on, go and have a look at the local paper to see what's on at the pictures and we'll go together one night this week. At least it might take your mind off the manhunt for a few hours.'

'What about Ronnie?'

'I don't see him every night.'

'Thanks, kid.'

'And Heather,' April began as her cousin turned to head for the house. 'You will find someone eventually. You're a nice-looking girl and any man would be lucky to have you. It will happen when the time is right. Just try and enjoy life a bit more and not be so desperate about finding a husband.'

'Oh,' said Heather with a surprised smile. 'Thanks. You're a good friend.'

April watched her go indoors wishing there was something constructive she could do to help. It was miserable for her cousin losing Arthur after such a long relationship. But sometimes Heather was her own worst enemy.

There were times when Ronnie was the sweetest of men and April was reminded of why she had fallen in love with him. But there were also instances when she could actually watch him disappear into himself and become a surly stranger.

Such an event happened when she was at his place for Sunday tea with his parents. Everything was fine; everyone chatting enjoyably then suddenly his part in the conversation ended abruptly, his eyes darkened and the atmosphere became strained. His mother and father were both dears and they soldiered on as though all was well, but it really wasn't.

'He isn't the same man who went away,' his mother confided to April when they were in the kitchen washing the dishes. 'He used to be a cheerful sort of a lad and it breaks my heart to see him when he goes into these terrible moods.'

April nodded, drying a cup and hanging it on a hook on the dresser. 'Have you spoken to him about it?' she asked.

'I've tried but he refuses to admit that anything is wrong,' said the older woman, who was wearing a carefully ironed pinafore over her blouse and skirt. 'I suggested that he see a doctor and he was absolutely furious.'

'Maybe I could have a word with him,' suggested April. 'I've told him that his moods upset me, as any girlfriend would, but it usually leads to an argument so I've tried to be patient and am hoping that he will improve over time. Naturally there have been occasions when I've thought he doesn't want to be with me anymore but in my heart I suspect that that isn't the problem. I must admit I find it hard to cope at times.'

'That's only natural but I hope you won't give up on him, dear.' His mother sounded worried.

April shook her head. 'Never, not while he still wants to be with me. I can promise you that.'

The older woman was a homely type with greying hair and soft brown eyes. Looking relieved, she said: 'He's never been like this before, not as a boy or a young man. The odd mood and bad temper, of course, like everyone, but generally speaking he had a happy disposition and was always very caring towards people. Never cold and distant as he is now. It's the war that's done it to him.'

'Yes I think it must be,' agreed April. 'I'll choose my time and try and get him to talk about it.'

'I'd be very grateful, dear,' she said and April's heart went out to her.

When Ronnie walked April home that evening he seemed to have shaken off his demons and was in a fairly amiable frame of mind so she saw the chance to raise the subject. 'Why are you so terribly sad sometimes?' she asked.

'I'm not,' he replied predictably.

'I know you put up a front but I can tell you're feeling miserable a lot of the time,' she said. 'Your mother knows it too and we are both worried.'

'So you've been talking about me?'

'Yes, we have as it happens,' she told him candidly. 'Because we both care about you.'

'I'm sorry, April,' he said. 'I know I'm difficult at times.'

'Why not let me help you?'

'You can't; no one can,' he said. 'It's up to me to pull myself together. No one can do it for me.'

'A little assistance wouldn't go amiss surely.'

'How can you or anyone else help when the whole thing is out of my control? he asked. 'It's inside me. Sometimes I think I'd rather be dead than feel like this.'

'Like what?'

'Fearful; in a blind panic and I have nothing to be afraid of,' he tried to explain. 'Half the time I'm knotted up and sweating, dry-mouthed and nauseous. I lose my concentration. I shall lose my job too if it carries on.'

'Does it come and go?' she asked.

He nodded. 'Usually eases up a bit in the evenings then it's back again in the morning or the middle of the night. I can't stop it. I feel as though I'm living in a nightmare.'

'Don't you think it might be a good idea to see a doctor about it?' she suggested. 'Maybe you can get some sort of medication to calm you down.'

'I'm not ill, April.'

'No, but—'

'It's within me,' he cut in. 'I have to fight it on my own.'

They stopped walking and she turned to him. 'Perhaps it might give you some relief if you talk to me about it when you are feeling bad.'

'I can't because I feel isolated from you, from everybody, when I'm like that so it won't help,' he said. 'I am in a grey world; you are all in a sunny one.'

'You are talking to me about it now,' she pointed out.

'Yeah and I shouldn't be,' he said. 'Now you are upset by it as well as me.'

'Not as upset as when you withdraw into yourself and shut me out,' she said.

'You'd be better off without me.'

'No I would not,' she said, her voice rising emotionally. 'Don't you ever say that to me again.'

'Sorry but most of the time I feel so distant from you.'

'Does it help having me around or is it more of a strain trying to be sociable?'

'Oh April, you are everything to me and I want to make you happy, not drag you down.'

'I'm made of strong stuff so you won't do that,' she said in a gentle but positive tone. 'I know there's not much I can do to change the way you feel inside but I'll be here for you, Ronnie. Always. Together we'll fight your demons.'

He held her close and they were both feeling too emotional to speak.

It was a glorious Sunday afternoon in early summer and April and her mother were both working at the allotment while Lily sat in her pram under the sun canopy, a picture of health with green eyes like her sister and spiky golden hair with a strong suggestion of red. April was hoeing at one side of the plot while Beryl was at the other sprinkling a mixture of soot and lime along the rows of plants to protect them from egg-laying pests.

'I'm beginning to understand why you enjoy being here so much,' said Beryl. 'And your father before you. It's not at all dismal but very peaceful.'

April laughed as a train rattled by noisily on its way into central London.

'All right, maybe not peaceful,' said Beryl. 'But I really find it soothing coming here and working with the soil.'

'And I'm very grateful for the help so we are both happy,' said April.

'It makes a nice break from the house for me.' Her mother paused, grinning. 'Even if you do make me work my fingers to the bone.'

'An allotment is no place for slackers or onlookers,' April said lightly. 'You were only allowed to sit and watch when you were pregnant.'

They worked for a while longer then Beryl finished the job and went over to the water tap near the communal hut to rinse the soot off her hands. She soon got into conversation with one of the men there. Being housebound with a baby for a lot of the time, she enjoyed company when she was out.

April was watching her mother, pleased that her grief seemed to be subsiding, when she had a visitor.

'I called at the house and Charlie told me I'd find you here,' said George, and she couldn't help noticing how handsome he looked in a checked shirt and light-coloured trousers. 'Quite a family affair then.' He looked across at Beryl by the water tap. 'I see you've got your mother at it.' He went over to the pram. 'You'd better be careful, Lily, or your sister will get you helping as soon as you can walk.'

'I shall rope you in if I have any more of your cheek,' she joshed, smiling at him.

Lily chuckled as George tickled her under the chin and made silly faces at her.

'What brings you here anyway?' April asked. 'I take it you're not just here to make daft faces at Lily.'

'I came to see how things are going and what we might expect from you this season for your home-grown corner in the shop.' He cast his eye over the beds. 'Everything seems to be coming along nicely.'

'So far so good,' she said.

'I'm trying to get as much stock as I possibly can,' he explained. 'I'm hoping to make sure the business is thriving before I go back to sea.'

103

'Will that be sometime soon then?' she asked, sad at the thought of him not being around and telling herself it was because her brother would miss him.

'Not as things are at the moment but I'm sure the time will come when Dad is well enough to take over again and I want him to come back to a flourishing business not a failing one. Anyway, it's satisfying to run a shop with decent stock to sell, especially in these times of shortages, and the customers can't get enough of your home-grown stuff.'

'I've put in a lot of peas and runner beans for later on,' she said, 'and fingers crossed for a good crop of new potatoes.'

'Those cabbages look promising,' he observed.

'I'll have some stuff for you soon so I'll be round with a pram-load.'

'I've been thinking about that and I reckon it would be better for me to collect the produce with the van when there's a lot to save you pushing that pram around.'

'Will that mean you'll pay a lower price?'

'Of course not,' he assured her. 'It's only a few minutes from the shop.'

'You won't make your fortune that way.'

'I can be a hard businessman when I have to be,' he said. 'You should see me at the wholesale market. I'm really tough there. I go to Covent Garden Market quite often now and that's no place for a pushover.'

'Covent Garden Market eh. I'd love to go there to see it in action. Since I've been doing the allotment I've developed an interest in greengrocery from seed to table.'

'Well . . . if you can be up and ready by five o'clock in the morning you can come with me,' he said lightly.

'Some time perhaps,' she said casually.

Sensing a note of sadness in her tone, he asked, 'Is everything all right?'

'Of course.'

'Boyfriend settling down?'

She glanced across at her mother, who was immersed in conversation with several men now. April desperately needed to talk to someone about Ronnie. If she mentioned it to Mum she got protective of her daughter and said that he ought to pull himself together; and Ronnie's mother was as worried as April.

'Strictly between us, he's finding it difficult as it happens.'

'I'm sorry to hear that.'

'His nervous system seems to be wrecked.'

'I'm not surprised after what the poor lads on the battlefields went through,' he said. 'There's a customer of ours at the shop; her son is in a terrible state. She was telling me about it the other day. On the quiet, of course, no one likes to talk about these things.'

'Exactly,' she said. 'He's very ashamed of the way he feels and that isn't right.'

'It certainly isn't, after what he's done for his country,' he proclaimed.

'What about you?' she began. 'You must have had your share of danger at sea.'

He nodded. 'Oh yeah, plenty of that. But we didn't have to kill people face to face in the merchant service. Ours was all about staying alive when our ship was under attack but there were some horrific moments even so. We lost a lot of men. One of my best buddies went down with the ship despite all my attempts to save him. That broke my heart and I thought my end had come plenty of times.' He seemed lost in thought. 'The sea can be as merciless as Hitler.'

'But you've managed to put it behind you,' she said.

'Up to a point but you never truly forget that sort of fear and I suppose it depends on your make-up how it affects you later. Anyway, mine was a different situation to that of a soldier. And your boy isn't the only one still suffering. Plenty of lads will be having nightmares. All you can do is be patient with him.' He looked at her. 'It must be a strain at times so if you ever need anyone to talk to, I'm your man. Anything you say won't go any further.'

'Thanks, George.'

He smiled at her and nothing seemed quite so bad.

'Oi oi, you two look nice and cosy,' joshed Beryl, returning from her socialising.

'Hark who's talking,' laughed April. 'What about you, getting all matey with the men.'

Beryl grinned. 'Well, I don't get out much and they are a friendly bunch,' she said. 'I've been talking to a chap called Frank and he's been showing me his lettuces. He's growing them in a cold frame and they look really lovely.'

'Frank's a nice bloke and a very good gardener,' said April. 'He does really well with his lettuce and cucumbers. He gave me a lettuce last year and it was lovely.'

'His plot looks very productive,' said Beryl.

'I'd like a cold frame,' April mentioned casually. 'They are very useful. Some things need to be under glass, for a while at least. Most people here have one.'

'Why don't you get one then, dear?' asked Beryl.

'Most gardeners make their own and you can't get the materials while everything is so short. The people here have had theirs since before the war, I think. I wouldn't even know where to start looking. Anyway these things cost money and any extra that I have goes into the fund that Ronnie and I have for our future.'

'So we won't be having any succulent salad items then,' said Beryl.

'Not from this plot,' April confirmed.

'That's a shame,' said George. 'I'd love to have some to offer the customers.'

'Never mind your customers,' said Beryl, laughing. 'I'd love to have some sliced cucumber in a sandwich with some nice juicy lettuce to go with it.'

They were all smiling and April thanked God for this place of sanctuary and a hobby that strengthened her and helped her to cope with Ronnie, who she would be seeing this evening. One of the worst things about his condition was the uncertainty; she never knew what sort of a mood he would be in or how long his current frame of mind would last. She felt herself tense in anticipation of their meeting later.

As it happened Ronnie seemed quite buoyant that evening, so much so that he wanted to set a date for the wedding which April saw as real progress. They hadn't spoken about that much at all since he'd been back.

'It's time we put plans into place,' he said as they strolled by the river in the setting sun.

'That's fine with me,' she said. 'But we'll have to discuss it with Mum as she'll be organising it. Traditional for the bride's people to do that.'

'How about just before Christmas,' he suggested.

'It might be a bit too soon to get everything ready.'

'We've waited long enough, April,' he said.

That was true and April wondered if it might be better for him if they were actually living together. Maybe having her around would give him some comfort. 'Yes you're quite right,' she said. 'We'll discuss it with Mum when we get back and, of course, see what your parents have to say about it.'

'We can live at my house until we can afford a place of our own,' he suggested. 'There's plenty of room with me being an only child.'

Naturally April wanted to start her married life in their own place but as the housing shortage in London was so acute because of the bombing she had already accepted that they would have to live at one of their family homes for a while. It wasn't ideal but many young couples started off this way.

'I'd rather we lived at mine,' she said. 'There isn't so much space but Mum will miss my contribution to the housekeeping when I leave.'

'Oh,' he said, seeming surprised and none too happy. 'You can't stay there forever, April, just to support your mother.'

'I know that but if we have to stay with anyone I'd sooner it was with my family.'

He was silent for a while and April was on edge, thinking that his mood was about to deteriorate. But he seemed to struggle for a few moments then said, 'If it means that much to you then that's all right with me. It won't be for long anyway. I've got a steady wage coming in so we can save up and it will be easier to do that when we are living together because we won't need to go out so much. I'll be happy to give your mother a helping hand financially when we do finally move on.'

'That's nice of you.'

'Once things in general start to get better in the country as a whole and building gets underway there will be more accommodation available.'

'You've got it all worked out, haven't you?'

'I certainly have,' he said. 'I've given you enough of a head-ache, it's time I made you happy.'

'Oh that is so sweet, Ronnie.' She guessed he had won some sort of a battle within himself when he had managed not to sink into despair just now.

'Let's go for a drink to celebrate,' he suggested. 'We can sit outside if there are any tables free.'

'Lovely,' she said and they walked towards the pub hand in hand.

'Are you sure it's what you really want April?' asked her mother later that night after Ronnie had gone home delighted that they had agreed a wedding date for a week before Christmas and had agreed to live at the Greens' at first.

'Of course, Mum,' said April, surprised by the question. 'Why do you ask?'

'It won't be easy spending the rest of your life with someone prone to such terrible depression.'

'That's a horrible thing to say!' April bristled because her mother was a little too close to what she herself had been worried about occasionally. 'Anyway, he seems better lately.'

'Tonight he was as nice as pie but tomorrow he might be in the depths and difficult again. As long as you're prepared for that.'

'Of course I'm prepared for it! If Dad had gone away to war and been changed by it, you wouldn't have turned away from him, would you?'

'You know the answer to that.'

'Then I don't know how you can even suggest such a thing as regards Ronnie.'

'You're my daughter and I want you to be happy, it's only

natural,' said Beryl. 'And since Ronnie has been back you've been edgy and tense with precious little happiness.'

'I don't suppose I'm the only woman to have her man return damaged,' said April. 'What about the poor souls whose men come home with limbs or sight missing. It's a reality of war, Mum, and we have to accept it. I love Ronnie and intend to make him a good wife.'

'In that case we'll get cracking with the wedding arrangements,' her mother said. 'Your dad had been saving since you were little to pay for it when the time came.'

'I don't want anything too fancy and expensive,' April was quick to assure her.

'You'll have the best I can possibly give you, shortages or not. And we'll have fun getting it organised.'

'Yes, Mum, we certainly will,' said April, feeling the first flutter of wedding excitement. It had taken a while to appear because of the problems with Ronnie but it was here now; she was officially a bride to be.

'That's good news, isn't it, Heather?' said her mother after April had paid them a visit with news about her wedding. 'It will be fun for you being a bridesmaid too.'

'Yeah, I suppose so,' said Heather who was extremely rattled by the news. She wanted to be the bride, not the bridesmaid, and the latter only exacerbated her misery and feeling of failure.

'It will be nice choosing the material for the dresses and having fittings and being a major part of it all,' said Peg, unaware that her daughter was deeply depressed about the whole thing. 'I shall have to get a new outfit too. It will give us all something to look forward to.'

'Mm.' There was another horrid aspect to this wedding for Heather; she didn't have a boyfriend to go with. The whole thing would be dreadful from beginning to end with everyone being happy for April and she herself prancing about in some soppy taffeta dress and no one to care what she looked like.

'Your turn will come, dear,' said her mother.

That sort of remark only twisted the knife. How could her turn come when she couldn't find anyone who wanted to marry her? What was she supposed to do, settle for someone like the goofy bloke who lived at the end of the street and made eyes at her every time she saw him? She wasn't that desperate. When she thought of all the years she had put into Arthur, it made her blood boil.

'Maybe,' she sighed and rapidly changed the subject. She'd had more than enough wedding talk with April coming round asking her to be bridesmaid. Why did everything always go right for her cousin and not for her? It was so unfair!

George turned up at the allotment out of the blue one Sunday afternoon and parked his van in the road nearby.

'I haven't got much for you today,' April said, looking up from the runner beans she was inspecting and throwing him a puzzled expression. 'It's only a few days since you last collected. I'm a gardener, not a miracle worker.'

'I'm delivering, not collecting,' he said, enjoying her sparky humour.

'Delivering,' she said, puzzled. 'What could you possibly have to deliver to me? Not unless you've been out collecting manure of course.'

'Nicer than that.' He beamed.

She couldn't help but catch his mood. 'Right. So how much is it going to cost me?'

'Nothing.'

She frowned. 'Ooh, I don't like the sound of that. There's always a catch.'

'No catch, I promise.'

'Don't keep me in suspense then,' she urged him. 'Let's see what you're on about.'

He went to the van and came back carrying a large window frame complete with glass. 'I found this in a pile of rubbish so I cleaned it up and am going to make you a cold frame with it,' he explained, sounding excited. 'I've managed to get a deep wooden box for underneath and don't worry – I know all about drainage in the bottom. It's for those salad items you are so keen to grow and anything else that needs to start under glass.' He looked at her. 'For your own use, not the shop. I know how much you fancy having a go with a cold frame.'

April's eyes filled with tears because it was such a sweet thing to do. She spent so much time and effort looking out for Ronnie, it was nice to have someone do something special for her. 'Oh, that is so kind of you,' she said. 'Thank you.'

Seeing her face was enough thanks for him. She was beaming and her eyes looked moist. 'It's a pleasure,' he said. 'I'll enjoy setting it up for you so that you can work your magic.'

'George, honestly, I don't know what to say.'

'It's only a pile of junk.'

But it was much more than that to her. To think that someone had gone to trouble to get something they knew would please her was so touching. She guessed he hadn't just come across the materials and had made an effort to find them. 'I'm absolutely thrilled.'

His grin broadened. 'I got you a few plants to start you off,' he said. 'Didn't want you to miss the boat completely for this year. I don't know if they'll work.'

She rushed over and hugged him.

'Hey, steady on,' he said jokingly. 'It's only a few old bits and pieces.'

'You are a real friend, George Benson; you and that lovely mum of yours.'

'I'm flattered you think so,' he said. 'I'll get some tools and put the cold frame together and leave the gardening part to you.' He gave her a wry grin. 'Get back to work then. We can't have you standing about.'

She was smiling as she went back to her beans. He really was a tonic.

Because young Charlie was such an exuberant person, he tended to be a bit garrulous at times and was particularly so at Sunday tea one day in summer.

'League football starts again on the first of September,' he announced excitedly to the assembled company of his mother, Ronnie, April and Lily in her high chair. 'The first Saturday League games since 1939. All those years it was stopped because of the war.'

'Do you remember going to see Chelsea play?' asked his mother wistfully. 'Your dad started taking you when you were really quite little.'

'I remember it all right,' he said. 'You don't forget something as important in your life as that.'

'Football isn't important,' Ronnie pronounced.

'It is to a lot of people,' said Charlie.

'All it is is a few blokes kicking a ball about.'

'It's much more than that.' Charlie took offence and flushed. 'It's about real skill and team spirit, bringing people together and giving them something to look forward to.'

'Worse things happened because of the war than League football being stopped.'

'I know that. Do you think I'm thick or something?' said Charlie crossly. 'I was just saying that it was a shame it was stopped, that's all.'

'People got killed and injured and all you care about is a stupid game,' said Ronnie irritably.

'It isn't all I care about but it is an interest of mine. Of course I'm sorry for all those people who lost their lives and I'm sorry that you had to go away to war,' said Charlie, his cheeks on fire now. 'It wasn't my fault I wasn't old enough to go away to fight.'

'I'm not saying it was but you should get your priorities right,' declared Ronnie.

'And you should get used to the fact that the war is over and people are trying to get some normality back into their lives,' retorted Charlie.

'Boys, boys,' Beryl intervened. 'That's enough. Calm down, the pair of you.'

April was cringing with embarrassment. She also found herself siding with her brother. She always trod very carefully around Ronnie and let him have his own way because he was such a sad character. But he couldn't be allowed to walk all over people just because he'd been damaged by the war.

'Charlie is right, Ronnie,' she said. 'Football is our national game and a lot of people have missed it. We need to move forward as a country and restoring one of our most popular traditions can only be a good thing.'

'Oh, so you're on his side.'

'It isn't a question of sides.'

'Seems that way to me.'

'Now you are being childish.'

Ronnie shot out of his seat. 'I'll go as the entire Green family has ganged up against me,' he said and marched across the room and out of the house, slamming the door behind him.

'Aren't you going to go after him, April?' asked Beryl.

'Not this time,' she replied thoughtfully. 'He's been very rude and it's up to him to apologise. We can't let him get away with it all of the time.'

'Sorry, sis,' said Charlie.

'You've nothing to apologise for,' she assured him. 'You're entitled to talk about anything at all that interests you in your own home.'

A horrible silence had fallen over the room though. April felt bad about not going after Ronnie but he had to realise that his views weren't the only ones or he would get into arguments at work, in shops and the pubs, everywhere. If he didn't appear within a couple of days, she would go round to his house. But not now!

He came round later that evening full of remorse. Charlie had gone out with his mates and Beryl was upstairs putting Lily to bed.

'Are you very angry with me, April?' he asked.

'Not so much angry as disappointed,' she replied. 'I want

you to get on with my family, especially as we'll be living here after the wedding.'

'I can't pretend to agree with their views just because we are going to be related.'

'Having different views is one thing, causing an argument and slamming out of the house in the middle of tea in a temper is quite another,' she said. 'I know you have problems but I can't always make allowances.'

'I know and I fully accept that I am in the wrong,' he said. 'What can I do to make it up to you?'

'You can apologise to my mother when she comes downstairs for ruining the tea she made for us and you can say sorry to my brother when you next see him.'

'He can be a bit irritating, you must admit.'

'We all are at times. Charlie is an enthusiastic person and football is the love of his life. All right, maybe he does go on about it at times but he is a good lad and I adore him so if you're thinking of making an enemy of him you'll make one of me too.'

'Of course I'm not going to make an enemy of him,' he said. 'I didn't intend to fly off the handle. Something came over me and the next thing I knew I was out of the house.'

'When you've made your apologies, I suggest we put it behind us and, as Charlie says, look to the future.'

'Yes,' he said but they both knew he was in the grip of something beyond his control again. She could see it in his eyes and the pallor of his skin. She felt enormous empathy for him but what was she to do? She couldn't make allowances for his behaviour indefinitely.

Chapter Six

'Only two weeks to go until the big day,' said Johnny, holding his billiard cue having just taken a shot, his gaze fixed on his ball as it rolled along the green baize and into the hole with a satisfying clunk. 'Saturday League football is being played for the first time for seven years.'

'Mm,' said George, seeming slightly wistful as he studied the table and got ready to have his turn.

'Well don't overdo the enthusiasm,' said Johnny with friendly sarcasm. 'I thought you were looking forward to it as much as I am. It will be just like the old days, mate, before you went away to sea. Young Charlie Green can come along too if he wants to.'

'The thing is, I don't think I'll be able to come to the match,' said George, placing his cue.

'Can't come to the first Saturday League game since 1939,' said Johnny in astonishment. 'I don't believe it.'

'It's the shop,' he explained, hitting the ball. 'It's busy all day Saturdays and I can't leave Mum to cope on her own.'

'But she managed well enough when you were away,' Johnny pointed out.

'She had an assistant then and when she left we didn't replace her because I was helping in the business by then and we thought we'd wait until food is plentiful again and our turnover goes up before we employ someone new.'

'Your mother is a very capable woman and she would hate you to miss the match.'

'Yeah, I know all that but I want her to do less in the shop, not more. In fact, I'd like her to have Saturdays off, the afternoon at least, on a permanent basis at some point. I don't want to impose on her just for the sake of a soccer match.'

'It isn't just any old soccer match though, is it?' Johnny reminded him. 'It's the first League game in a very long time. The atmosphere will be incredible.'

'Mm. I'm aware of that.'

'I'm sure your mum can manage for a few hours on her own, George, or you could always close for the afternoon.'

'On a Saturday, don't make me laugh,' George burst out. 'It's our best trading day. With things still being short we need to sell everything we put on sale.'

'So this means that you won't be able to go to any of the Saturday games because of the shop.'

'Mm, I suppose it does,' said George gloomily.

'You're entitled to some leisure time.'

'And I get it,' responded George defensively. 'I'm here playing billiards with you, aren't I? It's just Saturday during business hours that's difficult.'

'I'm really disappointed,' Johnny told him.

'Don't make me feel even worse,' said George. 'You and Charlie Green can still go.'

'It won't be the same without you.'

George was upset about it but his mother had had a rough

time after Dad got injured and George was trying to make her life easier, not pile more work and responsibility on her.

'I'm disappointed too but family comes first,' he said.

'I suppose so,' Johnny agreed finally. 'So if you can't come we'll just have to put up with it.'

'Shall we make this the last game here,' suggested George, feeling unsettled. 'I'm getting fed up with it.'

'Yeah, let's head off to the pub to get a few laughs,' agreed Johnny. 'Billiard halls are all right for a few games but you can't beat a pub for atmosphere.'

One Saturday afternoon April was just putting her garden tools away ready to leave when her brother appeared looking gloomy. He usually gravitated towards his sister when he had a problem.

'What's the matter with you?' she asked. 'You've got a face like a dead lupin.'

'George can't come to the match next week,' he announced bleakly.

'Is that all?' she said. 'I thought something serious had happened.'

'It is serious,' he said. 'It isn't just any old match.'

'I know which match it is,' she said, closing the shed door and turning the key in the lock. 'Why can't he go?'

'He has to stay and help his mother in the shop.'

'Oh, I see.'

'Johnny has been round to tell me and I'm going to the match with him but it won't be the same without George. It's a shame for him too because he loves footie and we've waited a long time for it to start up again. The first League match for years and he is going to miss it.'

119

'What about your mates? Will they be going?' she asked.

'Some of them. But George is such a good laugh and a true fan I was looking forward to going with him.'

'I expect he's disappointed too but he isn't the sort of man to shirk his responsibilities.'

'No, I suppose not,' agreed Charlie miserably.

'Hello, Winnie,' said April when she walked into the shop, having already greeted George who was serving from the outside display currently lush with plums, apples and raspberries. 'I've just popped in to say hello.'

'That's nice of you, dear,' she said. 'We're always pleased to see you.'

April did have an ulterior motive for being here but she needed to find the right moment to mention it.

'Is something the matter?' asked April, noticing that her friend seemed a little subdued. 'You don't seem your usual cheery self.'

Winnie glanced towards George, who was with a customer. 'It's that son of mine,' she said in a low voice. 'He's upset me good and proper.'

'What's he done?'

'He won't go to the football match next Saturday because he thinks I can't manage in the shop without him,' she explained. 'Never mind that I was running the place single-handed until he came back.'

'I'm sure it isn't because he thinks you can't manage,' said April. 'He's probably just being helpful.'

'What am I, some hopeless old biddy?' she said, close to tears. 'Is that what he thinks?'

'Of course not,' April assured her in a definite tone. 'It will be because he doesn't want to let you down, being that Saturdays are so busy in here.'

Customers were coming in so Winnie said to April, 'Put the kettle on, love, and we'll have a cuppa when things quieten down, if you have time.'

April did as she asked and George appeared when she was filling the kettle.

'Just came to see if there was any tea on the go,' he said. 'Glad to see you've got the job in hand.'

'You've upset your mother,' she informed him.

'And don't I know it,' he said. 'Honestly, I'm only trying to do what's right for her and she's gone all narked on me. What sort of a son would I be if I just cleared off on a Saturday afternoon and left her holding the fort? It gets busy in here then.'

'I know that but your mum is more than capable of coping,' she said.

'This has nothing to do with her ability, April,' he informed her. 'My mother spends most of her time working, either here in the shop or in the house, and ideally I would like her to have more time off at some point, not leave her alone when we're busy so that she has to work even harder.'

'If you're really worried about it why don't I help her out here while you're at the match?' April had waited for the right moment to propose the idea that had occurred to her when her brother had told her about George's problem. 'Or will she see that as a slur on her capabilities?'

He looked at her. 'Would you be prepared to do that?' he asked.

'Of course. I wouldn't have offered if I wasn't,' she said.

'We'd pay you of course.'

'Let's worry about that if she agrees,' she suggested, putting the cups out. 'I don't want to make things worse. She might see any offer of help as criticism.'

When his mother appeared he said, 'Right, Mum, this is the deal. I will go to the football match if you will agree to have April giving you a hand here while I'm gone. That's my final offer.'

Winnie wasn't prepared to submit without at least a token protest. 'I could manage perfectly well here on my own,' she made clear, then smiled and added, 'but it might be nice to have someone to help move the queue along, and there's no one I'd rather have than April.'

'I've never worked in a shop so you'll have to be patient with me,' said April.

'No trouble,' Winnie responded. 'So now that's sorted let's have a cup of tea.'

The shop bell rang so George went to see to it.

'Are you sure you're happy for me to help out?' April asked warily.

'Very,' she said. 'It will be nice to have company. I'd never have forgiven myself if he'd missed the first match of the new era because of loyalty to me. But what about your other commitments, April? Your allotment and your young man?'

'I don't see Ronnie until the evening and the allotment can do without me for a few hours.'

'If you're sure, that's settled then.' They were both smiling as the kettle boiled.

Ronnie wasn't quite so happy about the arrangement. 'But you're working all week in an office, why would you want to work in a greengrocer's at the weekend?' he asked that evening when he called for her to go out.

'I'm not doing it every weekend. It's just a one-off to help some friends,' she explained. 'A few hours, that's all.'

'It's a dirty job, selling potatoes,' he pointed out.

'They don't just sell potatoes. They sell lovely fruit and other vegetables as well. Anyway it's healthy dirt like the allotment and I thrive on it,' she said lightly. 'You can't live your life never helping anybody out, Ronnie. I can't anyway.'

'I'm not so sure that George Benson wouldn't like to be more than a friend to you,' he said and she realised where the source of his objection lay.

'In your heart you must know that isn't true,' she said. 'We've had one misunderstanding along those lines, please don't let's have another.'

'All right, I'll say no more about it.'

April felt as though Ronnie was permanently on the verge of despair and she tried to avoid this happening by maintaining a cheerful but firm attitude. It was a terrible strain and she was usually tense the whole time they were together but she coped as best as she could. He was worth any amount of effort.

'Are you two going out?' asked Charlie, bursting into the room with his usual exuberance.

'Yeah, why?' his sister replied.

'I wouldn't mind the sofa to myself.'

'You're in luck then because we're going to the pictures,' she said.

'Thanks for stepping in for George at the shop, sis,' Charlie mentioned. 'He'll be able to come to the match next week now. It's going to be really smashing. They're expecting record crowds at all the games, according to the paper.'

'I think that's our cue to leave,' said Ronnie, rising. 'We don't want to listen to any more soccer talk.'

'Suits me,' said Charlie, sitting down on the sofa with enthusiasm.

'See you later, Mum,' April called upstairs to her mother who was putting Lily to bed.

'Enjoy yourselves, kids,' Beryl shouted down the stairs but she didn't think Ronnie was capable of enjoying anything. He put up a front and she admired him for that but there was something very dark in his eyes.

They saw an American film called *The Best Years of Our Lives*, a moving story about the readjustment of servicemen and their families after their return home from the war, the tale featuring a man who comes back as a double amputee from war injuries.

Both April and Ronnie were quiet and thoughtful when they came out of the cinema.

'Imagine that,' said Ronnie as they walked home. 'It must be terrible to lose limbs.'

'Yes it must be,' she said.

'It makes me realise that I have nothing to complain about.'

'But you don't complain, Ronnie,' she pointed out, acknowledging as she spoke that it was true. 'You get withdrawn and miserable but you don't actually grumble.'

'I've no right to be miserable at all and a film like that makes me see how lucky I am.'

'Some people have scars that aren't visible in the same way,' she said and they walked home chatting about other aspects of the film. At times like this, when she seemed close to Ronnie, she felt privileged to be wearing his ring.

April was a bit slow with the weighing scales at first and got flustered when she managed to miss a customer's bag with the scale scoop and sent two pounds of shiny apples rolling all over the shop floor. But when she got into the swing of it she really enjoyed working at Benson's the following Saturday afternoon. It was so entirely different to her regular job it felt like fun. It was enjoyable chatting to the customers and Winnie instead of silent hours at the office working at her desk.

'You're doing well,' said Winnie towards the end of the shift when business was slowing down.

'Am I? That's good.'

'I'm surprised an office girl like you would offer to work in a greengrocer's shop.'

'I only offered because I wanted George to go to football,' she said. 'But now I've had a taste of it I'd rather do this sort of work for a living than what I do. The time has flown by. In the office I'm a real clock watcher.'

'It's been a pleasure to have you.'

Beryl appeared with Lily in her pushchair and some sticky buns for the two women to have with their tea. Winnie was chatty with Beryl, who she had got to know through April, and made a great fuss of Lily.

'I would have loved another child,' said Winnie wistfully. 'But, sadly, it wasn't to be.'

'I'll admit that I was none too happy when I realised I had another one on the way at my age and without Jim,' said Beryl.

'But I love Lily to bits and she's been the absolute making of me as a widow.'

'She's adorable.' Winnie smiled towards the little girl. 'You've got a wedding in the family to look forward to soon then.'

Beryl smiled back. 'We certainly have. It will soon come round. I hope we're ready in time.'

'People always think they won't be ready for weddings but they usually are,' Winnie reassured her.

A sudden surge of customers ended the discussion and Beryl and Lily went on their way.

When George got back from the match, jubilant because his team had won, Winnie said, 'We've got a natural in April here at the shop.'

'I've had a whale of a time,' added April.

George laughed heartily. 'You don't often hear someone say they've had a good time selling fruit and veg. But thanks ever so much for filling in for me. I so enjoyed the match.'

'Thank you,' she said as he took some money from the till and handed it to her. 'But there's no need.'

As he insisted she accepted the money graciously. On the way home she thought she had done a good afternoon's work and the money she had earned would go into the fund she and Ronnie were building for their future.

'Have you chosen your best man yet?' April enquired of Ronnie one evening in October when they were on the sofa at the Greens' house. Charlie was out and Beryl upstairs with Lily.

Her words came as something of a shock to him because he hadn't even thought about the wedding as a reality. Being married had been on his mind but not the actual nuptials. 'Er, no, not really,' he confessed.

'You need to get that organised soon, I should think,' she suggested. 'There's not long to go. Things are warming up into wedding fever around here. It's nice – I'm enjoying it.'

'I'll see to it.' He'd been something of a loner since he'd been back so his old mates had drifted away. He guessed they found him unsociable with his tendency to withdraw. Maybe he could ask one of the chaps at work. He wasn't close to anyone there but they seemed a decent lot. How awful that he didn't have a mate to stand by his side when he got married because he'd driven them all away. His stomach knotted and he felt tight as the symptoms of panic began to take hold. He was trapped in a vicious circle because it was fear of the fear that made it come and he didn't know how to make it go away. The truth was he couldn't so he had to bluff his way through life.

'Once you've chosen someone he'll arrange your stag night for you,' April was saying. 'That's the usual procedure I think.'

He nodded, feeling even worse as he realised that he didn't have anyone to ask to his stag night either. Why was he like this, afraid to go out, afraid to stay in? In a state of misery most of the time and acting his way through life simply to survive.

'Yes, I'll get it organised,' he said.

Beryl entered the room. 'Wotcha, Ronnie, I didn't realise you were here.'

'Hello, Mrs Green.'

'How are you love, looking forward to the big day?'

'Yeah not half.' Actually he was dreading the whole thing. Being married to April would be good because maybe he wouldn't feel so lonely but the actual wedding celebrations were just something to be endured.

'So are we,' she said. 'The happiest day of a girl's life so they say and I'll do my best to make it so for April.'

'Me too,' he said, terrified he might ruin the whole thing for her because of something that was out of his control.

'She'll take your breath away when you see her in her wedding dress,' said Beryl. 'I can promise you that.'

'She takes my breath away anyway,' he said, managing to sound normal.

'Aah, that is so sweet,' approved April.

'Shall we go for a walk?' he suggested because exercise sometimes calmed him.

'Yeah, I'll get my coat.' She was unaware of the agony he was going through because he was becoming something of an expert at hiding it.

'Lily, please keep still so that the lady can fit your dress for you,' urged Beryl.

In reply Lily trotted around the room chuckling.

'Come here, you horror,' said April, scooping her sister up and standing her on a chair so that the dressmaker could put some pins into the dress which was blue satin. 'Be a good girl and stand still. Just a few minutes and the lady will be finished.'

A neighbour, a trained dressmaker, was making the dresses for the wedding. At little more than a year old, Lily was really too young to be a flower girl but April wanted her to take part so much and there would be plenty of people to look after her. If they managed to contain her during some of the service and for the photos, she could run about as she liked after that.

'Right that's you done, young Lily,' said the dressmaker. 'Let's have the bridesmaid now.'

Heather got up in her half-finished bridesmaid dress in pale blue satin. She thought she looked hideous, like an overgrown schoolgirl in a party dress, but was forced to pretend to enjoy it for April's sake; her cousin who had a charmed life with everything Heather had always wanted and didn't have. The dressmaker pinned and pleated until it was finally April's turn and her dress was long, white and lovely.

Even Mum was here to join in the wedding preparations and was piling the praise on to April. There were compliments from Auntie Beryl and the dressmaker too and Heather wanted to die. But she said, 'You look lovely, April, and when it's finished it will be even more gorgeous.'

'Thanks, kid,' she said, unaware of her cousin's envy.

April had a good harvest: cabbages and cauliflowers, beetroot, carrots and potatoes and much more.

'You've done us proud,' said George when he came to collect one Saturday afternoon towards the end of the season.

'I wasn't lucky with everything,' she said. 'My runner beans didn't do very well. That's the way it goes sometimes.'

'I suppose everybody must have some failures as there are so many enemies to gardeners: pests and our unpredictable weather to name just a couple.'

'Nature is a hard taskmaster. You can challenge it but you can't always win. Still, next season I shall get the full use of my lovely cold frame to help me.' She smiled towards the large glass-topped piece of equipment he had made for her. 'That's my prize possession.'

Never had the joy of giving been more acutely felt. 'Glad you're pleased,' he said in a matter-of-fact tone though her pleasure made him feel warm inside 'Thanks for the wedding invitation by the way. Mum will reply.'

'Hope you can come.'

'We wouldn't miss it for the world.'

'Good.'

'Is everything going to plan?'

'Sort of.'

'I don't envy your intended,' he said. 'I've heard that women get into a real state when they are organising a wedding.'

'I don't know about a state but we are very full of it at the moment,' she said. 'That's why it's nice to come to the allotment; calms me down and gives me space.'

He finished loading the vegetables into the van in rough wooden crates and paid her for them. 'I'll leave you to it then, April. See you soon.'

She waved him off and had just got back to weeding the turnip beds when someone said, 'Hello there, April, you're still at it then.'

'Hello, Frank,' she said, rising to her feet and smiling at the gardening enthusiast who looked to be in his mid to late fifties; a man of stocky build with greying brown hair and a warm smile. 'Yes I'm still at it. Our house is in a bit of a frenzy with wedding plans at the moment. I'm enjoying all the preparations but it can get a bit much at times so I've escaped for a while.'

'Your mother not with you today then,' he remarked.

'No. She's at home with my little sister. Now that Lily is running around she's into everything so an allotment isn't really suitable for her.'

'I hope that isn't the last we'll see of them.'

'It won't be, don't worry. Mum enjoys helping me here so she'll be around at some point.'

'That's good.'

They talked about gardening, which was their mutual interest, and she said she still had a lot to learn.

'You never stop learning with vegetable growing,' he said. 'But I've been at it longer than you so if you ever need any help or advice you know where to come.'

'Thank you.'

'Give my best regards to you mother,' he said.

'I'll do that,' she said thoughtfully.

'You've got an admirer at the allotments,' April told Beryl when she got home.

'Don't be soft,' said Beryl predictably.

'Well, Frank was asking about you and sent his regards,' said April.

'I've chatted to him a few times down there, that's all,' she said defensively. 'Only about gardening.'

'You are allowed to speak to members of the opposite sex without explaining yourself you know, Mum.'

'I wouldn't want anyone to think there was anything untoward,' said Beryl, flushing.

'And no one does think that but he seems a nice enough chap to me,' said April.

'I expect he is but that is of no interest to me.'

'Dad has been gone for nearly two years, Mum,' April reminded her.

'I don't care if he's been gone twenty-two years,' said Beryl. 'I am not interested in anyone else.'

'Steady on, Mum, he only asked me to give you his regards, nothing more.'

'That's all right then,' she said. 'I hope I haven't given him the wrong idea by chatting to him.'

'Of course you haven't,' said April. 'He's probably married anyway.'

'He's a widower,' said Beryl.

'Oh I see,' said April. 'But I'm sure he's harmless. Anyway, you can't spend the rest of your life never speaking to a man, can you? That would be ridiculous.'

'I can if they are going to get the wrong idea.'

'I wouldn't have said anything if I'd known you were so sensitive,' said April.

'I'm not particularly sensitive,' denied Beryl hotly. 'I just don't want any man sniffing around. At my age, no fear.'

'You're not exactly in your dotage, you know. Anyway the poor man hasn't done anything beyond wishing you well,' April pointed out.

'He'd better not either,' she said fiercely. 'From now on the subject is closed. I want you to help me work out the menu for the wedding reception. I've been to the church and arranged to hire some trestle tables and chairs.'

In common with most people of their ilk they were having the wedding reception at home. The furniture in the back room would be cleared and trestle tables put in, white cloths covering them, and food prepared by Beryl and her sister Peg with offers of help from Ronnie's mother, the two families having met recently over Sunday tea at the Greens' house when Mr and Mrs Bailey had offered to pay for the flowers and the photographs.

'Well done, Mum.'

'I'm thinking in terms of boiled ham and vegetables, as we can't get salad at this time of year, with trifle to follow and the wedding cake of course. Naturally there will be plenty of booze.'

'Sounds good to me.'

'That's settled then.'

April was excited now that things were happening. It was supposed to be a woman's happiest day and she was determined that it would be hers. She wasn't so wrapped up in herself as to have forgotten about Heather in all the excitement though. She'd noticed that she'd been a bit quiet lately and thought it might be hard for her having been let down so badly by Arthur. So April decided to set aside some time for her.

'I'm going to ask Heather if she'd like to go out for the evening next Saturday,' April said to Ronnie. 'You don't mind being without me just for once, do you?'

'No, of course not.'

'I thought Heather and I might go to the West End and have a meal somewhere,' she said. 'My getting married might be quite hard for her as her own plans fell apart. I don't want her to feel left out.'

'A night out together is a good idea.'

'There's only a couple of weeks left before the big day and things will get really hectic then so I want to do it now in case it gets forgotten but I wanted to check with you first.'

'You have my full approval and I hope you have a good time,' he said amicably.

'Aaw, that's nice,' she said, putting her hand on his. 'You're a good bloke and I'm very lucky to have you.'

'I won't argue with you about that,' he said jokingly.

He seemed to be in good spirits but for a moment she thought she had seen a hint of relief in his eyes at the idea of Saturday night without her. She must have been mistaken, though, because she knew how much he relied on her company. Yes, her imagination was getting as sensitive as his moods. She was pleased that he seemed to be more like his old self though and able to enter into the spirit of the pre-wedding excitement.

'This is nice, April,' said Heather as the two women settled down at a table in one of the restaurants in Lyons Corner House in the West End, having had a stroll around first enjoying the lights, the crowds and the atmosphere.

'I thought we should have a night out together before the wedding,' she said. 'The men have their stag do so why shouldn't we have a treat? Ours might not be as boozy as theirs but we'll have a good time.'

'Thank you for suggesting it,' said Heather, studying the menu and feeling bad about all the evil thoughts she had about her cousin as April was being so kind to her now.

'Shall we have some wine?' suggested April.

'I've never tasted wine,' said Heather.

'Neither have I but it might be fun.'

The women decided to give the house wine a try and after a couple of glasses the evening began to go with a swing.

'I want you to know, Heather,' began April after the main course of delicious braised steak, 'that I'll still be around for you after I get married.'

'How can you be?' enquired Heather. 'You'll be with Ronnie all the time.'

'Most of the time, yes that's true, but I shall still find time to see you.'

'There's no need to patronise me, April.' Heather sounded extremely miffed. 'I will actually be able to go on living without you, you know.'

'Sorry I didn't mean to sound condescending,' she said. 'I suppose I am just trying to make sure you know that I will still have my friends.' She reached across and put her hand on Heather's. 'Honestly, I would never knowingly do anything to hurt you. I suppose I'm trying to convince myself as well as you that things will stay the same between us.'

'It's all right,' said Heather in a softer tone. 'I shouldn't have jumped down your throat.'

'It's such a huge thing I'm going to be doing, I have moments when I get scared,' April confessed.

'I think that's quite usual for a bride, isn't it?' said Heather. 'I've heard it said before. But you are so lucky. I'd give anything to be in your shoes.'

'Marrying Ronnie?'

'Marrying someone, anyone.'

'You wouldn't settle for just anyone, surely.'

'Who knows what I might do if I get too desperate. But I'd have to fancy them, of course. The longer I have to wait the less fussy I'll be, I suppose.'

'I'm sure someone you like will turn up.'

'God knows when,' Heather said. 'I'm hopeless with men. I either frighten them away by being too keen or I don't fancy them at all. I suppose I'd been with Arthur so for long I lost the technique if I ever had it in the first place, with us knowing each other for such ages.'

April didn't know what to say that might be of comfort.

She knew Heather wasn't happy and she felt as though she was deserting her. 'I suppose when you meet someone and click with them, technique won't matter.'

'Maybe not,' said Heather, feeling nicely relaxed by the wine and a little giggly.

'Shall we have another glass,' suggested April. 'It is a special occasion.'

'Yes let's,' agreed Heather.

By the time they left the restaurant they were both quite tiddly.

'I've had a lovely time,' said Heather when they got off the train and started to walk home a little unsteadily.

April hiccupped. 'Me too,' she said.

'Funny how a man goes out drinking with his mates the night before the wedding and the woman traditionally stays at home. No one ever suggests that the bride goes out.'

'It's the way of things but we've had our own hen night so I'm not complaining.'

'They should bring it in as the norm for women.'

'Maybe they will have by the time you tie the knot,' suggested April.

'Surely I'm not going to have to wait that long,' said Heather, laughing helplessly.

'I didn't mean that,' said April, giggling.

'I know you didn't,' said Heather. 'I know one thing, kid, when I do find someone to marry, you and me are having a hen night just like this one. Why should men have all the fun?'

'Yeah, I'll second that.'

They reached the end of Heather's road.

'Are you all right to walk that bit on your own?' asked April because neither of them was too steady on their feet.

'Course I am. What about you?'

'I'll be fine. G'night, kid.'

'Night, April. Thanks for a smashing night.'

'You're welcome.'

They tottered off their separate ways, both a bit wobbly but happy.

Because April was a little tipsy when she got home it didn't strike her as odd to see Ronnie's father sitting in the living room with her mother and brother.

'Hello, Mr Bailey,' she said with a boozy smile. 'You're out late tonight. Come to pay us a visit, have you? Is it something to do with the wedding?'

'You've been drinking, April,' said her mother accusingly.

'I certainly have. Heather and I have had a hen night. We're starting a trend and there's nothing wrong with that. At least I've got time to sober up before the wedding, unlike Ronnie who's having his stag do the night before.'

She flopped down in an armchair and looked from one to the other. 'You're all looking a bit grim. Surely a hen night isn't that much of a sin, is it? So we've had a few drinks. So what? Men do that all the time.'

'April,' began her mother, going and sitting beside her. 'Mr Bailey is here because something has happened.'

She focused her eyes on Ronnie's father, perceiving that he looked upset. Sitting up and leaning forward, she said, 'What's the matter? Is Mrs Bailey not well?'

'It isn't Mrs Bailey, April,' her mother said, taking hold of her hand in both of hers.

'Who then?'

'It's Ronnie dear . . .'

'Ronnie, what about him?' asked April. 'Has he gone down with something?'

Beryl swallowed hard. 'It's worse than that.' She paused and took a breath. 'I'm sorry to have to tell you, dear, but Ronnie, well I'm afraid he's dead.'

'Dead! Don't be daft. He can't be. I was with him last night and he wasn't even ill.'

Mr Bailey came over to her chair and she stood up, feeling sober suddenly.

'Ronnie he . . . er, well, it's so hard for me to say this but . . . he took his own life,' he choked out.

April stared at him. 'What?' she said dumbly.

'My wife and I went to visit relatives this afternoon and when we got home we found him in the kitchen on the floor by the gas oven. The room was filled with gas.'

April's legs turned to jelly and for a moment she wasn't able to utter a word. She just sunk down in the chair. 'But why?' she asked when her powers of speech returned. 'Why would he do a terrible thing like that?'

'He left you a letter,' he said, handing her an envelope, 'and one for us.'

Trembling all over, she knew that she must somehow be strong for poor Mr Bailey who was ashen-faced and shaky. Oh Ronnie, what have you done? she cried inwardly, barely aware that her brother had come over to her chair and put his arms around her.

Chapter Seven

Despite strong opposition from her mother, brother and Mr Bailey, April insisted on escorting Ronnie's father home. The poor man was devastated and seemed achingly fragile. Of course, she couldn't ease his pain but maybe some company on the way home might help in some small way.

It was too late for the last bus so they had to walk but she was glad of the fresh air and exercise, barely noticing the cold weather in her distressed state.

'I'm so ashamed,' he said as they walked through the streets.

His remark surprised her. Sadness, agonising grief she could understand. But shame? 'Why is that, Mr Bailey?' she asked.

'Because suicide is a sin,' he replied. 'We won't even be able to bury him in consecrated ground.'

'Your son must have been suffering dreadfully to do such a thing. He was ill I think, even though he wouldn't accept it,' she said. 'So you shouldn't feel ashamed.'

'How can I not when it's generally accepted as a sin as well as illegal?' he said. 'If he'd survived he'd have had the police after him.'

'But I suppose it depends on the circumstances as to how you judge him yourself.'

'My son was the easiest-going bloke you could wish to meet before he went away to war that last time,' he reminisced. 'I don't think he'd been in combat before that, though he never went into detail about what he actually did so we can't be sure.'

'I know he used to be an amiable sort of person because that was the man I fell in love with,' she said. 'I still loved him, though, when he came back and had changed so much. I thought he'd seemed a bit better recently but I suppose he just got better at hiding his true feelings.'

'He shouldn't have done it,' said Mr Bailey thickly. 'His mother will never get over it.'

'I don't suppose any of us will but it's a terrible thing for a mother to have to endure.'

When they reached the house they found Mrs Bailey looking weepy but April sensed that the couple needed to be alone so she didn't stay to offer comfort. They looked so vulnerable and older than before somehow. She would keep in touch with them later on after the funeral when the initial shock had eased. It seemed only right that she should as she had so nearly been related to them.

Walking home in the deserted streets, as it was now the early hours, she was thinking about how dreadful Ronnie must have been feeling to do such a thing. He'd been tormented beyond endurance. She wasn't angry with him; just desperately sad and concerned about her own part in it. Could she perhaps have done more to stop this happening? Had she always been as patient as she might have been with his moods? But in some truthful corner of her mind she suspected that this was almost destined to happen from the moment he had got back from the war. He had been mentally tortured and living in hell. His scribbled note to her had read simply:

Forgive me April but I just can't go on.

She doubted if he had planned it and the hurried note seemed to confirm this. She thought it more likely he had found himself at a point of despair while alone in the house and, desperate, had seen an instant way out. The thought of it made her cry and she let the tears fall. She was about ten minutes from home when she saw Charlie coming to meet her. 'What are you doing out at this hour?' she asked.

'Mum is worried to death about you being out on the streets on your own so late,' he explained. 'I wasn't happy about it either so here I am.'

'Sorry about that. I shouldn't have gone off like that but I felt so sorry for poor Mr Bailey.'

'That's all right,' he said as she linked arms with him. 'What a terrible thing to happen. I'm so sorry, sis.'

'Thanks, kid,' she said. 'I'm still trying to take it in. His poor parents, how will they ever get over it?'

'How will you?'

'I don't know the answer to that and it will take a while I expect, but I'm young and resilient so I suppose I'll get through it somehow. How his mum and dad will ever come to terms with it though, I have no idea. I mean to lose a child . . . It isn't the way it should happen.'

'It shouldn't have happened anyway,' stated Charlie. 'I think it's a terrible thing to do, causing people such pain.'

'He wouldn't have done it if he'd been in his right mind,'

she said. 'He's not been himself since he got back from the war. He was a victim of his experiences.'

'Even so . . .'

'Please don't judge him,' she urged. 'He isn't here to speak up for himself. None of us know what was going on in his mind. I mean, ask yourself, he had everything to live for. He was about to get married.'

'Naturally my sympathies lie with you.'

'I realise that but it would really please me if you could try and show a little compassion for him,' she said. 'It hurts me to hear ill of him.'

'Fair enough, sis,' he said and they walked home arm in arm barely saying a word.

April hardly slept that night. She kept turning the events of her life with Ronnie these past few months over and wondering if perhaps he'd been worried about coping with the responsibility of marriage given the state of his nerves? Had that driven him over the edge?

Fortunately the next day was Sunday so she didn't have to go to work in her exhausted state and she didn't even have the heart to go to the allotment. It was a dark, dismal day and didn't inspire her to venture outside, which was unusual for someone who liked to be outdoors whatever the weather. In her depressed state, her little sister's noisy exuberance grated on her nerves and she found herself snapping at her.

'Don't take it out on her,' admonished her mother. 'She hasn't done anything wrong.'

Immediately filled with compunction, April lifted Lily on to her lap and gave her a cuddle. 'Shall I take her to the swings,

Mum?' she suggested, spurred into action by guilt. 'If I wrap her up well.'

Her mother agreed so, swathed in coats, scarves and gloves, they set out for the park, April wheeling Lily in the pushchair. She supposed this was what Sundays would be like in future for her with no Ronnie to see, or married life to look forward to.

They were just about to enter the park when they came face to face with a neighbour and April realised that news really did travel fast around here.

'I heard about your trouble dear, and I'm very sorry for your loss,' said the woman, who was on her way out of the park with a young boy.

'Thank you,' said April politely, not really in the mood for a chat.

'What a shocking thing for him to do to you.'

'Not very nice for him either,' said April defensively.

'He had the choice, you didn't,' said the woman. 'And you with your wedding plans all in place.'

April wanted to slap her but she just said, 'Wedding plans are nothing. They can easily be cancelled. But I must ask you not to speak ill of my intended.'

'I won't be the only one,' she said smugly. 'It's wrong to take your own life; everyone knows that.'

'Then I will tell anyone who feels the need to make any nasty comments about my late fiancé not to do so,' April stated. 'I won't have him maligned.'

'Yeah, all right,' said the woman.

'Good,' said April. 'So let's start again, shall we? Are there many at the swings?'

'It's too cold for most people to venture out,' she said, looking at Lily. 'So she won't have to wait long for a turn.'

As they went on their way, April felt a dragging sensation in the pit of her stomach as the reality of her life hit home. Yesterday she had been a bride to be, brimming over with excitement. Now she was just a single woman with nothing special to look forward to, and if her first outing was anything to go by she was going to have a fight on her hands because she simply wouldn't let anyone speak ill of Ronnie in her hearing.

'So you're not on your own on the shelf now, Heather,' said April to her cousin who was at the house with Auntie Peg when she and Lily got back. 'You've got me perched up there right beside you. And if you say one bad word about Ronnie, I won't be responsible for my actions.'

'I wasn't going to,' said Heather.

'Try not to be so sensitive, April dear,' her mother advised. 'People will say things, it's only natural.'

'Whatever happened to not speaking ill of the dead?' she asked.

'That still applies but the circumstances in this case are rather different,' said Beryl.

'People are sorry for you so they take their feelings out on him,' suggested Auntie Peg.

'Well I don't want their sympathy and I won't tolerate criticism of him.'

'All right, dear,' said Beryl with an air of weary patience and April saw a look pass between her mother and Auntie Peg. 'Please try not to be so sharp with everyone.'

'While we are on the subject,' April went on determinedly. 'I will not be wearing black except perhaps for the funeral or going into mourning. I shall carry on with my life as best as I can in the normal way.'

At that moment there was a knock at the door. Charlie answered it and came back into the room with George Benson who immediately sensed the tension.

'Is this a bad time?' he asked gingerly. 'Shall I come back another day?'

'Surely the news hasn't reached the High Road already,' said April brusquely.

'April,' said her mother in a tone of admonition. 'Don't be so rude.'

'News, what news?' George asked, puzzled. 'I just came round to see Charlie about football and to ask a favour of April.' He looked round. 'But as I am obviously interrupting something I'll leave and come back some other time.'

'No, George, don't go,' urged April. 'We've had some bad news. I'm sorry I was so rude.'

She looked at her mother, who told him what had happened, adding, 'But my daughter will bite your head off if you make any negative comments about Ronnie.'

'I wouldn't dream of it,' he said, looking concerned. 'But I am very sorry for your loss, April.'

'Thank you,' she said graciously, feeling calmer presumably because his arrival had eased the tension in that it had interrupted it. 'So what's the favour? Let me guess. You want me to help in the shop while you go to football.'

'No, not now,' he said adamantly. 'I wouldn't dream of imposing on you at a time like this.'

'What do you think I'm going to do, sit indoors crying for the rest of my life?'

'Of course not, but—'

'So tell me what it is you want.'

'There's a match in a couple of weeks . . .'

'That's fine, I'll fill in for you.'

'Cor, smashing,' said Charlie, beaming. 'Thanks, sis.' He stopped smiling abruptly. 'Sorry, everyone.'

'Being pleased about something isn't wrong, Charlie,' said April.

'A bit inappropriate at the moment though,' he said.

'Look, everyone, Ronnie is where he wants to be and I have to get on with my life without him. I am not going to go around with a long face for the next ten years so will you all please stop walking on eggshells around me,' she said, then rushed from the room and headed upstairs to her bedroom.

When Heather went to go after her Beryl said, 'Leave her be for the moment, love, she needs to be on her own.'

George made a diplomatic exit and Beryl did what she always did in times of stress: she put the kettle on.

April couldn't stop crying. She was sitting on the bed sobbing and trying to keep the noise down for fear anyone should hear. She barely remembered what had happened in the time since she'd heard the news but she suspected she'd been horrid to all and sundry. But she had meant what she'd said about not wearing black and not hearing a word against Ronnie.

Perhaps she had been too abrasive, so she needed to put things right with people she had upset. She did actually experience moments of anger towards Ronnie herself even though she wouldn't allow others to voice their negative thoughts. Now that the initial shock was beginning to wear off she had times when she was deeply hurt that Ronnie had chosen to leave her. Of course, the balance of his mind had been upset but it still felt like a rejection. She was bitterly disappointed that her wedding plans were to be cancelled and that her future life partner was no longer with her. The pain was almost physical, gnawing away in the pit of her stomach so hard that she felt ill.

Heather was trying desperately hard not to be pleased about April's misfortune. It was a shocking thing that had happened to her cousin and she wanted to feel sorry for her. She really did. But there was always a little corner of her brain that sent selfish thoughts and feelings to her.

She didn't want April to be unhappy exactly but it was comforting for Heather to know that her cousin was now in the same boat as herself. Single. April would be more available too, which was good news. Suicide though! Heather had never known anyone who had done such a terrible thing. It was creepy. So awful she could hardly bear to think about the details.

But it was an ill wind. She had her cousin back and she herself was no longer the only spinster in the family, so things were looking up for her personally. Anyway, April would get over it. She wouldn't stay down for long. She wasn't the type. Meanwhile Heather would enjoy giving her cousin some comfort and having company herself at the same time.

It was instinctive to April to offer support to Ronnie's parents. Empathy came naturally to her and she could only imagine how devastated they must be at their son's passing so she was still planning on visiting them regularly with the idea of providing comfort. She was Ronnie's chosen one and he had been a part of them so she hoped they could find some sort of solace in each other.

The Baileys had arranged the funeral, which was the bleakest event April had ever been to. A cold and foggy day; no mourners apart from family because of the nature of the death and no place for him in the consecrated part of the cemetery.

A week or so after this most miserable occasion April called round to see the Baileys on a Sunday afternoon and Ronnie's father answered the door. She waited for him to usher her inside as usual but he left her standing outside and stepped out, half closing the door behind him and looking uncomfortable.

'Have I called at a bad time?' she asked. 'I've just popped round to see how you and Mrs Bailey are.'

'It's a bit awkward actually,' he said. 'Er, my wife . . .'

'Is she not very well?' asked April.

'She's all right but . . .' He cleared his throat. 'We think it would be best if you didn't call here again.'

It was like ice in her face. 'Oh. Have I done something to upset Mrs Bailey then?' she asked.

'No, nothing like that, dear,' he said, sounding awkward. 'It's just that you remind her of what might have been and she just can't take it. Ronnie's death has really knocked the stuffing out of her, especially the manner of it, and seeing you upsets her even more.'

'I'm so sorry,' she said. 'I didn't think. I suppose I should have realised.'

'Not at all,' he said. 'You weren't to know.'

'I'll say cheerio then.'

'Yes, I think it's for the best. Ta-ta.'

April turned and walked down the path, absolutely shattered by a feeling of rejection.

★   ★   ★

'Oh Mum, how could I have been so insensitive?' she said when she got home, still burning with embarrassment. 'I should have known they wouldn't want to see me.'

'How could you know that?' asked Beryl. 'Most people in their sad position would have been pleased to see their son's intended. They would have welcomed your support with open arms. But bereavement affects people in different ways.'

'Maybe I was just trying to ease my own pain by giving them support.'

'You were just doing what comes naturally to you, you were being kind. Now try to put it to the back of your mind; you've got quite enough on your plate without worrying about people who don't want to be helped.'

'I know I've been a bit difficult since it happened, Mum,' said April. 'Will you promise to tell me if I step out of line again?'

'You don't need to ask that.'

'No, I suppose not. My confidence has taken a bit of a knock, though. Rejection does that.'

'It wasn't rejection in the usual sense so try not to think of it in that way,' her mother advised. 'Go and sit down and read the paper to take your mind off it.'

April went into the living room and sat in an armchair, the quiet boredom of Sunday afternoon sweeping over her, along with the lingering aroma of the traditional roast meal they'd had for lunch. It was the comforting, but slightly claustrophobic, feeling of home. Outside everywhere was silent and all the shops in the town would be closed. The weather was cold, the light already beginning to fade. In normal times on a Sunday afternoon Ronnie would be here and they would have gone for a walk together before tea. Now she would stay at home and think about what might have been.

She could hear Lily stirring from her afternoon nap and calling for her mother.

'I'll go and get her, Mum,' she said to Beryl in the kitchen and hurried up the stairs.

Lily was standing up in her cot, her cheeks pink from sleep. She beamed when she saw her sister and lifted her arms. April picked her up, holding her close, her aching heart soothed. 'How did we ever manage without you in our family, Lily?' She kissed her. 'You are our bright and shining star.'

The following Sunday afternoon, April tried to outwit the blues by going to the allotment, despite the weather which was damp and raw. December wasn't the most exciting month for gardeners but there were always jobs to be done. She got the fork out of the shed and began to dig. The soil needed turning over as many times as possible during winter in vacant ground, according to her father's chart.

'Good grief,' said George Benson, striding up to her. 'I could hardly believe it when your mother told me this is where I'd find you. But you really are here. What sort of a lunatic goes out digging in this weather?'

'Either a gardening fanatic or someone looking for solace in the soil,' she suggested.

'I think there's a bit of both of those in you,' he said in a friendly manner. 'But today I suspect it's most likely the latter.'

'You're probably right. The ground isn't actually freezing though or I wouldn't be digging,' she said, 'and the exercise is keeping me warm.'

She was wearing a blue coat and matching knitted hat with trousers tucked into wellington boots. Her cheeks were glowing from the cold and the exertion.

'You should be at home by the fire in this weather,' he told her.

'Maybe but I prefer to be here. Weekends are hard, and working at the allotment helps me. I don't know why but it does.'

'It's good that you have a way of finding comfort.' He had thought of not asking her to fill in for him at the shop given the circumstances but after mulling it over he had decided that it might help to take her mind of things. 'Talking of weekends, I came over to confirm your shift at the shop on Saturday afternoon. You were a bit preoccupied when we spoke about it before.'

'I hadn't forgotten,' she said. 'How could I with my brother counting the days to the match?'

He smiled, hugging himself against the cold. 'I probably drive them mad at home about it too.'

'Don't stand about in this weather, George. You'll freeze.'

'Aren't you going to offer me a spade and tell me to get digging to keep warm?'

'Of course not.' She grinned.

'Thank God for that,' he said. 'But if you were thinking of inviting me into your shed for a cuppa, I doubt if I could refuse. I know you keep a flask in there.'

'That isn't a bad idea actually,' she said. 'I've got enough tea for two. It isn't exactly the Ritz but at least we'll be out of the wind.'

She dug her fork in the ground and headed for the shed with him following.

★　　★　　★

'I don't like the idea of George going off on a Saturday afternoon and leaving you to look after the shop on your own,' Percy Benson complained to his wife.

'He's arranging cover,' said Winnie, defensive as ever of her son. 'Young April Green is coming in to help me.'

'Even so, he shouldn't be going,' stated Percy. 'I never went off enjoying myself during shop hours.'

'Maybe you should have,' suggested Winnie. 'You wouldn't be quite so lost without the shop now if you'd had other interests.'

'You and the shop were all I ever wanted.'

Winnie was imbued with conflicting emotions. While it was warming to know that she was everything to her husband, the responsibility of it sometimes weighed heavily upon her. Now that he didn't have the shop to occupy him he focused totally on her, which could be suffocating at times.

'What about George, surely you wanted him.'

'Of course.'

'You've never been very warm towards him,' she said, not for the first time.

'You know why that is, Winnie. Boys grow up to be men who have to make their way in the world so mollycoddling them does them no good at all. I've always had his best interests at heart.'

'I suppose so. It's just that it makes me sad that the two of you aren't close.'

'We're men and that's how we do things,' he said. 'It's different for women.'

'Fathers and sons can sometimes be good mates when the son is an adult,' she said. 'I know of families where that is so.'

His wife had no way of knowing that Percy could never be close to his son and it was best left that way. Even if he did have any idea of how to put things right between himself and

George he wouldn't do it. A man had to stand by the consequences of his actions and what he believed was right.

'What happens in other families is no business of ours,' he said. 'So let's just leave it at that.'

She shrugged. 'Fair enough.' She finished her tea and leaned back in her armchair, closing her eyes.

'You should have more time off from the shop,' he said. 'You're dead tired.'

'George is always telling me the same thing and I can have more time to myself if I want but the shop is what keeps me going. Right now it's a Sunday afternoon and I'm relaxing, that's all. You have a nap every day after lunch and I don't go on at you about it.'

'George is overworking you and I shall have a few words with him about it.'

'Look, Percy, one day you will be able to take your place in the business again, God willing,' she said. 'Until then please don't make an issue when there's no need. George is doing a good job so leave him alone.'

He fell silent rather sulkily and when he next looked at her she was fast asleep.

Having brushed the cobwebs off the deckchairs, April and George were sitting in the shed drinking tea and chatting. She seemed able to talk to him easily about what had happened and how all the wedding arrangements had now been cancelled. It was less emotional to talk about the practical side of things.

'We only lost money on the dresses; everything else we were able to cancel.'

'I don't suppose you care about the money.'

'Absolutely not. It's just so dreadfully sad. You know, that a young man in the prime of life felt driven to do a thing like that.' She told him what had happened with Ronnie's parents. 'That really turned the knife, even though I can understand why. I'm wondering if I can get anything right ever again.'

'You've done nothing wrong.'

'That's what Mum says but I can't help thinking that I should have been able to stop Ronnie getting so low and I should have guessed how his parents were feeling.'

She looked so achingly vulnerable he wanted to hold her and stop her from hurting.

'April, you can't take that blame,' he said. 'You're not being fair to yourself. None of it was your fault.'

She finished her tea and put the cup down. 'It sometimes feels as though it was . . . here,' she said, pointing to her heart.

'No, I can't let you do that to yourself,' he said, leaning forward and taking her hand and holding it with both of his. He pointed to his head. 'In there you must know you are not to blame. Please think about it. You can't read people's thoughts. How could you know what Ronnie was going to do or that his parents didn't want you around.'

Then it happened. She welled up and started to cry uncontrollably. He gave her his handkerchief and held her hand until the tears finally abated.

'I should have given you a spade and got you digging to keep you warm, not given you tea while you gave me sympathy,' she said, feeling better.

'I've been all over the world and in all sorts of situations but I've never taken tea with a girl in a garden shed in the middle of an English winter before,' he said, hoping to make her laugh.

She managed a watery smile. She wasn't out of the wood

154

by a long way but she'd had a glimpse of light in her dark world and that had to be a good sign.

'Do you fancy having a wander around the shops on Saturday afternoon, April?' asked Heather when she called round to the Greens' one evening after work. 'I've still got some Christmas shopping to do.'

'I'm working at Benson's,' she replied.

'Oh, it's this Saturday is it?' said Heather. 'That's a bit dismal for you.'

'Not at all,' said April. 'I enjoy working there as you know and at least I'll feel as though I'm doing something useful.'

'Christmas shopping is useful in that it has to be done,' said Heather. 'And everything you buy is for someone else so it's not a selfish occupation.'

Heather had an answer for everything when she wanted something. 'You know exactly what I mean,' said April.

'I suppose so,' said Heather. 'But it's so miserable for you being stuck in a freezing cold greengrocer's shop on a Saturday afternoon when you've been working all week.'

'Don't you mean that it's a bit dismal for you Christmas shopping on your own?'

'That's a horrible thing to say,' Heather protested. 'I was thinking it might be nice for you to capture the atmosphere of Saturday afternoon shopping, especially at this time of the year.'

April gave her a steady stare.

'All right, maybe I would like it for me too,' she admitted. 'I've missed you while you've been tied up with Ronnie. Even without him you have these peculiar commitments like vege-table growing and working in a blasted greengrocer's shop.'

She thought for a moment. 'What about Saturday evening? Surely you'll not be digging or selling spuds then.'

'Of course not,' said April. 'So I'll be free to do something with you. But I'm not going to a dance hall.'

'As if I would suggest something like that at this time,' Heather objected. 'Honestly. What do you take me for?'

'I wouldn't put it past you,' said April with a wry grin.

'Oh April, that's mean.'

'All right, I'm sorry, but I know how you enjoy a bit of a twirl and all that goes with it.'

'Not so much that I would drag a recently bereaved person there.'

April sighed. Her cousin could be infuriating at times but she supposed her heart was in the right place.

'George, can you bring some more spuds up from the cellar to make sure we have enough for this afternoon?' Winnie asked her son on Saturday morning, the day of the match.

'Will do, Mum,' he said pleasantly. 'I'll have a look round the shop to see if there's anything else you might need too.'

'Thanks, love.'

George made his way down the cellar steps, a shiver running up his spine. It didn't matter how many times he came down here; it still stirred up memories and made his flesh creep. He remembered the sound of the door closing behind him and the way his stomach used to lurch and his heart beat faster. To this day he never shut the cellar door when he was down here.

Still, that was a long while ago and it was time he stopped allowing it to affect him. Concentrate on the job in hand,

George; potatoes, carrots and turnips were needed upstairs. He reached the stone floor and headed for the potato sacks, thinking about the present and the football match this afternoon. That was better. The past was best forgotten.

April enjoyed her shift at Benson's. It was cold in the shop but they had a paraffin heater out the back and she and Winnie huddled around it at regular intervals.

'How is Mr Benson these days?' April asked during a break. 'Is his back any better?'

'Not really, dear. He manages to shuffle around upstairs with the help of a stick but I can't see him being ready to come back to work at any time in the near future. If it was possible for him to do so he would. He's a very active man, my Percy, and he hates not being actively involved in the business.'

'Is there nothing that can be done for him?'

'Not without money,' Winnie replied. 'If you're poor you don't have to pay for medical treatment but if you've an income you have to make a contribution and we can't afford hospitals and specialists. Going to the doctor's is expensive if you go too often. So we don't go there unless we absolutely have to.'

'There is talk of some sort of government health scheme so that everybody gets medical treatment free.'

Winnie nodded. 'Yeah, I remember hearing something about that. It's part of the Labour Government's programme of reform they talked about when they were campaigning for votes at the General Election just after the war when they trounced Churchill and his Tories. It's all part of the building a better Britain campaign I think. God knows we need it but whether or not it will actually happen is anyone's guess.'

'There was something on the wireless about it the other day,' said April. 'Mum was talking about it. Apparently even dentists and opticians will be free for all of us as well as doctors and hospital treatment. If it does come to be it will be an absolute godsend for us with little Lily. You know how kids of that age are always going down with something or other and we can't afford the doctor unless we suspect she has something really serious. So we usually just manage with a bottle of something from the chemist.'

'It would be wonderful if it did come to be,' said Winnie. 'We might even be able to get some proper treatment for my Percy's back. Something more effective than rubbing liniment on it and hoping it will get better.'

'At least they are talking about it so you never know,' said April optimistically.

A rush of customers brought the conversation to a halt and the rest of the afternoon flew past.

Johnny was with George and Charlie when they arrived back, all of them full of beans and hugging the heater. It was closing time, so April and Winnie had already started bringing in the outside display and George took over. Charlie said he would wait for April so that they could walk home together.

'I'm so sorry to hear about your loss, April,' said Johnny who was seeing her for the first time since Ronnie's death. 'How are you feeling?'

'I'm not so bad, thanks,' she replied. 'There's nothing like keeping busy to keep the miseries at bay.'

'I'm sure,' he said.

'She's a proper little trouper,' said Winnie.

'I'll second that,' agreed George.

The Apple of Her Eye

'Are you all coming upstairs for a cuppa?' Winnie asked. 'You'll be very welcome.'

April said she wouldn't because she liked to bath her little sister on a Saturday and Charlie said he'd go home with her while Johnny accepted the invitation but set to and helped George to finish closing up.

'April really is something else,' he said to George after the latter had cashed up and the two of them headed upstairs. 'An absolute peach.'

'You don't have to tell me that,' said George.

'You're smitten, you old bugger.'

'Maybe I am but I hope I'm not making it too obvious,' said George.

'Only to me because I'm your mate and I can read you like a book.'

'Yeah well, I can't do anything about it can I, not after what's happened,' he said.

'Obviously not now you can't,' agreed Johnny. 'But when some time has passed maybe you could make a gentle move in that direction.'

'I don't think she sees me in that light,' said George.

'That could change with a little encouragement.'

'Possibly, but we're just mates at the moment and that's good enough for me if that's what she wants,' George told him. 'She needs a good friend now.'

'Good luck with that,' said Johnny with sincerity. George hadn't had an easy life by any means when he was younger but he'd never complained and he had always been a good friend so Johnny wished the best for him.

Chapter Eight

Christmas passed quietly for the Green family with Lily creating the festive spirit even though she still wasn't old enough to understand the reason for all the treats.

Not long after the New Year of 1947 the people of southeast England found themselves in the grip of what was to become the worst winter since records began. The temperatures soon plummeted in the rest of Britain too so the whole country was freezing. Heavy and continuous snowfalls caused a fuel crisis in the capital because the coal bound for London couldn't get through to coal merchants or power stations. The skies were continuously dark and even the Thames froze over. Blizzards, gales and snowdrifts crippled the roads and railways, bringing the country almost to a standstill.

'And we thought peace would bring us good times,' Beryl said to April when they were feeling their way around the unheated house by candlelight during a power cut. 'We're as bad off as we were in wartime.'

'No, Mum, we can't be because we don't have bombs falling on us,' April pointed out.

'When you put it like that, you're right of course,' Beryl conceded.

It took a lot to keep April away from the allotment but even she was defeated by the weather because the ground was frozen hard. People were expected to turn up for work despite the dreadful conditions but many workers had to operate by the light of a candle when the power went off. April thought this was rather a lark, especially as it encouraged a little more social chat in the office. Even the hard-faced head of her department became almost human.

It was March before the thaw finally came and it was so drastic the rivers overflowed, then a violent storm in the middle of the month added to the floodwaters until finally the weather got back to normal. It had been a harsh winter and was a damaging spring so people were looking forward to the summer with more than usual ardour.

April was glad to get back to the allotment, which had been unavoidably neglected, but once she'd cleared up and got rid of all the rubbish there was nothing that couldn't be put right. With the weather back on track she got to work in earnest. Oh, how she enjoyed it! It felt so good to be outdoors again. There was a lot to be done though, so much that her mother helped out one Sunday afternoon while Auntie Peg was looking after Lily, something Peg enjoyed enormously.

'Wotcha, ladies,' said Frank, coming over. 'Haven't seen you for ages, especially you, Beryl.'

'It hasn't been the weather for gardening has it,' she responded.

'It certainly hasn't,' he agreed. 'Where's the nipper?'

'She's with my sister for the afternoon so I thought I'd show willing and come and give April a hand.'

'Lucky you, April,' he said, smiling. 'If you don't need her send her over to me. There's plenty to do on my patch.' He looked across the allotment area where there was a lot of work in progress. 'Everyone is at it today.'

'They need to be after all that time off in the bad weather,' said April. 'Nature runs wild left to itself.'

'It certainly does,' agreed Frank mildly. 'Well, I'll leave you to get on while I do the same. Cheerio.'

'Ta-ta,' the women chorused.

'I told you he was harmless, didn't I?' said April as soon as he was out of earshot.

'You did indeed,' her mother said thoughtfully. 'It was stupid of me to think otherwise I suppose and I didn't, not really. I just had a moment of panic because I really wouldn't know what to do with a pass from a man, it's been so long since anything like that has happened to me.'

'It's not beyond the realms of possibility that you might get some male interest,' suggested April. 'You're not even quite turned fifty yet.'

'Fifty being the operative word,' Beryl said. 'I'm far too old to want any of that old malarkey. But at least now that I know there won't be any of that, I can enjoy a chat with Frank when I see him. He's a nice bloke.'

'I've always thought so,' agreed April.

The two women carried on working with enthusiasm in the pale sunshine.

'I've got a proposition for you,' George told April when he called at the house one evening in the late spring.

'Ooh that sounds wonderfully sinful,' she said laughing, glad of the humour after the trauma of Ronnie's death and the long and punishing winter.

'I'm far too much of a gentleman for anything untoward with regards to you, April,' he said, enjoying the banter. 'But I can change my ways if you wish.'

'Should we leave the two of them alone, Charlie?' suggested Beryl jokingly.

'No, we're all right, Mum,' he responded. 'George won't step out of line. He's a mate.'

'He won't but I might,' chuckled April and they all smiled. 'So, what is it you want to ask me, George?'

'I wondered if you might be interested in doing a Saturday afternoon shift at the shop for us on a regular basis,' he explained. 'Two o'clock until five should be about right. No need to stay until closing time.'

'Oh,' she said, surprised. 'Are you having Saturday afternoons off then?'

'No, I'm not. But Mum is. I want her to have a longer weekend, a bit of time to herself. I've been trying to persuade her for ages but she wouldn't hear of it. Now Dad's getting on to her about it as well so she's finally agreed to have Saturday afternoons off as long as I can get someone she approves of to stand in for her. Naturally my first choice is you but I'll understand if you don't want to do it. You already have a full-time job and the allotment to look after.'

'I'll do it,' she said without hesitation. 'I'll be happy to. Weekends are far too long for me now that Ronnie isn't around. I'll still have Saturday mornings and Sunday to work at the allotment and anything else I want to do.'

He couldn't hide his joy at the prospect of working with her but they would all assume that he was pleased merely to have filled the vacancy. 'That is marvellous, April,' he said. 'Obviously we'll make sure you are well paid.'

'What about football?' asked Charlie, looking worried. 'Will you still be able to come when there's a match on if your mum isn't working in the shop?'

'Don't worry, that's all taken care of,' George assured him. 'Mum will step in for me then.' He looked at April. 'Same thing applies if you have anything you want to do at any time. Mum will cover.' He gave a wry grin. 'She'll probably jump at the chance. Dad isn't the most cheerful company because of his bad back. I've suggested that she go to visit her sister for the afternoon so that she has a real break.'

They all nodded diplomatically but didn't make any comment.

'So when would you like me to start?' asked April.

'This Saturday?'

'I'll be there.'

They were all looking pleased when Beryl went to put the kettle on.

'I don't believe it,' said Heather disapprovingly on hearing about her cousin's Saturday job. 'Are you stark raving mad or something, April? Why on earth would you want to work in a flamin' greengrocer's shop at a weekend on a regular basis? It isn't as though you aren't reasonably paid in your proper job.'

'I don't know why I want to do it but I do and it's only a few hours a week,' explained April. 'Anyway the extra money is always handy.'

'So you'll never be around to go for a look round the shops and have a cup of tea in Lyons with me then?'

'We can do that on a Saturday morning if you want,' suggested April.

'There isn't the same atmosphere in the morning.'

'You are being very juvenile if you don't mind my saying, Heather,' said April firmly. 'We did all that Saturday afternoon hanging around the shops when we were younger.'

'Blimey, hark at the old codger,' said Heather sarcastically. 'And I do mind you saying.'

'I'm sorry about that but there it is. Surely you can go round the shops on your own or with someone else.'

Heather shrugged. 'I shall have to, won't I?'

'Yes, I'm afraid you will,' said April, tired of the constant battle she had with her cousin whenever she wanted to do anything that didn't involve her.

April threw herself into the job at Benson's with gusto and enjoyed every minute. She and George worked well together and they had plenty of banter. For a while after Ronnie's death she had felt guilty if she'd laughed; as though what had happened was so awful that to indulge in humour was disrespectful. She now realised that life went on and she had to embrace it. There was no point in two young lives being wasted.

Summer came at last and was a series of sunny days and balmy nights. It was like living in a different country to the frozen, flooded place they had inhabited all winter.

It was during the nice weather that April got to know George's father, who had always been rather a distant figure, a little better. Between them George and his mother would sometimes bring Percy downstairs and into the small, paved back garden where he would sit for a while with a cup of tea

165

and the newspaper. Because of his disability, the journey up and down the stairs was difficult and George and Winnie used humour to help things along.

'It would be easier to drop you out of the window to get you down,' said George, grinning. 'We could tie you to a sheet and ease you down gently.'

'Or perhaps a little parachute might do the trick,' added Winnie. 'You could float down then.'

'I'm glad you find it so funny,' Percy objected mildly. 'You wouldn't be laughing if you were in my shoes.'

'I certainly wouldn't,' said George. 'My feet are bigger than yours.'

And so it went on. April heard all this when she was working there on a Saturday and found it amusing. When George suggested that she take her tea break outside one sunny afternoon she was worried about invading the older man's privacy but George said some young company might do him good.

'Mind if I join you for ten minutes or so, Mr Benson,' she asked warily.

He didn't look too happy but said it would be fine.

'I understand you lost your father in the Blue Rabbit bombing,' he said.

'Yeah, that's right,' she confirmed. 'You were there too, I believe.'

'Mm. I was in the saloon bar, which was fortunate for me as it happened as that was the only part not destroyed completely. It was a terrible thing to live through, though,' he said, shaking his head slowly. 'I shall never ever forget that night.'

'I can imagine.'

'I suppose you think I'm very lucky to be around considering what happened to your father.'

'All of us who survived the war are lucky, I reckon,' she said. 'But it isn't up to us to make those sorts of judgements, is it?'

'That's true I suppose, but I think perhaps your dad should have been spared instead of me what with your mother having the little one to bring up.'

'Oh Mr Benson, that's a terrible thing to say! You mustn't think like that,' she said, sensing a kind of desolation about him. 'My dad dying has nothing to do with you being alive. It's just pot luck in an air raid.'

'Still, you can't help thoughts, can you?' he said. 'I bet he was a good man. I can tell by the way you are.'

'I don't know of anyone who didn't like my dad,' she said. 'He was a very gentle sort of a person but a real man's man too. He had lots of mates.'

'I'm sure he is much missed.'

'Every single day,' she confirmed. 'We talk about him all the time.'

The conversation ended there because George shouted from the door that the shop was full and he needed her so she hurried away.

'How did you find the old man?' George asked April when things calmed down a bit later on.

'He's rather nice,' she said. 'I've never had much to do with him before but he was quite warm and friendly towards me.'

'Blimey, things are looking up,' said George. 'He's usually a miserable old git.'

'George, that's not a nice thing to say about your father,' she admonished.

'It's true though,' he said. 'He's got a bad back so I suppose it's understandable.'

'He's a troubled man.'

'He would be, as he's in a lot of pain.'

'I got the impression there was something more than that,' she said. 'He seems to be full of regret . . . about himself, his life.'

'That's the first I've heard of it.' George sounded surprised. 'As far as I know he thinks he's right about everything. His way is the only way.'

'You don't get on with him then.'

'We tolerate each other for Mum's sake.'

'Oh that's a shame.'

'Yeah but that's the way it is. Not all families are warm and cosy like yours, unfortunately, April,' he said.

'No, I suppose not,' she said. 'We are very lucky even though we lost Dad.'

He stared at her, her beautiful feline eyes as green as spring leaves, and he was in awe. She had lost her father in tragic circumstances and been to hell and back with her fiancé before he had also died in a dreadful way. But here she was saying that she was lucky.

'Aye aye, you two are looking very cosy,' said someone and turning they saw Johnny, grinning at them.

'We were just talking,' said April, colouring up.

'Take no notice of him, April; he's got a one-track mind,' said George. 'What are you doing here anyway? I'm guessing you haven't come to buy vegetables since you've got your mother doing all that sort of thing for you.'

'Spot on mate,' he said. 'I've come to see if you fancy coming out for a few drinks tonight.'

'Yeah, I might as well.'

'I'll come round about eight o'clock then,' he said and headed for the door just as Heather was on the way in, dressed to the nines in high heels and a summer dress.

'Here's another one who won't be buying,' said April.

'Too true I won't,' Heather confirmed. 'The only way I like potatoes is baked and on the plate with gravy.'

'A woman after my own heart,' said Johnny. 'See you later, George.'

'So Heather,' began April after Johnny had gone. 'I should imagine you've come to ask me if I'll go to the pictures with you tonight.'

'How did you know?'

'Just a lucky guess,' said April inwardly, smiling at her cousin's transparency. 'But yes, I'll come with you. Why not?'

'You and George Benson seem very friendly,' remarked Heather as the two women walked to the bus stop that evening.

'Yes, we do get on well.'

'You don't mean . . .'

'Of course I don't,' confirmed April.

'He's very good-looking,' said Heather.

'Indeed.'

'So are you hoping something will come of it eventually then?' asked Heather.

'No. Just because I think he looks good it doesn't mean I automatically want to fall into bed with him,' she said. 'Ronnie hasn't been gone for a year yet so I am not thinking along those lines with anyone at the moment.'

'All right, don't bite my head off.'

'Just want to make things clear.'

'And you have.'

'His friend is single if you are still keen to find someone, though. He was on the way out of the shop as you came in this afternoon.'

'I didn't notice.' Heather had been far too busy looking and wondering about April and George.

'Who was that woman who came into the shop as I was going out this afternoon?' Johnny enquired of George that evening. 'Dark hair, high heels. Well turned out.'

'That's Heather, April's cousin.'

'Is she spoken for?'

'No not now; she was engaged to her long-term boyfriend but he ditched her when he came back from the war.'

'Mm, interesting.'

'I would steer clear if I were you, mate, she's trouble, that one,' said George.

'What makes you say that?'

'It's just the impression I get. April has never spoken ill of her but I've seen the way she gets April to do what she wants. She seems like a girl who likes her own way and is determined to get it.'

'Not bad-looking though.'

'She makes the best of herself. She's not in the same league as April as regards that but she's all right, I suppose. Definitely not my type but I could act as intermediary if you want to get to know her better.'

'I'll think about it,' Johnny said.

★   ★   ★

It was a glorious sunny Sunday and the gardeners were out in force at the allotments. There was so much to do April had recruited the rest of the family. Mum had come along with Lily asleep in the pushchair and was busy with the hoe; Charlie was weeding while April was attending to her lettuces.

'The Greens are out in force today then,' Frank remarked to Beryl when she went to the tap with the watering can.

'Yeah, she's roped us all in,' she said. 'Though I can only work until Lily wakes up. She'll be all over the place then, getting into everyone's way and into all sorts of mischief. Lightning Lily we should call her. She runs like the wind now that she's found her legs. I'll take her over the park when we leave here. She can run some of her energy off there.'

'She keeps you on your toes then.'

'Not half. We have to be very careful to close outside doors at home. If the front door is left open she's out, gone up the street. The children play out there and they're like a magnet to her. But she's too little to go out there to play yet. She won't be two until later in the year.'

'Kids keep you young though, so they say,' he remarked.

'I don't know so much about that,' she said. 'I'm a bit past the antics of a toddler full time. I was thinking more in terms of grandchildren than another one of my own before she came along. Still, she's here, and we all love the bones of her even if she does run rings around us.'

'My daughter is grown up now and grandchildren are still a thing of the unknown future so I don't have any little ones around to keep me youthful,' he said.

'Has she left home yet?' she asked.

'I should be so lucky,' he said, grinning.

'Go on. You know you'll miss her when she does eventually leave.'

'I won't miss the noise and the clutter but yes of course I enjoy having her around.'

She smiled. Now that she had got used to Frank it was nice having someone outside the family to talk to. Someone of her own age. But the high-pitched sound of Lily calling for her mother cut the conversation short.

'Madam is awake so I have to dash, Frank,' she said. 'See you another time.'

He nodded and she hurried back to the allotment with the filled watering can for April, feeling good about herself somehow; she was imbued with the warm feeling of having a friend.

George was looking very pleased with himself when April arrived at the shop for her shift one Saturday afternoon.

'You look like the cat that got the cream,' she observed.

'Better than that, I'm the man who got the oranges,' he said, 'and a few bananas as well.'

'Oh well done. Where did you find them?'

'Covent Garden Market. That's the place to go. More goods from abroad are beginning to come in now that the ships can get through but supplies aren't anywhere near what they should be. So we'll still have to ration them, I'm afraid. First come first served but only to people who can prove they have young children by showing their ration book. Take some for Lily, of course.'

'Thank you,' she said.

'This is just the tip of the iceberg, April. The greengrocery trade is going to be so exciting when goods get plentiful again,' he enthused. 'It's a long time coming but it will arrive eventually and then business will really start to move. Benson's will have the most colourful displays in London.'

'You're going back to sea though, aren't you, when your dad comes back to work so you'll miss it,' she reminded him.

'Mm, that's true, I suppose. But if I was staying I could really do things with this business. I know it seems as though we're stuck in austerity forever but good times are coming.'

'Are you naturally an optimist?'

'Definitely but it isn't so much that,' he said. 'Things always go in cycles and they are bound to change for the better because they have been bad for so long and it will be good times for shopkeepers as well as everybody else. And by God the people of this country deserve it.'

'We certainly do.'

'If it was up to me I'd have more than one shop,' he went on buoyantly. 'That's the way forward in the new Britain when it finally does arrive. I've learned a lot about business since I've been back. I was never interested before, probably because I was just a kid when I went away.'

She lapsed into thought for a moment then asked, 'What's it like at Covent Garden Market?'

'Jam-packed with people and atmosphere. You see some real characters and you have to be sharp to get the best prices. It's no place for an amateur.'

'Sounds exciting.'

'It is, especially if you're in the trade,' he told her. 'I'd ask you to come along with me one morning to see for yourself but you'd have to get up at the crack of dawn because, as you know, I leave at five o'clock.'

'I could do that, as long as I'm back in time to get to work by nine,' she said.

173

'You'll be home well before then because I have to get back with the new stock in time for the day's business.'

'If you're sure I won't be a hindrance, perhaps I could come one day next week then.'

'You're on,' he said.

'I must be mad to be out at some unearthly hour when I could be tucked up in bed,' said April as she and George headed for Covent Garden in the van.

'That's what comes of having a lively mind,' he said lightly. 'You are interested enough in things to put yourself out.'

'And there was me thinking I was showing signs of lunacy,' she said.

He laughed. 'But now that you're up and out, doesn't it feel good?'

'Yes it does actually,' she agreed. 'I feel pleased with myself for making the effort and there is a special freshness in the air. Very invigorating!'

'You should try it in the middle of winter,' he said with a wry grin. 'It's fresh all right then; freezing more like.'

'Maybe I'll give that a miss then.'

'Wise girl.'

When they arrived at the market there were vehicles of all sorts already there. Vans, cars, trucks and horse-drawn carts. As they entered the market April was struck by the blast of noise, the clamour of human conversation rising to the roof. People milled around among the sellers, examining the goods and doing business. Groups of men in caps and trilby hats were standing about chatting among themselves.

Lots of them seemed to know George. 'How's it going, son.

The Apple of Her Eye

How's your dad,' he was asked as they made their way slowly among the crates of fruit and vegetables on sale.

'There are bananas over there,' she said, excited by the flash of yellow next to the boxes of cabbages and was surprised when he moved on without showing interest.

'If one seller has them there'll be others,' he said. 'If I look too eager they might get a bit cheeky with the price.'

George looked at everything on offer before he started buying and then he bartered for all the goods he eventually bought, sometimes getting his price, other times not quite.

'It's another world,' she remarked on the way home. 'Quite friendly and sociable.'

'Don't be deceived,' he said. 'Hard business goes on from both sides. Buyers and sellers will barter to the last farthing. But yes there is a good feeling there, probably because we're all in the same line of business.'

'Heaven knows what I'm doing here.'

'You came to have a look,' he said. 'Anyway you're a grower so you're part of it.'

'Not really. Greengrocery is a business; gardening is a hobby.'

'You sell some of what you grow so that's business.'

'In a very tiny sort of way. I should think greengrocery is something that's handed down in families.'

'That's how I'm involved certainly. It isn't a thing I would have chosen to go into even though I've grown to enjoy it.'

'I took over Dad's allotment so you could say it was handed down. I hadn't given vegetables much of a thought before except when they were on my plate. So I have something to thank the government's "dig for victory" campaign for. I wouldn't mind being involved in the selling side of it though. That's the sociable part.'

'That's unusual for a girl I should think. Unless they are born or marry into it, women aren't usually interested in selling greengrocery as an occupation. It's a cold job and your hands get dirty. Not at all glamorous.'

'I like the idea of it for some reason. It's odd because I like to look smart yet I spend half my life in my scruffy gardening clothes,' she said. 'I think it might be because greengrocery is something you can touch and smell and look forward to eating. And of course growing it is very creative.'

'But when you get home this morning you'll get changed into your smart office clothes and do something entirely different.'

'Yeah and the day will seem endless.'

'All jobs seem like that sometimes, it's only natural, but not often for me these days. I never get a chance to get bored because I'm either out buying or serving or thinking of what we can do to improve the business. The job was forced on me by Dad's bad health and I wasn't at all happy about it at first but I really enjoy it now.'

'So you won't want to go back to sea then.'

'Oh, I don't know about that,' he said truthfully because the situation was so uncertain he wasn't sure how he felt about it. 'We'll have to wait and see what happens about Dad. He tries to do a bit in the shop every now and again but it's too much for him so he never stays. He can't stand for long or lift anything so greengrocery is the last thing he should be doing.'

'It must be quite a worry for you and your mother.'

'A constant one.'

'Surely there must be something the doctors can do for him,' she suggested.

'Dad never goes to see the doctor,' he told her. 'I think he did go once earlier on but the doc just examined him and gave him pills for the pain. So he gets something from the chemist now to save money.'

'What did he actually do to his back?'

'He was hit by debris and broken glass cut his back and some of the glass got lodged near his spine so they had to open him up to get it out,' he explained. 'It healed but he was still in pain. The doctor thought he must have pulled a muscle and said it will cure itself with rest but no luck so far. The hospitals were very overcrowded at the time he was injured because of the flying bomb casualties so they tried to get everyone in and out as soon as possible. Dad doesn't have anything life-threatening so his case was never considered urgent and still isn't so he just lives with it and hopes it might improve at some point. Basically it's just a very bad backache.'

'Debilitating though.'

'Exactly, and it must get him down,' said George. 'I've told him I'll pay for him to go to the doctor but he says there's no point as nothing can be done and lots of people have backache when they get a bit older.'

'To that degree?'

'According to him they do but I shouldn't think so,' said George. 'All I know is, it doesn't seem to be getting any better.' He mulled this over. 'But, thinking about it, he can just about get around now and he couldn't do that when I first came home so there must have been some improvement. But he's still in a lot of pain and not able to work.'

'It must be awful for him,' she said. 'It's no wonder he's miserable.'

'Mm.'

'Anyway, this is where I get off,' she said as he turned into her street. 'Thanks ever so much for letting me come along. It's been a real eye-opener and I enjoyed it.'

'Me too.'

He was smiling as he ran round and opened the passenger door for her. What a lovely way to start the day, with April by his side. If only it could be like that every day!

Talking to April about the family business had made George realise that he needed to have a serious discussion with his parents. Benson's did, after all, belong to them.

He raised the subject that night over their evening meal.

'The fact is that the business can only show a profit and support all three of us for any length of time if we open another shop,' he said when he had finished his steak and kidney pie and was looking forward to his mother's baked rice pudding. 'We are barely breaking even at the moment; well, you do the books so you'll already know that.'

'It's hard enough trying to stock one shop let alone two,' said Percy.

'At the moment it is, yes,' agreed George. 'But the shortages aren't going to last forever and when the time of plenty comes we need to be ready. Anyway, I do go out looking for stock so we usually manage to put on a reasonably decent show under the circumstances.'

'I thought you wanted to go back to sea as soon as possible, George, yet here you are talking about opening another shop,' his mother objected.

'I can't go back to sea at the moment, can I, because I'm needed here,' he reminded them. 'But while I am running the business I want to make a good job of it and that means expansion as soon as the time is right.'

'So, what if we take on another shop and then you bugger off back to sea,' said Percy. 'How will we manage then, especially with me in my state of health?'

'That's something that we need to think about.' George mulled it over and made a sudden decision. 'Right. If we do expand the business I'll see that as a commitment and I won't go back to sea. You have my word.'

Winnie's face was wreathed in smiles. 'Oh George, that would make me a very happy woman.' She paused, becoming serious. 'But you mustn't stay here just for us. You must only stay if it's what you want.'

George didn't reply right away because if he seriously agreed to stay it was a huge undertaking on his part. But he couldn't see any alternative. They all talked about his father's return to health in a positive manner but was there a realistic chance of that ever happening? He doubted it, especially as Percy wouldn't even seek medical help.

'I never thought I would ever hear myself say this but I do actually enjoy the job,' he told them. 'So I will stay for as long as you need me.'

'That's marvellous news,' said Winnie, beaming. 'You've made your mother very happy.'

'Dad,' said George, looking at his father in a questioning manner.

'So long as you realise that I'll be running the show again as soon as I'm able,' he said gruffly.

'Percy,' admonished Winnie. 'Fancy saying a thing like that to him after all he's done.'

'No, he's right to mention it, Mum,' George assured her. 'Of course Dad will want his place back at the head of the firm,

I understand that. But if we have two shops there'll be room for us both. I'll run the new one if you want. If you're still not too good, Dad, Mum will have to run this one again but with a full-time assistant, not on her own again. That's too much.'

'So what about the location of this second shop?' asked Percy with interest. 'Where do you have in mind?'

'Not too far away because it would be difficult to manage both shops if they were at too much of a distance from each other. Hammersmith, Shepherds Bush, somewhere like that. It depends where there's a shop available when we're ready to proceed. We need to give it some more time. But as we've agreed in principle I think we could probably start looking around for an empty shop in the early part of next year. The war will have been over for three years then so surely the food situation will start to get easier at some point soon.'

'Sounds good to me,' said Winnie. 'It will give us all something to look forward to.'

'Indeed,' agreed George.

Never an enthusiast, Percy stayed silent, mulling things over with a serious expression.

It was harvest time for April so she was very busy at the allotment.

'I haven't really got time to go to work at this time of the year,' she remarked lightly to George when he came to collect some produce from the allotment. 'There's far too for me much to do here.'

'Give up the office job and become a grower full time,' he said jokingly. 'That's the answer to that.'

'I wish I could,' she said wistfully. 'Office work really isn't for me but we all need a steady income and I wouldn't get that from the allotment.'

'It's a shame you have to do a job you don't enjoy as you spend so much time there.'

'Me and most other people,' she said thoughtfully. 'Work is work isn't it? How many people do you know who are earning a living doing something they really enjoy. That sort of luxury is for film stars and musicians and the like and they have to suffer for their art, doing menial jobs until the lucky ones get established. Most of us have to do what we can find. I don't hate it or anything; just find it a bit boring and unfulfilling.'

'I must be one of the lucky ones then,' he said. 'I've only ever done two things, worked on ships in the merchant navy and greengrocery, and I enjoy them both.'

'You are fortunate,' she said, picking some runner beans and adding them to those already in the wooden crate for George to take. 'I probably enjoy growing because it's a hobby. If I did it full time I might not like it so much. Hobbies are supposed to be pastimes of enjoyment aren't they?'

'Oh yes. Football is mine which is far less hard work than yours.' He paused thoughtfully. 'That reminds me, I must speak to Charlie about a home game that's coming up. Find out if he wants to come along with Johnny and me.'

'You already know the answer to that, don't you, George?' she said.

'Yeah, your brother loves his football all right. So I'll call round sometime soon and talk to him about the next match. I haven't seen your mum and Lily for a while either so it will be nice to say hello to them as well.'

'They'll enjoy that.'

He lifted the boxes she had ready for him and carried them out to the van with a cheery 'Ta-ta'.

He had such a marvellous physique, she thought, as she watched him go.

Chapter Nine

There was often quite a crowd at the Greens' house on a Sunday morning. Charlie's mates usually congregated there, Heather often came to see April and Aunt Peg put her own Sunday roast in the oven and came for a cup of tea and a chat with her sister. Several conversations would be in progress simultaneously and Lily received attention from one and all while the savoury aroma of roasting potatoes filled the house. Charlie's crowd usually assembled in the living room, Beryl entertained her sister in the kitchen while keeping an eye on the oven and making tea for the visitors and April and Heather found a seat where they could.

This Sunday morning was no different but the cousins were in the small back garden because April was tidying the flower beds. It was only a little area but April liked to keep it looking nice. Heather, in full flow as usual, was moving around with her cousin relating the story of how she'd had high hopes of the young man who came to fix the typewriter at the office where she worked and was sure he was going to ask her out.

'I could have sworn he was interested,' she said. 'He definitely gave me the eye but then off he went without a word. It's enough to make me lose all confidence in myself.'

'It's difficult for a stranger to make a date with someone when he's visiting an office,' said April, hoping to comfort her cousin. 'He might have got into trouble with his firm if he was seen chatting to you.'

'He could have found a way,' said Heather. 'No. It's me, April. Men just don't fancy me anymore. On the odd occasion that I meet any that is, since you won't go dancing with me.'

'Don't start that again for goodness' sake,' said April, snipping a dead flower.

'Honestly, April, you are wasting your life away with all this gardening,' said Heather reprovingly. 'It's all you seem to think about.'

'I'm only tidying up out here to save Mum having to do it. Anyway, how can I be wasting my life when I'm doing something so useful and fulfilling?'

'It isn't natural for a young woman to spend all her spare time gardening. It will be a year soon since Ronnie died so you should be out with me looking for men. All dressed up and full make-up. Instead of which you are always in shorts or trousers and not so much as a smudge of lipstick. We are both in the same boat now so we have to make an effort.'

'Oh do change the record, for goodness' sake, Heather,' sighed April. 'Let me live my life how I want to.'

'I'm only saying . . .'

'Well, I don't want to hear it, thank you.'

'The way I'm going on,' said Heather, undeterred by April's comments. 'The only interest I'll get is from those mates of your brothers who can't keep their eyes off my chest.'

April chuckled. 'They're at that age. I don't think they can help themselves. They're nice lads though.'

'They certainly know how to gawp.'

'Well, I'm just about done here,' said April after a final glance around. 'So let's go inside and have a cup of something, shall we?'

'Thank God for that,' said Heather. 'I thought I was going to have to watch you work all day.'

As they went in the back door to the kitchen they were greeted by the sound of laughter and conversation and the inviting smell of food cooking as Beryl turned the roast potatoes over; they were golden brown on one side.

'No, you're not having one,' said Beryl in anticipation. 'I've just had Charlie and his mates trying to nick them and they are going straight back in the oven.'

'They do look good though, Mum,' said April with longing.

'They'll look even better on your plate with the meat and gravy,' her mother said firmly.

'You're not going to win that one dear,' said Peg.

'We'll settle for just for a cup of Camp coffee then,' said April, going to the sink to wash the dirt of her hands.

'I'll put the kettle on,' said Peg as Heather sat down at the kitchen table.

April felt the familiarity of a Sunday morning at home sweep over her. Sometimes it felt suffocating because she was at an age to want to broaden her horizons. Today it felt good. 'George is coming round to see Charlie this morning so could you put a cup and saucer out for him please, Auntie Peg?' she asked.

'The rest of the neighbourhood seems to be here so he might as well join the party,' said Beryl smiling; she enjoyed a houseful.

'Where's Lily?' asked April.

'She's with Charlie and the boys,' said Beryl.

'I might have guessed,' said April. 'She likes the men, does our Lily.'

'They let her climb all over them, that's the attraction; they are very good with her and spoil her rotten.'

April dried her hands and sat at the table to drink her coffee. She was aware of a pleasant feeling of anticipation and realised it must be because George would be here soon. She did so enjoy his company.

George was feeling oddly excited as he got in the van to drive to the Greens'. Mostly because he would be seeing April, he readily admitted that, but he liked the rest of the family too. Their house was always so full of life, probably because of the three siblings. Being an only child himself, he enjoyed the youthful banter.

The family had had their share of sadness recently though, losing their father and then Ronnie's death, but there was always a great warmth there which reached out to visitors. April was the main attraction for him though, there was no denying it. He was becoming increasingly drawn to her but now wasn't the time to do anything about it. She seemed to have recovered from her bereavement but it wasn't a year yet so he didn't want to impose. He needed to wait a while longer and enjoy her friendship meanwhile.

But beneath all the chat and the laughs and the good manners was underlying passion. He was a man after all, and she a beautiful woman. It wasn't just lust though. He wanted to love and look after her and have her by her side for the rest of his life.

Pushing such thoughts to the back of his mind he turned on the engine and drove away.

Charlie's pals were about to leave and moved noisily towards the front door, arranging to meet in the park later on for a kick about. Full of youthful exuberance, they were laughing and joshing boisterously.

'Ta-ta, Mrs Green,' they shouted towards the kitchen. 'Thanks for the tea.'

'You're welcome, boys. Cheerio for now, see you again soon I hope,' she replied.

Charlie opened the door and the lads went out but stood around talking. So engrossed in each other, no one noticed a small figure in a pink frock slip out. Lily reached the gap where the iron gate used to be before it was taken away during the war to be made into weapons, and paused, looking back and grinning as though daring them to come after her.

'Lily, come back here this minute,' her brother shouted at which point she darted out into the street in sheer devilment, with Charlie and his mates in hot pursuit.

George always drove carefully in the side streets because these were the children's playground. There weren't many kids about, this being a Sunday morning; some people went to church, other families kept the kids in on a Sunday, but he took it slowly anyway.

As he turned the corner into the Greens' street he saw the flash of a pink frock as a child ran into the road in front of him. Lily, he gasped as recognition dawned and he slammed on his brakes so hard the steering wheel went into his chest, squeezing the breath out of him. He caught a glimpse of Charlie before he blacked out.

'Mrs Green, come quick,' said one of Charlie's pals in alarm. 'There's been an accident.'

It was chaos outside. All the neighbours were out on the street; someone had already gone to the phone box to call an ambulance and Lily was sobbing with fright in the arms of one of Charlie's pals. Auntie Peg took her indoors with Heather while April and her mother tried to take in the sight of Charlie lying in the road with his leg under Benson's green van and George slumped over the steering wheel.

One of Charlie's pals was on his knees beside him. 'He's alive, Mrs Green,' he said.

'Oh thank God,' said Beryl, kneeling by her son.

'It's my foot, Mum,' said Charlie faintly. 'I think the wheel went over it.'

There were people crowding around the driver's seat of the van, trying to open the door to get at George.

'It's jammed,' said a neighbour. 'So we can't get at him to get a pulse. Looks like he's a goner to me though.'

April had had some bad moments in her young life but this had to be the worst.

April went in the ambulance with her brother so that her mother could stay with Lily, who wouldn't be pacified by Auntie Peg and was practically hysterical. George had been knocked out by the impact but had now recovered consciousness and went with them to be checked over at the hospital.

Charlie had been screaming with pain so the medics gave him something to relieve it and he was quiet now.

'Thank God he's alive,' George said to April. 'I'd have had blood on my hands if he hadn't made it.'

'It was an accident,' said April.

'You didn't stand a chance mate,' said Charlie weakly. 'Lily ran right in your path. I threw myself after her to push her out of the way. It's lucky we weren't both killed and none of it your fault. If anyone is to blame it's me for letting her get out. She slipped past me while the lads and me were talking.'

'No one was to blame except, of course, Lily and she's too young to take responsibility,' April told them. 'So stop going on about it and thank God you're all alive.'

No one said much for the rest of the journey. Charlie was drowsy from the medicine.

After being checked over George was discharged from hospital later that day. He'd been interviewed by the police while he was there and they seemed satisfied with his version of events, especially as they had also spoken to Charlie whose account matched his. So there were to be no charges made against him.

The news wasn't so good for Charlie, who had broken several bones in his foot and ankle and was in terrible pain. An operation was needed to try and straighten the ankle but there was no guarantee of success and he could have a disability for life.

'I feel as though I shouldn't be behind a wheel,' George confessed to April and her mother that night after they had all been to visit Charlie in hospital. 'But I know that I have to.'

'Of course you have to; your living depends on it,' said April. 'Who else is going to go to the market to get the stock?'

'Perhaps I should revert back to a horse and cart,' he suggested with a wry grin. 'Plenty of business people did that when petrol rationing came in.'

'Those things aren't entirely safe either,' said Beryl. 'I know someone who got kicked and badly hurt by a milkman's horse one day when she was walking down the street. The horse was upset by an air raid apparently. If you feel that blame is necessary, you should point your finger in Lily's direction but I'm sure none of us want to do that.'

'Certainly not,' he confirmed.

'We'll all have to keep more of an eye on her, though, until she's old enough to be trusted not to go in the road,' said Beryl.

They all agreed on that but George was still feeling guilty when he went home and was thinking about it when he went to bed. Then he realised that there was something he could do to help and decided he would organise it as soon as possible.

April had a few hard words to say to George when she arrived at the shop for her afternoon shift on Saturday.

'What's all this about you offering to pay Charlie's hospital expenses?' she asked. 'Mum told me you've been round to see her about it.'

'I know you have to pay a contribution towards the cost unless you are very poor,' he said. 'So I want to take care of it. I think it's the least I can do, under the circumstances. Please don't be offended, April.'

'Don't tell me you still think it was your fault, is that why you're doing it?'

190

'No, well not entirely,' he said. 'Charlie is only a lad and he's a mate; he doesn't want to be worrying about money on top of everything else. He has enough to contend with, worrying about if and how he's going to walk again. I thought if the financial problem was removed he could concentrate on getting better.'

'Well, it's very good of you but between us the family would find the money,' she said.

'You won't have to now. Please accept it in the spirit it is offered.'

'If you're sure, thank you very much.'

'The least I can do. So what's the latest news?' He hadn't been to visit Charlie for a few days because visiting was restricted so he left it clear for the family.

'Not the worst but not brilliant.'

'Oh?'

'The operation itself went well but there is only so much they can do apparently,' she said. 'He should be able to walk eventually but only very awkwardly which means he won't be able to take part in any sport because he won't be able to run properly.'

This news stabbed at George's heart. No matter how much he reasoned with himself about it being an accident, he still blamed himself. 'Oh dear, I'm so sorry, April. Poor Charlie. He's such an active boy too.'

She nodded. 'Still, he's alive, that's the main thing, and Mum went to see his boss at work and he was sympathetic. He said they will try to find something for him when he's ready to go back to work if he isn't able to do his old job which involves a lot of walking about. But it will be quite a while before he's able to go back. He can't do much until after the plaster comes off and even then we're not sure exactly how disabled he will be in the long term.'

It was almost physically painful to George. To have injured someone this way felt like torture. It was a blessing he hadn't had to fight in the war; he'd never have survived the mental anguish. It was no wonder poor Ronnie had done himself in.

'When will he be coming out of hospital, do you know?' he asked.

'A couple of weeks, I think, but he'll have to rest at home for a good while.'

'Maybe I can find a match to take him to when he's well enough.'

'I'm sure that will cheer him up,' she said. 'But he's being pretty good and taking it all in his stride. You know Charlie. He's cheerful by nature.'

George wondered about this. Charlie was a lovely lad but at sixteen and suddenly disabled he was going to have a lot to put up with. But he just said, 'Yeah, he is.'

'Anyway, how did the last lot of produce you collected from me sell?' she asked.

'It flew out of the shop as usual,' he replied. 'There's nothing else for it April. You'll have to grow more.'

She smiled at his joke, pleased to be talking about something other than broken bones and hospitals which was all the conversations seemed to consist of at home at the moment. Some customers came into the shop so she went to serve them, feeling better than she had all week.

Beryl was waiting for a bus to Hammersmith one evening when a familiar voice said, 'Hello, Beryl.'

'Wotcha, Frank,' she said, turning to face the man from the allotment who looked entirely different; he was very smart in a suit and tie and trilby hat. 'How are you?'

'Not so dusty.' He frowned. 'But how is that boy of yours? I was very sorry to hear about what happened.'

'He's coming along now,' she said. 'I'm just going to visit him at the hospital actually. April is looking after Lily.'

He nodded.

'Thank God for April,' she said 'I don't know what I'd do without her.'

'I'm sure,' he said kindly. 'If there's anything I can do to help don't hesitate to ask.'

'Thank you.'

'I mean it,' he said and she knew that he did.

'You're looking very smart, Frank,' she remarked. 'Going anywhere nice?'

'I'm going to meet some old mates,' he said. 'We're going to have a few drinks and a chat.'

'That will be fun.'

He nodded. 'You need a night out every now and again when you're on your own, don't you?'

Beryl couldn't remember the last time she'd been out of an evening except to the hospital to visit Charlie but she said politely, 'I suppose you do.'

'I like to get out from under my daughter's feet every so often,' he told her. 'So that she doesn't worry about me getting lonely. Kids can get a bit protective when you lose your partner. Well you'd know all about that.'

Beryl had managed to put on a cheerful face ever since the accident, assuring everyone she was fine and everything was going to be all right for Charlie. But at that moment something awful happened and she was utterly powerless to stop it. She felt a lump rise in her throat and she tried to choke back the tears but the flow wouldn't stop. At that moment the bus arrived and they moved forward with the queue but Frank offered her his handkerchief and ushered her protectively on to the bus and into a seat, sitting next to her.

'I don't know what came over me,' she said, embarrassed. 'I don't usually bawl my eyes out in public. I'm so sorry.'

'You've nothing to apologise for,' he assured her kindly. 'So stop worrying.'

She cried discreetly into his handkerchief until they reached Hammersmith where they both wanted to get off at the same stop.

'Thanks for being so nice,' she said thickly.

'Look, you don't want your son to see you looking all puffy eyed so why don't we go in Lyons for a cup of tea so that you can recover. If you've time that is.'

'I always come very early so I can spare ten minutes but what about your friends?'

'They'll wait,' he said.

'I've tried to keep cheerful for April and especially Charlie but I'm so worried about him, Frank,' she confided over a cup of tea in Lyons. 'I mean he's sixteen and not going to be able to walk properly, let alone run. He's always been such an active boy; plays football at an amateur level. All that's finished for him now. He won't be able to walk up the street without crutches or maybe a stick later on. You know how cruel people can be towards anyone who seems a bit different.'

Frank was at a loss to know how to comfort her but wanted

to do his best. 'Not everyone is unkind,' he pointed out. 'Maybe the injury won't be as bad as you think.'

'There is no way he will be able to walk normally; they've told us that,' she said, sipping her tea.

'Remember, the young are very resilient so don't underestimate him,' he advised her. 'I have a suspicion that your boy is going to make you proud.'

She thought about this seriously for a few moments, suddenly seeing the whole problem in a new light. 'Yes, of course, thank you.' She was smiling now. 'I was looking at the situation from a general point of view, reckoning without Charlie's spirit.'

'Feeling a bit better now?'

'Thank you, yes,' she said. 'Much better. You've been very kind. I hope you won't be too late meeting your friends.'

'Don't worry about that,' he said.

She looked at the clock on the wall. 'I must be going anyway. I'm usually waiting outside the ward for ages before they let the visitors in. I'll be right on time today.'

They walked to the door of the tea shop together. 'If you need anything at all, don't hesitate to let me know,' he said. 'Anyone at the allotment will tell you where to find me.'

'Thank you,' she said, warmed by his kindness.

Then she was thrown into complete confusion when he said, 'Do you fancy going to the pictures one evening?'

Flustered, she turned scarlet. 'Oh, I don't think so, Frank. I don't go out at night. I have the little one to consider. But thank you for asking.'

'I only thought it might be a break for you when the initial worry about your son is over,' he said, looking as embarrassed as she was. 'No offence meant.'

195

'None taken,' she assured him. 'It was kind of you to ask. Thank you for the tea and sympathy.'

'Pleasure.'

'Ta-ta then,' she said. 'I'll probably see you at the allotments some time.'

'Cheerio.' He watched her hurry away, her fading red hair looking bright against her blue coat.

He was as surprised as she was about the invitation to the cinema and he'd obviously ruined any chance of getting to know her better. What had possessed him when she was so worried about her son? The words had come out of his mouth as if of their own volition. It was the first time he'd even noticed a woman since he'd lost his wife eight years ago. But he'd discerned something special in Beryl the first time he'd seen her at the allotment. Now he had ruined everything and caused them both embarrassment. He went on his way, the pleasurable anticipation of his night out with his mates very much depleted.

'So he asked you if you'd like to go to the pictures with him, what's so terrible about that, Mum?' asked April.

'I'm a married woman with a young child,' she said.

'You are a widow with a young child,' corrected April. 'Anyway, so what? Dad's been gone for nearly three years now, Mum. Life moves on.'

'Surely you're not suggesting that I consider having another man in my life,' said Beryl, horrified.

'No. Not if you don't want to. But I can see no harm in a night out at the pictures with one. A little light relief might do you good. Take your mind off things, which is probably what Frank had in mind when he suggested it. I'll look after Lily.'

'Going to the pictures with a man is a date. It used to be when I was young anyway.'

'Usually but not always,' said April. 'Anyone would think he'd asked you to go to Brighton with him for a dirty weekend the way you are carrying on.'

'Don't be so disgusting, April,' admonished her mother.

'You're the one who is making it seem disgusting,' said April. 'Frank always seems like a very decent chap to me. Anyway, if it was a date, would that be so terrible?'

'It isn't appropriate.'

'So you no longer think he's a decent bloke, even though he was so kind to you.'

'He spoiled it all by asking me out.'

'Some women would be flattered, not offended.'

'I'm not offended as much as disappointed,' Beryl said. 'I used to enjoy a chat with Frank at the allotments.'

'In the past tense?'

'Of course. I won't be able to face him now, after making such a complete fool of myself.'

'So you are embarrassed by your own behaviour rather than annoyed with him.'

'I'm annoyed with him for putting me in such an awkward position.'

'In that case the best thing you can do is forget all about it and act as though nothing happened when you next see him.'

'I'd sooner avoid him altogether.'

'What about in the spring when I need you to help me at the allotment?' asked April.

'I'll worry about that when the time comes.'

'I think it's quite sweet actually.'

'You go out with him then.'

'A little too mature for me, Mum,' she laughed. 'Anyway, forget all about it and tell me about Charlie.'

'He's about the same really,' she said. 'Still in pain and still putting up a front.'

'Once we get him home we'll soon cheer him up.' But April too was worried about how her brother was going to adapt to his disability.

It was cold and a yellowish London fog was swirling over everything and keeping people indoors. Except for April, who was at the allotment doing some maintenance work, removing bean poles and pea sticks ready for winter storage. None of the work was so urgent it had to be done in such horrible weather conditions but she needed to be here to help her cope with what was on her mind: her brother Charlie.

He was being discharged from hospital next week and she was worried about how he was going to cope. It was one thing being looked after by trained people and quite another being at home away from a protective environment and plunged into a new world which didn't involve going out whenever he felt like it as he used to. How was he going to feel with life going on as normal for everyone else and not him in these early days of recovery? Somehow they needed to show him how much he was loved and cheer him up.

She cleaned the bean poles with a rag and stored them neatly in the shed, then did the same with the pea sticks. It was then that she had an idea.

* * *

'You're suggesting a surprise homecoming party for Charlie,' said Beryl, taken aback. 'Do you think that's a good idea with him being a bit below par?'

'Not so much a party as a small gathering of family and his friends to welcome him home,' explained April. 'Nothing fancy or formal, just a few bottles and some sandwiches and sausage rolls. Maybe the gramophone won't be such a good idea as Charlie won't be able to jig around as people do at parties when the music is on so we'll keep that turned off. We don't want him to feel left out as the whole thing will be for him.'

'Yes I think you're probably right about that, April,' agreed Beryl. 'Charlie loves a party so maybe it isn't such a bad idea. Nothing he likes more than company and he's bound to feel a bit lonely being stuck indoors without his pals. If we invite all his mates and George and Johnny who he's friendly with and your Auntie Peg and Heather, that'll be enough I should think.'

'We'll make it a surprise party but better not spring it on him the day he comes home because he might be tired. I was thinking in terms of the first Saturday night. You and I can get it ready in the kitchen. We'll tell him Auntie Peg and Heather are coming round if he wonders why we are making sandwiches. We'll hide the booze in the garden. He'll only just be able to hobble around the house on his crutches so he won't go out there.'

'I'll pop round to his mate Freddie's house and tell him to put the word around,' said Beryl.

'And I'll mention it to George.'

'Right, we're on then.'

★　　★　　★

April was delighted when everything went as planned. Having resigned himself to a Saturday evening at home with only his mother, his sisters and the wireless for company, her brother suddenly found himself surrounded by people. The drinks flowed, the sandwiches were handed around and the place was buzzing with laughter and conversation.

Then Charlie unexpectedly asked for quiet and said to the gathering, 'If this is supposed to be a party where the hell is the music?'

'We thought . . . er, I mean, it didn't seem appropriate,' said April.

'Do you really think I don't want music on just because I can't get up and dance? Get the gramophone going, someone. Let's get this party started properly.'

'You couldn't dance even before you did your foot in,' joshed one of his mates.

'There is that,' he said without taking offence. 'But I used to be an expert in shuffling about. And I will be again in the future; you just wait and see. Meanwhile put something lively on and dance your socks off, everyone.'

Suddenly the room was filled with the sound of Frankie Laine booming out 'All of Me'. April and her mother started the ball rolling by jigging around with Lily, who had been allowed to stay up later for the occasion. April felt uplifted by the atmosphere. They all needed cheering up and the little gathering seemed to be doing the trick. There were a couple of girls in Charlie's clique and they took to the floor with the boys doing a jive. The Greens' living room was small but with the furniture pushed to the sides and the music going it felt to April as good as the Hammersmith Palais.

* * *

'You are April's cousin then,' Johnny said to Heather.

'That's right', she said coolly.

'I'm Johnny, George's mate,' he said. 'I saw you in passing once at Benson's shop.'

'Did you?' she said, sounding bored. 'I don't remember.'

'Fancy a dance?'

'If you like.'

Her blatant lack of interest only increased Johnny's ardour. There was something about her that intrigued him despite her supercilious attitude or possibly even because of it. He remembered George's warning about her and guessed she was difficult and selfish to the core, but he felt drawn to her even so.

There was something about the hard look in her eyes and the unconcealed petulance that he found rather attractive. Behind all that arrogance there was probably a decent human being, given the right encouragement. But being young and male he was thinking more in terms of the fact that she had curves in all the right places.

Heather wasn't so desperate to find a husband that she was interested in just anyone and this bloke she was dancing with didn't do much for her. He wasn't bad-looking and seemed like a decent sort though, so if he asked her out she might consider it just to pass the time. He was better than nothing.

Anyway, she was too preoccupied with April and George, who were dancing together, to think much about her own dance partner. What was April up to? All that stuff about her and George being good friends was just baloney. They certainly didn't look like just friends now. Trust that cousin of hers to nab one of the best-looking blokes in Chiswick. Heather actually felt quite ill with jealousy. How could April cause her so much pain without even realising it?

'It all seems to be going quite well,' April said to George as they moved about to the music.

'Yeah, it does.'

'Charlie seems to be enjoying himself anyway and that's the whole point of it.'

'Whose idea was it?' he asked.

'Mine originally but Mum was all for it when I mentioned it,' she replied. 'It's hard to know what to do to help him, the poor lad. He enjoys company so we thought it was the best way to celebrate his homecoming.'

He smiled, looking at her. 'You're looking very pretty tonight, April,' he said.

'Thank you.' She was wearing a blue blouse with a black skirt, her red hair freshly washed and a little make-up adding the finishing touches to her face. 'It's a real change for you to see me smartened up.'

'You always look nice.'

'Thank you. You're not so bad yourself.'

They looked at each other and there was sudden awkwardness. They were such good friends, uneasiness never arose but it was there now and she knew why. She was falling in love with him and the process was almost complete.

'Are you flirting with me, April Green?' he asked jokingly.

'Maybe just a little,' she replied.

'Flirt away,' he said. 'You won't hear me complaining.'

They were laughing when the music ended. April felt something good emerging from the bad. It had been such a terrible few weeks it had seemed as though nothing would ever be fun again but here she was enjoying herself at a party put on to cheer her brother up.

Then she noticed that Charlie was missing.

'He's probably gone to answer a call of nature,' she said to George. 'He can get about very slowly on the crutches.'

'I'll be back in a minute,' he said and went in search of Charlie.

'What are you doing out here all on your own?' asked George when he tracked Charlie down in the back garden, sitting on an old wooden bench that had seen better days. 'You'll get cold without a coat on.'

'Just taking a break,' he said. 'There only so much jollity I can take.'

'Oh, so you didn't want a party then?'

'Like hell I did. It's the last thing I wanted. I don't know what possessed them to organise it.'

'I think they need to feel they are doing something to help,' suggested George.

'So it's all about making them feel better, is it?' said Charlie. 'Well it's doing bugger all for me except make me feel even more depressed.'

'You're putting on a really good show for them,' said George. 'No one would guess that you're feeling miserable.'

'I know they mean well and love them both to bits but a party, under the circumstances, I ask you.'

'Perhaps they thought you might enjoy the company as you're stuck indoors.'

'When all I want to do is be on my own feeling sorry for

myself, yes, wallow in it,' he said. 'The truth is, George, I can't take being out of action, not being able to walk properly or play football or just go out of the door any time I want to. Even when this first recovery period is over I'll never walk normally again and I hate the idea of looking weird, being different to other people. I'm not putting a brave face on it at all, that's just an act. I'm furious that it's happened to me. Sometimes I even feel angry with Lily for causing it, and that isn't right, is it? Blaming a two-year-old child, I'm ashamed.'

'You never show it in your behaviour towards her though do you?' said George.

'Of course not.'

'Then stop feeling bad about it.'

'But George, I don't know how I'm going to cope with a lifetime of restriction. I just don't have the bottle. My dad, he was a man who could cope with anything life threw at him. If this had happened to him he wouldn't have been sinking into despair, he'd have just got on with it. And what about all the servicemen who have come home with terrible disabilities and they just carry on as best they can. All I have is a damaged foot and I feel as though my life is over.'

'You don't know how those people feel inside, do you? They might be feeling just as sorry for themselves as you are. It's the getting on with it that's the brave part and that's what you are doing by seeming to be cheerful at a party you don't want.'

'There's no great courage in that.'

'There's strength of character though, which is a kind of courage.'

'Is it?'

'I think so. Anyway, you haven't had a chance to really

challenge yourself yet as you've only just come home from hospital. But I think you've made a good start.'

'I doubt if I'll have the guts to put on a brave face when I have to limp down the road to go to work, or when I have to watch my mates playing football and I can't join in. Or when I can't get a girl because I'm that bloke who walks funny.'

'OK, so you'll be a miserable bugger about it all but you'll still be alive. You won't be able to play football again but you might be able to have a gentle kick about with me in the park, later on when the injury is healed.'

'I know I'm being pathetic,' said Charlie. 'But I feel so miserable and alone, George. There is a house full of people who care about me but I feel on my own. I know I'm being ungrateful and I can't seem to do anything about it.'

'Look, don't you think you are expecting too much of yourself at this early stage. It's all so new, of course you are overwhelmed by it. But they don't know you are miserable, that's the important thing. You haven't spoiled it for anyone and that takes a certain kind of guts.'

'I want to be as good a man as my dad was but I don't think I have it in me,' he said.

'Just be yourself and you'll be fine,' said George.

'You reckon?'

'Absolutely!'

An interruption ended the conversation. 'Oh, there you are,' said April. 'I've been looking for you. What on earth are you doing out here in the cold?'

'I needed a breath of air,' said Charlie.

'We'll be in in a minute,' said George. 'I promise I won't let him stay out here for long.'

'Oh,' said April sensing that she was in the way. 'I'll see you inside then.'

When she was out of earshot George said, 'Don't be too hard on yourself, kid. It's all right to feel sorry for yourself sometimes and show it.' He grinned and added, 'But maybe not tonight, eh?'

'No, not tonight, I promise,' Charlie said, getting his crutches and pulling himself up with some difficulty. 'I'm the only male in an all-female household so I know a bit about holding my tongue at the right times.'

They were both smiling as they went inside, Charlie taking it very cautiously and George, being a sensitive man, careful not to try and help him.

Seeing them looking happy as they entered the living room, April felt a sense of relief and gratitude to George for taking on the role of older brother to Charlie. He could give him something neither she nor his mother or pals could do. He could give him the mature male perspective he had had from his father.

Charlie saw himself as the man of the house but he was still immature and especially vulnerable at the moment. She sensed that George could reach out to that vulnerability in a way that neither she nor her mother could because they were both too emotionally involved with him. Charlie's mates were a decent bunch but there was always an element of competition between teenage boys. George was outside all of that but still young enough to know what it felt like.

He really had become an asset to their family and she was so glad they had him in their lives.

Chapter Ten

Although the party didn't flag, neither did it go on until the early hours because everyone was mindful of the fact that Charlie wasn't on top form. People started leaving around midnight, which proved to be a bewitching hour for April because that was when she and George had their first kiss.

She was seeing the guests out at the front door and George was the last. As soon as Charlie and Beryl had gone inside, April and George moved towards each other instinctively. The entire evening, which had been vibrant with light-hearted flirting, had been leading up to this moment.

'I'll be on my way then,' he said, surprising her by leaving so soon after a tender embrace. 'Thank you for a lovely party I'll see you soon.'

'I do hope so,' she said and watched him stride off down the street.

As the weather was reasonably mild the next day April went to the allotment in the afternoon and got busy with her spade as the soil was damp and manageable. She also needed the fresh air and exercise to calm her after the excitement of what had happened last night with George. Strange how he had hurried away like that!

She heard the soft thud of footsteps on the damp earth and, looking up, he was there. 'Hello, April,' he said, smiling a little uncertainly.

'Is this when you tell me that what happened last night was a mistake?' she asked.

'Well no . . .'

'Why did you rush off ?'

'I don't know,' he said. 'I think I was a little overwhelmed and not sure if I'd overstepped the mark.'

'After the way I'd been flirting with you all evening, don't make me laugh.' She looked at him. 'Come here,' she said, leaving her work and opening her arms to him.

There weren't many other gardeners at the allotments but the few who were there smiled then looked away discreetly.

Sharing a flask of tea with him in the shed a bit later on April said, 'I'm so happy things have changed between us, George. When you've been friends with someone for a while, the transition to the other thing could be awkward I should think. But last night it just seemed to change naturally.'

'It's always been the other thing for me,' he admitted with a wry grin. 'From the moment I first set eyes on you. But you were engaged to Ronnie so I settled for friendship.'

'And after Ronnie died?'

'It wouldn't have been decent to try to change things then,' he said. 'I was waiting until the time was right. Fortunately for me you pre-empted the situation last night.'

'I fancied you from the start,' she confessed. 'But I wasn't in a position to do anything about it so I enjoyed just being your friend. Last night I suppose nature took its course.'

He nodded.

'Perhaps we shouldn't make too big a thing of it to the others, though,' she suggested more seriously, 'with life not being too grand for Charlie at the moment.'

'I hope you're not suggesting that we keep it secret because I want everyone to know.'

'We can tell people, of course, but perhaps we shouldn't shove our happiness down Charlie's throat.'

'He'll be pleased for us,' said George.

'I'm sure he will but I don't want to overdo it.'

'I doubt if I'll be able to hide my feelings.'

'Try to tone it down in public just until Charlie is at least a little bit more mobile.'

'Perhaps we can take him out with us sometimes,' he suggested. 'If I've got enough petrol I'll take us to the cinema in the van.'

'That's nice of you and it will be a break for him,' she said. 'But he needs to be with his mates as soon as he's able. That's what will give him his confidence back.'

'You're probably right,' he agreed. 'But I've a few things lined up for him in the meantime.'

'Football matches?'

'Exactly. He'll forget all about his injuries when he's watching a game.'

Her eyes filled with tears. 'It's so sad that he won't be able to play again.'

He squeezed her hand. 'I'll take him to the park as soon as he is up to it so at least he'll get to kick a ball, even if it is only with his left foot.'

'You're such a good bloke, George Benson,' she said.

'I inherited my mother's good genes.'

'Only your mother's?'

'I don't think my father has any good ones,' he said lightly, adding quickly, 'But come on, let's go home and start spreading the good news.'

He helped her to clear up and they headed for the Greens' house.

While April was out there was a knock at the door and when Beryl answered it she saw Frank standing on the doorstep.

'Sorry to call on you unannounced,' he said. 'I got your address from someone at the allotments'.

Although a little flustered, she remembered her manners and invited him in but he declined politely saying he would only be a few minutes.

'I know it's a bit overdue but I've come to apologise for embarrassing you that night when we met at the bus stop and went to Lyons,' he explained. 'It's been bothering me ever since.'

'Oh don't give it another thought,' she said, assuming a casual air. 'I'd forgotten all about it. I wasn't embarrassed, well, maybe just a little.'

'I don't know what came over me,' he said. 'The words were out before I realised.'

'It doesn't matter,' she said. 'I probably made too much of it.' She paused for a moment, deciding that an explanation was necessary. 'The truth is, Frank, most women of my age have their children off their hands but I still have a little one so evenings out aren't really on the agenda for me and I'm completely out of the habit of that sort of thing.' Lily appeared as though to validate her explanation and was told by her mother to go to the living room with her brother. 'If you see what I mean.'

'Oh absolutely,' he said. 'I hope you don't mind my coming round but I didn't want things to be awkward between us if you were at the allotment any time.'

'I'm glad you came,' she said. 'I was concerned about that too. I enjoy our little chats.'

'So you'll be at the allotments at some point then?'

'I certainly hope so but Lily is at an age to be into everything so I can't be absolutely sure.'

'You'll have to give her bit of ground to dig in and a little spade; kids love playing with mud.'

'We'll see,' she said.

'I'll be on my way then.'

'Thanks for coming round.'

He nodded. 'Cheerio,' he said, smiling.

Beryl felt almost light-hearted as she headed back to the kitchen, relieved that the silly business was cleared up. She hated awkwardness with anyone and especially someone as nice as Frank. Here she was fifty years old and had been a mother for so long her own personality had been completely absorbed into it. A part of her wanted to go out to the pictures with Frank, to be carefree for a few hours. Had Jim still been alive and Lily not come along, her life would be very different now.

But she had lost her life partner and Lily had happened and Beryl would be tied for a long time to come. But although she would always be lonely for Jim, she felt blessed to have Lily and adored her youngest child. Indeed her family was everything to her. It was just that now and again it might be nice to be just Beryl.

'Who was it at the door, Mum?' called Charlie.

'Just a friend from the allotments,' she said.

Lily appeared and asked for a drink and a biscuit. Beryl picked her up and smothered her in kisses, almost as though to wash away the thoughts she'd had about wanting a little freedom. Home and family was what she did best; that was her life and she wouldn't want it any other way.

'There must be romance in the air what with Princess Elizabeth marrying Prince Philip a week or two ago, and now you two getting together,' said Beryl when April and George came in with the news that they were courting. 'About bloomin' time too. You've been long enough getting to it. You were made for each other and it's been obvious to the rest of us for months.'

'That was only because of Ronnie,' April explained. 'I had to show him some respect.'

'I know that, love. But I'm very pleased for you now. Good news, isn't it, Charlie?'

'As long as they aren't going to be soppy over each other all the time,' he said.

'I can't promise not to be, now and again,' said April.

'I think we almost certainly will be quite often,' added George, grinning. 'But don't worry, kid; you and I will still do our man stuff. I'm going to get tickets for the first home match after Christmas. You should be up to it by then.'

Charlie grinned back. 'Thanks, George.'

April noticed that his enthusiasm was very much muted, which was only natural, but he was making an effort, which was a good sign. She hoped that eventually they would have the old Charlie back but it was still very early days. All they could do was support and encourage him. The rest was up to him. In her heart though she knew her brother had it in him to overcome this setback. They were a tough lot, the Greens.

'I can't say I'm surprised. I thought you and George looked very cosy together at the party on Saturday,' said Heather when April called to see her cousin after work on Monday night to tell her about the developments with George.

'That was because we were finally admitting our feelings for each other.'

'Good. I'm pleased for you,' lied Heather. 'It's high time you put the Ronnie business behind you.'

'There'll always be a place in my heart for Ronnie but, yes, life does move on.'

'Actually I'm going out with George's pal Johnny on Saturday night,' mentioned Heather.

'Oh really, that's good,' said April. 'He seems like a nice sort of bloke.'

'Maybe we could make it a double date.'

'It's too soon, Heather,' she said frankly. 'I need time on my own with George to get to know him.'

'You've known him for ages.'

'Not as a boyfriend though; you know what I mean. But later on if you are still going out with Johnny maybe we could make up a foursome sometime.'

'That would be really good.' Heather hadn't been exactly delighted about her date for Saturday night but now realised that Johnny would be an asset to her in that he could keep her involved with April and George, particularly the latter. They'd all get to be friends and who knew what might happen? Yes, that put a whole new light on her arrangements for Saturday. She was tired of always being on the outside looking in at her cousin's life. She wanted to be the main attraction for a change.

April was invited to Sunday tea at the Bensons' as a result of the news.

'We're ever so pleased for you, aren't we, Percy?' enthused Winnie.

'Are we?' said Percy, then receiving optical orders from his wife added quickly, 'Yeah, of course, absolutely delighted, it's time George settled down.'

This produced another disapproving look from with his wife and April felt embarrassed. 'We're only going out, Mr Benson. Nothing more at the moment.'

'Er, quite so, I meant it's nice for him to have one girl in particular.'

'How many does he usually have then?' asked April as Percy dug himself ever deeper into a hole.

'Not many . . . er I mean, well, none,' he stuttered. 'Only one at a time anyway.'

''Struth,' exclaimed April, looking at George. 'Are you a serial womaniser or something?'

'Take no notice of Percy,' said Winnie. 'He can't say right for saying wrong.'

April smiled. 'Just teasing. George is twenty-five. I know he will have history. I myself almost got married.'

'So, now that we've got the embarrassment out of the way shall we enjoy our tea?' suggested George.

'Good idea son,' agreed Winnie.

It was traditional Sunday teatime fare: a variety of sandwiches, a homemade jam sponge and apple tart. Winnie asked after April's family, especially her brother, and April brought them up to date.

'I suppose George will have told you about his plans for business expansion,' said Percy, who had cushions supporting his back but still looked to be creased with pain.

'He has mentioned something about it but I thought it was for the future rather than now.'

'Yes it is but the future is almost here I think as far as that's concerned,' he said. 'If only I could get rid of my back problem I'd be all for it right away so that we'll be ready when the tide begins to turn.'

'How is your back now, Mr Benson?' she asked politely.

'Killing me most of the time. I'm full of aspirin and covered in liniment.'

'Maybe if this new Health Service scheme they are talking about does come to be you could see the doctor about it,' she suggested. 'We won't have to pay then.'

'I don't see much point in seeing doctors,' was his firm response to that.

'Well I do,' Winnie declared. 'If it was up to me you'd have been long before this, never mind that we have to pay. When it's free I shall drag you there, kicking and screaming if necessary.'

'They've told me what the problem is so there's no point in cluttering up a doctor's waiting room,' he said. 'I have a war wound like thousands of other people.'

'They might be able to do something about it now that things have calmed down,' she pointed out. 'The hospital was packed with bomb victims when you were in there and the staff were rushed off their feet. Yours wasn't a life-threatening case so you weren't given priority treatment.'

'Mm, well, that's enough about that,' said Percy and changed the subject. 'Maybe next year might be the time to start looking for another shop. You'll have to take someone on, George, if I'm still laid up. We need to be ready at the beginning of better times.'

'All right, Dad. I'm sure April doesn't want to hear about our greengrocery business.'

'On the contrary,' she said. 'I'm interested. It will be lovely for us all when things are plentiful again.'

'Not half,' agreed Winnie. 'Meanwhile there's plenty of apple tart if you'd like another piece.'

'Thank you,' said April. 'That would be lovely.'

Although the conversation was flowing easily and April felt at home here, there was an air of sadness about Percy Benson that worried her. He seemed to be a nice man but deeply troubled. The obvious reason for this was his back injury but she thought it was something more than physical pain, a kind of sorrow. George didn't seem to be fond of him either which wasn't good. There must be a reason but she would never ask George about it because it was private family business. She couldn't imagine not getting along with her own father but she knew that these things happened among relatives sometimes. The Greens were lucky that way; they had their arguments like all families but they were a close knit unit.

'How's your allotment doing?' asked Percy by way of conversation.

'Fine, thank you,' she replied. 'Now isn't the busiest time of the year for gardening but I keep going and enjoy what I do. I'm already looking forward to the new season and we haven't even had Christmas yet.'

'She hides away there, Dad,' said George, teasing her. 'She goes there to escape and think things over.'

'I do actually,' said April, smiling. 'When there's anything wrong or I'm worried, as I have been lately about my brother, I find solace in the soil if that doesn't sound too pretentious.'

'Not in the least,' Percy assured her. 'I think it's nice that you have something worthwhile to do that you get pleasure from.'

April sensed that George's father liked her; she had felt a connection at other times when they had spoken. He was quite paternal towards her.

'You could do with some sort of hobby, Dad,' George suggested thoughtfully.

'I could do with getting back to work,' said Percy. 'That would soon put me right.'

'We all want that for you, love,' said Winnie, leaning over and touching his hand.

April felt a lump rise in her throat because it reminded her of her own parents before Dad died. After many years together they were still devoted. Whatever Mr Benson's faults might be, his wife still thought the world of him.

Christmas passed sweetly for April because of her new relationship with George. They made things official by getting their families together. George brought his parents round to the Greens' in the van on Christmas night for a few festive drinks. Peg and Heather were there too and it was all quite jolly. April and George were so engrossed in each, April had to admit that everything else was rather a blur but she was glad all went well. It gave their relationship a kind of authenticity. This was the first Christmas since they had lost her father that she felt optimistic about the New Year. Whatever came she would embrace it with George by her side.

It was March before Charlie finally got rid of his crutches, but he still had to walk with a stick. His foot was so deformed that his limp was exceptionally pronounced, which made him vulnerable. He became no stranger to verbal abuse and that was when his stick came in handy. 'Hoplalong' and 'Cripple' were just a few of the names that were hurled at him when he was out on his own, mostly by young yobbish types who wouldn't have the courage to do it if he was with his mates.

The name-calling hurt but he never let it show. He raised his stick as if to bring it down on his persecutors but they didn't wait to find out if he actually would. He kept quiet at home about this, partly because he knew it would worry them and also because talking about it made him even more sensitive about his disability and feel somehow lesser than other people. He kept it from his pals too because he didn't want them to see him as a figure of fun.

In March he went back to work and was very disappointed with his new position.

'How did it go, Charlie?' asked April over their evening meal on his first day back.

'All right,' he said, sounding miserable.

'Doesn't sound as though it was all right,' remarked his mother.

'Well, they've given me a different job.'

'But they told you they were going to do that, son, so it

couldn't have been a surprise,' said Beryl. 'You need a sitting-down job now that walking is a problem.'

'I didn't know they were going to put me in with two old women in the accounts office,' he said. 'I'm a junior clerk, which really means dogsbody. It's a sissy sort of a job.'

'It isn't at all,' his mother disagreed. 'Anyway, you were always good at arithmetic at school.'

'That doesn't mean I want to be cooped up with two old spinsters all day,' he said. 'I've got no one to talk to.'

'It's only the first day,' said April. 'It might not seem so bad when you get used to it.'

'How can it not be so bad when the old girls aren't going to turn into people of my own age, are they?'

'You shouldn't be rude about older people, Charlie,' admonished his mother.

'I'm not rude to their faces; I wouldn't do that and I've nothing against them personally,' he said. 'But I don't like it there now. I don't want to work in an office.'

'I know the feeling,' said April.

'Don't encourage him, April dear,' tutted Beryl quickly. 'It's very good of the firm to find a place for him under the circumstances.'

'Yes, you're right,' agreed April. 'Give it a chance, Charlie, and think of pay day. That will keep you going.'

'I suppose I'll just have to grin and bear it,' said Charlie dismally.

'That's my boy,' said Beryl. 'By the end of the week you'll be used to it and might feel a whole lot better.'

One week passed and he still came home miserable; two weeks the same thing. Then at the end of the first month the complaining grew less and one day he came home with the news that he was going to sign up at night school for a course in bookkeeping.

'Ivy and Maude think I have a good head for figures so I ought to get myself a qualification,' he said.

'Ivy and Maude?' inquired April.

'The misses. Miss Brown and Miss Wilkins, but I sometimes push my luck and call them by their Christian names when no one else is listening. They tell me off about it but I think they quite like it really.'

'So what happened to the horrible old spinsters?'

'They're not horrible at all when you get to know them,' he said. 'They are really nice. They are ancient but they are quite kind and ever so clever.'

'They can't be all that old or they'd be retired,' April remarked.

'Not as old as that, but I should think they might be about your age, Mum.'

'Thanks for reminding me of what an antique I am,' said Beryl with a wry grin.

'I didn't mean . . .'

'Just kidding, son.'

'The misses have worked there since they were young; they were at school together.'

'They sound lovely,' said April. 'So you do like office work after all?'

'Now I've got used to it, yeah.'

'And do you really want to get this qualification or do you just want to please the ladies?' she continued.

'I'm not that soft, sis,' he said. 'I really want to do it. It'll take quite a long time but I could end up with a good job if I stick at it. The misses say that if you are good with figures you should nurture it because it's a gift only a few people have.'

Well thank you Ivy and Maude for putting my boy on the right track, thought Beryl, and said, 'You'd better find out about the evening classes then, hadn't you?'

'I already have, or rather the misses found out for me,' he told them. 'The class I would need is on a Wednesday night. I have to find out if they will let me start mid-course or wait until September. Either way I want to do it. It will give me something to do to pass the time while my mates are away doing their National Service once they turn eighteen; obviously the army won't want someone with a stupid limp like mine. The lads think I'm very lucky to get out of it.' He gave a wry grin. 'I think I'd rather do the service than walk about like a circus act.'

'We'll be glad you don't have to go away, from a purely selfish point of view,' said Beryl.

'Hear hear,' added April.

Her brother was beginning to show the spirit she knew he had in him. She guessed that he sometimes had a hard time; she'd seen the way people looked at him when he was with her – some with blatant curiosity, a few with sympathy and a rough element saw him as the perfect candidate to bully – and she dreaded to think what might happen when he was out on his own. But he had to learn to cope outside the protective arms of the family and he seemed to take it all in his stride; he'd certainly taken on the job with spirit now that he was used to it.

'Everybody is going to the doctor's now that it's free,' declared Winnie one evening in July over their meal. 'The dentist and optician's are free of charge too. The customers are full of it.

They are getting new glasses as well as new teeth. Some people are having all their teeth out so that they can have brand new false ones. All for nothing. Isn't it wonderful?'

'It isn't actually free,' Percy pointed out gruffly. 'We'll be paying for it in one way and another.'

'Well yes, of course, the money has to come from somewhere, but we can get medical treatment whenever we need it now without worrying about the cost,' she enthused. 'I'm going to get you an appointment at the doctor's, Percy, and the sooner the better.'

'Me?'

'Of course you. You're the only one in the family with something wrong with your health. And don't even think of saying you're not going because you are and I shall go with you and tell him exactly how much you've been suffering.'

'Good for you, Mum,' said George. 'I'm all for that.'

'How many more times must I tell you, woman, there is nothing to be done about my back. If there was the doctors would have done it at the time.'

'What are you so scared of anyway?' asked George bluntly. 'Are you afraid they will tell you that there is no cure and you'll be like that for the rest of your life?'

'Of course not,' he retorted.

'Ooh not much,' said George, goading his father because he wanted him to get medical advice. 'You've come through a war and narrowly escaped death and you're frightened to go and see the local doc.'

'Because it will be pointless, that's why,' he explained irritably. 'A waste of everybody's time. They didn't bring in the National Health Service so that people can go rushing to the doctor's for no genuine reason.'

'So Mum and I have got to put up with you moaning about your back for the rest of your life, have we?'

'I don't moan.'

'We are aware that you are suffering, put it that way.' George wasn't close to his father but sympathised with him and knew that soft words wouldn't persuade him to seek professional help. 'At least go and see the doctor and if there is nothing to be done then we'll all accept it and carry on as we are. Even if he just gives you tablets for the pain, it will help. They are bound to be more effective than the pills and potions you get from the chemist. You'll want to be functioning normally when we expand the business, won't you?'

'Of course, but I don't believe in miracles.'

'Neither do we but a thorough examination by the doctor can do no harm,' said Winnie.

'That's what he's afraid of,' said George. 'God knows what he thinks the doc will find.'

'How many more times must I tell you, I have a minor wartime injury and that's all,' insisted Percy.

'We'll get that confirmed by a professional anyway,' said Winnie in a tone of authority. 'I shall call in at the surgery tomorrow to get you an appointment.'

'Humph,' snorted Percy. 'A man's life isn't his own.'

'A married one's certainly isn't,' agreed Winnie.

It was a glorious summer evening and April and George were walking along the riverside hand in hand towards Kew Bridge because there was a particularly pretty pub there that they liked to visit. The sun was sinking behind some trees and the blue sky was flushed with pink and reflecting on the water which was tinted green in places in the evening light.

'Mum is dragging Dad off to see the doctor now that the new scheme is in place,' mentioned George. 'The poor bloke is scared stiff.'

'In case they find something bad?'

'I'm not sure if it is that,' he said. 'I think it might be that he's afraid the doctor will say that nothing can be done so he'll have to accept it.'

'I think he has accepted it anyway, George; that's the impression I've got when I've spoken to him.'

'But hearing a professional actually say it makes it definite,' he said. 'As it is now there's always a chance he can find a new cream or pill from the chemist and hope it works.'

'Poor thing. I always feel very sorry for your dad.'

'Because of his back trouble?'

'No, because he always seems so sad,' she said. 'It's as though he doesn't like himself.'

'I've never noticed anything like that,' said George, surprised by her comment.

'You must have done.'

'No. Just the opposite in fact,' he told her. 'He always seems very fond of himself to me. Quite the big I am. Always has been.'

'I suppose you see him with different eyes being closely related but that could be just a front. He wouldn't want to seem lacking in self-confidence in front of his son because it might rub off on you. Every parent wants to set an example. Men always like to seem strong and fathers probably bluff it out in front of their sons.'

'Could be I suppose,' said George quickly, not wishing to

dwell on his father's character. 'Anyway, I'll let you know what happens. Meanwhile, did you have a good day?'

'At the office in this lovely weather, are you insane?' she said lightly. 'Did you?'

'Yeah, I did as it happens,' he said. 'I really enjoy going to work.'

She turned to him and smiled. 'You are a one-off, do you know that, George Benson.'

'Because I enjoy my job?'

'Among other things, yes,' she said. 'But mainly because you are such an enthusiast.'

'We're two of a kind then.'

'I don't enthuse about my day job.'

'You do about everything else though and I absolutely adore you,' he said.

'Likewise,' she said and they proceeded to move away from the towpath to somewhere a little more private.

'So the doctor is sending you to the hospital for an X-ray then, Dad; that's good,' said George, having been told all about his father's appointment at the surgery. 'That's the best news I've heard in ages.'

'I don't have to go and have it done,' his father pointed out. 'It isn't compulsory.'

'It's what the doctor suggests though,' put in Winnie. 'Just so they can see what's going on in your back and maybe find out what is causing the pain.'

'At last something is being done,' George approved.

'No it isn't, because I'm not going,' stated Percy.

'Yes you are,' George retorted. 'I shall take you myself in the van so you can't claim it's too far for you to walk.'

'The inside of a person's body is his own business and best left private.'

'They're not going to put your X-ray on a placard in the High Road, Dad. It will just be between you and the doctor.'

'Even so.'

'Stop moaning and thank God for Mr Bevan's new health service.'

'Don't be rude to your father.' Winnie spoke as though George was five years old.

Oh well, thought George, accepting the fact that he would always be just a boy in his mother's eyes. Fortunately for him his father was well aware that he was now a fully grown adult and a strong man.

'So your dad had an X-ray then, George,' said Beryl at Sunday tea at the Greens'. 'All under the new scheme.'

'That's right,' he confirmed.

'Marvellous isn't it that such things are available to us now?' she said. 'So when will he get the results?'

'A few weeks or so I think. We have to call in at the surgery to find out but these things take time. It's only standard procedure anyway. They probably do X-rays as routine now. If we don't hear anything we'll know there's nothing untoward but we'll still follow it up to make sure.'

'I'm sure there's nothing to worry about but it's good to get it looked at,' said Beryl. 'Fancy going to the hospital and not having to pay.'

'It is pretty amazing,' George agreed. 'Anyway, how is your course going, Charlie?'

'Pretty good thanks. A lot of homework and extra reading up to do as they let me start early instead of waiting until September,' said Charlie. 'So I have plenty to do in the evenings. I don't mind though, especially as some of the lads have gone into the army so there's not many left to hang around with. There's nothing much for us to do anyway.'

'No there isn't for people of your age,' agreed George. 'You're in between. There's the youth club, I suppose.'

'They're all kids of about fifteen,'

'Mm, I expect they would be.'

'The pictures?'

'Not every night.'

'I suppose not.'

'What did you used to do in your spare time when you were my age, George?' asked Charlie.

'I was away at sea,' said George. 'So it was a different sort of life altogether.'

'Sounds marvellous, going to all those exciting foreign places.'

'Yeah, I enjoyed it at the time. Plenty of camaraderie and new places to see. But it wasn't all fun and games by any means. Some of it was very hard and boring work on board the ship and a storm at sea is something I wouldn't recommend to anyone.'

'That's one thing I'll miss through not doing the service,' said Charlie. 'The chance to travel. Some of my mates are being posted abroad.'

A part of George still felt guilty about Charlie's accident; even though in his heart he knew it wasn't his fault. 'Still, you've taken up another chance that's arisen and that will be more useful to you in the long run.'

Even he could hear the ring of empty words to a lad of

seventeen. Boys of that age wanted adventure. He remembered that he certainly had.

'Yeah, I suppose so,' agreed Charlie, handing George the fish paste sandwiches.

A week or so later a letter in the post gave Winnie and Percy Benson a fright.

'George, come quick,' Winnie shouted down the cellar where George had gone to get some potatoes for the shop. 'Hurry up, please.'

'What's the matter?' asked George, rushing up the steps. 'Is somebody hurt?'

In reply she handed him a piece of paper which requested that Mr Percy Benson report to the doctor's surgery with regard to his X-ray results as a matter of urgency.

'Don't panic,' said George though he himself was alarmed and trying not to show it. 'They probably want Dad to go back for another X-ray. Perhaps the first one didn't come out properly. I think that does happen. One of the customers had to go back a second time.'

'Yeah, I expect that's what it will be,' said Percy but he was looking very pale and shaken.

Chapter Eleven

It was half day closing for the shops in Chiswick and George was in the cellar checking stock and making a list for the market. His thoughts were of the worrying event tomorrow. As George had predicted, his father did have to go back for another X-ray but the second only confirmed what the first had indicated. There was something on his spine that needed investigation so he was going into hospital for a major operation first thing in the morning.

The doctor was noncommittal about exactly what the problem might be but all three of them feared it was cancer, a word barely uttered in most circles because of its alarming seriousness. But George's father had surprised him in a good way recently. Having shown such cowardice about seeking medical advice initially, now that he had to face surgery and its consequences he'd done so with courage, his main concern seeming to be his wife and son and his beloved shop. He'd been busy making sure his affairs were all in order in case the worst happened and been kindness itself to Winnie, who was clearly terrified but putting on her usual brave face.

George was amazed at his own reaction to this turn of

events. Having never got along with his father, the news of a possible early death aged fifty-four shouldn't have affected him. But he was absolutely devastated by the prospect. A world without Percy Benson in it was unthinkable and he couldn't begin to imagine his mother bereft of her husband. She wasn't soppy or sentimental towards him but she was devoted.

He heard someone coming down the cellar steps, very slowly and carefully. 'I thought I'd come and have a few words with you, son,' said his father.

'You've shut the door,' said George, hurrying towards the stairs to rectify this. 'You know I always leave it open.'

'Leave it closed, please,' demanded Percy. 'What I have to say won't take long but I don't want your mother to hear it.'

'Just like old times then,' said George in a bitter tone. 'You always used to lock the door back then so Mum wouldn't hear, just in case I cried out. But I never did. I wouldn't give you the satisfaction. That's why I never shut that door now. It brings back too many painful memories.'

George could hear his own words echoing in this dismal place and could hardly believe he had uttered them. In all the years that had passed since, the beatings he had taken from his father as a boy had never been mentioned until now. The dark memories had stood between him and his father, a tacit barrier.

'I want to make my peace with you, son, just in case anything goes wrong tomorrow,' said Percy. 'What happened wasn't right. I know that now and I'm sorry.' He paused, looking sheepish. 'I thought it was the best way to bring a boy up. It was what my father did to me to make me behave.'

'I wasn't bad. No worse than any other boy. You could have given me a clip round the ear and left it at that,' said George.

'But the ritual, the secrecy, the cellar door being firmly locked.' He shivered. 'Ugh, even the thought of it makes me feel sick. Still to this day.'

'I wanted to make it feel like a punishment so you would learn from it.'

'I did that all right,' said George. 'I learned what cruelty was from an early age.'

'Your mother wouldn't allow me to raise a hand to you so it had to be in secret,' Percy told him. 'A boy needs discipline. Anyway, I never hit you very hard.'

That was actually true, George now realised as he cast his mind back. The physical pain had been minimal. It was the disgrace of it that had hurt so much. 'It was the humiliation you enjoyed, was it, Dad?'

'I didn't enjoy any of it. Of course I didn't. I'm not that much of a monster,' said Percy in a definite tone. 'But it had to be done, or so I thought. If you have boys of your own you'll understand.'

'I would never do that to any child of mine,' said George adamantly.

'I should wait until you're in that position before you make such claims,' advised Percy. 'Bringing up a child is no easy thing.'

'Spare the rod and spoil the child, eh Dad, is that what you think?'

'It's certainly what I used to think. Anyway, you turned out all right, didn't you?'

'I survived but I've hated you for most of my life,' said George. 'You were the reason I went away to sea. I couldn't bear to live in the same house as you even though the cellar sessions had long since stopped by then.'

'Oh,' his father said, clearly surprised.

'Surely you realised.'

'I thought you went away because you wanted adventure.'

'I did but I wanted to get away from you more.' He paused thoughtfully. 'The beatings stopped when I got bigger, didn't they, Dad? Was that because you were afraid I'd retaliate once I had the strength?'

'Of course not,' his father denied hotly. 'I felt that sort of discipline was no longer necessary once you got to a certain age.'

'You're a bully.'

'Maybe I was. Actually I hated the cellar beatings as much as you did but I thought they were necessary. Left to your mother you'd have done exactly as you liked.'

George wondered if there might be some truth in that. He'd always felt adored by his mother and knew he could get away with murder. 'She doesn't have a cruel bone in her body. But she's strong. I did as she told me. I respected her, which is more than I can say for you.'

'Oh!'

The light in here wasn't brilliant but George saw his father wince. 'Surely you didn't think that form of punishment was going to earn you respect, did you?'

'Maybe I did.' He shrugged rather helplessly. 'It's the way things are done. I bet your mates have all felt their father's belt a good few times.'

'I don't know about that but I doubt if they would be locked away in a cellar while it was going on.'

'I'm not a wicked man, George, I was just an ordinary bloke bringing up a boy as best as I could,' he said wearily. 'I wanted to make a man of you.'

'It's a wonder I'm not a nervous wreck,' said George.

'You're not though, are you? You're a fine man.'

'And I suppose you're taking the credit for that.'

'No, not at all. I'm just stating a fact.'

'You ruined the chances of us ever having a bond,' said George. 'Do you realise that since I've been an adult you and I have never been to see a football match together, we've never been for a pint or even shaken hands. We have no rapport whatsoever. We just exist together under the same roof for the sake of Mum.'

'You were away for so long.'

'That's true but it isn't the reason,' said George. 'If I'd stayed it would have been the same. There's a barrier between us because of your coldness towards me when I was a lad.'

'Yeah, I've realised that I wasn't as warm as I might have been towards you,' admitted Percy, looking very forlorn. 'Like many other men, I left all that sort of thing to your mother. I haven't known how to make things right.'

'I'm not sure that you can,' said George, wanting to end this painful conversation and mindful of his father's current ordeal. 'What's done is done and it was a long time ago.' He paused, choosing his words carefully and softening his tone. 'Look, Dad, you have enough to worry about with the surgery tomorrow so concentrate on that and forget about the past. I'll look after Mum while you're away.'

'I know that, son.'

'I'm sorry you've got this operation to face,' said George, feeling awkward and inadequate to the situation because he and his father had always been so distant when they were alone together and not putting on an act in front of Winnie. 'I'm sure it will be fine. These doctors know what they are doing.'

'We all know that it's serious and I have to take what comes,' Percy said. 'I'm prepared for that.'

George suspected that his father wanted more from him than he knew how to give. 'Mum will be wondering where you are,' he said awkwardly.

'Yeah, I'll let you get on then.'

'See you in a bit,' said George and his father limped laboriously towards the stairs which he had to climb very slowly. 'Leave the door open, please.'

'Will do.'

Sorting through potato sacks, boxes of cabbages and crates of apples from abroad, George's eyes burned with tears. He felt as though he had failed his father over the last few minutes and he didn't know what to do about it.

April had been on edge all day worrying about George's father who was having his operation today. By four o'clock she felt as though she would scream if she had to file one more piece of paper. But they just kept on coming because it was her job. If she was out in the fresh air working on the allotment she might be more able to cope; being stuck in this office, though, was purgatory.

George had said he would let her know as soon as there was any news and she hoped he might be waiting for her outside the office when she left since she wasn't allowed phone calls at work. But there was no sign of him so she guessed that he hadn't been able to leave the shop, probably because Winnie had stayed at the hospital.

Instead of going home she headed for the High Road only to find Benson's shop closed. This didn't bode well because they never shut the shop during working hours. She knew that George had planned to take his parents to the hospital early and come back and look after the business for the day. So something awful must have happened!

She headed home with the vague hope that he might be there waiting for her.

'He's probably gone to collect his mother from the hospital and closed the shop early,' suggested Beryl, seeing how worried her daughter was.

'The operation was scheduled for this morning,' said April. 'There should be some news by now.'

'Perhaps they were late doing it,' Beryl suggested. 'I doubt if things always go according to plan in hospitals with emergencies and such like.'

'Wotcha,' said Charlie, home from work.

'You're early,' Beryl remarked.

'George came along as I was walking and gave me a lift,' he explained.

'Where is he now?'

'Outside, locking the van.'

April tore from the house to meet him.

'So all those years of pain were caused by a little piece of shrapnel pressing on your dad's spine,' said April when a beaming George had told them about the result of the operation.

'That's right,' he confirmed, looking pleased, 'and now they've removed it so he won't have any more pain, once the operation wound has healed up.'

'That's marvellous,' said Beryl.

'I'll say,' added Charlie.

'It's such a relief,' said April, who had grown rather fond of

Percy. 'I have to admit I wasn't expecting good news. I've been worried sick, especially when the shop was shut.'

'Sorry about that,' he said. 'I had to go back to the hospital at four o'clock to see the surgeon so I closed up early.'

'So why wasn't the shrapnel removed when he actually got the injury and was in hospital?' asked April.

'Human error, I suppose. They must have thought they'd got it all out but missed a bit. They were frantically busy at the time with bomb victims, and of course Dad's hardly ever been to see the doctor since until the new scheme came in so it's never been checked.'

'Thank goodness it's been sorted out at last.'

'Not half. Anyway, I have to dash,' he said. 'I'm going back to the hospital when I've had a bite to eat, for visiting time. Mum wanted to stay there so I'll take her some grub too. See you later.' He kissed April, picked Lily up and planted a smacker on her cheek before he dashed off.

'That must be such a relief for that family,' said Beryl.

April nodded in agreement.

'It is good news,' added Charlie. 'But now that we know that all is well, I'm starving, Mum, and it's my class night.'

'There's a shepherd's pie in the oven which will be on the table in less than two minutes,' said Beryl happily. She loved this time of day when the older children got home from work and they were all together. April and Charlie usually went out somewhere later on but the time in between was pure joy for Beryl. Lily always enjoyed it too; she adored her older siblings.

George had been amazed by the strength of his feelings towards his father during the past couple of days and he was mulling this over as he drove to the hospital that evening. The rush of emotion had started with the confrontation with Percy in the cellar and had been a rollercoaster ever since. The worry of the operation and what the findings might be had been fierce and the absolute joy when the good news came was indescribable.

He didn't know if he could ever put the memory of what used to happen in the cellar out of his mind but he did want some sort of a relationship with his father. Having thought he might lose him had certainly clarified his priorities. Yes, his father had been cruel when George was a lad and he would always hold that view but the reality was that many fathers used violence on their sons in the name of discipline and Percy was following his own father's example. George would never subject any child that he might have to that sort of punishment but it was a long while ago and it was time to put it behind him.

It would be nice to get rid of the barrier that had stood between them for so long and have some sort of companion-ship. It might not happen overnight but maybe it would be possible with time if he made the effort. If it was what his father wanted, of course. He had seemed repentant yesterday when he'd thought he was not long for this world. Now he'd had a reprieve it might be a whole lot different.

'You're not going to get rid of me after all then,' said Percy when George and Winnie sat down by his bed in the ward. 'Not because of my back injury anyway and hopefully not for a while yet.'

'You old bugger, scaring us like that,' said George in the jovially insulting manner that men used towards each other when they were friends. Now, though, his attitude was genuine and not just to please his mother.

'You could have got it sorted years ago if only you'd gone to see the doctor,' said Winnie.

'What's done is done so there's no point in going on about it. It's been put right now, thanks to this marvellous new health scheme,' he said.

'That you were originally so cynical about,' George reminded him.

'Well I've changed my mind, haven't I?'

Winnie took her husband's hand. 'I'm so pleased you're going to be all right, Percy. Have they told you yet when you'll be coming home?'

'No, but I shouldn't think it will be very long,' he said. 'The doctor said I'll be a bit sore while the wound heals but eventually that will go.'

'So we might see a few smiles about the place then,' said George, maintaining a jovial air.

'Ooh, I'm not sure I can go that far,' joshed Percy.

'He's probably forgotten how, it's been that long,' added Winnie, affectionately joining in the joke.

'Yeah, I've got so used to being a miserable bugger, I might not be able to break the habit. And don't make me laugh now because of my stitches. I have had an operation, you know.'

'Yeah course you have, dear,' said Winnie sympathetically. 'Is it very sore?'

'Very.'

'Don't milk it, Dad,' said George jokingly. 'You've had enough sympathy these last few years to last a lifetime.'

'Precious little from you though.'

'We're men, aren't we? We don't do soft stuff,' said George. 'Anyway I've been too busy running your business for you.'

'I'll be back on form soon,'

'So I'll be out of a job.'

'Not on your life,' said Percy. 'We're not letting you run away to sea again, are we, Winnie?'

'Not likely.'

'Not unless he really wants to go, of course,' added Percy carefully.

'We'd never stand in your way,' said Winnie.

There was a tight silence which George smoothed over by saying, 'Well, I'll let you two have a bit of time on your own.' He looked at his mother, grinning. 'But you mustn't get in the bed with him, Mum. It's against hospital rules.'

'Oh George, you are awful,' laughed Winnie.

He was still smiling as he walked out of the ward.

'So your dad will be able to go back to work then once he's recovered from the operation,' said April later that same evening when she was saying goodnight to George at the front door.

'That's right,' he confirmed. 'He should be completely back to normal after some recovery time.'

'How will that work out practically then?' she asked. 'You can't both run the shop.'

'I'm not absolutely sure what will happen yet but I think it might be time to expand. I'll probably run the new shop and he and Mum can look after the other. We'll work out the details when he's back home.'

April became thoughtful. 'I know your original idea was to go back to sea when your dad came back to work.'

'Yes it was, but things have changed since that was the plan,' he said, giving her a tender smile.

'If you did want to revert to that idea for any reason, don't let me stand in your way,' she said. 'I would still want to be your girlfriend. Obviously it wouldn't be ideal but I'd go along with it if it was what you wanted.'

'Do you really think I would go away and leave you?' he said sharply. 'I'm not that stupid.'

'All right,' she said. 'No need to get narked. I just wanted you to know that I'm not the sort of woman to be clingy.'

'I know that and I wouldn't mind if you were,' he told her. 'In fact, it might be rather nice if you were a little bit more dependent on me.'

'You wouldn't really like it if I was, would you?' she asked.

'I think I would,' he said thoughtfully. 'But on the other hand, one of the many things I love about you is your independent spirit.'

'I'm not thinking of changing that so we'll both be happy,' she said, smiling.

'Well, it's been quite a day,' he said. 'It started so badly too with Mum and I worried sick about Dad.'

'And now you're both up there on cloud nine.'

'It's especially good for Mum. Dad's been a worry to her since the injury happened. Once he's better she'll be able to lean on him a little again. Anyway, it's very early days. Let's give him time to recover before we start making plans.'

'You'll all sleep better tonight,' she said.

'Not half.'

'Give us a kiss then and be on your way.'

He did as she asked, lingered a while longer then headed for home, leaving April feeling happy for him.

* * *

240

'How are things with you and Johnny?' April asked her cousin as Heather sat in a deckchair watching April work on the allotment one evening as the sun went down; she was harvesting some peas and beans for the shop.

'All right,' she replied.

'Does he fit the bill as a future husband?'

'Oh April, fancy saying a thing like that,' Heather objected.

'I thought you saw all men in those terms,' said April. 'You've never made any secret of the fact that marriage is your aim in life. As you're going out with him quite regularly I assumed that's what you had in mind.'

'Well it isn't. You have to let these things take their course.'

April laughed heartily. 'That's what I've been telling you for years but ever since Arthur you've been desperate to find a husband.'

'Well I'm not now,' Heather made clear. 'I've decided there is more to life than marriage.'

'Blimey you've changed your tune,' said April.

'Yeah, I'm all for having fun now.'

'Thank goodness for that. That will take the pressure off the male population of London.'

'Honestly, April, you are horrible to me sometimes,' objected Heather, though even she could see the joke. 'You'd never dream we are cousins, the way you treat me.'

'What about the way you treat me? Always telling me I'm a disgrace to womanhood with my muddy hands from working this allotment.'

'Well, it's true,' said Heather. 'I bet your fingernails are black with mud.'

'Occupational hazard I'm afraid,' said April. 'They'll be all right when I've given them a good scrub with a nailbrush.'

'I should hope so too,' said Heather. 'I'd hate to think of you going into the office tomorrow with dirty fingernails.' She studied her own hands. 'My nails are looking really good as it happens. I managed to get some nice nail polish in Woolworths the other day. I'll show you when I can get you away from those damned vegetables. I really will have to take you in hand.'

'You can do what you like but you'll never get me to give this allotment up,' April said. 'This gets the office boredom out of my system.'

'I can't think of anything more boring than growing vegetables,' said Heather. 'Office work is interesting in comparison. Obviously when I do eventually get married I shall give up work and I can't wait for that part. But an office job suits me for now. I mean, what else is there for women like us except a factory or a shop.'

'Mm,' agreed April. 'So you do still have the marriage bug?'

'It isn't a bug, it's just the normal course of events and I don't want to be left behind. But I'm not quite so desperate now, probably because I do have a boyfriend of sorts so I'm not stuck indoors listening to the wireless with my mum on a Saturday night.'

'A boyfriend of sorts?'

'Yeah, I like Johnny but it isn't serious at the moment.'

'Oh well, that's your business.'

'Exactly.'

April finished what she was doing and stood up with the wooden crate of vegetables. The sun had disappeared and there was a chill in the air. 'I'll just put these in the shed ready for George to collect then I'm off home,' she said. 'Are you coming?'

'Might as well. It's Thursday, the night Johnny and George go out for a few beers so neither of us has a date.'

'That's right.'

'Talking of dates why don't we make up a foursome on Saturday night,' suggested Heather.

Oh dear. April really wished she hadn't made the suggestion because she knew George wouldn't want to do it. He liked to have her to himself, he said. They'd been out on a few foursomes with Heather and Johnny and April thought they had been quite good fun. But George seemed reluctant to do it again.

'I'm not sure, Heather. George has a lot on his mind at the moment with his dad having been in hospital and running the business and everything.'

'How old is George, sixty-five?'

'That isn't very nice, Heather.'

'Well, wanting it to be just the two of you, that is so staid.'

'There's nothing staid about George and I think you know that,' said April. 'Anyway I like it to be just us two as well.'

'Oh well suit yourself,' said Heather sulkily. 'Johnny and I will have fun without you.'

'I'm sure you will,' said April, closing the shed door. 'Meanwhile let's go home.'

'Good news about your dad, George,' said Johnny as the two men stood at the bar of the local pub drinking their beer. 'Who would have thought he would have a lump of metal inside him all this time? But I suppose that sort of thing does happen in wartime. God knows what they'll find inside patients now that people can actually afford to go to the doctor's.'

'I think that's a bit of an exaggeration, mate,' protested George. 'Dad's is an unusual case.'

'He's the only one we know of,' said Johnny. 'I bet there are others.'

'Maybe. So how are things going with you and Heather?' asked George as a way of changing the subject.

'All right but she blows hot and cold so I never quite know where I am with her.'

'I did warn you about her.'

'Yeah, you did. She isn't an easy woman to be with, I admit. The trouble is, mate, I'm really keen on her so all the common sense in the world won't change that.'

'Has she asked you to name the date yet?'

'Of course she hasn't,' said Johnny defensively. 'She isn't that bad.'

'She used to be marriage mad,' said George. 'But she's probably got over all that now.'

'I know she can be a bit pushy and attention-seeking,' said Johnny. 'I think that's because she's so jealous of April. When she lets go of that, she's lovely.'

'I'm sure she's a nice girl,' said George and changed the subject to football as the new season was imminent.

Women, relationships and work were all cast aside as they discussed their favourite topic.

As the season of mists and mellow fruitfulness arrived again, April visited the allotment one Saturday morning and looked back on the year and thought the allotment had done quite well despite having lost a crop of cabbages to some determined slugs. All in all it had been a good season; she had managed to feed the family and maintain a reasonable supply to Benson's. It would soon be time for the winter work but there were still some nice crops to harvest. She pulled a cauliflower and some parsnips for their dinner tonight, feeling pleased with her efforts though there was always room for improvement. She could never explain to anyone the pleasure this little piece of ground gave her.

'I was thinking, George,' began April that evening on their way home from the cinema. 'When your dad comes back to work full time, you won't need me at the shop on a Saturday afternoon, will you?'

'As things are at the moment, I don't suppose we will,' he confirmed.

'That's a shame, I'll miss my shift,' she confessed. 'I always enjoy it.'

'Thinking about it, though, it might be best to leave things as they are so that Mum and Dad can have Saturday afternoons off together.'

'That's fine with me.'

'While we're on the subject of your employment, I have another idea in mind for the future that I'd like to talk to you about,' he said. 'I wasn't going to mention it until nearer the time but while we're talking shop I might as well tell you.'

'Sound interesting.'

'I was wondering, and don't be afraid to say no if you don't want to do this. But when we open our second shop, I wondered if you might consider a full-time job helping me to run it. I know you're not keen on office work and we would more than match the wages you get there. The job wouldn't just be shop assistant because you'd be helping to manage it.'

She was taken aback but happily so. At last there was a way out of office work.

'You'd have to work on a Saturday but you would have time off during the week to make up for it,' he went on. 'I know it isn't exactly a glamorous job but I'd love it if you felt you could take it.'

April had thought of a potential drawback. 'I would love to run the new shop with you, George, but don't you think working together might spoil our relationship?'

'That never even crossed my mind,' he told her. 'Mum and Dad have worked together for years and they haven't murdered each other yet. A lot of shops are run by couples and they all seem to be still talking to each other.'

'The answer is yes then,' she said. 'But when is this going to be happening?'

'We're going to start looking for an empty shop right away,' he explained. 'So it depends what comes up.'

'Soon then?'

'Oh yes. I've been talking about it for long enough. It's time to get on with it. Now that Dad is feeling better he's all for it too.'

'That's really good news,' she said. 'Things seem to be going well for me lately. The allotment is flourishing and now I have a chance to escape from the dreaded filing cabinets. So everything in the garden is rosy.'

'Good,' he said. 'And long may it continue.'

It didn't continue. A few days later April received a letter in the post from the council to say that the allotments were closing next year.

'"The land is needed for building,"' April read to her mother and Charlie. 'That's a joke in itself since no building has been done around here since before the war.'

246

'There will be in the near future I suppose,' said Beryl. 'Housing is so badly needed after the bombing to ease the terrible housing shortage. They have to start sometime.'

'There are plenty of bombsites everywhere for them to build on,' said April. 'They don't need to take the allotments. There were never houses on that piece of ground anyway. We need to have some green space.'

'We have Duke's Meadows,' Beryl reminded her.

'I mean somewhere for people to grow things,' said April. 'A lot of people round here don't have gardens.'

'The builders are going to be in seventh heaven when building does start again,' remarked Charlie. 'They'll make an absolute fortune.'

'Money will probably be behind this decision rather than the good of the people,' said an outraged April. 'I know we desperately need homes but you look along any street at any bombsite and you'll not see a builder in sight; just weeds. They need to build on those before they start taking allotments. Well, I'm not going to accept it.'

'I don't see what else you can do, dear.' Beryl was realistic.

'Neither do I at the moment but I'll find a way. I am not just going to sit back and let a tradition be wiped out.'

'I don't expect they'll build over all allotments in the area,' said Beryl in an attempt to calm her daughter. 'They'll probably suggest an alternative.'

'They are not building over ours, Mum,' she stated firmly. 'I have to go to work now but this isn't the end of it, not by a long way. If the suffragettes got us women the vote, I am sure I can save our allotments.'

★   ★   ★

'Let me see if I can find out more about it before you start organising protests,' said George when she told him the news in a fury. 'People are desperate for housing so you might get opposition if you walk about with a banner. There are protests about the housing shortage so allotments might not get the same sympathy.'

'There is plenty of space for housing, George, but where are the houses, tell me that,' she said furiously. 'They've put up a few pre-fabs but bugger all else around here. There is a lot of talk about new towns outside London but what about people who don't want to move away?'

'I thought it was the allotments you wanted to save,' he said.

'It is but I recognise that there is a terrible housing shortage too. We're lucky. We managed not to lose our home but thousands of Londoners lost theirs. The bombed sites are everywhere so let them build on those. Why choose a small piece of land that never had houses on it? That land was allotments in my father's day and probably even before that. I can't understand why they would want to wipe out a tradition.'

'Neither can I but I aim to find out.'

'How?'

'I know a lot of people in the town and Dad has contacts in various trade associations,' he said. 'We'll get to the bottom of it and when we know a bit more I'll be right by your side in taking action if that is necessary.'

'I knew it would take drastic measures to get you away from that damned allotment but I never thought it would be the council who finally did it,' chortled Heather with her special brand of caustic humour when she called round to the Greens' after work the following evening.

'They haven't done it yet,' April reminded her.

'I thought you said they are closing the allotments next year.'

'That's what they are planning but I have other ideas.'

'Oh no, you're not going to organise a protest are you, with a banner and placards and all the rest of the paraphernalia? Please tell me you're not.'

'I doubt if it will come to that but if that's what it takes, yes, most definitely.'

'How embarrassing,' Heather complained. 'I hope you are not expecting me to join in.'

'It would be nice to have your support.'

'But I don't care if they close the allotments so how can I truthfully protest about it.'

'You could do it to support me but I suppose that would be a bit dishonest.'

Heather tutted. 'Why can't you be like any normal woman and be content with ordinary things like clothes and men instead of getting involved in stuff like this?'

'I don't know,' April admitted. 'It must just be the way I'm made, I suppose.'

Heather could see that she was genuinely upset so she softened her tone. Despite her ferocious jealousy, she was actually rather fond of her cousin. 'Look, although I can't see the attraction of growing vegetables when there are farmers to do it for us, I know how much you love your bloomin' allotment so I'll do what I can to help.'

'Thanks,' said April and collapsed into tears.

'Dad knows one of the chaps on the council,' George told April later when he came round. 'He's going to see what he can find out. I think someone at the town hall might be on the fiddle.'

'Really? In what way?'

'Taking a backhander from someone who wants to buy the land.'

'A builder?'

'Or speculator. Someone who makes it their business to know councillors and the like. The land isn't big enough for an estate and council houses are the priority,' he said. 'But further down the line when regulations are lifted someone could put up a few private houses and make a lot of money.'

'It's a good location, being near to the shops and the station and a stone's throw from central London,' said April.

'Exactly,' said George. 'In a few years' time posh houses in that area will be worth a fortune. So who's to say someone isn't negotiating to buy the land as an investment for the future.'

'Why don't I just go to the council and ask them outright?' she suggested.

'Because you can't throw accusations around without evidence,' he said.

'I suppose not.'

'But talk to the others at the allotments and see what they think.'

'They'll be as upset as I am.'

'You can bet your life on it. So the more of you the better if you are going to make a stand against this.'

'We'll be doing that all right,' she said. 'That much I am certain of.'

Chapter Twelve

'What's all this, Frank, are you skiving off work?' asked Beryl lightly that afternoon when she noticed that he was busy at his allotment on her way home from the park with Lily, who had fallen asleep in the pushchair.

'No, not really, because I'll be out on my rounds this evening,' explained Frank, who was an insurance agent and cycled around the area collecting premiums. 'I catch the ones I missed during the day around teatime. So I can afford an hour or so off in the afternoon.'

'Seems as though you won't have your allotment for much longer.' Her voice was serious.

He dug his fork into the ground and folded his arms, looking grim. 'If certain people have their way, no I won't, but I don't see how they can get away with it. This isn't building land. Never has been to my knowledge.'

'April is absolutely furious about it and her boyfriend is looking into it. His father knows someone on the council apparently. Once we know more, she is going to try and get it stopped. God knows how but she isn't prepared to sit back and let them get away with it.'

'She won't be the only one. Once everybody has digested the contents of the letter there'll be a few who will want to rebel against it, myself included. The only reason I know of for them to have grounds to close the allotments is if they are not being looked after properly.' He cast a critical eye around. 'No one can say that about these here. One or two plot holders perhaps don't do as much work as they might but everyone else is diligent, your daughter included. Anyway, we need the food we grow since supplies are still short.'

'We do indeed,' agreed Beryl. 'April has kept us fed well from hers.'

'Tell April that I am not going to accept it without a fight,' he said. 'I shall speak to some of the others and get a meeting arranged.'

'She'll be right behind you, if not in front,' said Beryl. 'Knowing her she'll go to the council to protest.'

'It'll be best if a few of us go but people are at work during the time the council office is open. I could go due to my flexible working hours.'

'I'll tell her,' she said.

He looked at her in a friendly manner. 'How are you keeping, Beryl?'

'All right thanks, Frank.' Since he'd paid her that apologetic visit, she'd got better acquainted with him and now counted him as a friend. She often had a chat with him and found him to be pleasant company. Occasionally she wondered what might have happened if she'd accepted that ill-timed invitation to the cinema. Would they still be friends if she had?

'How is your boy coming along now?' He always asked about Charlie and she was touched by it.

'He's doing all right thanks,' she replied. 'Naturally he gets a bit frustrated with his limitations at times, I think, but not very often and he doesn't say much about it. He's getting on well at night school too. Having a qualification will boost his confidence as well as help him to get a better job.'

'Mm, it certainly will.'

The suggestion of a frown passed across her face. 'It's just that he was such an active boy, always playing football or taking part in some sort of sport. It hurts me that he can't do it now.'

'I'm sure it must do but he's obviously come to terms with it so I suppose you'll have to try and do the same.' He raised his eyes and gave a wry grin. 'Kids eh. Who'd have 'em? You're vulnerable from the minute they are born because their problems are yours too.' He pointed to his heart. 'In here.' He looked at Lily fast asleep. 'When they're that age you think you won't worry about them when they're grown but nothing changes.'

'You are absolutely right,' she told him. 'Right now I'm all upset on April's behalf about her losing her allotment. She loves it and will miss it like mad.'

'She hasn't lost it yet, Beryl,' he reminded her. 'Tell her I shall be looking into it and we'll have a chat when I see her.'

'Will do,' she said. 'I'll get my little one home and let you get on. Ta-ta Frank.'

'Cheerio.'

He watched her walk away, pushing the pram with that special energy she had which he also saw in her daughter. There was such a sense of life and purpose about Beryl Green somehow. What a lovely woman she was. It was a pity he'd blown his chances with her by being too presumptuous too soon. He took hold of his fork as if to resume digging then changed his mind, put the fork in the shed, and headed for the Town Hall.

★　　★　　★

'I suppose it could be possible that some ambitious builders might make a point of getting to know someone at the council in the hope of getting planning permission through in return for some sort of payment,' said Percy to his wife and son one night over their evening meal. 'But we have no proof that anything of that sort goes on and certainly not in the case of the proposed allotments closure. I've spoken to a pal of mine on the council and he doesn't think any money has changed hands. I reckon it's more a matter of the urgent need for housing that's caused them to consider the idea of selling the land to a builder who will, of course, apply for permission to build on it at some point. The council needs to be seen to be doing something about the chronic housing shortage.'

'They need to build on the bombsites before they start taking over the allotments.'

'In normal times I don't think building on allotments would even be considered but perhaps the rules have changed because of the need for housing.'

'That point needs checking out then,' said George.

'Oh yes, tell April that her and her pals need to nip this idea in the bud and organise a formal protest if they can't get any joy through the normal channels,' said Percy. 'We can't have the council selling off land willy-nilly. Those allotments are needed in the area. You can't wipe out a piece of local culture.'

'Don't worry, Dad, April is ready for a fight over this,' said George. 'There'll be no stopping her once they've made a few enquiries.'

Questions were asked at the Town Hall, meetings were held and still the allotment holders couldn't get the council to reconsider their decision.

'We shall have to arrange a protest march,' Frank said to April when they were both at the allotment one weekend in October. 'It's the only thing we can do.'

'I agree but let's do it properly; tell the police and let the local paper know so that we get some publicity,' she suggested. 'And make sure we get as many people as possible to join us.'

'That's the spirit,' said Frank. 'I'll go knocking on a few doors tonight to let the others know about it. I'll tell them to come here next Saturday so that we can set a date.'

'The sooner the better,' said April.

'I've never been so embarrassed in my life,' Heather said to Johnny as she marched beside him carrying a board saying SAVE OUR ALLOTMENTS – OUR HERITAGE.

'A bit of embarrassment won't hurt you,' he responded. 'And bear in mind the fact that you are doing something unselfish for a change.'

'Only because April nagged me into it,' she said. 'I don't want to be here making a show of myself. Does my hair look all right and is my lipstick smudged?'

'You look fine,' he said after glancing at her face. 'No one has come to look at you anyway.'

'No, but they are seeing me aren't they? Here in the middle of the road. There are plenty of people watching.' The neighbourhood had turned out in force to support the allotment holders and were cheering and clapping. 'I feel like I'm in show business.'

'I bet you're lapping it up.'

'I certainly am not,' she denied.

'The support is all due to April,' he said. 'April and Frank. And the fact that it is a good cause. They've been putting up notices and knocking on doors to spread the word about the march. I believe the reporter from the local paper is here somewhere too.'

'Will we be in the paper?' she asked excitedly.

'We won't be unless they do a random shot of the marchers but April will be I should think.'

'Trust her to be in the limelight.'

'Now, Heather, don't spoil your good deed by being bitchy,' he admonished. 'Of course she's centre stage. She organised it and it's her cause.'

'I suppose so,' she agreed reluctantly. 'It's freezing cold. Not the weather for this sort of carry-on.'

'You can't choose the weather when you have a point to make.'

'Why did I agree to do this, Johnny?'

'Because, my dear Heather, you do actually have a heart buried deep somewhere beneath your enormous capacity for self-interest,' he said, gently teasing her.

'I don't know why you go out with me as you are always finding fault,' she said.

'It must be because I enjoy a challenge,' he said, again teasing her, 'and you are that all right.'

'I shall slap you in a minute,' she threatened. 'I don't need criticism on top of all the punishment this march is giving me, what with me making fool of myself and being frozen half to death.'

'You don't half exaggerate. Anyway, I think you are secretly enjoying it.'

'You're deluded if you think that,' she said but somewhere deep inside her something resembling pleasure was slowly rising above the discomfort. It felt good to be a part of something that people cared about. Personally she didn't give a damn if they covered the allotments with ten-storey blocks of flats but April and her vegetable-growing cronies cared so it felt worthwhile and, almost despite herself, she was beginning to have fun.

'Is that a smile trying to break through?' asked Johnny.

'It most certainly is not,' she denied hotly. 'If you think I enjoy making a spectacle of myself in the middle of winter you don't know me at all.'

'I know you better than you know yourself.'

'Not a chance,' she came back at him but he did sometimes seem to be very much in tune with her way of thinking and wasn't backward in telling her. Johnny was a really nice bloke. He wasn't in the same league as his friend George but he'd do as a boyfriend for now.

Heather's mother caught up with them. 'Wotcha, you two. It's going well, isn't it? An excellent turnout.'

'Very good,' said Johnny. 'Your daughter is really enjoying herself.'

'Of course I'm not. Take no notice of him, Mum,' said Heather. 'He gets a kick out of annoying me.'

'You're not here to enjoy yourself anyway,' Peg reminded her. 'But you are here, that's the important thing.'

'Not much chance of getting out of it with everyone making such a big fuss about it.'

'Even your cousin Charlie is here,' observed Peggy, spotting him right at the end. 'And that really does take guts. So just be grateful that you have both your legs and feet intact and put your heart and soul into it.'

'Don't push it, Mum.' Even so, Heather did march with a little more enthusiasm.

Charlie had only agreed to come on the march on the under-standing that he was left alone to walk at his own pace at the end with no one feeling they must lag behind to keep him company. 'If anyone feels sorry for me and drops back to walk with me I shall go straight home.'

People thought that he had accepted his injury and wasn't in the least bothered by it. That was the impression he purposely created. In truth he was still embarrassed by it and often felt very irritated because he couldn't lead such an active life as before. He had dreaded this march because his peculiar way of walking would be on show but he hadn't felt able to refuse; not only because he felt driven by loyalty to his sister, though naturally he wanted to support her. But his own personality wouldn't allow him to fail to rise to the challenge. He believed that once he gave in to negative feelings he was done for.

Even apart from the embarrassment of walking in such a laboured way, the physical effort it took was enormous and his legs ached and his feet got very sore. He managed to get about well enough from day to day, to the bus stop for work and his evening class. But today's event was really punishing and he felt pushed to his limit. Still, though, he managed a smile and a wave for the well-wishers.

'Mind if I join you?' asked someone and turning he saw a girl who looked to be about his age with dark curly hair and big brown eyes.

'I'm quite happy walking on my own, thanks,' he said.

'Fortunately for me you don't own the road so I can walk wherever I choose, which happens to be next to you.'

'Oh,' he said, taken aback. 'Why would you want to be a straggler when you can be at the front with the others?'

'Because you happen to be the only other person of my age on the march so I thought we might have something to talk about,' she explained.

'Oh, I see.'

'I'm Susie and I'm seventeen,' she informed him brightly. 'I'm here because of my father. He's the one of the allotment holders. I thought I'd better give him some support. He's a smashing dad and a very keen gardener.'

'I'm Charlie. My sister is the gardener in our family,' he said. 'She took over the allotment after my father got killed by a bomb.'

The conversation flowed after that. She told him she worked in an office, he told her what he did and about his evening class. Then they got on to films and music and discovered that they both loved popular songs and the swing and jazz music from America that was all the rage at the moment. Charlie forgot about his limp and his embarrassment and really began to enjoy himself.

'A good turnout, Frank,' remarked Beryl, walking beside him. 'You and April did well to organise it.'

'It's the people who turned up that have done well,' he said. 'It wouldn't have been much of a protest with only us gardeners.'

'But you and April made sure people knew about it, didn't you?' she pointed out.

'That's true,' he said. 'I'd be lost without my allotment. Where would I go to get out of the house and escape from my daughter if I didn't have it?'

She laughed. 'I know the feeling. We all need some space but I don't get much, if any.' She looked ahead to Lily, who was sitting on George's shoulders as he marched next to April at the front. 'I wouldn't be without them, though, and Lily has been the making of me since I lost Jim. I shall miss her when she goes to school.'

'I can imagine. I wouldn't be without my girl either but sometimes I need a bit of distance, especially from the gramophone she has on all the time.'

'Charlie is the same with ours but I rather like it,' she told him. 'It's nice to have music about the place and I enjoy the modern stuff.'

'I'm happy with the wireless myself.'

'I like the wireless too but you don't get much in the way of dance music on there, do you?' she said. 'So a spot of swing around the house is nice.'

'The young ones love it, don't they?'

'They certainly do,' she agreed. 'Most of Charlie's mates are away doing their national service at the moment. He must miss them but he doesn't make a big thing about it. That's another thing that might make him feel different, the fact that he can't go away to do his service. I know all the lads complain about having to do it but when you are not able to, I suppose that could make you feel less like one of the boys.'

'I don't think any of his mates would see it in that light but I know what you mean.'

'Has your daughter come today to give you some support?' Beryl asked.

'Yeah, she's here somewhere.' He turned, looking around. 'There's Susie. She's right at the end . . . with your Charlie as it happens.'

Beryl swung round. 'The dark-haired girl?'

'That's right.'

'Well would you believe it,' she said. 'He told us he didn't want anyone walking with him at the back because they felt sorry for him and he would go home if anyone tried it.'

'He looks happy enough now, they both do,' Frank observed

'They certainly do,' she said. 'She must have managed to convince him that she doesn't pity him.'

'It's something to do with them being youngsters I expect,' Frank said casually. 'It's one thing walking with a parent and quite another if you're with someone in your own age group.'

'The fact that she is a pretty girl might have helped too,' she said, laughing.

Given the gravity of the situation, Beryl wasn't sure if she should be having fun but a serious issue had proved to be a happy occasion for her because there was so much support and spirit here among the crowds. She was enjoying Frank's company too. It felt like a day out.

'As soon as you've had enough, Percy, let me know and we'll go home,' Winnie told her husband.

'Why would I have had enough?' he asked.

'Because you've had an operation, of course.'

'Which was months ago,' he reminded her. 'I'm well over that. Anyway we're only walking through the town, not hiking across country for miles.'

'That's true.'

'I think some of these people would climb mountains if that's what it took, they're so enthusiastic,' he said. 'I'm glad they've turned out for April.'

'Do you think it will do any good?'

'It must do good to bring something that isn't right to the public attention but whether the council will change their mind or not is anyone's guess.'

'Isn't it lovely that you've been able to come to support

it,' enthused Winnie. 'A few months ago it would have been unthinkable.'

'Yes, it's very good. When I think about all that pain I was in I still can't believe how lucky I've been,' he said. 'I feel as though I'm a new man.'

'You seem to be getting on better with George lately too,' she ventured.

It was true that he and George had more of a rapport now but it had nothing to do with the state of Percy's health even though it was the operation that had brought the situation out into the open. Things seemed to have improved since then without either of them making a big performance of it. George had been warmer and Percy now felt able to be less restrained towards his son since they'd talked about the past and he'd confronted his shame. But his wife didn't need to know the details. What had caused the rift was long ago and no good could possibly come from telling Winnie. That would always stay just between himself and George.

'Yes I suppose I am,' he said now.

'It's nice for us to be able to go out together, Percy,' she said, taking his hand.

'Especially as it's in such a good cause,' he said, smiling at her.

April had captured the spirit of the occasion too and was enjoying herself. It was a serious event but the support from the crowds made it feel like fun. She and George were leading the march as some of the others dropped back. There were a few policemen around to keep order though it was all very peaceful so they hadn't really been needed.

When they got to the Town Hall the protesters raised

the banners and began chanting 'Save our allotments' and as the rest of the march arrived the volume increased. There was a reporter and photographer from the local paper and April found herself being snapped and asked questions. Just as she had begun to tell the journalist some details, she felt someone pulling her from behind and swinging round she found herself staring into the face of a man with fury in his eyes.

'You and your bloody allotments,' he said. 'It's houses we need, not gardening. So take your friends and clear off and let the council do its work.'

'The town has plenty of space for house building,' she said. 'We can't let them build over everything.'

'They can build where they like as far as I'm concerned because I want somewhere for my family to live,' he burst out emotionally. 'I bet you're all right, you'll have a house and be very comfortable thanks very much. Well some of us ain't so lucky so take your band of gardeners and bugger off.'

'Oi,' said George, who still had Lily on his shoulders. 'Leave her alone.'

'It's all right, George, I can handle this,' she said. 'You look after Lily. Keep her out of the way.'

George couldn't really do anything else because the crowds were pushing in and the man had supporters so things were beginning to get ugly as opposing sides of the argument clashed. The man was shaking with anger and looking at April with sheer hatred.

'It won't be affordable housing that will go up on the allotments,' she said. 'It will be offices or posh houses. Whoever is after the land is probably a speculative builder. He'll bide his time and do what he likes when he's ready.'

'Don't tell lies,' he said furiously. 'There must be laws about that sort of thing.'

'Most laws have a way of being broken if you are in the know,' she said. 'The allotments take up a small piece of land. Surely you don't begrudge us growing food on it.'

'You can't put gardening in the same league as housing in terms of importance,' he said and she could see that he was shaking with rage and almost at breaking point.

'We grow food, not roses,' she pointed out.

'We've got farmers to do that.'

'These allotments helped to keep people fed during the war,' she said.

'The war is over, in case you haven't heard.'

'We still need the allotments, we always will.'

'Not like we need houses, you silly bitch,' he said, then his temper finally snapped and he lashed out at her and she felt a blow to her face which knocked her back so that she stumbled but didn't quite lose her balance.

Chaos ensued. People were shouting. Arguments broke out. The police came on to the scene and April's attacker was led away still shouting abuse at her. George appeared and tried to go after him but she held him back because she didn't want any more violence. In a dazed state she gave the policeman her name and address as requested and assured him that she was all right and didn't need to go to hospital to be checked over, though she could feel her eye swelling from the blow. Then she gathered as many of the supporters as she could find and thanked them for coming. Finally she said to George and the family, 'Let's go home.'

Sadly they all headed homewards carrying their boards and banners.

★   ★   ★

'I can't believe that you are not going to bring charges against that maniac,' said George, later that afternoon when they were at the Greens' and the police had been to see April about what happened. 'He attacked you and gave you a black eye.'

'He's right,' added Johnny, who had come to the house with Heather and her mother. 'He can't be allowed to get away with a thing like that.'

'He was provoked,' she reminded them.

'Not by you?'

'By what I was campaigning for. He feels as strongly about housing as I do about the allotments. And housing is a priority, he's right about that.'

'So are you are going to drop your opposition to the closing of the allotments,' asked Beryl, who was sitting next to Lily playing with her dolls, the adult conversation going over her head.

'Of course not; they are our heritage,' she assured them. 'There is plenty of land for house building and taking our allotments won't make any difference because it isn't very big and the builder who is trying to buy it won't have the public interest at heart. Only profit. But I can see how hard it is for people like that man; people who don't have anywhere to live so I will not bring any charges against him no matter how much that upsets you all. The poor bloke probably has young kids and has enough on his plate, which was why he was in such a fury.'

'Well, I can't say I'm pleased that he'll get away with it,' said George. 'But it's your decision.'

'It certainly is,' she agreed. 'We could so easily be in the same position as he is. We were lucky that we didn't get bombed out and we should be grateful.'

'I agree with you entirely,' said Charlie who had as strong

a social conscience as his sister. 'Being taken to court is the last thing that fella needs.'

'Thank you, Charlie,' she said. 'I'll never forget the despair on that man's face.'

'I saw it as pure spite,' said George.

'That's because you are protective of me.'

'Very probably.'

'Anyway, it was a good protest despite the miserable ending,' she said. 'The scuffle won't make any difference to the end result I shouldn't think.'

'It will probably get more column inches because of it,' said George. 'The photographer was having a field day.'

'Shame on you, George, for even thinking such a thing,' admonished April.

'A man is going to get away with punching my girlfriend,' he reminded her. 'There has to be something in it for us. Anyway you are not fighting a personal battle and wanting publicity for yourself. You are doing it for your community.'

'That's true.'

'When is tea, Mum?' asked Charlie.

'Soon love, why, are you hungry as usual?'

'Naturally, but it's more that I'm going out afterwards so I don't want to be late,' he said, smiling a little coyly.

'You got a date, kid?' asked George.

'I have as it happens,' he replied, surprising them all.

This produced an outburst of interest.

'Is it the girl you were walking with, Frank's daughter?' asked Beryl.

He nodded and there was a chorus of approval.

'Good for you, kid,' said George and added, grinning, 'Johnny is the one to ask if you need any tips on how to make a date go with a swing. He's had plenty of experience.'

'Don't listen to him,' said Johnny, entering into the banter. 'George is the real expert. All those years abroad; a girl in every port and all that.'

'That is just a myth, as you very well know. I've seen you work your magic with a few young ladies in my time.'

'I think I'll be able to manage without the benefit of your experience, thanks lads,' said Charlie drily. 'She's such a nice girl and we get on so well, I don't think I'll need tactics.'

'Good for you,' said April. 'Take no notice of these two who think they are such experts on women.'

'The man hasn't been born who is an expert on women,' laughed George.

'I don't know so much,' said Heather. 'I think Johnny has got me pretty well worked out. He thinks he has anyway.'

'I bet he hasn't,' said George. 'Women are far too complicated for a mere man to understand.'

'So long as you realise that, we can all get along with you recognising our superiority,' joked April.

This caused a roar of good-humoured disapproval from the men but everyone was laughing.

Heather was thinking how shocked Johnny would be if he knew what really went on in her head. He was well aware that she was selfish and jealous of April but he could never guess how violent her thoughts towards her cousin sometimes were. She frightened herself at times with the ferociousness of her envy. She comforted herself with the knowledge that as long as the thoughts didn't become deeds no one would get hurt.

She was recalled to the present by April telling her mother she would help to get the tea.

'Will you lay the table please, Heather?' April asked.

'Of course,' she said and went over to the sideboard drawer where she knew they kept the tablecloth. This house was almost as familiar to her as her own, she'd spent so much time here during her life. Perhaps that was why she was so envious of April, because they had grown up in such close proximity. Sometimes she wished she could move away from here so that she could escape from the torment of being in someone else's shadow. But she knew she never would. She didn't have the courage to leave the things and people she knew and loved.

She spread the cloth on the table and went to the kitchen for the crockery.

One of the many things April treasured about her relationship with George was that she could talk to him about such delicate matters as issues of conscience and he listened and gave her his true opinion, even if it wasn't what she wanted to hear.

'I can't help thinking about that man,' she told him when she was seeing him off at the door later, the visitors having left after tea and Charlie not home from his date yet.

'Me too,' he said. 'Every time I look at your eye I'm reminded of the rotten thug.'

She brushed his concern aside. 'He isn't a thug, George, just a very angry and frustrated man. My eye will be fine in a few days but he still won't have anywhere decent to live. His terrible fury has made me wonder if I'm right to be campaigning to keep allotments when there are people with nowhere to live.'

'You are absolutely right to fight for what you believe in,' he said. 'You can't save the world, April, and there are other people protesting about the lack of housing. Once building gets underway, there will be more places for Londoners to live and people will calm down. Our country needs rebuilding and it's all taking longer than everyone expected since the end of the war. But if the council sell off the allotments to a builder where will it end? Ask yourself that. Parks and recreation grounds might be next. You are doing the right thing and I admire you for it. Your dad would be very proud.'

'Thanks, George,' she said, feeling better.

'Maybe you should go to bed now,' he said. 'You need to rest after the day you've had.'

She wanted to weep with the comfort of his concern for her and she adored him.

'Yeah, I'll go straight up when you've gone,' she agreed, kissing him goodnight.

As George walked home he was aware of a lowering of mood because it was becoming increasingly difficult for him to leave April at night. He wanted to be with her all of the time, not just part of it and usually with other people around. But this was what courting was like for everyone, he supposed, intense pleasure punctuated by periods of agonising frustration.

He comforted himself in the thought that it wouldn't be forever. There was something on his mind that he had never thought he would even consider: marriage. It was a huge commitment and he hadn't got the details properly organised in his head yet so he wasn't ready to ask her, but it was very much in his thoughts. He hoped most ardently that it was what April wanted too when the time came for him to propose.

Chapter Thirteen

'You made the front page, love,' said Beryl excitedly, waving the local paper at April when she got home from work one evening the following week. 'Well done!'

Warily, April took the newspaper from her mother and looked at the picture on the front. The photographer had captured the exact moment her attacker's fist had hit her face. Her legs felt weak suddenly. She knew she would never forget the terrible hostility in that man's dark eyes.

'It isn't something to be proud of, Mum,' she said.

'Not for him.'

'Or me, I didn't want to incite violence.'

'You wanted to make your cause known, though, and you've certainly done that.'

'I'd rather not have done it that way.'

'You weren't the one being violent.'

'It was my fault that he was,' she said.

'All in a good cause,' said Beryl. 'You can't be held responsible for other people's behaviour.

'Maybe not but it's left a nasty taste in my mouth.'

'You'll have to toughen up if you're going to stand up for things so openly.'

'I'm not thinking of becoming a regular campaigner, Mum,' she pointed out. 'Only if I feel really strongly about something.'

'Anyway, there's a good write-up,' said Beryl. 'Read it, it'll make you feel more cheerful.'

The reporter had indeed done them proud. All the points she had wanted mentioned were there and the article sympathetic towards the allotment holders.

'Yeah, he's done a good job,' she agreed, having read it. 'We'll have to wait and see if it has the desired effect. The issue does have a lot of local support now, as a result of the march, so let's hope so.'

'Will you read me a story when I go to bed, April?' asked Lily, bringing things down to earth and clarifying April's priorities.

'Of course I will,' said April. 'You find the storybook that you fancy.'

'Not going to bed yet,' protested the little girl, predictably appalled at the idea.

April laughed. 'I know, sweetie,' she said. 'I meant choose a book ready for bedtime.'

What would they do without this three-year-old redhead with her bouncy curls and dimpled cheeks? She brightened up every day in the Green household and kept their feet firmly planted on the ground.

A few weeks later there was an announcement in the local paper about the land bordering the railway line and now used as allotments. It stated quite categorically that the area would not be sold so the allotments would stay.

'This calls for a celebration,' said George when he went to the Greens' house that evening. 'Let's all go down the pub for a drink.'

'I can't go because of Lily,' said Beryl. 'But you go and enjoy yourselves.'

'Why don't I stay with Lily?' suggested Charlie. 'Susie is coming round later; we'll babysit together.'

'There you are, Mum,' enthused April. 'That's an offer you can't refuse.'

Beryl flushed up. 'I don't go out of an evening,' she said predictably. 'I haven't been in a pub for years. Women didn't used to go in very much.'

'The war changed all that,' said April. 'So now's the time for you come along and see for yourself.'

'Yeah, get your glad rags on Mrs G and come and have a snifter,' encouraged George.

It was a poor choice of words as it happened because Beryl immediately started fretting that she didn't have any suitable clothes for 'going out'.

'We're only going to the pub, Mum. You don't need anything special,' said April. 'Just take your pinny off and get your coat on and you'll be fine.'

'If you insist then,' said Beryl uncertainly.

'They twisted my arm something awful,' Beryl told Frank, who was also in the pub as well as some of the other allotments crowd. 'I don't usually go out at night, as you know.'

'It's a nice change for you then.'

'I must say I'm rather enjoying myself,' she said, flushed from the sherry. 'And it is a special occasion.'

'Very special,' he agreed. 'So who is looking after Lily?'

'Charlie and Susie.' She paused, frowning. 'I hope that's all right with you. Susie will come to no harm with my Charlie.'

'I'm sure she'll be fine,' he said. 'She's been going out dancing since she was fifteen and I'm sure she's kissed a few boys along the way. If I worried every time she went out of the door, I'd be a nervous wreck.'

'They seem very keen on each other,' she said.

'Yeah, that was the impression I got.'

'I think it's rather sweet,' said Beryl.

'Mm, it is. She's a good girl, my Susie. She's got plenty to say for herself though.'

'They have their own ideas at that age.'

'Ooh, not half,' he said. 'They think us old codgers know nothing.'

'You're telling me. You should have heard Charlie carrying on when he found out I was pregnant with Lily. Anyone would think that sex was invented just for their generation.'

He laughed. 'Gawd knows how they think they got here,' he chortled.

'They can't bear to think about that side of it in relation to a parent,' she said. 'I suppose we were the same at that age.'

'Are you two enjoying yourselves?' enquired April, coming over to join them.

'Yes, dear, very much,' replied Beryl. 'It's nice to be out of the house of an evening for a change.'

'We had to get tough with her to get her out of the door, Frank,' said April.

'I'm glad you did,' he said.

'You should do it again sometime soon, Mum,' suggested April. 'Everyone needs a night out now and again.'

Beryl threw her a warning look and said, 'This will keep me going for a while thanks.'

'Yes of course.'

George and some of the other allotment people came over and the conversation became general. But when Beryl and April were at home alone later, after George had left and while Charlie was walking Susie home, Beryl said to her daughter, 'I know you mean well, dear, trying to get Frank to ask me out again, but it's most embarrassing and I want you to stop doing it.'

'Sorry, Mum, I thought it might be nice for you both,' she apologised.

'It probably would be. But if the two of us ever do have an evening out together, to the pictures or something, it will be because we both want it and not because someone else has tried to push us into it. Frank is a friend and that's how it will always be so don't get any romantic notions. I am perfectly happy with my life as it is and have no plans to change anything.'

'Sorry,' April said again.

'That's all right,' said Beryl. 'But I had to say something, especially as Charlie's going out with Frank's daughter which might mean we see more of him. So long as we understand each other about this. I'm not just being coy, I really mean it.' She paused. 'Now give us a hug to show there's no ill feeling.'

April did as she asked and was very much aware that her mother knew her own mind. She had grown in confidence over time since Dad died and seemed stronger altogether. April guessed it hadn't been easy for her but she'd kept going and come through it. It would be nice if she would take some time for herself every now and again though and have a little fun. But she was adamantly against it so who was to say that looking after the home and family wasn't totally fulfilling for her? She certainly seemed to enjoy it. Whatever the truth of the matter, April wouldn't try to bring her and Frank together again.

The Greens' house was as crowded as ever on Christmas Day with people coming and going. George was there for most of it, Winnie and Percy called in, Heather and Johnny arrived on Christmas night with Peg and Susie came for a while in the afternoon but went home after tea to be with her father. April's own father was still especially missed during the festive season but time did heal to a certain extent.

One Saturday morning early in the New Year of 1949 April went to the allotment to check on things. It was too cold and the ground too hard to work on but she wanted to prepare her seed boxes, work out which seeds to order and generally plan things for the new season. She missed the allotment when the weather was too bad to do any physical work at all but she could always find a job of some sort. It was deserted here today, apart from her. The other allotment holders were obviously not quite as attached to their hobby as she was in the chilly weather.

Having done what she intended in the shed, she looked around the plot then turned towards the path to go home. As she did so she saw a movement out of the side of her eye and realised there was a man in a dark coat and trilby hat standing by the gates, looking this way. He was too far away for her to make out who he was but he was obviously a stranger or he would have called out to her. Even as she saw him he hurried away, which was a bit creepy.

It wasn't until she was on her way home and about to turn into her road that she heard steps behind her. She turned quickly and the man was there but ran away, though not before she saw his face and knew who he was. It was the man who had attacked her at the protest march. Her legs weakened and she felt rooted to the spot. He disappeared round the corner before she gathered her wits sufficiently to think straight and go after him.

What did he want with her and why didn't he wait and tell her what it was? He must still be holding a grudge; that was the only explanation. Perhaps he'd seen the local paper so knew the allotments were here to stay and his temper was inflamed again. But he hadn't seemed the type to hold back so why had he run away? She was very unnerved but it was more than just that. It was a lonely, isolating feeling to know that someone wished you ill. Why hadn't he confronted her? That was peculiar!

During lunch Beryl noticed that her daughter wasn't as chatty as usual. 'Are you all right, dear?' she asked.

'I'm fine, Mum.' She had no intention of worrying her mother with what was on her mind. 'I might not have time to help you with the washing-up though because of my shift at the shop.'

'That's all right, love,' she said. 'Take your time eating your food though.' She looked at Charlie. 'I'll get love's young dream here to give me a hand with the dishes.'

'I don't mind helping, Mum,' said the ever-amiable Charlie.

'I wanna do the dishes,' Lily piped up.

'You can help me with the drying,' said Charlie, who had endless patience with his little sister.

When Lily smiled she could light up Wembley Stadium and when she did so now she melted April's heart. She decided there and then that she mustn't allow the prowler to frighten her and spoil her life; she was going to confront him if he appeared again and find out what he wanted with her.

The shop was busy that afternoon, customers wanting sprouts for their Sunday roast and winter vegetables to make stew. It was cold in the shop and she and George had a paraffin heater at the back which they huddled over every so often between customers.

George had heard of a shop that was expected to become vacant in the next few months. It was across the river in Barnes and he was very excited about it.

'It might be just right for us. It's situated in a very good position and already trading as a greengrocer's so we wouldn't have to apply for change of use or have it refitted, though of course we'd smarten it up a bit if we can get hold of any paint. Naturally I'll want to do it up properly when materials aren't so short. Mum and Dad have had a look and are all for it.'

'Mm.'

'It might not be easy to keep both shops stocked at first but things will get easier soon and if we get it on a long lease at a fixed rent for a certain length of time we should manage to hold our own till the good times come.'

'Yeah, right.'

'April,' he said. 'Are you listening to me?'

'Of course.'

'You don't sound very interested.'

'You know I'm always interested in what you have to say,' she assured him.

'So do you think it's a good idea to take on another shop at this time?'

She forced herself to concentrate, despite the 'other thing' that was dominating her thoughts. 'I'm not an expert on business. That's your forte.'

'You're a sensible girl though,' he said. 'It would be nice to have your opinion.'

'Well,' she said, making herself focus on the subject in progress. 'Things have to get more plentiful again at some point soon and if you can get this shop at an affordable rent I can't see it failing, not with you in charge.'

He gave her a studious look. 'Are you all right?' he asked. 'You look a bit pale and seem preoccupied.'

'How can I be preoccupied when I've just given you a valid opinion about something as important as your business?' she said sharply.

'All right, there's no need to bite my head off,' he retorted. 'What's the matter?'

She wanted to confide in him about what was troubling her but deemed it unwise because he would be worried and might insist on going everywhere with her until the man turned up again. Then the sparks would really fly. So this was something she had to deal with on her own, for the moment anyway.

'Sorry, George,' she said. 'I have a bit of a headache.'

'Oh you poor thing.' He was immediately concerned. 'You'd

better go home and put your feet up. I can manage here for the last couple of hours.'

'No, I'm not bad enough for that,' she said quickly, hating herself for lying to him.

'Just as you like,' he said. 'Do you fancy going to the pictures tonight to take your mind off it, or will the cinema make your headache worse?'

'I'd like that very much.' She leaned up and kissed him instinctively.

'Oi oi,' said a middle-aged woman in curlers and a turban. 'That'll be enough of that sort of carry-on, thanks very much. You'll make me jealous.'

'Don't give us that, Marge,' said George, who knew the woman well. 'I'm sure that you and your Bert can beat us in that department.'

'About thirty years ago, maybe,' she said, cackling. 'We're both a bit past it now.'

'Not on your life,' said George and went on to serve her, keeping the chat going.

He was an excellent communicator, April thought, watching him in action. He could melt the coldest heart and make people actually enjoy spending their money. It was a gift he had inherited from his mother.

That evening they went to the cinema and for a drink afterwards. Wrapped in the warmth of his company, she relaxed and thoughts of the protest man faded to the back of her mind.

When a few weeks had passed without a sign of the man April began to lower her guard and enjoy life again. The allotment was beginning to get more interesting as she prepared the ground for sowing. She had kept the soot from the last time the chimney was swept and worked that into the ground as it was beneficial to the soil in several ways.

Engrossed in her labours one sunny day in February, she looked up and saw the man standing by the gates. She dropped everything and tore towards him. He turned and fled but she was faster and managed to catch up with him.

'What do you want with me,' she demanded, grabbing his arm and pulling him back. 'I could get the police on to you for harassment, you know. So what's your game?'

'All right, calm down,' he said, struggling to get away. 'Let go of me and I'll tell you.'

'You'd better start talking quick,' she said, letting go of him.

'I saw the picture in the paper . . .'

'And I assume you saw the later announcement about the allotments staying,' she said. 'So you'll have to accept it and get over it.'

'I have,' he said, surprising her.

'So why are you pursuing me?'

'I wanted to make sure you were all right. When I saw the picture and realised how rough I'd been with you I was shocked and knew I had to find you and try to make things right. But I didn't know where you lived. The only thing I had to go on was the allotments. I knew that if I went there often enough sooner or later you would turn up.'

'Are you seriously asking me to believe that you are concerned for my well-being?'

He nodded. 'I'm not normally a violent man. But when I came back from the war to find my wife and kids bombed out and living in a dingy room with damp walls and no hope of us finding anything better, I got angry. The list for council housing is so long it's hardly worth putting your name down. You have to have lots of kids before you have nearly enough points to get considered. That day at the protest I'd had a few drinks and I was enraged about people trying to save the allotments when there are so many of us without decent homes in London. I just saw red and hit out at you. I realise now that you are right; of course, the allotments mustn't be built over.'

'So why scare me by making yourself seen then running away?' she asked.

'I wanted to apologise but lost my bottle when it came to it and scarpered,' he explained. 'I'm very ashamed of what I did to you and my wife gave me hell when she saw the picture in the paper. I really am very sorry. I've never hit a woman before in my life.'

April was briefly lost for words. After she'd thought about it she decided to go easy on him. 'There was no permanent damage but my eye was swollen and painful for a week or so. It could have been worse.'

'Sorry.'

'Apology accepted.' She gave him a studious look, now believing him to be genuine. 'So is there no hope of you getting a place?'

He smiled and his whole face changed; became softer and less threatening though there was a tough look about him, being square-jawed and broad-shouldered with those very dark eyes. 'Yeah, there is now, as it happens,' he said. 'We've decided to take the plunge and move out to one of the new towns that are being built outside London. We're going to Hemel Hempstead.'

'Oh. Where is that exactly?' she asked.

'In Hertfordshire.'

'Blimey, that's a long way out. Will you be all right with that?'

'It isn't what we wanted at all,' he said. 'The wife and I are both Londoners through and through but if we are prepared to make the move we can have a house with a garden which will be lovely for the kids.'

'Might you be homesick though? We Londoners tend to think our town is the only place to be.'

'We're sure to miss London but we've decided to look at it as the chance of a new life. We'll hate not being near our relatives here, of course, but we can't stay in conditions like the ones we are living in now. It's damp and the kids get bad chests in winter.'

'So when will you be going?'

'They are moving the first residents in later this year so we're hoping we won't have to wait too long as our living accommodation here is so dire.'

'What about work?' she asked.

'I'm a skilled worker, an electrician,' he replied. 'So I'll be all right in Hemel with all the building work that's going on there; especially as it will be ongoing in the area for a good few years to come. They need people like me.'

April had heard about the New Town Scheme to ease the housing crisis in London but until now she hadn't known of anyone who was going to take the plunge.

'Well, I wish you all the best,' she said.

'Thanks.' He offered his hand. 'I'm really sorry about what happened. No hard feelings.'

'No hard feelings,' she repeated. 'Good luck.'

'Thanks.' He smiled. 'You take care.'

'You too.'

He turned and walked away with a slight swagger to his step. Oddly enough she felt a pang. Not because she was sorry to see him go in particular but because of all the Londoners who would be forced to make the same decision out of necessity. They had all heard a lot about the Bright New Britain. Maybe this was the first sign of it.

She was thoughtful as she walked back into the allotments. What a strange meeting it had been. Instinctively she knew she was going to keep it to herself. There was no point in upsetting her loved ones by telling them. Their reaction would be anger because of what he had done to her and they would be cross that he'd turned up again.

They hadn't seen the pain behind the anger in his eyes when he'd struck her or the genuine remorse just now and that was something she couldn't describe. She was very glad he'd found her. He'd made her see that her cause wasn't the only one worth considering and it was a relief to know that she could now draw a line under the whole thing.

In February 1949 the British people were given a boost when clothes rationing was abolished.

'About time too,' said Beryl.

'It's a welcome sign that things are getting better,' said April, delighted.

'It certainly is,' agreed Beryl. 'It will certainly cheer everyone up. It's a big step forward.'

'Just at the right time for me, too,' said April, 'because George and I are going out to dinner in the West End next Saturday night so now I can get something new to wear.'

'Ooh that will be nice,' said Beryl. 'What's the occasion?'

'Nothing special,' she said airily. 'He says he thinks it's time we had a good night out together, and he's found a shop over at Barnes for their expansion plan so that's something to celebrate.'

'Be lovely for you, dear.'

'I'll go to Oxford Street on Saturday morning and have a look round the dress shops. I'll mention it to Heather. She might like to come. You too if you like, Mum. No coupons, hooray!'

'I've got Lily to think of and I don't think she is quite up to a clothes shopping trip with you. The amount of shops you go in before you make your decision.'

'I'll look after her if you want to go, Mum,' offered Charlie.

'I'll pass on this one, thanks, son, and leave it to the young ones,' said Beryl with a wry grin.

'The New Look has gone out, hasn't it,' said Heather as she and April trawled the shops on crowded Oxford Street.

'Yeah, I think I heard something about that,' said April. 'But skirts still seem to be quite long. New Look, old look. When I see something I like that I can afford, I shall have it whatever look it is.'

They went into shop after shop, looking in the windows and sorting through the rails inside and trying to ignore the pushy sales assistants who hated any potential customer to leave the shop without buying. It was too early for summer dresses but April eventually found a mid-calf skirt in green and a white satin blouse with full long sleeves.

To celebrate the end of rationing Heather bought a black skirt and floral blouse.

'It seems funny not having to worry about coupons, doesn't it,' said April when they went into Lyons for a cup of tea and a bun before going home.

'It seems flippin' lovely to me,' said Heather. 'All we need now is the money to buy the things.'

'Exactly.' April smiled.

'What you got is really nice,' remarked Heather, unusually complimentary. 'You have the special occasion to wear it too. Lucky thing.'

'It isn't a special occasion as such,' said April. 'Just a night out in the West End.'

'You're going somewhere worth dressing up for, that's what I mean,' Heather pointed out. 'I just got something for every day. Though I think I might suggest to Johnny that we go dancing at the Palais tonight. I fancy a bit of a jive. And I can wear an ordinary blouse and skirt there. Plenty of make-up and a sparkly necklace and I'll look as good as anyone else.'

'I wouldn't mind going dancing,' said April.

'Tell George that you fancy it and come with us instead of going to the posh restaurant,' suggested Heather. 'It will be a darned sight more fun.'

'He's booked the table so I'd better not,' she said. 'He seems very keen to do it too.'

Heather shrugged and drank her tea as the queue at the self-service counter grew ever longer. It seemed to April as though the entire population of London had come to Oxford Street today.

George was very quiet at the shop that afternoon.

'Is anything wrong?' April asked him.

'No. Why?'

'You seem a bit fed up.'

'I'm fine.'

'If you've changed your mind about the restaurant, I don't mind,' she said. 'We can go dancing at the Palais instead. I'll be happy with that.'

'I haven't changed my mind. Why would I?'

'The expense, the bother, I don't know. But something is troubling you.'

'There is nothing bothering me,' he insisted brusquely. 'Nothing at all.'

'All right, don't bite my head off,' she said. 'I hope your mood has improved by tonight.'

'Sorry, April.'

'I'll forgive you so long as you cheer up now.'

'I'll try.'

George was actually in a state of nervous apprehension. As well as having made the decision with his parents to go ahead with the shop in Barnes, he had also made another personal and far more important choice. He'd decided to do something that at one time was unthinkable because of his way of life. Now it was possible and he was as nervous as hell about it. The plans were made; everything was in place. All he had to do was get on with it.

They went to a very stylish restaurant near Leicester Square. It was all starched tablecloths and waiters in tails.

'This is lovely, George,' said April as they settled at the table. 'I've never been anywhere as posh as this before.'

'I wanted it to be special,' he said, thinking how lovely she looked, the white satin blouse enhancing the flame colour of her hair which was shiny and lustrous.

She narrowed her eyes. 'Why? Why does everything have to be special tonight?'

It was supposed to be later, after their dessert. He'd got it planned to the last detail so that it would be the perfect moment. But he could hold back no longer. He dipped his hand in his pocket and produced a small box.

'April,' he said opening the box with a shaky hand and reaching over to her. 'I love you. Will you marry me?' He looked at her, his eyes seeming depthless. 'Please.'

Such was the rush of emotion, she thought she was going to collapse into tears but she managed to control herself. 'Yes, George,' she said, smiling. 'I would love to.'

He really thought he must be the happiest man in London as he slipped the ring on to her finger. He'd been so afraid she would say no. Because she was such an independent woman he'd wondered if she would want to take on such a huge commitment as marriage. He'd sailed the world, weathered many a storm at sea and been close to death on various sinking ships that had been bombed. But nothing had scared him as much as making that proposal.

'This calls for champagne.' He raised his hand towards the waiter.

Chapter Fourteen

'I thought that might have been what he had in mind but I didn't say anything in case I was wrong,' said Beryl the next day when April told the family the good news as everyone had been in bed when she'd got home last night.

'Funnily enough I didn't,' said April. 'He hadn't given any hint of that so I thought the posh dinner was because of the new shop being definite as he's been so full of that lately. We'd never really talked about marriage, not in a serious way anyway.'

'You were serious about each other, though, so surely you must have thought that's what it would lead to,' said Charlie.

'Of course. I was hoping he would ask me at some point soon but I didn't think it would be at this particular time because he's been so wrapped up in the business expansion lately. Naturally I thought that was the only thing on his mind.'

'Obviously not and it's very good news,' said Beryl, hugging her. 'Congratulations, love.'

'Yeah, from me too,' said Charlie, no longer the young boy who dismissed romance as pathetic now that he had a girlfriend of his own.

'Thanks, both of you,' said April, picking up her little sister. 'And you'll be my bridesmaid at the wedding.'

'Don't start planning the wedding yet for Gawd's sake,' implored Beryl. 'We've got the engagement party to organise first.'

'We don't need a party, Mum,' April protested. 'It will be too much work, too expensive.'

Beryl looked at her. 'Do you really think this family would let an event like this go by without a party?'

'I suppose not,' said April with a wry grin.

So April had done it again, Heather thought miserably, after hearing the news. The wretched woman had got the best-looking bloke in town, the diamond solitaire, an engagement party planned: the whole damned package. Once again April was the cousin in the limelight while Heather walked in her shadow.

Heather surveyed her own situation gloomily. She had a regular boyfriend but Johnny was never likely to give her a romantic proposal and all that went with it. He wasn't the type for grand gestures. He would never take her to a posh restaurant to pop the question. She doubted if he'd ever pop the question at all, even if she wanted him to. He'd never mentioned anything about them having a future together.

Oh well, Heather, pull yourself together and act like you're pleased for her. 'The ring is lovely, just gorgeous,' she said as April held out her left hand for inspection.

'He even got my size right, bless him,' said April, unaware that she was turning the knife.

He would, thought Heather bitterly. He would never do anything less than perfect for April, damn her. 'He's thoughtful like that then,' she said.

'Very.'

'So, have you a date in mind for the wedding?'

'Oh no. One thing at a time and I want to enjoy this part before we start thinking about the next stage.'

Thank God for that, thought Heather. She really couldn't stomach wedding talk just yet. 'Good idea,' was all she said.

'We're having an engagement party next Saturday at our place,' said April. 'Naturally, I hope you and Johnny and your mum will be there.'

With a sinking heart Heather accepted that there was no way she could get out of it without making a complete fool of herself. So she would be forced to endure an evening with the entire gathering drooling over April's ring and a general outpouring of good wishes for her. It would be absolute hell. 'We wouldn't miss it for the world,' she said, forcing herself to look pleased.

As always when there was something to celebrate in the Green family, their little terraced house became a palace of fun and entertainment. Furniture was moved around, sandwiches, cheese straws and other savoury nibbles were made and drinks delivered from the off-licence. George's parents insisted on contributing with ration books and expense so there was no shortage of goodies on offer here tonight.

Johnny brought a supply of records so the house was filled with the music of Glenn Miller and other popular tunes to dance to. Lily had been allowed to stay up later than usual but had fallen asleep in the chair early on so had been carried up to bed and the party was now in full swing.

April was ecstatic. Everyone she loved was here to wish her and George well.

'Wonderful isn't it,' she said to George as they smooched to 'Moonlight Serenade'. 'I'm so happy, George.'

'Me too,' he said, holding her close and feeling truly blessed. 'Me too.'

'Made for each other aren't they,' Johnny said to Heather as they danced nearby.

'Yes, they certainly are,' she said with an edge to her voice, having said the same thing in numerous ways umpteen times during the evening because the 'happy couple' was the subject on everyone's lips.

'At least it's stopped him going back to sea so I get to keep my best mate around.'

'That isn't very romantic.'

'I'll leave the romance to April,' he said. 'I'm just glad to have George here in London because he's such a good friend. What with the war and him being away at sea for all those years we hardly saw each other after we left school. It'll be nice to have him close by.'

'Mm.'

So, not only did she have to put up with April being praised to the heavens; now her own boyfriend was effusing about George as though he was some sort of a saint. Were there no other people on this planet worth mentioning apart from April and George? Not at this ghastly party; that was for sure.

★   ★   ★

'Do you like parties, Frank?' asked Beryl, who had seen him standing on his own and wanted to make sure no one felt excluded.

'Yeah, I enjoy a get-together and this one is a cracker,' he said. 'You've done a good job in organising it, Beryl.'

'Thank you,' she said graciously.

'I used to be a bit of a dancer in my day too,' he remarked casually.

'Jim and I could hold our own on a dance floor, when we were young.'

'I don't think it's actually illegal to dance when you've hit fifty, is it?' he said drily.

She smiled. 'I'm sure it isn't.'

'Shall we have a go then?' he asked.

'Yes, let's.'

It wasn't really dancing as such because the room was too small; it was more of an amble to music but it was very companionable and the younger guests used the lack of space for romantic purposes. As she and Frank moved with the rest, Beryl realised that she was having a wonderful time.

Percy was in charge of the bar in the kitchen and Winnie was keeping him company.

'Good party, isn't it?' she said.

'Yeah very good. George couldn't have chosen a better girl than April. She's a real sweetheart.'

'She was my friend before she was George's girlfriend so I couldn't have asked for more.'

'She fits in with us just right.'

She looked at her husband. 'There's no one wanting drinks at the moment so shall we go and have a dance?'

'Ooh I don't know about that. It's years since I had a bit of a jig.'

'It's time you put that right then.'

'I've had a bad back.'

'Had being the operative word. There's nothing wrong with you now.'

'Come on then,' he said with a hint of a grin. 'But don't you start getting all lovey-dovey with me.'

'Don't flatter yourself.' She smiled.

The two of them headed towards the music but not before Percy had had a swig of whisky.

'Blimey,' said Charlie to Susie. 'My mother is dancing . . . with your dad.'

'What of it?' said Susie lightly.

'Mum doesn't usually do things like that,' said Charlie, who could now just about manage to hobble in time to the music.

'Neither does Dad so it will do him the world of good,' she said. 'At least he's thinking about something other than his bloomin' allotment.'

'Don't you like the allotment?'

'I've got nothing against it, as such, and it gives Dad something to do but since Mum died it's all he ever seems to think about outside of work. Apart from me, of course. He's a very devoted dad.'

'People do seem to get very keen on growing things once they start doing it. My sister is the same.'

'Yeah. That's surprising with her being so young and gorgeous and everything. I always used to think it was something that appealed to old people.'

'I think it generally is. In your dad's case I expect it's something for him to do now he doesn't have your mum and it gets him out of the house. My mum has Lily to fill her time.'

'Oh well, this shindig is a change for him anyway. Lovely party, Charlie. A smashing atmosphere.'

'I'm enjoying it too,' he told her.

Everyone had had a good few to drink and things really livened up later on when they played some jazz records and people jived. Even Beryl and Frank did their own version of it and Peg danced along too. Nobody cared that the steps weren't right.

'Don't you think you've had enough to drink, Heather,' asked Johnny when she downed yet another gin and orange.

'If I thought that I wouldn't have any more, would I? But I don't so I will,' she said.

'I'll have to carry you home at this rate.'

'Stop being such a misery and let's dance,' she said. 'I'm fine, honest.'

She was too. There was nothing like a good few large gins to lift her spirits and help her to see things from a different and more positive perspective.

No party at the Greens' house would be complete without the conga and the hokey-cokey and the congregation rose to the occasion when the party was coming to an end. George wasn't in the circle for the latter and April hoped he wouldn't miss it all because it was traditional and always rounded off any get-together. Heather wasn't here either, she noticed vaguely. Where on earth had they got to?

The singing ended suddenly when Heather's voice could be heard shouting loudly in the kitchen. As April and the other guests rushed in to see what the commotion was about, they were confronted with the vision of Heather leaning back against the sink and George towering over her, clutching her arm.

'Get your hands off me,' she cried with a catch in her voice. 'He's trying to kiss me.'

'Who is?' asked April in confusion.

'Who do you think,' she said. 'Your precious George. He's been chasing me for months and now tonight he thought he could try it on again.'

'George,' muttered April into the hushed silence. 'He wouldn't do a thing like that.'

'He would and he has,' Heather announced and as George stepped away from her, she added, 'Ask him yourself.'

'Is it true, George?' enquired April though dry lips.

'Of course it isn't true,' he said, looking shocked. 'Surely you don't even need to ask. You can't possibly believe that I would want to kiss her.'

Frank intervened. 'I think we should all leave and let these good people sort out their private business,' he suggested. 'It's very late anyway.'

There was a murmur of agreement and people began to get their coats. The house that had rung with music and laughter was now horribly quiet.

★   ★   ★

'So what were you doing, George?' asked April when only the two couples were left in the room.

'I went into the kitchen to get a glass of water and I found Heather holding your engagement ring up to the light. I thought she was going to steal it so I reached out to grab her arm and the next thing I knew she was all over me. I pushed her away and then she just started screaming. I was holding her away from me when you came in. You don't really think I would be interested in Heather when I have you?' he said. 'She's been chasing me for months. Why do you think I never wanted to go out in a foursome? Because she would never miss a chance. If we went to the Palais and swapped partners for the odd dance she would come on to me, every single time. It drove me mad.'

'That's such a lie, George Benson,' sneered Heather. 'You know you were trying to kiss me just now.'

'That's not true. It's as though you are trying to hurt April by breaking us up.'

'No,' gasped April. 'She wouldn't do a thing like that. She's my cousin.'

'Related or not she is jealous of you, April,' he said. 'Surely you must know that.'

'Why would I be jealous of her?' asked Heather.

'Because she is strong and independent and popular and now she has an engagement ring that you were coveting, maybe that's the reason. By the way, April, why was your engagement ring in the kitchen?'

'I'd taken it off to wash some glasses towards the end of the evening. I never thought it would lead to this.'

'I think we should leave it at that for tonight because it's very late,' suggested Johnny. 'Sleep on it and we'll sort it out tomorrow when we are not so tired and are sober. We've all had quite a bit to drink.'

'There is no need to sleep on it as far as I'm concerned,' said George, looking directly at his fiancée. 'You either believe your cousin or you believe me, April. I did not try to kiss her tonight, or ever. Those are the facts and they won't have changed tomorrow.'

April was traumatised almost beyond feeling, all the joy of her engagement tainted by the accusation. 'I believe you George,' she said, squeezing his hand.

'Thank you.'

She turned to Heather and spoke from the heart. 'I've let you get away with all the criticism over the years, never quite sure why you always wanted to spoil anything good that ever happened to me. Well now you've gone too far and this is where it ends. I don't want to see you again, Heather, not ever, so please leave and never come back.'

'Oh, that's a fine thing when you turn your back on your own flesh and blood,' said Heather, whose face and neck were suffused with strawberry-coloured blotches. 'Well, don't come running to me when he tries it on with someone else.'

'I don't think I've ever come running to you over anything,' said April. 'It has always been the other way round.'

'Ooh, of all the cheek.' Heather lunged towards April as though to inflict a blow but was held back by Johnny.

'Come on, let's go home,' he said, standing between the two women. 'Could you get our coats please, George?'

'Yeah, of course, mate.'

A few minutes later April and George were alone. 'Well, what a horrid ending to a lovely evening,' she said. 'How could my own cousin do a thing like that?'

'You must have known that she was jealous of you.'

'I knew she had a nasty streak but didn't realise she could be so cruel.'

'Well it's all over now,' he sighed. 'The whole thing is best forgotten.'

'You're probably right,' she agreed but she knew she would never forget how horrible she felt now. Her beautiful engagement night was ruined.

'So, does the fact that you are still with me mean that you believe me over George?' asked Heather as Johnny walked her home.

'No, it doesn't mean that,' he replied. 'I've known from the start that you're no angel and I wouldn't put it past you to try to ruin things for April. But I won't desert you. You need someone. The way you carry on you'll end up with no one at all because you have so little confidence in yourself you are jealous and resentful.'

'So you do think I was making it up,' she said.

'I think it's possible.'

'What about George?' she asked. 'Won't he turn against you for staying with me?'

'I shouldn't think so because we've been mates a long time.' He paused. 'If you did make it up, please put it right. He doesn't deserve it.'

'Oh Johnny, I'm so miserable,' she said, sobbing. 'April has always been my best friend and now I've lost her, and all because of that bloody George Benson.'

He held her comfortingly but said nothing.

★ ★ ★

The next morning they had a visitor who made April horribly aware of the consequences of Heather's behaviour.

'So you believe George Benson didn't try it on with Heather,' said Auntie Peg accusingly,

'Well yes, I'm afraid I do,' said April.

'You'd turn your back on your own family for some stranger,' she roared.

'George isn't a stranger,' she reminded her. 'He is my fiancé.'

'You ought to be ashamed of yourself, agreeing to marry someone who clearly has his eye on your cousin,' Peg bellowed, incandescent with rage.

'Here, you watch your mouth, Peg,' Beryl intervened. 'That's my daughter you're talking to and George is the most decent bloke you'll ever come across.'

'You shouldn't be defending her after what she did, turning her back on her own cousin.'

'Heather was lying. We all know that.'

'Well that does it,' huffed Peg on the verge of angry tears. 'I want nothing more to do with any of you. From now on you're no relatives of mine.'

'Peg,' said Beryl, her voice breaking. 'Don't go blowing things out of all proportion. We can sort it out.'

'If you want April to go ahead and marry him that's up to you, but Heather and I will not be seeing you again.'

'April has already given Heather her marching orders anyway,' Charlie reminded her.

'And I'm giving you yours,' she said and stormed out of the house.

Beryl was trembling.

'Oh Mum, I'm so sorry about all this,' said April, her nerves shattered.

'It isn't your fault, dear,' she said, copious tears falling. 'It's just that she's my sister and we've always been so close. Like best friends really.'

'I know,' she said sadly. 'Look Mum, I truly believe that George is telling the truth but if it's going to make it awkward for you my being here, I'm sure I could go and stay with the Bensons. Then you might be able to put things right with Auntie Peg.'

'The last thing I want is for you to move out. That time will come soon enough when you get married,' she said. 'It would make no difference to my relationship with Peg anyway because I would still believe George over Heather whether you're here or not.'

'Mm, there is that.'

Charlie got up and put his arms around his mother. 'Together we are strong, Mum, remember that.'

'I know, son,' she said. 'I know.'

April felt as though her whole world was collapsing around her but she still believed that George had done nothing wrong.

'Men can be vulnerable when it comes to this sort of thing,' said Percy to George and Winnie over a late breakfast. 'I know women are supposed to be the fragile ones and us men beasts but some women are wicked.'

'It's just my word against hers,' said George. 'And I still feel as though I'm under suspicion. Thankfully April believes me and that's all that really matters but it still rankles.'

'Those of us who matter to you believe you so keep that in mind if you get any snide remarks,' his mother said. 'You have April and your family backing you.'

'It'll blow over anyway,' said Percy. 'Give it a few days and it will all be forgotten.'

'Not by me,' said George. 'I hate having my integrity put into question when it's just a pack of lies and there's nothing I can do about it. If I go to see Heather to try to persuade her to tell the truth, she'll accuse me of harassment. I have never been so angry in my life.'

'No one who knows you will believe it,' said Johnny when he came round to see George later that morning. 'I certainly don't.'

'Does that mean you finished with Heather then?'

'No, I can't do that, mate,' he said. 'The girl is a walking disaster. If I drop her she'll have no friends and God knows what trouble she will get into.'

'So, you'll still go out with her knowing that she lied to hurt April and me?' George was astonished.

'I am not taking her side against you,' Johnny pointed out firmly. 'I just don't feel able to desert her, whatever she's done. I think she's quite a nice person if she wasn't so jealous of April. That's what all this is about, though she hasn't even admitted to me that she made it up.'

'Far be it from me to interfere with a man and the woman in his life but make sure you keep her well away from me, unless of course she wants to admit the truth and clear my name.'

'If anyone can persuade her to do that it's me.'

'Are you in love with her?' George enquired.

'I do have feelings for her, God help me. She's her own worst enemy.'

'Of course you must feel something for her or you wouldn't be going out with her.'

'Are we still mates, George?'

'I'm not going to fall out with you over it,' George said. 'We're not six years old.'

'So Thursday night is still our night out then?'

'Of course.'

'George . . .' Johnny began.

'Yeah?'

'I'm really sorry about what happened.'

'So am I.' George paused in thought, shaking his head slowly. 'How can things change so suddenly? And all because some stupid girl wants to make trouble,' he said angrily.

At that moment Johnny knew that their friendship would be untenable with things as they were because his instinct was to defend Heather no matter what she'd said. So something had to be done and the sooner the better.

Johnny went straight from the Bensons' to Heather's where he found both her and her mother red-eyed and weepy.

'Get your coat, Heather,' he said in an authoritative manner. 'We're going out for a walk.'

'I'm not going out anywhere,' she declared. 'I'm far too upset.'

'We're both upset,' added her mother.

'I realise that and I'm sorry,' he said, looking at Peg. 'But I need to speak to Heather alone.'

'No,' said Heather.

'Right, let me put it this way,' he said. 'Either you come with me or I walk away and I don't come back . . . ever!'

She stared at him incredulously. He had never spoken to her this way before. 'Oh all right. Just a minute. I'll get my jacket.'

* * *

The Apple of Her Eye

There were a lot of people around on the towpath, this being Sunday; some walking, others standing watching the river activity; boats, barges and oarsmen training, boatmen working on their craft. Johnny led her to a quiet stretch in Duke's Meadows and they sat on a bench.

'What's this all about,' she asked as Johnny had stayed determinedly silent on the way there.

'It's about this business of George supposedly trying to kiss you. It's gone far enough and he is furious about it,' he said. 'You and I both know he didn't do anything so do the decent thing and apologise and make it generally known that it was you trying to spoil April's engagement party, nothing more.'

'Are you calling me a liar?'

'I'm saying that you'd had a good few to drink and you got carried away.'

'Well that's a fine thing when your own boyfriend doesn't believe you.'

'Look, I know you, Heather. I know how you are about April. A spot of healthy rivalry between cousins is one thing but you take it to a whole new level and it's now got out of control and caused George and April a lot of pain. I'm sorry if it upsets you but that's how it is,' he said. 'I've known George a long time.'

'And you believe him over me now.'

'I'm afraid I do. I thought I could still be mates with George, and have you in my life as well whatever you'd done, but I now know that I can't.'

'So you get rid of him,' she said.

'I don't want to do that.'

'So you're going to give me the push.'

303

'If you will come with me now and apologise to George and tell April the truth, we can carry on as we are.'

'And if I don't?'

'Then you and I are finished,' he said. 'It won't work with this standing between us.'

'That's emotional blackmail.'

'No. Just plain fact. Anyway what you did wasn't exactly a good deed.'

'You don't have the right to judge me.'

'No I don't, but I do have the right to choose who I go out with. Look, Heather, we both know you tried to upset the applecart for April and George and you're probably regretting it because deep down you're not a bad person. You just have a serious problem with your cousin. Put it right before any more harm is done and you and I can carry on as before.'

'There is nothing for me to put right,' she insisted, her cheeks red and blotchy in her pale face. 'You should be giving your mate a hard time for trying to take advantage of me, not taking his side.'

He looked at her, almost wishing he could believe her. 'Is this your last word?'

For a moment he thought she was going to weaken because she hesitated and her face worked but she said in a defiant manner, 'Yeah, absolutely.'

'Oh, in that case there's nothing more to say then,' he said, rising. 'I'm sure you can find your own way home. Goodbye, Heather.'

She didn't reply; just sat stiffly on the seat staring unseeingly at the river as he walked away, pale-faced and sad.

* * *

'Hello, George,' said April when he appeared at the allotment that afternoon while she was on her knees planting. 'I didn't think I was seeing you until tonight.'

'That was the arrangement but I wanted to see you sooner and thought you might feel the same.'

'You're absolutely right,' she said, standing up. 'I'd give you a hug if I wasn't so muddy.'

'A bit of mud won't hurt me,' he said.

She dropped the trowel and went into his arms. 'Oh George, I'm so glad you've come. Auntie Peg has fallen out with us and poor Mum is devastated. They've always been such mates.'

This news stabbed at George's heart; he'd done nothing wrong but if he hadn't tried to stop Heather stealing April's ring, Heather wouldn't have felt the need to say what she'd said and Mrs Green and her sister wouldn't have fallen out.

'That is awful. This whole wretched thing is spiralling out of control.'

'I know,' she said. 'And there doesn't seem to be anything we can do about it.'

'One thing is for sure, April, we have to stay strong and united or it might start to come between us.'

'We mustn't let that happen.'

'Absolutely not!'

'I've got a flask of tea and I could do with a break so let's get the deckchairs out and have a sit down while we talk. We might even be able to sit outside as we are wrapped up.'

George followed her towards the shed, so thankful that she believed him and they were together.

Chapter Fifteen

Although the incident at the engagement party changed the pattern of life for the Green family, they did their best to adjust to the absence of their relatives. For all Heather's faults, April missed her but suspected that the rift must be more painful for her mother because she had been so reliant on Auntie Peg's company since Dad died. April had heard from George that it was all off between Johnny and Heather so she guessed that her cousin would be feeling lonely and this bothered her a lot. But there could be no olive branch offered from this side of the family after what had happened. April had been too deeply hurt to think that her own cousin would try to kiss her fiancé. George didn't seem to want to talk about it so she respected this.

In early May they had a welcome diversion when George came round with the news that they had signed for the shop in Barnes and would be opening in a few weeks.

'You're going up in the world then,' said Beryl. 'It's posh over the river in Barnes.'

'Some of it is a bit classy,' agreed George. 'But all the better for business. The toffs need their spuds and sprouts the same as everybody else.'

'Course they do,' enthused Beryl. 'The better off they are the more they'll spend in your shop.'

'Exactly,' he said. 'It's not such a busy place as Chiswick but there is less competition and we reckon there'll be more than enough trade for us and scope to build up. I reckon the people in the big houses will want their stuff delivered so we'll oblige with that.'

'Sounds lovely, George, and good news is just what we need,' said Beryl.

'I'm feeling very positive about it myself,' said George then went on to have a chat with Charlie about football while April went to finish getting ready to go out.

'So now that the second shop is a reality, I need you to make an important decision, April,' said George later as they sat on the riverside terrace of The Dove with their drinks in the setting sun. 'Do you still want to swap your smart office clothes for an overall and come and work with me?'

'Try stopping me.'

'Seriously, April, it isn't a glamorous job.'

'And you think office work is?'

'It's congenial, warm in winter and you don't get your hands dirty.'

'That's true and most people thoroughly enjoy it,' she said. 'But not me. The way you're carrying on I'm beginning to think you might be trying to put me off?'

'Don't be daft. I just want you to be quite sure it's what you want. On the plus side of working with me, you'll have no one breathing down your neck and as much responsibility as you like because I shall want you to take an interest.'

'When do you want me to start?' she asked.

He beamed at her. 'That's what I hoped you'd say,' he said happily. 'We're hoping to be ready to open at the beginning of June.'

'I shall make sure I hand in my notice in good time then,' she said excitedly. 'I can't wait, George. A new challenge is just what I need.'

'Yes,' he said slowly. He knew she was still hurting from the rift with Heather and he wished he could do something to help. He had told her that she didn't have to stay estranged from her cousin on his account and he wouldn't see any reconciliation as disloyalty to him so long as he didn't have to see Heather. But April was adamant that there could be no reunion. He did sometimes sense tension between April and himself when they kissed each other and occasionally he wondered if she ever doubted him; did she ever think Heather might have been telling the truth? But he didn't allow such thoughts to take root because in his heart he knew she trusted him. That was the awful thing about accusations; they created doubts, no matter how untrue. 'I think it will probably do us both good.'

She raised her glass. 'Here's to our new adventure, George.'

'Cheers.' They chinked glasses as the sun finally slipped away behind the trees and a breeze from the river created a sudden chill, making them shiver.

'I thought I might find you here, Frank,' said Beryl, arriving at the allotments to find him busy with a hoe. 'I know you sometimes do an hour or so here in the afternoons before your evening round.'

The Apple of Her Eye

'Hello, Beryl, where's the little 'un?'

'She's gone to play with a neighbour's little girl so I thought 'd have a wander down here to see if you were about.'

'How are you?'

She made a face. 'Missing my sister,' she said. 'We used to ee each other most days.'

'Mm, it's a shame,' he said. 'Is there no way things can be ut right?'

'No, not really. I never talk to April about it because I don't vant her worrying about me. She's still upset about it herself, hough she would never admit it. Her cousin was never a good riend to her but she must miss her because they saw such a ot of each other. Have done all their lives.'

'She's sure to feel it.'

'But she's starting a new job next week; she's going to help George run Benson's new shop so I'm hoping that will take er mind off things.'

'Which still leaves you missing your sister.'

'That's right.'

'Well if it's any help, you can count on me for company,' e told her.

'That's what I hoped you'd say,' she said. 'Do you have time or a cuppa?'

'I have the time but not the tea, not here anyway.'

'I do though,' she said. 'I've brought a flask.'

'Oh well done. I'll get some chairs out of the shed and we an have a proper chat.'

'I feel better already,' she said and meant it. There was some-hing so comforting about Frank. The more she got to know im the more she valued his friendship.

★   ★   ★

309

When April went to work at the shop in Barnes, it was such complete change from her previous job she felt as though sh was on holiday. There were no orders to obey. Just conversation with George about what needed to be done. She was always the shop long before it opened because she liked to do the outsic display, polishing the apples until they shone, and arranging all th fruit and vegetables into a colourful and inviting presentation.

It was a pretty shop in a parade near Barnes pond with red and white striped awning and BENSON'S AND SOI proudly on display in black lettering over the shop fron Relieved of the dread of going into the office, April was happ in her work and this made her appealing to the customers.

Because George was up so early for market, he took a extended lunch break to rest and she held the fort on her ow The responsibility suited her and she already had a proprietar air towards the shop. If the weather was nice when she took he own break she would sit on a bench near the pond and eat he sandwiches, never minding when it was time to go back to wor

Within days she got to know the regulars' names an everyone was given a warm greeting. The good thing was sh didn't have to pretend. She really was pleased to see them.

'I feel as though I have been given a new lease of life,' sh told George at the end of the first week when he gave her lift home in the van on the Saturday.

'No regrets then.'

'None at all but I knew I wouldn't. You were the one wit doubts.'

'I'll ask you again in the middle of winter, shall I?'

'You can do but the answer will be the same,' she said wit confidence.

'I'll take your word for it then.'

'It's Sunday tomorrow and our day off so why don't we do something special to celebrate the end of my first week?' she suggested impulsively.

'I'm all for that. We could go to Brighton for the day on the train as the weather is nice.'

'Let's take Lily,' she added with enthusiasm. 'She'd love that. There's no sand but she'll be thrilled to see the sea. Mum could come as well. Or did you want it to be just us?'

'I don't mind sharing you just this once,' he said, entering into the spirit. 'So the more the merrier as far as I'm concerned. I'll ask Mum and Dad if they'd like to tag along. Johnny might fancy a day out too.'

'Smashing,' she enthused. 'A day out at the seaside. Whoopee!'

In the event a whole gang of them headed for Victoria Station and Lily was almost beside herself with excitement. Charlie came with his girlfriend and Susie invited her dad too. Winnie and Percy joined the party and of course Beryl was there.

Since the end of the war when the barbed wire and Keep Out signs were removed from Britain's beaches and they were given back to the people, the seaside was hugely popular and day trippers flocked there which meant there was a very long queue at the station, snaking out and curling around London's bombed streets.

'By the time we get on a train it will be time to come home,' said Percy.

'But we are not downhearted, are we folks?' said Winnie.

There was a chorus led by Frank. 'Of course not. We're Londoners.'

★   ★   ★

Brighton seafront was a heaving mass of people determined to enjoy themselves, the beach covered with deckchairs, the pubs, cafés and pier all crammed. It was vibrant and gaudy, the brine in the air heavily spiced with the smell of frying. The crowds were gregarious, noisy and here to have fun.

April and the others packed as much as they could into the few hours they had; spent time on the pebble beach where April took her excited little sister paddling. The appearance of the sun was the signal for Frank and Percy to roll up their trouser legs and protect their heads with knotted handkerchiefs, the younger men telling them they looked like something from a seaside postcard.

They had sandwiches on the beach, visited the amusements, had fish and chips at a seafront café before heading for the station to catch the train home, having used their sweet coupons to buy Brighton rock.

'Have you enjoyed yourself, Beryl?' asked Frank as they waited in the queue for the train back to London.

'I've had a lovely time thanks. It's been a real tonic.'

'You needed something to give you a lift.'

'Thanks for being such good friend,' she said.

'Likewise,' he said. 'Now that I know you a bit better, one of these days I might get really cheeky again and invite you to the pictures.'

'I can't promise anything but I might be able to improve on the reaction you got last time.' She smiled.

'I'll bear that in mind.'

Whenever the Green family were out together Lily never left her sister's side and she fell asleep on April's lap on the train back to London.

'She's spark out,' said Johnny, who was sitting next to April while George was further down with his parents, the carriage full of the Green party. 'She's had a good day.'

'We all have.'

'I've certainly enjoyed myself,' said Johnny.

'What do you do with yourself these days now that you are not with Heather?' she asked. 'Do you have a new girlfriend yet?'

'No, nobody at the moment.'

'I'm sure you will soon rectify that.'

'I'm in no hurry.'

'You're going to settle for the bachelor life then, are you?'

'I wouldn't go that far,' he said. 'I might go abroad. See something of the world.'

'Weren't you overseas in the war?'

'Yeah, but it might be nice to go to another country as a civilian. There are all sorts of opportunities for a young single man like myself. I might as well. I have no ties here.'

There was a wistful note to his voice and she thought he had probably felt the break-up with Heather more than he had ever admitted.

'We'll miss you if you go,' she said.

'I don't suppose I ever will. It's just an idea, a spot of wanderlust,' he said. 'How about you and George? How is the new shop working out?'

'Everything is going well and I just love working with him. We make a great team. Probably because we both have such enthusiasm for the business.'

'Or because you love the bones of each other,' he suggested.

'There is that too,' she said, smiling. 'But working there feels like a great weight has been lifted off my shoulders. I just wasn't cut out for office work. No more of that awful Monday morning feeling for me. I actually enjoy going to work now.'

'It was a really good day,' said George later when April was saying goodnight to him at the front door. 'Everyone enjoyed it so it was a good suggestion of yours.'

'I didn't realise there would be so many of us but it seemed to work.'

'It really did but I'd better be on my way as I have the market in the morning.'

'Yes, that's the only drawback of your job, the fact that you have to get up so early.'

'I wouldn't miss it for the world,' he said.

'No chance of my doing it for you every so often to give you a break when I get better acquainted with the business then?'

'You are very welcome to come with me any time you like. But that's one responsibility I won't be handing over. Especially now that things are getting more plentiful. I just love the buzz of the market.'

'So you'd even refuse the offer of a lie-in.'

'That's right.' He smiled at her. 'But I have an extra bonus at work now to make up for my early mornings.'

'Which is?'

'I get to be with you all day.'

She laughed. 'That's a treat for me too.'

He put his arms around her and kissed her, the happy atmosphere of the day and his love for her making him more passionate than usual. For some reason the thought of him kissing Heather popped into her head and she found herself drawing back.

314

'Sorry, is everything all right?'

'Of course everything's all right.'

'I'd better be on my way,' he said gruffly.

He hurried away, leaving her feeling disappointed and worried.

Heather and her mother were drinking cocoa and listening to the wireless. Neither of them had said much all evening. Sunday was the worst day of the week when you were lonely, thought Heather. It was endless hours of nothing to do but while the time away. At least when evening came her mother stopped coming up with places where Heather could go to find company.

'Why don't you go for a walk in the park,' she'd suggested several times. 'Better than being stuck indoors all day.'

'I'd look a right dope walking around on my own,' she'd responded. 'Everyone is with someone on a Sunday.'

'I'll go with you,' her mother had offered.

'That would make me look even more of a prune, being out with my mother.'

Mum had finally given up trying to help and somehow the day had passed. Thank God for work tomorrow, she thought. At least she would have people to talk to even if they were all going on about what a wonderful weekend they'd had with their boyfriend or husband.

She knew that her mother was missing Auntie Beryl too, though she didn't say much about it. Mum had the capacity to get on with things without complaining, a trait she hadn't passed on to her daughter, unfortunately. Heather felt a stab of pain when she thought of how lonely her mother must be without her sister but she was too sorry for herself to spare much sympathy for anyone else. She missed April more than she cared to admit. Her cousin wasn't easy to have as a friend because she was annoyingly lucky but they had been together all their lives and not having her around was painful. Irritatingly she missed Johnny a lot too. It had been a shock when he had deserted her on top of everything else. She had no man in her life and no real friends. There were workmates she could go to the pictures with during the week but they were all busy at weekends.

So this was it for her. At home with Mum. That was her life. And it was all her fault.

Because April worked all day Saturday she had Wednesdays off which gave her a chance to catch up with things at the allotment. She was there in the afternoon on the Wednesday after the outing, weeding and watering and arming her beds against pests which would have a whale of a time at this time of the year with everything flourishing.

Her thoughts were of George. While she loved him with all her heart and trusted him implicitly, she also recognised the fact that he was human and therefore very occasionally the unthinkable crept in. Could it be that Heather hadn't been lying and therefore George's guilt was causing these strained episodes between them?

If he thought for a moment that she believed Heather over him, it would be over between them forever. And she absolutely did not believe Heather. It was just that sometimes when he kissed her, she couldn't help wondering what had actually happened in the kitchen between him and her cousin.

She would just have to forget it. Everything else in her life was fine. She enjoyed her new job and she and George worked well together. As always her allotment was a joy. She worried about her mother, who she knew was still missing Auntie Peg, and was glad Mum seemed to have made a friend of Frank. If April was totally honest with herself, she missed Heather a lot for all her spite and jealousy. When she hadn't been in a nasty mood, and there had been those times, she'd been fun.

'Even on your day off you're working,' said George, appearing at the plot.

'This isn't work,' she said. 'This is relaxation.'

'I think someone needs to show you what relaxation really is,' he said, smiling. 'So let's go to the West End tonight to see a film. Have a bite to eat somewhere.'

'Have you finished your paperwork?' she enquired. It was half-day closing at the shop and George had decided he would put Wednesday afternoons to good use by catching up on the administration.

'Yeah, all done.'

'Leicester Square here we come then,' she said with enthusiasm.

Because they weren't working so could leave early they didn't have to queue for too long for the cinema where they saw *The Third Man*, a spy thriller with Orson Welles and haunting background music. They went for a meal afterwards in Lyons Corner House.

'I've got something to tell you,' he said over braised beef and carrots.

'Oh no,' she said, in a moment of panic thinking he was going to make some sort of a confession.

He frowned, noticing that she had turned pale 'April, what is it, why are you so on edge?' he asked. 'It's nothing bad.'

'Thank heavens for that,' she said, the colour returning to her cheeks.

'Why would it be anything bad?'

'I don't know why I said that, George,' she fibbed. 'Take no notice of me.'

He gave her a studious look then said, 'It's good news actually. I've just heard that the flat above the Barnes shop is going to become vacant soon and I've decided to move in. It's time I was out from under Mum and Dad's feet.'

'What a good idea,' she approved. 'What's it like? I've never been up there.'

'It's nice. Not huge but big enough,' he said. 'You must come and have a look as soon as I can get it arranged with the tenants who are in there at the moment.'

'I can't wait.'

'The thing is,' he began. 'I was wondering if you might consider moving in with me.'

As her mouth opened and her eyes bulged, he laughed and said, 'Your face is a picture. I mean after we're married, of course.'

'Oh you are rotten, teasing me like that,' she said. 'I think my mother would die of shame if I moved in before then. The scandal would sweep across Chiswick like an autumn gale.'

'Seriously though, I'm thinking that it's about time we set a date for the wedding,' he said. 'The flat above the shop will be ideal as a starting point for us. I'll do it up and make it into a little palace. As we have somewhere to live there's no real point in waiting. Not as far as I'm concerned anyway.'

'Slow down, George,' she said, deterred by the moment of awkwardness between them which bothered her. 'There's a lot going on at the moment with the new business and us getting used to working together. Let's wait until things calm down a bit before we start planning the wedding.'

'Oh.' He looked as though she had slapped his face.

She reached for his hand. 'One of us has to keep our feet on the ground,' she said. 'I'm not saying we shouldn't start thinking about setting a date and I will give it some serious thought but planning a wedding is a big job and I think we should wait until the new shop gets properly underway and you move into the flat before we start arranging it.'

'I can't pretend not to be disappointed.'

'I'm not suggesting we wait long,' she explained, eager to appease him. 'Just until things are a bit less hectic for you; a couple of months at the most.'

'I don't see why we can't get on with it but if that's what you want, then that's what we'll do.'

'I'm sure it's for the best,' she said. 'We'll enjoy it all more if we have time.'

He sighed. 'Fair enough,' he said, finally accepting it. 'So finish your meal and we'll see what delicious desserts they have.'

'Rationing is still on remember so there won't be anything too fancy,' she said, adding quickly, 'but it will be lovely whatever it is because it's a treat to eat out and I'm having such a nice time. Thank you, George.'

'It's a pleasure even if you have dashed my hopes about setting a date.'

'Don't be such a child,' she teased him. 'I haven't dashed your hopes. I've just slowed things down a bit.'

'I'll forgive you,' he said, turning his attention to his meal and changing the subject.

'Blimey, you've got a face like a dead rabbit that's been put through the wringer,' said Johnny when he met George in the pub on Thursday night as usual. 'There's only one thing that makes a man look like that and there's always a woman involved.'

'Mm, you're right, it's April,' George said gloomily, having ordered Johnny a pint. 'She doesn't want to marry me.'

'What, not at all?'

'She doesn't seem to be in any hurry.'

'Oh. It's not all off then?'

'No, not yet, but I can see it heading for the rocks the way things are going. I think she might believe all that rubbish Heather came out with at the party.'

'April's a sensible girl,' he said. 'I'm sure she wouldn't be that naive.'

'Why has she gone cold on me then?'

'Has she though?'

'Seems to have done. Draws back quite often when I touch her. Something happens between us. She pulls back, I get tense and there's this awkwardness.'

'Complicated creatures, women,' Johnny said. 'Perhaps it's the time of the month.'

'No. It's been going on for a while.'

'All the time?'

'No, but quite often,' said George.

'Why don't you talk to her about it?'

'It isn't the sort of thing you can talk about, but something isn't right, I know it. I mean, I suggested that we set a date for the wedding, as I'm going to be moving into the flat, and she put me off; said we should wait. I thought women liked a man to be impulsive, to sweep them off their feet.'

'That's the general opinion but they are also known to be very unpredictable,' said Johnny. 'There's just no knowing which way they will swing.'

'You're right.'

'I think you should bring it out in the open.' Johnny had April's remarks in mind. 'Ask her outright what's the matter and if she believes Heather's version of events.'

'I shouldn't have to. Surely she must know me well enough to take my word for it.'

'That's a bit unrealistic, mate. The idea has been planted and she's only human. The way I see it the best thing you can do is to have it out with her. But only you can decide.'

'I'll see how it goes,' said George.

'Shall we go and have a game of billiards after we've had this drink?' suggested Johnny. 'It might help to take your mind off things.'

'Good idea, mate, let's do that.'

The two men drank their beer, the conversation becoming general.

'I need a favour,' said Beryl to her offspring over their evening meal a few days later.

'That's a first,' said April. 'I don't remember you ever asking us to do anything for you before.'

'What is it?' asked Charlie.

'I need one of you to look after Lily one evening while I go out.'

'Oh,' said April, surprised. 'I'll be happy to do that.'

'I don't mind either,' added Charlie. 'So long as it isn't my class night.'

'Unusual for you to go out of an evening, Mum,' said April in an enquiring tone.

'I thought I'd go to the cinema,' she said, feigning a casual air. 'Frank asked if I'd like to go actually.'

'Oh that is good news,' April approved. 'It's about time you had a night out, isn't it Charlie.'

'Most definitely.'

'It's only a one-off,' said Beryl quickly. 'I won't be making a habit of it.'

'I can't see why not,' said April.

'Because I don't want to, that's why.' She flushed up. 'My place is here and that's where I want to be. I'm only going with Frank because he doesn't want to go on his own. That's the sort of thing friends do for each other.'

'All right, Mum,' said April. 'No need to get upset about it. Charlie and I aren't going to force you out of the house once a week to go to the pictures with Frank, are we, kid?'

Her brother laughed. 'Not unless you've been misbehaving,' he joked.

'I don't want the two of you getting any daft ideas,' warned Beryl.

'We won't,' said April.

'Didn't Frank ought to ask my permission to take you to the pictures as I'm the man of the house,' said Charlie, teasing his mother.

'He isn't taking me,' she pointed out firmly, too embarrassed to see the joke. 'I am going with him, walking on my own two feet, and I shall pay for myself.'

April threw her brother a warning look then said, 'Good for you, Mum.'

'Right, as that's settled, I'll go ahead and get it arranged,' she said.

'Any night is all right with me,' said April.

'What about your arrangements with George?'

'He'll probably come over to keep me company. He won't mind what we do. You know George, he's easy-going.'

'Thanks, dear,' said Beryl, glad that her daughter was settled with such a lovely man.

When the tenant moved out of the flat and George took April up to see it, she fell in love with it. It was an old building with high ceilings, large bay windows to the front and a small balcony leading from French windows in the sitting room. It overlooked other buildings but there was a glimpse of the river between the rooftops. Even in its bare state April felt right here.

'Oh George,' she said. 'It's gorgeous.'

'I shall do it up if I can get hold of the materials,' he said. 'I might have to pay the extra on the black market but it will be worth it to see it looking nice.'

'Some paint and wallpaper and a few bits of furniture and you'll be very comfortable here,' she said.

He stared at her, frowning.

'What's the matter?'

'It's for us, April, not just me; you said I'll be comfortable here, just me.'

'Oh, did I? It must have been a slip of the tongue. But it will be just you at first. I suppose that's what I meant.'

'But I want it to be nice for you,' he said. 'I want you to choose the wallpaper and furnishings.'

'I'd love that.'

'Mum and Dad have got a few bits of furniture we can have and we'll have to look around to see what else we can find.'

'We'll have fun doing that.'

'Good. I'm pleased you're happy with it,' he said.

'I adore it,' she assured him, standing on the balcony looking at the view, unaware that her earlier comment had added to his feeling of insecurity about her feelings for him.

George managed to get hold of the materials so started work on the flat right away. There wasn't much of a choice of wallpaper but they settled for a fairly plain design with a light background. He spent all his spare time working there.

'I shall begin to feel like a grass widow if this goes on much longer,' said April one evening to her mother when George was working at the flat and Charlie was out with Susie.

'Still, it's all in a good cause,' said Beryl.

'Oh yes, and it will be lovely when it's finished.'

'I suppose you will be setting a date for the wedding now that you've got somewhere to live.'

'Yes. We need to get on and do that. As soon as he's finished the decorating and is not quite so busy we'll get together with you and his parents and work out when suits us all.'

'I'll look forward to that,' said Beryl.

'Second time lucky.' April was remembering her wedding plans to Ronnie. 'But I don't even want to think about that.'

'I should hope not.'

'What about you, Mum?' said April. 'Any more plans to go to the cinema?'

'I wouldn't mind.' Having established the fact that she and Frank were just friends she was quite happy for another trip to the cinema. 'I enjoyed it last time. It made a nice change.'

'Well, you can rely on me for babysitting. So if you and Frank fancy a night out I'm your girl.'

'Thanks, dear.'

The underlying tension between April and George remained. This meant that the smallest criticism was magnified out of all proportion and turned into an argument. This happened one day in the summer when the two of them were working together in the shop, something they managed to do quite peaceably as a rule.

'Did that customer show you her green ration book, George?' April asked. 'I noticed you served her with bananas.'

'Yeah, I didn't bother to look at her ration book because I know she has young kids.'

'I thought we had a rule in this shop that customers were only served with bananas if they showed a child's ration book,' she stated.

'Yeah, that's right. Until supplies get back to normal, priority goes to people with young children and that's what we do. Obviously I don't need to see the ration book if I know the customer's circumstances. That would be completely ridiculous.'

April heard herself say, 'Rules are rules and we should obey them.'

He looked at her in astonishment. 'I am obeying them,' he

said. 'That customer has young kids. And I'd rather you didn't breathe down my neck and criticise my way of working if you don't mind. I know the greengrocery business inside out so I think I'm quite capable of conducting myself properly, thank you very much.'

'I was only saying—'

'You were criticising,' he snapped.

'No I wasn't.'

'Yes you were. I'm quite happy to be told when I do something wrong. In fact I encourage it but I don't welcome nasty sniping at every opportunity.'

'I wasn't sniping.'

'You were and it isn't the first time, April,' he said. 'Every opportunity you get you're at me lately.'

Now they were both red-faced and shouting.

'Should I come back later,' said a customer who had walked in on them.'

'No, of course not,' said George. 'Just a slight disagreement. What can I get for you?'

April's heart was pounding. She knew she had started the quarrel and was entirely at fault but she didn't know why because she had every faith in George's ability to conduct his business properly. She would apologise as soon as the shop was empty. But there was something deeper and more serious wrong between her and George and it needed to be brought out into the open, in private outside of working hours.

Chapter Sixteen

As soon as the shop closed, April came straight to the point.

'George, I really am sorry that I criticised you,' she said. 'I was wrong to do that and it was most unfair. I don't know what came over me.'

'You've already apologised so forget about it,' he answered coolly.

'What's happening to us?' she asked miserably.

'You tell me, April.' He looked at her grimly. 'All I know is that it's one niggle after another.'

'Perhaps we're not suited to working together.'

He shook his head. 'It started before we took over this shop,' he said. 'In fact, I can tell you exactly when things began to go wrong. It was directly after our engagement party when your cousin poisoned your mind with that evil tongue of hers.'

'I don't know why because I didn't believe her; still don't.'

'I can tell you why. Because your trust in me was tested and while you say that you don't believe her I'm not so sure.'

'What exactly are you suggesting?'

'That a part of you thinks Heather could've been telling the truth.'

'That isn't fair,' she protested. 'I've told you I don't believe a word of it.'

'Oh come on, let's be ruthlessly honest about this. You may not want to believe it but sometimes you just can't help yourself. I can sense it in the way you are with me now; you freeze every time I kiss you.'

'I'm sure I don't.'

'Maybe not intentionally but you do.'

'Are you sure this isn't your guilty conscience making you imagine things?' she blurted out.

He stared at her, looking hurt. 'There, at last you've said it out loud. You do believe I tried to kiss her. If you only knew how repellent she is to me you would never even have thought such a thing, let alone said it.'

'I'm sorry.'

'Not good enough I'm afraid, April,' he said bitterly. 'It can never work between us without mutual trust and you've now proved that you don't have it in me. You weren't there with Heather and me that night so you can't actually know what happened. All there is is belief and you obviously don't have that in me.'

'All right, I never wanted ever to have such thoughts but just occasionally, and against my will, I might have had the tiniest suspicion something may have happened. And with this awful tension between us lately, I suppose it's all got too much for me.'

'Well it's all out in the open now and we both know where we stand,' he said. 'How can a marriage survive without trust?'

'I do trust you,' she told him, her voice rising. 'It was just an occasional niggle because I am a human being and not a machine.'

'How could you have doubted me, April?' he asked.

'I didn't, not for more than a second now and again anyway. I am only human and so are you and we'd all had quite a lot to drink that night.'

'So now I am a drunkard too, am I?'

'Don't be so ridiculous and stop twisting everything I say,' she said.

'Sorry.' His neck and ears were flushed and his eyes ice hard. 'But I don't see how we can come back from this. You'll never know the actual truth because you weren't there so there's always going to be a doubt at the back of your mind that maybe Heather wasn't lying. I can't live with that, April. You're not the girl I fell in love with any more.'

She twisted her engagement ring off her finger and handed it to him. 'You'd better have this back then.'

'There's no need for that.'

'Take it,' she screamed at him. 'It has no place on my finger now. I don't want to be in the life of a man who can't forgive me for having normal human doubts.' She put the ring on the counter by the till. 'Obviously, I can't work with you any longer so I won't be coming in to the shop again.'

She turned and marched out of the premises and he didn't go after her; just watched sadly as she headed off down the street, a slight figure in a summer dress and sandals, her red hair flowing loosely. When she was out of sight he concentrated on the job in hand and started cashing up, his hands trembling slightly.

As soon as April got home she said to her mother, 'George and I have split up and I can't talk about it yet. I need to be on my own for a while so would you mind if I went up to my room.'

'Of course not, love,' said Beryl, looking anxious. 'I'll warm your meal up when you're ready.'

Charlie and his mother exchanged worried glances, Lily was told not to follow her sister upstairs and a deep gloom descended on the house.

Johnny found George standing at the bar in the local.

'Your dad came round to the house and told me what's happened,' he explained. 'He thought you might need a friend just now.'

'It's always better getting drunk with someone than on your own,' said George. 'But thanks, mate.'

'Do you want to talk about it?'

'There's not much to say really,' said George. 'Things haven't been right between April and me since the engagement party when that cousin of hers shot her mouth off. It's been there all the time, coming between us. Heather might as well have built a wall between us when she came out with that rubbish.'

'April believes it, does she?'

'She said she sometimes wonders if there was anything in it, very briefly,' he explained. 'As she wasn't there, she'll never actually know for sure so the doubt will always be there and I can't live with that.'

Johnny was thoughtful. 'I have somewhere to go,' he said suddenly. 'I won't be very long. I'll be back long before you start to get legless.'

'Take as long as you need,' said George, imbibing a large swallow of his beer.

*   *   *

Heather answered the door.

'I need to speak to you on your own,' Johnny announced grimly.

'Mum's gone to the pictures with her friend so you'd better come in,' she said.

'I'll come straight to point,' he said as she showed him into the living room. 'I just wanted to let you know that you've got what you wanted. April and George have split up because of your lies so I hope that makes you happy.'

'Why would I want them to split up?' she asked innocently.

'To spoil things for April because of your insane jealousy of her. But why you are so jealous is beyond me. I mean, you and I were getting along fine together and given time it might have led to something. But you're not content with that; you have to put your oar in and ruin everything for us all. April and George have tried to make it work but your lies have finally caused them to break their engagement and I wanted you to know that just in case, somewhere in that cold little heart of yours, you might have a stab of conscience.'

She was very pale and still as she listened to him. She would never admit it but she had missed him terribly, had been bereft without April too. 'I'll get you a cup of tea or something, we can talk about this.'

'Don't you realise the enormity of what you have done,' he shouted, almost beside himself with rage. 'You've ruined two people's lives and a cup of tea and a chat isn't going to put that right.'

'You're making more of it than it is,' she said defensively. 'If their relationship was strong it would have survived.'

'I don't think you realise the seriousness of what you did that night,' he told her.

'Not for a second did you consider the idea that I might be telling the truth. I was your girlfriend, Johnny. You should have taken my side,' she said, her voice rising.

'I knew you too well for that,' he said. 'I was well aware of how much you hated April to be happy and in the limelight.'

'Why did you go out with me if you thought I was such a horrible person?'

'I liked you for all your faults and enjoyed being with you. You were good fun a lot of the time. So I accepted your bad points, since none of us is perfect; but when you did that to your cousin it was too much and I knew I couldn't stay with you after that.' He headed for the door. 'Anyway, I have a mate with a broken heart to console so must be on my way. Cheerio, Heather. I'm sorry it's all ended so horribly for George and April. You are the only person who can put things right.'

He was quite a distance down the street when she caught up with him. 'Please come back, Johnny, so that I can talk to you properly,' she implored.

'What would be the point of that?' he asked coldly.

'All right, I admit it. I lied,' she said, her voice shaking. 'George didn't touch me. I was stupid to say he did. Please can you help me to put things right for them? I'm very sorry about what I've done and I've been so miserable.'

'You've admitted it at last, that's a start I suppose,' he said with a sigh of relief.

'Will you help me?'

'I'll come back for ten minutes and we'll talk about it,' he agreed. 'That's my best offer.'

'Thank you, Johnny,' she said.

★   ★   ★

'Didn't you ought to go into the shop, April?' Beryl suggested the next morning when April, looking pale and puffy-eyed, stayed in her dressing gown. 'I mean you do work there and you didn't give notice. George will find it hard to manage without you.'

'George is the most competent person I've ever met,' said April, putting up a front though she was actually in pieces. 'He'll manage. I promise you, he won't want to see me. I'll hurt him if I go in and I don't want to do that."

'You know best I suppose,' sighed Beryl, who was very upset at the news of her daughter's broken engagement. They'd seemed so perfect together. But April was adamant there was no going back so her mother had to accept it.

'I shall have to find a job quickly because I need the money but I'm not going back to office work if I can possibly help it. I'm just not cut out for it.'

'There's no need to worry about it today,' said Beryl.

'I suppose I could leave it for just a day,' agreed April, who had loved her job at the Barnes shop and knew nothing else would come close to it in terms of job satisfaction. But she couldn't be out of work for long because she had to pay her way. 'I'll do some work at the allotment today and go to the labour exchange first thing tomorrow.'

'Good idea.' Beryl knew her daughter went to the allotment when she was feeling bad. She also knew she was a lot more miserable than she was letting on.

George was rushed off his feet without April at the shop, but he was glad to be busy to take his mind off things. Strictly speaking he should go round to her house and demand that she work out her notice. Yet being with her and not together would be hard to bear. He hardly knew how to cope with his feelings as it was. She would feel awkward too. So he would go it alone. Still, the shop only seemed half alive without her cheery presence about the place.

His inebriation last night had left him with a headache this morning, which served him right. The evening was something of a blur. Johnny had disappeared for a while then reappeared with a verbal invitation to a get-together at Heather's house tomorrow night. He'd told Johnny he would sooner eat Thames mud than spend a moment in her home but Johnny had begged him to go as a special favour to him so he'd agreed to call in for half an hour.

Meanwhile he had to get through the day without April in his life, a depressing thought indeed!

'So you are saying that you want us to go to a party at Auntie Peg's place tomorrow night,' said April when Johnny called at the house on his way home from work to say that the whole family was invited and their presence would be very much appreciated.

'Yeah, that is what I'm saying.'

'That's very odd, seeing as we are not on speaking terms with them. Why would they invite us to a party and why would we want to go?'

'It will be more of a small get-together than a party,' he explained.

'How do you know about it?' April enquired. 'Don't tell me this is about you and her getting back together?'

'I happened to see her and she asked me to pass the invitation on.' He looked at her pleadingly. 'I know it seems odd but please don't ask questions, just trust me.'

'But we've fallen out with them in a big way.'

'Can you tolerate them just this once?' he asked.

'We can't all go because of Lily,' Beryl pointed out.

'Is there a neighbour who might help out? It really is important that you are all there.'

Sensing the urgency, April said, 'All right, I'll see what I can do. But it's very short notice.'

'Do we need to dress up?' asked Beryl.

'Definitely not; it isn't that sort of thing.'

'Will there be many people there?'

'Quite a few I believe.'

'It's all very peculiar,' said April. 'If you weren't such a good friend you wouldn't get me to agree to go anywhere near the place, never in a million years.'

'But I am a good friend, aren't I, April?' he said, teasing her. 'So can I say that you'll be there?'

'Heaven knows what we're letting ourselves in for but I suppose so.' In spite of herself she couldn't help being curious.

April didn't know what to say when Heather opened the door to them the following evening.

'Thanks for coming,' said her cousin, looking nervous.

'We can't stay long because Lily is with a neighbour,' April said coolly while her mother nodded towards her sister Peg.

'I understand,' said Heather.

They were shown into the front room, which was crowded with people; all of whom the Green family knew because they had been guests at April and George's engagement party. Frank and Susie, Percy and Winnie, Johnny and some friends of April and George, though there was no sign of the latter. People had drinks as at any party but there was no music.

'What is this?' asked April. 'Why do I feel as though we've been set up in some way?'

'There's just one more guest to come and we'll get started,' said Peg. 'Sit yourselves down and I'll get you some drinks. Gin and orange, April dear?'

'Just the orange please,' she said because she wanted to keep a clear head.

'Ah good, that will be our final guest,' said Peg as the door-bell rang.

When George walked in April was unprepared for the sheer joy of seeing him, her reaction sharper, warmer and more lustful than ever before. If he'd asked her to go with him at that moment she would have gone and to hell with their differences. But of course he didn't. He nodded towards her and smiled briefly. When the host had made sure that everyone had a drink, Johnny led the proceedings.

'You're probably all wondering why you've been invited here tonight and I apologise for the short notice but it is rather an urgent matter. Heather asked me to help her gather you all together, everyone who was at April and George's engagement party is here; this is where my part in the proceedings ends so I'll hand you over to Heather.'

She stood near the door so that she could see and be heard by everyone. April observed that she was trembling slightly and had a very high colour.

'As you will remember, the last time we were all together at April and George's engagement party, there was an incident that took place between me and George in the kitchen.'

There was a murmur of agreement.

'I've got you all here this evening to tell you that I lied when I said he was trying to kiss me. He was right when he said he found me trying on April's engagement ring that had been left by the sink. When he ordered me to give it back, I refused, which is why he was holding my arm, and it was then that I tried to kiss him. He held me off and at that point I started to scream and you all came running in.'

The silence rocked the room; then there was a critical outburst towards Heather, who held up her hands and asked them to bear with her for a short time longer.

'I know you're all shocked that anyone could be so cruel but I've always been very jealous of my cousin because she's prettier, brighter and nicer than me. She and George shone together that night and I just couldn't bear to see her so happy so when I found her ring lying in the kitchen I did think about stealing it. I regretted it at once and am deeply ashamed. When I heard recently that they'd split up because of my lies I knew I had to try to make things right for them, so I hope that now the truth is out they will get back together with any slur on George's reputation erased.' She looked directly at April with tears in her eyes. 'I'm so sorry, kid. I'm a nasty bitch, I know.' She cleared her throat. 'That's it, folks, thank you all for coming.'

There was an outpouring of noise. People shook George's hand and said they'd never believed a word of it anyway. Even Heather's mother was shocked but proud of her daughter for having the mettle to do what she had tonight. It couldn't have been easy.

'I've missed you, Beryl,' Peg said to her sister as people began to depart. 'All of you.'

337

'Likewise, Peg,' said Beryl. 'It's been awful.'

'I'm sorry I turned on you.'

'You were just being loyal to your daughter,' said Beryl. 'As I was to mine.'

'I'd love for us to get back to normal.'

'Me too,' said Beryl. 'Why don't you come round for a cuppa tomorrow? Lily has missed you too.'

'I'd love that,' said Peg, wet-eyed.

'I've been so miserable without you,' said George to April. 'I wouldn't have lasted another day.'

'Me neither,' she said.

'If Heather hadn't done the decent thing and cleared me, I would have asked you to have me back and blow all the complications.'

'When you came in tonight I nearly melted.'

'You had the same effect on me.'

'All right, you two,' said Beryl. 'Save all the canoodling until you're on your own. We're going now.'

'I'd like to see Heather before I go,' said April. 'She did the right thing in the end and it took some courage to admit the truth in front of everyone. So I think it's time we made up. Where is she, Auntie Peg? In the kitchen?'

'I don't know, dear,' said Peg. 'I haven't seen her since her big speech. Have you, Johnny?'

'No, not since then.'

A tour of the house showed no sign of Heather.

'I expect she went for a walk to cool down after such a public apology,' said April. 'When she comes back will you tell her I'll see her tomorrow, please, Auntie. I'll come round after work.'

'I'll tell her,' said Peg, smiling. She was so pleased that the family were to be reunited.

'I'm glad you made it up with your sister, Beryl,' said Frank as they walked home.

'Me too, Frank,' she said. 'I'm glad the truth is out for April and George too. Heather's never been an easy girl but I didn't know her resentment towards April went that deep. Still, it's all out in the open now so she'll probably feel better as well as the rest of us.'

'You won't need me to go to the pictures with now you have your sister back.'

'Oh Frank, don't say that,' she said in concern. 'Of course I will. I enjoy our evenings at the flicks ever so much. I'll have plenty of time for both of you.'

'I'm glad about that,' he said.

'I didn't expect that, did you, Charlie,' said Susie as they walked home arm in arm. 'Your cousin must be really mixed up to do a thing like that. And fancy getting everybody together to own up to it.'

'I suppose she wanted to make sure everyone who heard her original allegation learned the truth,' he said. 'She's got some bottle, I'll say that much for her.'

'Yeah. I hope I never get that twisted.'

'You're far too nice.'

'You make me sound really boring,' she said.

'That's the last thing . . .'

'I know,' she said, squeezing his arm. 'We are what we are.

I don't suppose your cousin wanted to be jealous. It must have been something in her personality.'

'Mm, I suppose so.' They walked in silence for a while then he said, 'My mum still seems to be getting on well with your dad.'

'Yeah, I'm pleased about that. He needs a friend of his own age.'

'Do you think they'll ever be more than friends?' he asked.

'Don't be ridiculous,' she said. 'They are far too old for that sort of thing.'

'Yeah, that's what I thought,' he said and they moved on to talk about other matters.

'I'll stick around until Heather gets back if you like,' Johnny suggested to Peg. 'I can see you're upset and it's no time to be on your own. I don't suppose she'll be long.'

'That's nice of you, thank you,' she said. 'I must say I'm bothered by what's happened. It's a shock to find out your own daughter has done such a horrible thing.'

'I can imagine.'

'It's made me wonder if Heather was more damaged than I thought by her father's death,' she said. 'She was the apple of his eye. He absolutely adored her and she him. I thought she seemed to get over it but it could have left its mark. I mean, it isn't normal to be so viciously jealous of someone as she obviously is of April. Something must have made her like it.'

'What age was Heather when her father died?' he asked.

'She was seven. He had a heart attack; hadn't even been ill. Just dropped dead while he was looking after Heather. She watched him go, the poor mite. I'd gone next door to a neighbour's for something when it happened. Heather was near hysterical when she came to get me.'

Johnny was surprised. 'She's never mentioned anything about it to me. I knew her dad wasn't around but I've never known any details. She hasn't ever spoken about it and that seems odd considering the circumstances. You'd think she would have said something about a thing like that. She's the sort of girl to be partial to a spot of drama.'

'Yes, I'm surprised she hasn't mentioned it as it's probably the most awful thing that's ever happened to her, though it was a long time ago and she was quite young,' she said. 'She was very quiet for a long time afterwards, then she seemed to get back to normal so I thought she was all right. But to have someone adore you as much as he did not be around anymore, it must have been hard for her. I mean she's never been short of love from me but her dad was very special to her.'

'It's sad.'

'Very. It's no excuse for her to have done what she did to April, of course, but it might have something to do with the jealousy even though she probably isn't aware of it.'

He nodded.

'Would you like a drink while we're waiting?' she asked.

'A cup of tea would be nice.'

Heather had had to get out of the house, away from all the eyes full of shock and disapproval. Now she was on Chiswick Bridge, leaning on the wall and staring into the dark waters, visible only because of the splintered reflection of the moon. Still smarting from the humiliation of her confession, she felt bleak and unloved by everyone. Friends were few and far between for her anyway and the chance of making any new ones very remote because she just wasn't a likeable person.

But why had she done such a horrible thing to April and George in the first place? Why was she so spiteful? She didn't want to be; she really didn't. Other people seemed to be able to function harmoniously with their fellow kind. But not her! There was an ache somewhere inside her that made her long to shine and be special but somehow she never was. Not since Dad died anyway. She always said the wrong thing; behaved inappropriately. She never looked as good as other girls, especially April. So she hit out and hurt people, her cousin in particular. She was a thoroughly bad lot and she hated herself.

Returning to the present she realised that her mother would be wondering where she was. So it was time to go home and face the music. She was so deeply immersed in her thoughts she was barely aware of her surroundings and crossed the road with her head down, right in the path of an oncoming bus.

Peg and Johnny were still talking about Heather.

'She must have been feeling very low to do such a horrible thing to her cousin,' said Peg. 'I can't help but wonder if I failed her in some way.'

'Oh no, you mustn't think that,' Johnny was quick to assure her. 'I'm sure she never lacked in any way at home. She's an adult and responsible for her own actions.'

'I know. But such vindictiveness probably stems from the past. Perhaps I should have done more for her after her dad died,' she said. 'Been more sensitive to her feelings.'

'I'm sure you did everything you should have. You couldn't get into her mind and change how she was feeling. She was very young. Children are resilient, so I'm told, and they have short memories.'

'Oh I don't know, Johnny,' she sighed. 'I'm angry with her for doing such an awful thing to April and George but I'm very sad too. She must have been feeling very unhappy to sink to such depths.'

A knock at the door interrupted the conversation.

'That'll be Heather,' said Peg. 'She must have forgotten her key.'

'I'll go,' said Johnny.

When he returned he had two policemen with him.

'Hello, Johnny,' greeted April when she answered the door to find her fiancé's friend standing there. 'Have you come to join the celebrations?'

He shook his head. 'I'm afraid not,' he said gravely. 'I need to see your mum.'

'Come on in then,' she said and showed him into the living room where George, Beryl, Frank, Charlie and Susie were gathered.

'Sorry to break up the party,' he apologised. 'I'm afraid there's been an accident.' He looked directly at Beryl. 'Heather has been knocked down by a bus and I think her mother could really do with you by her side, Mrs G. I've got the van outside. I'll drive you to the hospital.'

'Of course,' said Beryl without question or hesitation. 'I'll come right away.'

★   ★   ★

'The bus driver said there was nothing he could do,' Peg tol
Beryl tearfully. 'She just stepped into the road without lookin
Luckily she had her identity card on her so they were able t
find us quickly.'

'Do you think . . .?'

'Suicide? Oh no, Heather wouldn't do a thing like that,' sai
Peg. 'I think she was just deep in thought about what ha
happened and wasn't paying attention to what she was doing

'So, how is she?'

'I don't know. The doctor is with her now.' Peg looke
at her sister, her eyes filling with tears. 'Oh Beryl, I'm s
glad you're here with me, I don't think I can get throug
it without you.'

'Don't worry. I'm not going anywhere, not ever again,' sh
said emotionally.

'Well, you certainly went to extreme lengths this time to g
the limelight,' said Johnny, sitting by Heather's hospital bed.

'I didn't get knocked down by a bus on purpose, you know

'Just kidding.'

'I'm a complete disaster,' she told him. 'For myself as we
as other people.'

'You've been lucky to get away with just bruises and
broken arm, so why not make this a new start.'

'How can I do that?' she asked. 'I mean, April is speakin
to me again and I'm really pleased about that but how lon
before I ruin everything again? I am who I am, Johnny.'

'We can all change our ways and you could if you were t
start liking yourself and stop wanting to be April,' he advise
'Stop thinking everyone else is better, prettier and luckier tha

you and enjoy being yourself. You're a healthy, attractive woman with a good sense of humour when you're in the right mood. Just be grateful.'

'I always feel so lonely, Johnny,' she confessed. 'I drive people away. You left me because of the way I am.'

'Yes that's true. But I think you and I could have had something special given a bit more time,' he said. 'I'm willing to give it another try, if you are. Maybe you wouldn't feel so lonely with me by your side, keeping you on the straight and narrow.'

'You mean you would take me back after everything I've done,' she said, astounded.

He nodded. 'You have made a public apology and that is a step in the right direction because I know it couldn't have been easy. Besides, you need someone to keep you in order and I enjoy a challenge. So yes, I'll take on the job so long as you stop being envious of all and sundry.'

'I'll try.'

'You'll have me to deal with if you don't try hard enough,' he said, resting his hand on hers.'

'I'm so lucky,' she said.

'That's a start anyway. That's the first time I've ever heard you say that.'

Lily almost stole the show at the wedding of April and George on a cold and bright December day. She was so cute in a red velvet dress, her hands enclosed in a white fluffy muff. But even she couldn't outshine April today. In a long white dress of a simple design and an elegant headdress, green eyes shining against her flame-coloured hair, she was stunning.

Posing for the photographs outside the church after the service April felt complete, her husband by her side, handsome and smart, friends and family around her. She smiled at her mother with Frank, glad they had progressed slightly from an occasional cinema visit to a night out at the theatre in the West End. Just being friends obviously suited them but it was obvious that they were fond of one another.

Heather was beaming at her and her smile looked genuine. April had forgiven her, but learning to trust her again would take more time and she had been frank with her cousin about that. Heather had been easier company since the confession. Johnny was obviously a good influence on her.

But today belonged to herself and George and she was cherishing every moment.